NOAH'S RAINY DAY

FOURTH IN THE LIV BERGEN MYSTERY SERIES

SANDRA BRANNAN

GREENLEAF
BOOK GROUP PRESS

Published by Greenleaf Book Group Press
Austin, Texas
www.gbgpress.com

Copyright ©2013 Sandra Brannan

Distributed by Greenleaf Book Group LLC

For ordering information or special discounts for bulk purchases, please contact Greenleaf Book Group LLC at PO Box 91869, Austin, TX 78709, 512.891.6100.

Design, cover design and composition by Greenleaf Book Group LLC
Cover image: ©iStockphoto.com/Sergeeva-Elena Alyukova-Sergeeva

Publisher's Cataloging-In-Publication Data
(Prepared by The Donohue Group, Inc.)

Brannan, Sandra.
Noah's rainy day / Sandra Brannan.—1st ed.

p. ; cm.—(The Liv Bergen mystery series ; 4)

Issued also as an ebook.
ISBN: 978-1-62634-017-6

1. Missing children—United States—Fiction. 2. Kidnapping—Investigation—United States—Fiction. 3. Cerebral palsied children—United States—Fiction. 4. Suspense fiction. 5. Spy stories. I. Title. II. Series: Brannan, Sandra. Liv Bergen mystery ; 4.

PS3602.R36485 N63 2013
813/.6   2013939126

Part of the Tree Neutral® program, which offsets the number of trees consumed in the production and printing of this book by taking proactive steps, such as planting trees in direct proportion to the number of trees used: www.treeneutral.com
Printed in the United States of America on acid-free paper

13 14 15 16 17   10 9 8 7 6 5 4 3 2 1

First Edition

TreeNeutral®

To Jake
A warrior, raised by angels

Sandra Brannan's Liv Bergen Mystery Thriller Series:

In The Belly Of Jonah, 2010

Lot's Return To Sodom, 2011

Widow's Might, 2012

Noah's Rainy Day, 2013

PROLOGUE

Noah

THE GOOD NEWS IS I think I broke my leg.

The bad news is I don't know if anyone at school would ever believe how it happened. Or worse, I'm not sure if anyone will ever figure out how I got here.

It's getting cold now and I don't do so hot when I get cold. Ha! I made a funny. Emma would have laughed at that one. I wish she were here right now. Well, not really. I'm glad she's not. She's safe, at home where she's warm and not somewhere so moldy and smelly. And dark. I just meant I wish I could tell her my story. She's the fastest at listening to me with her "five-finger" method, and she'd understand why I think it's so cool that I broke my leg, even though Mom would be sad and Dad would be worried.

Emma didn't listen to me yesterday. Maybe if she had, I wouldn't be in this pickle. That's what my dad calls a sticky situation. A pickle. It makes me laugh, the way he says it. My foot keeps sliding on the ground beneath me like I'm standing on a slippery pickle, which helps me forget about the pain in my other leg. And the sound of whimpering beneath the pile of clothes nearby. Right now I can barely hear the whimpering. My ears keep plugging up because I can't stop wrinkling my nose at the rotten smell. Not like pickles. Worse. But I try to listen. Listening is important, especially for a spy like me.

My little sister didn't not listen to me because she was mad or anything; she was just distracted. That's the word my mom always uses for Emma when she's too busy to spend time with me. Distracted. Since it was Christmas and knowing how hard it is for me to focus on anything but Santa this time of year, my mom might be right.

But normally she's not. Not about Emma being too distracted when it comes to me. I know better.

Emma has a life, too. It shouldn't always be about me. We've talked about that. Emma and me, when Mom and Dad aren't around. Well, not really talked. More like Emma talks for the both of us. But at least she's honest about what I'm trying to say even if she disagrees, and she gets it right more than she gets it wrong.

She's pretty good for a nine-year-old whose older brother is trapped in his own body.

Let me back up because I think I'm getting ahead of myself. Story of my life. Getting ahead of myself. It's my destiny, considering my mind is constantly outpacing my body.

I'm twelve, almost a teenager. I'm in the same grade as my little sister, Emma, who's nine. Mainstreamed. I was born premature and weighed less than two pounds.

I have severe cerebral palsy.

My brain works like any other kid in my grade. Maybe better, according to one of my doctors, since the gray matter seems to be the only part of my anatomy that works normally. Nothing else seems to. My mind tells my hand to move or my mouth to open, but for some reason, the signal gets lost somewhere along the way. My body won't cooperate. My stomach doesn't work so good with food going in or all that other stuff coming out. I have trouble swallowing. And I overheard a teacher say that an older kid with cerebral palsy died of a heart attack in her class a few years ago. My hearing is better than people think, although my sight isn't so great. I was born so early that I had to be on oxygen therapy, so I have only a little vision with one eye and see only shadows with the other. Unless I have my contact in. Then I can see great. It's like a bionic eye.

I can't run.

I can't walk.

I can't even crawl.

If I work at it—concentrate really hard—I can roll over on my own. It takes every bit of my strength and if I land wrong, my muscles are too tired to move. Sometimes I pin my arm beneath my body and it starts tingling really bad. And sometimes when I flip over I land on my nose, which makes my eyes water and my contact lens pop out. Then I'm nearly blind again.

My muscles stay all bunched up and tight. "Contracted muscles" is what the adults say when they talk. But they also talk about contracting a disease, which I know I don't have, or signing a contract, which I couldn't do even if I wanted to. So it's just easier to talk about muscles being bunched up. At least that's how Emma describes it. So I do, too.

One time, a specialist warned my parents that my contracted muscles would someday shorten so much that the bones in my wrists and arms would break. My mom covered my ears, but it was too late. I heard her scolding the specialist as my dad wheeled me out to the waiting room. She asked him what he was thinking and why he felt it was his place to have such an adult conversation in front of me. I heard her remind him that I wasn't deaf and that I was just a kid.

But I heard it all the same. And I've felt my muscles getting tighter—can almost hear them growing shorter—which makes me wonder when my bones will snap like twigs. SNAP! SNAP! I never dreamed I'd be lucky enough to have my first broken bone from such an exciting event like tonight. Or last night. It might be after midnight. I can't tell what time it is anymore.

As I grow colder, the only thing that runs through my head is that awful bedtime prayer about "if I should die before I wake."

If I *should* die before I wake—and I am hoping I'll eventually fall asleep so I can forget about the cold for a little while—I know I will die happy, because I broke my leg doing the best I could to protect the boy who was kidnapped, the one from TV who everyone's talking about.

I don't want to die.

I want to live.

And after thinking about my life, after hours of sniffles and tears in the dark, I can honestly say I tried my hardest to save the little boy.

Now it's up to Auntie Liv to find me. To save the day.

I've decided to call this my rainy day. Mom always told Emma and me to save up for a rainy day, so I've saved up all my hopes and prayers for today. I've prayed hard several times already for God to let Auntie Liv figure out my story. The story I've been trying to tell all day. Since Christmas morning.

As the night keeps getting colder and darker, I've been trying to find a sliver of sunlight, something that will bring me hope. And in the dark, I feel thankful for what my parents told me about my birth. They said when they laid eyes on me they understood how Noah must have felt seeing that first ray of sunshine after forty days and nights of rain.

And if I had to be honest, I'd admit that I'm scared. Really, really scared.

And it feels like I'm trapped in the rainiest of all days.

My name is Noah.

CHAPTER 1

WALL-TO-WALL PEOPLE. Everyone was too busy to notice each other, let alone him.

Perfect.

A tinny version of "Jingle Bells" scraped through the airport PA system. Occasional reminders that smoking was not allowed in the airport punctuated the obnoxious and too-frequent warnings—"Trains from other terminals are arriving. Please stand clear of the doors to allow passengers to disembark before boarding"—that floated up the escalator from the floor below.

He hated the holidays. The loneliness. Everyone but him feeling so happy.

Tugging at the blue vest that had ridden up over his expansive belly, he pushed the empty candy wrapper with his broom and watched the crowd scurrying about through the main terminal. He kept a careful eye on the smallest of holiday travelers, particularly any whose parents made detours to the nearby restrooms.

Just one. He only needed one.

The tattered candy wrapper, companion to the sentinel line of dust gathered by his push broom, had tumbled across every inch of the tiled floor over the past three hours as he backtracked over this particular section at least a dozen times. The same wrapper. A wrapper that once contained his breakfast. This wrapper never quite made it from the floor to the garbage can, despite his diligence and effort to sweep it away.

No one noticed.

No one ever noticed a janitor. The simple disguise was his favorite, like an invisible cape. He could have chosen scrubs, a park ranger outfit, a construction vest, or a security guard's shirt and cap and gone somewhere else. But nothing was more effective than pretending to be a janitor.

And he needed today to go well.

He was nervous enough as it was, forced to try again. He had vowed to himself it was over. Never again. Especially after what had happened last year. He couldn't afford to lose another one. Couldn't afford to choose unwisely. Couldn't afford to make a mistake. But he knew it was the right thing to do. For them. Even if no one had come to save him when he was a child.

He needed to give a child the best Christmas gift that could ever be given to another human being. A better life. With him.

So above all else, today he needed to be at his best.

A janitor. Invisible. He'd felt no indecision this morning as he rifled through the choices in his basement. Today he needed to be expedient and effective. He needed a win. Not even those who legitimately worked at the airport would notice him, especially since he had no intention of going anywhere near the watchful eyes of the TSA agents at security screening. If they realized his blue vest wasn't quite the same color as theirs or that his name badge wasn't quite the same size, they may ask Denver International Airport employees whether they recognized him, revealing him as an imposter.

That wouldn't do.

He planned to linger between the ticketing entrance near short-term parking and the security screening area just above the escalators that led down to the trains. Plenty of shops and restaurants in the main terminal rimmed the restricted rope lines that led to security screening, which was crowded with travelers who were awaiting security checks before they headed toward the concourses.

And there were plenty of bathrooms.

On the occasions when he could no longer resist his duty to help free a child from its situation, his cover as a janitor had been his most successful to date. Particularly in crowded public places—at the Rockies stadium, at Larimer Square, and at Cherry Creek Mall. His past experiences had helped bolster his confidence this morning, along with the good fortune of finding an open parking spot in short-term parking right near the door. It was just yards from a family bathroom with a door that he could lock from the inside.

Perfect.

When he had sat in his parked car hours ago, readying himself by pulling on the blue vest over his coveralls and slipping on the glasses with white tape wrapped around the plastic frame between the lenses, he had noticed the gleam of excitement in his eyes and the angle of the nearest security camera mounted on the concrete wall nearby. It had a busted lens—a good omen. He would succeed today, he had thought. And this would be the last time. He'd get it right. Prove his father wrong. Possibly in record time.

But he hadn't expected it to take this long. And as his confidence had dwindled, he felt his anxiety growing. Only his resolve to help those who suffered as he had as a child compelled him to keep looking. And the idea of being successful on Christmas Eve further motivated him.

Holidays sucked. Christmas was the worst. Too many people. Too many smiles. Too many packages being tenderly carried to their rightful places under countless trees. Didn't he deserve a little something under the tree this year?

Yes. Of course. That was why he was here. He just had to have patience, patience and discretion.

The longer he remained huddled against the wall, the more likely it would be that someone would notice his ineffectual labors. But he was safe here under the overhang, away from the cameras' ranges. He had escaped his cover being blown about thirty minutes ago when he was over by the food court beyond the ticketing counters. Only feet from where he had stood, pushing his broom in the shadows, some old bat had dropped her bag of popcorn in her awkward attempt to rise from a dining table. Several travelers had glared in his direction as they stepped over the spilled pop-corn. He had pretended not to notice. He had turned his back as he pushed the candy wrapper in the opposite direction, away from the food court where he'd be expected to sweep up a real line of food wrappers.

He wore his navy blue stocking cap, pulled down on his forehead. His thick, black-rimmed glasses obscured much of his face and certainly his eyes from being recognized. The pretense of limited peripheral vision was complete. Believable. The earpieces of his headphones were jammed deep in his protruding ears, which gave him the excuse to ignore any demands for his services. Just to be on the safe side, he meandered toward the bank of restrooms, hugging the wall under the overhang and pushing the tumbling candy wrapper.

But he was safe, invisible. Just a janitor gripping his broom. A shiver crawled up his spine. Gripping a broom. A child's grip. In the closet. The closet filled with mops and brooms. Locked. Where his father had kept him. Where he had imagined growing up to be a janitor just to keep his mind off the darkness. And loneliness. In a way, his father was to thank for this clever disguise, he supposed. Especially since as an adult, he now had so many to choose from compared to the three sets of identical uniforms his father had forced him to wear throughout his childhood—a pair of blue denim husky dungarees, a white beefy T, and a crisp, white button-down shirt. He might as well have been wearing a "kick me" sign to school.

His stomach growled.

It had been too long since he last ate and he simply hadn't eaten enough then. His large, doughy fingers uncurled from the broom handle and reached between the ties of his blue vest into the pocket of his olive-drab coveralls. Just as his fingertips reached the edge of the king-sized package of peanut M&M's, he saw him.

Like a camouflaged hunter spotting a trophy elk in his scope, he kept his movements slow and deliberate. He eased the candy from his pocket without making a sound while he studied his prey.

A tall, lanky man wearing a BlueSky Airlines uniform was walking—more like prancing—off the escalator that brought arriving passengers from the underground trains. The man headed toward the Buckhorn Bar and Grill. The bar was across from his safe haven under the overhang by the restrooms. It was less than thirty yards away.

The airline employee carried himself as if he were tethered to electric voltage. He was all jitters and nerves hidden by a phony smile plastered on his face. The man made a beeline toward a perturbed woman standing just beyond the row of barstools that separated the restaurant from the main terminal. She didn't look happy. Her fists were planted on her hips. Her foot was tapping and her eyes looked angry.

Perfect. A lovers' quarrel. There was no better distraction.

As the airline employee approached, he gave the irritated woman a quick peck on the cheek and leapt into a long, animated explanation trying to appease the irritated, foot-tapping, ball-fisted lover awaiting him. It was not important what the two lovers were so worked up about on this otherwise peaceful Christmas Eve. What was important was that Santa had not forgotten him this year. His Christmas gift had just arrived.

Delivered by a BlueSky Airlines employee, one of Santa's elves.

It was a little boy. A beautiful, blond boy. A sad boy who needed him. Like a puppy from the pound. He'd save him.

The airline employee had long since released the little boy's hand. The boy was lingering beside the quarreling couple, circling around the area. Just beyond the bar, busy pedestrian traffic was ebbing and flowing through the main terminal from the ticketing area to security and from the underground trains to the baggage claim areas.

Dressed in a beautiful hunter-green Christmas outfit, the boy danced about, oblivious to the tide of travelers. The boy was oblivious to his distracted escort, oblivious to the woman's fury, and oblivious to the invisible janitor across from the bar who was fixated on his every movement.

An unaccompanied minor.

He spied the airline wings pinned to the little boy's vest lapel that confirmed his assumption. It explained the tall, nervous man and his inattention to the boy. The child was traveling alone from one place to another and just passing through Denver International Airport.

What good fortune!

He closed the distance between them, careful to stay close to the wall yet out of the spatting lovers' peripheral vision. He stood between the boy and the small family bathroom that was nestled between the expansive bathrooms dedicated to men and women only. The family room, which was really just an oversized restroom intended for mothers and fathers to help their young, offered him privacy with its locking door.

Pushing the small line of gray dust and the well-traveled candy wrapper toward the door, he felt the weight of his concealed backpack against the small of his back, under his blue vest, and smiled. Opening the door, he set the broom just inside and turned back toward the child. He rattled the bag of M&M's. The child looked up. And stopped dancing.

The child saw the bright yellow bag and a dimpled grin spread across his smooth, white cheeks. After cutting a quick glance in his escort's direction, the boy tiptoed toward the man with the bag of candy.

"What Child Is This?" was playing on the PA overhead, and he scanned the airport before he ducked, unseen, into the bathroom with the bag of M&M's.

The boy followed.

CHAPTER 2

SPECIAL AGENT LIV BERGEN, my ass.

As I was yanked off my feet and my teeth were sinking into Rocky Mountain turf, I wasn't looking very agent-like and I certainly wasn't feeling very special despite my new credentials from Quantico.

I might be new at all of this—formally trained as an FBI agent, specifically assigned to be the handler for this tracking hound—but I wasn't born yesterday. In fact, I am quite confident in my abilities as one of the youngest managers ever promoted in the mining and mineral processing industry. And soon turning thirty, I can confidently say I know what I'm doing. An expert. In mining. Not as a first office agent with the Bureau.

That's my problem.

Having given up my quarrying experience and knowledge to work closely as an investigator with Special Agent Streeter Pierce, a legend at the Bureau, I am hell-bent on proving to him that his confidence in me at replacing my friend Lisa Henry—God rest her soul—in her official capacity as Beulah's handler was not in vain. So I've spent every waking hour of my personal time since returning to Colorado from Quantico out training with this bloodhound, relying on the help of my brother-in-law Michael or one of many family members to be "lost" so I could track them.

I had expected more from my Christmas Eve than this.

I spat out the pine needles and attempted to free my hands from underneath me. The same hands that by sheer instinct should have reached out to break my fall but didn't. I just could not make myself let go of the lead, afraid Beulah might get away from me. I wriggled my body off my hands and let the lead pull my arms above my head. Rocks, sticks, icy snow, and mossy dirt scraped into my jeans as my belly dragged across the forest floor.

The taut lead between us held snug against a pine tree as she bolted in a different direction. She hesitated for an instant and I jumped on the opportunity of the angled lead. Scrambling to my knees and scampering around the tree, I levered myself against Beulah's mighty force so I could regain my footing, my composure, and my dignity.

I muttered, "What's gotten into you?"

She ignored me, baying at something up the hill, pulling hard against her harness. In all my training with her, I hadn't seen her behave like this. I wondered where my brother-in-law Michael was, hoping it was he that Beulah was marking. But something about her behavior made me think not. So what had Beulah winded? And why was she off Michael's scent?

I had intentionally interrupted Beulah's momentum by tying her leash to a tree while I caught my breath. That would make this particular search inadmissible in court if we were tracking a criminal for real, but I was getting better. And the true benefit of spending my free time like today in the field with Beulah was so that she could train me to better understand her signals for when it really counted.

We'd both been working so hard every day since I'd been home that I felt like the two of us—dog and handler—were becoming one. We were thinking alike, moving together, and honing our skills as a specialized trailing team. And thanks to Michael, who was willing to get lost every time I asked, we were getting better.

I was so grateful to my brother-in-law. Especially on Christmas Eve. I knew he and my sister Elizabeth had better things to do, considering they weren't home in Louisville, Colorado, much these days, spending every moment possible building the future facilities for the Lost Boys, an outdoor campus for at-risk youth, in Rochford, South Dakota. I didn't want

Michael to think he'd wasted his holiday break on me if I'd missed Beulah's signals. So to say I was frustrated would be a gross understatement. How could I ever impress Streeter with my newly acquired skills if I didn't have a clue about what was setting Beulah off?

As I brushed off my clothes and scooped the mossy decay out of my waistband, my eyes looked ahead to see if I could see what Beulah was howling at.

And I saw it.

In a tree less than ten yards ahead of my bloodhound, fifteen yards from where I stood, were two remarkably green eyes peering down at me. Beulah was bobbing stiff-legged and baying so loudly my ears were pounding. I debated whether my head hurt from her baying or from crashing to the ground when I was trying to keep up with Beulah's sudden and mighty sprint up this hill. I was thinking back, wondering if maybe I'd hit my head on something. After all, this was the Rocky Mountains and there was nothing but trees and rocks and mountain lions out here.

A mountain lion.

I suppose that's where my wonderment should have been focused. Not on whether or not I had hit my head on a rock a minute ago. But it was all so surreal to me. I blinked and rubbed my eyes with my free fist.

About twelve feet from the ground in the crook of a heavy branch, the cat was crouched. Its eyes shifted from me to Beulah, it laid its ears back, and it hissed, baring its teeth. Beulah kept bobbing and baying, excited by the strange creature she had marked. The cat crouched lower, lifting its hind end higher in the tree. It was positioning itself to pounce. I had never seen a mountain lion, even though I grew up in the Black Hills of South Dakota. I don't know what I expected in a face-to-face encounter, but this wasn't it. I didn't think I would find the animal so beautiful, so mesmerizing. So scary.

I had read somewhere, or Michael had told me, that over the past few decades, the mountain lions had evolved to be fearless of dogs and would eventually be fearless of humans. With the expansion of the suburbs into the pristine areas west of Denver and along the Rocky Mountains, the cats had been pushed out of their natural habitat. With the ban on mountain lion hunting, the roaming acreage available to the cat population had plummeted, leaving the young male cats no other option but to double back into the populated areas. At least, this is how the experts justified the increase in kills attributed to mountain lions over the past five years. Humans, flipped over, filleted, entrails eaten, and discarded for other predators or later eating if times got tough. We had come to expect at least one death a year of a hiker or runner in the foothills.

We were nothing but lunch for this cat, if I didn't do something.

Fast.

The cat could have gone further up the tree or outrun us. But instead, it crouched and readied itself for Beulah. My hand slipped to my waist, searching for my six-inch hunting knife. My breath caught when I realized it was gone. As if the cat could read my mind, its gaze slid back to me, ignoring Beulah for the moment. I did not want to take my eyes off the cat for fear I'd miss something. Our eyes locked, and I let the lead ease through my fingers, giving myself just enough slack so that I could back up but not enough to let Beulah lurch forward. I reached the end of the lead, took a cleansing breath, and waited.

The cat grew tired of my stillness and directed its gaze back to Beulah. I took advantage of the moment, searching around my feet for the knife. Nothing. I must have lost it farther back. I looked up at the cat and it was still studying Beulah, but it had shifted its weight. The cat's back was swayed, and its tail twitched back and forth. I had to find that knife. Or something.

My eyes scanned the forest floor, looking for anything I could use as a weapon. Just behind me and off to the right, I saw a small bit of brown that did not blend with the other drab browns and grays in the shadows and snow. It was the leather sheath with my knife. I eased down to a squatting position, hoping beyond hope that the cat wouldn't see my vulnerability. Clutching the lead with one hand, I reached behind me with the other, my fingers searching the pine needles and rocks for the knife.

Just as my fingers touched the cold handle, the cat's deep green eyes shifted to me, and it stopped moving its tail. I snatched the knife and bolted upright, making myself look as big as I could by holding my arms above my head, tugging the lead accidentally as I did. Beulah's head jerked back and the cat's attention returned to her, sensing her momentary weakness.

My only thought was I had to get Beulah closer to me, away from the tree. I clipped my knife back onto my pants and clasped the lead with every ounce of strength I had. I circled the tree that I'd used as a pulley device, unwinding Beulah. I tightened the lead and pulled harder against Beulah's weight, coaxing her to be calm.

"Good girl, Beulah. You found your mark. Super. Come here now, Beulah. Come to me, baby."

Beulah stood still, no longer howling.

"That's it, Beulah," I said, tugging on her lead.

Beulah backed up several steps, her nose still pointed up at the tree. The cat stared at Beulah, crouching lower on its haunches, twitching its tail in stuttered movements. What had I done? This wasn't working right. Or I hadn't thought this through carefully enough. Mountain lions hated the sound of dogs baying and howling. Evidently, it was one of the last introductions of civilization that mountain lions feared. And I had stopped Beulah from howling.

I had to get training kicked back into gear, hers and mine.

Gripping the lead, I wrapped it around my hips and yelled, "Find!"

Beulah stiffened and lunged forward, closing the distance to the cat by a few feet. I leaned back. Beulah strained on the lead, bobbing up and down on stiffened legs, sounding again. It worked. The cat cowered into the crook of the tree. I inched along the lead for what seemed like hours. The cat was intimidated by Beulah's howl but looked a bit more perturbed by my closeness. It was studying me now. The only thing that stood between it and me was Beulah's howling. And I wanted to keep it that way.

I resisted the urge to touch Beulah. That was our signal that training was over and Beulah could stand down. I thought about trying to back out of here but that would require Beulah to stay on her mark and howl, me to be strong enough to pull her back the entire time, and both of us to be far enough away to outrun the mountain lion. We needed to stand our ground and somehow finish this. Alive. I had to ready my knife but needed both hands to hold Beulah back. Without taking my eyes off the cat, I edged closer to the nearest tree and struggled to tie Beulah to it.

I pulled my knife from the sheath and eased closer to Beulah. I spotted a broken tree branch big enough to whack the cat and inched in that direction. Just as I eased into a squat to pick up the branch, Beulah's lead loosened and she bounded toward the tree where the cat crouched.

"No!" I yelled, snatching the branch and posturing myself in a menacing stance. "Beulah, here!"

The cat leapt from the tree.

Beulah had reared up, her front paws against the tree to get her nose as close as she could to the mark, not quite seeing what she had treed or knowing the danger we were in, driven only by animal instinct.

For a moment, I couldn't move.

I know now everything happens in slow motion in a crisis like this, just as people claim. Every instant was in freeze-frame, not unlike my whole body during this split second of tragedy. The horror of imagining that cat flying through the air and landing on Beulah's back was too much for me. My shock was only intensified when I saw the cat land on the ground behind Beulah, not on her.

That's when I realized I'd had it all wrong. The cat was coming for me.

With the mountain lion between me and Beulah, sprinting toward me with tremendous speed and intent, I did what any sane person would do at that moment. I dropped the branch and the knife.

And ran like hell.

CHAPTER 3

FEAR TASTES FUNNY.

The bile that rose in my throat as I turned to run burned in my mouth with the taste of iron. That knife and tree branch sure would have come in handy right about now. And what the hell was I thinking with the running? Sure as shit I was looking like prey to the cat. My legs were racing faster than I thought possible. I didn't get very far before I felt the expected push from behind as the cat's huge paws hammered against my shoulder blades.

This was it.

I heard Beulah's growling howl and a loud crack. Run Beulah, was my last thought as my body slammed to the forest floor for the second time today. The whoosh of air from my body sounded unnatural. My world went dark for a moment, which I could only assume was from losing all my breath; oxygen rushed out of me as I struck frozen ground. I felt the weight of something rolling up the back of my legs and across my back as if I were laundry in a washerwoman's ringer.

I assumed the lion was simply toying with me, claiming me as its spoils, until I felt its hot breath against the back of my neck. Any minute its teeth would sink into the base of my skull and sever my spine. I must have been having another one of those slow-motion moments, which really didn't sit well with me considering my predicament. I wanted this moment to be quick. And over. But it wasn't. I lay there waiting for the moment to pass, waiting for the cat's teeth to sink into the soft skin behind my neck, crunching through bone to leave me paralyzed. And dead. All I felt was its weight and movement.

"Liv?" The voice, breathless but familiar, pierced the gray that crowded my senses. "You okay?"

It sounded like Michael.

What in God's name made him ask such a stupid question when clearly I was not okay? I had a huge mountain lion on my back about to eat me. Definitely not okay.

I tried to speak and realized I hadn't recovered my breath yet. I started to cough and felt movement on my back. Am I supposed to fight mountain lions? Play dead? Or is that bears? The weight on my back shifted, moved off. Something was trying to reach beneath me—the cat's paw!—to flip me over. I knew what would come next. It would slice me up the middle and eat my insides, leaving my carcass for later. I squeezed my eyes shut, pretending to be dead, just as the cat flipped me over onto my back.

Then I punched, clawed, and jabbed my thumbs toward its eyes, letting out a cry that echoed off the mountains around me.

"Liv! What the hell's wrong with you?"

I felt a warm tongue lick my cheek. I opened my eyes. Beulah was standing over me and Michael was kneeling by my side, holding the side of his face. There was no mountain lion. Just Michael nearby and Beulah sitting beside me.

"Geez, that hurt," Michael was saying, his hand pressed to his cheek.

He pulled his hand away from his face and I saw the scratches I had made, thinking he was the cat.

"I'm sorry," I whispered. My breath recovered.

Beulah wagged her tail and licked my face again. I coughed.

"Way to go, pooch," Michael said to the dog. He stood up and tucked his pistol back into his holster. I followed his gaze off into the woods. "Come on. Before that mountain lion comes back."

"So there *was* a cat."

I remembered the loud crack, wondering if what I had heard was a gunshot. But I didn't see any blood, other than from the scratch I'd made to Michael's cheek. I assumed his shooting would have at least injured the mountain lion. I wondered if Michael had missed completely.

Looking a lot like a young, thin Wilford Brimley in an old cowboy flick, Michael stood over me, petting Beulah's knobby head. Glancing at his pistol, he said, "Just scared him off. My granddaddy told me that when he was a boy, he used to walk to and from school five miles each way in the woods. His daddy gave him a small pistol. Not big enough to shoot at the mountain lions, but loud enough that when he shot into the air, the report would scare off any big cats that might be preying on him. He said it always worked."

I stared at him, incredulously. My mouth dropped open. "And what if it hadn't?"

Michael shrugged, a rascally grin tugging at the corners of his mouth. Then I realized he'd been messing with me. Michael knew what he was doing. In that split second when the cat had pounced, he had made a decision about leveling his sights on the beast. First, the large, young male likely outsized Michael's ammunition. Second, the cat was moving, and so was I, which meant Michael would either miss altogether or possibly hit me or Beulah with the bullet.

I realized Michael had decided to aim his pistol in the air intentionally to scare off the cat, rather than taking aim at him. And I realized the mountain lion had probably changed its mind when it bowled me over and decided to run right past me when I hit the ground hard enough to lose my breath and injure my ribs. Beulah must have lunged for the cat and landed on top of me, her massive weight crushing my back. It hadn't been the lion's hot breath I had felt against my neck, but Beulah's.

I suppose Beulah thought she was standing guard over me, protecting her master. But I could barely breathe with her eighty-five pound mass sitting on my back. She stuck so close to me, I could actually tell what flavor Dog Chow she'd had for breakfast.

"You saved my life."

I sat dazed, assessing the damage. My palms stung and I felt a sharp pain in my lower chest.

Michael shrugged. "You saved mine."

I plunged my hands in the snow for relief and wished Mom were here to lift me up onto the washing machine, spray my skinned palms with Bactine, and blow on them to take out the sting.

Michael was stroking the bloodhound's ears. "Well, maybe not you. More like Beulah saved my life. That mountain lion was stalking me. In broad daylight."

"I think I broke a rib."

"Good girl."

"How sensitive of you," I said, shifting my weight to lessen the pain.

"I meant Beulah, not you. Don't be stingy with those dog treats."

As I offered Beulah a fistful, Michael spread his fingers over Beulah's knobby skull again and added, "Don't tell me—now that you have a taste for cats, you're spoiled on humans?"

Beulah panted, enjoying his attention.

"Help me up," I said.

Michael reached down and yanked me to my feet. Pain shot across my back and down my leg and I doubled over.

"Damn. I really think I broke a rib."

Michael was rolling up the lead and removing Beulah's harness for me. "Probably need to call this in to the Game, Fish, and Parks, Boots."

I wasn't too pleased with the idea, but Michael was right.

If I ever thought I had a chance to be called out on search and rescue, I needed local and federal support. Not reporting to GFP that I'd had an encounter with a mountain lion during a training session wasn't exactly the way to win friends and influence people. Even if the cat had run away with no harm to any of the parties involved.

"I know."

Then, something worse dawned on me.

"Don't tell Elizabeth."

Michael just laughed at me.

I had eight siblings: Elizabeth was fifth born. I was seventh. Frances is the closest in age to me at eighteen months older and my little brother Jens is two years younger. We all had our own personalities, but the same general value system. I was the neat freak growing up. Obnoxiously

Check Out Receipt

Aberdeen Public Library
605-626-7097

Wednesday, September 27, 2017 1:36:26 PM

Title: Second chance summer
Material: Book
Due: 10/11/2017

Title: Sea glass
Material: Book
Due: 10/11/2017

Title: Solomon's whisper
Material: Book
Due: 10/11/2017

Title: Widow's might
Material: Book
Due: 10/11/2017

Title: In the belly of Jonah : a Liv Bergen myst
ery
Material: Book
Due: 10/11/2017

Title: Lot's return to Sodom : a Liv Bergen myst
ery
Material: Book
Due: 10/11/2017

Title: Noah's rainy day
Material: Book
Due: 10/11/2017

Total items: 7

Have A Great Day!!!

impeccable, my oldest sister Agatha always called me. And practical. Lacking pizzazz, as Ida says. I'd like to think of myself as more of a minimalist. Barbara might call me cheap. She'd be right. I don't like spending money if it isn't necessary or spending time if it's only to improve my looks. Everything I have must have a purpose and I like everything in its place. That's me. My sister Catherine calls me "The Big O," for organized. Eight siblings with strong opinions. Even stronger minds and backbones. And immense hearts.

"I'm serious." I really didn't want my sister Elizabeth calling me Critical Mass, or CM for short, again. She'd taken to calling me that this summer when my world had seemed to become a magnet for all things evil. Luckily, Frances defended me. I was staying with Frances and her family now, temporarily, while I found an apartment. I had leased out my house in Fort Collins when I went to Quantico and now I'm trying to sell the place. It's too far to justify coming into Denver every day, now that I'm a special agent.

Frances would be the most sensitive, compassionate, and kindest soul among us. Ole calls her the iron marshmallow, soft and squishy like a favorite teddy bear, but tough as nails when circumstances call for it. Elizabeth says she's the Bergen version of Mother Theresa, which particularly irks Catherine, considering she's the only nun in the family.

We all agree, Frances is the glue.

I collect rocks with characteristics that best describe my family members. Frances is my gypsum. In its purest form, gypsum is transparent, like Frances. Frances doesn't have a phony bone in her body; she's always the same wonderful soul no matter who she's with. She can conform within a crowd, making everyone feel at ease, yet she is the first to stand up against the injustices or the toughest of circumstances. Although gypsum from the quarries is normally quite pliable, sculptors prefer alabaster—a variety of gypsum—to nearly any other medium since it's forgiving. Gypsum also is the ingredient that gives cement its compressive strength. The iron marshmallow of the rock world.

God knew what he was doing. Noah needed a mother like Frances.

"The whole CM thing?" Michael asked.

"Yeah, for starters."

Michael pulled out his GPS and marked the location of the tree in which the mountain lion had been. I went back to retrieve the knife I'd dropped and noticed something lying under the scrub nearby. The brush was prickly and I earned further scrapes on my hands, arms, and cheeks going after the prize tucked deep beneath it. I pulled on the strap and came out with a backpack. A small, camouflage backpack.

"What'd you find?"

I lifted the pack and felt its weight.

"A hunter's?" Michael asked, stepping up behind me.

I unzipped the bag and peered inside, finding schoolbooks and candy wrappers and a couple of Matchbox cars. "A child's. A boy's backpack."

I slung the backpack over my shoulder and decided I'd see if I could find the owner to return it. I couldn't count the number of times I'd misplaced my school bag when I was a kid and wished an adult would've returned it to me. Maybe I'd get Noah to help me. He likes these types of games, solving puzzles. Like last year when we found a girl's sandal near the swing set. We talked for hours—well, more like I asked questions and he answered yes or no—about what might have happened, creating all sorts of ideas about the lost sandal before turning it over to the lost and found.

As we started heading toward the campground where we had parked, I imagined how Noah would smile when I told him about the mystery of the backpack when I got home. Beulah stayed close by my side. The exertion of the walk sent a searing pain through my rib cage, making my knees buckle. Michael steadied me. The situation hadn't quite sunk in with either of us yet. We had both almost been killed by a mountain lion, a big, hungry male nearly as long as I was tall. After getting a good look at his paw prints in the snow, neither one of us wanted to talk about that yet.

We just wanted to go home.

Beulah licked my hand. "Come here and let me give you some loving, Beulah," I said, realizing I hadn't given her any praise for the expert way she'd handled the situation.

"You okay?" Michael asked, peering over at me

"I guess."

After walking in silence and in considerable pain for the next two miles toward the campground, Michael started fidgeting with his cowboy hat.

"Can I ask what the hell you were thinking, trying to outrun a mountain lion?"

I kept walking, ignoring him.

"And where's your Sig?"

"In the fitted holster you made for me so I'd have no excuse not to have a gun with me at all times," I answered. "Under the seat of my SUV."

He grinned.

"What if that cat hadn't been spooked off by your shot? He'd have bitten through my neck before you had a chance to realize what was happening."

"Probably," he said.

We walked the rest of the way without saying a word. Maybe Elizabeth was right. Shit does seem to happen when I'm around.

No wonder she calls me Critical Mass.

CHAPTER 4

"**ANSWER THE PHONE,**" **MELISSA** said as she turned her delicate wrist and noted the time on her watch, her irritation growing with every ring she counted. She stared at her reflection in the shiny gold placards that paneled the columns in the airport baggage claim area. Smoothing her skin-tight dress and primping her long, blond hair, she added, "Come on, Max."

"Hey, that's Melissa Williams," she heard someone holler. "Melissa! Can I take my picture with you?"

Without ending her call or removing her sunglasses, she turned and smiled at the fan rushing up beside her as he shoved his cell phone toward a woman and hurriedly gave instructions on how to take their picture. Melissa's smile never waned, even when the creep slipped his hand around her waist and let it linger near her butt. How she hated this part of fame. But how she loved the publicity on the social networks. This guy would brag for weeks about groping her, make up all sorts of lies about what they did together, and plaster the picture—this picture—of them all over the Internet.

The more creeps like him, the more buzz for her.

Besides, it was her choice to come in here. Melissa's driver had offered to collect little Max at the airport for her, but she missed the little guy, wanted to surprise him. Plus in the process, if the paparazzi happened to catch her in a loving embrace at LAX with her son on Christmas Eve, showcasing her rocking body and her practiced expression of alarm that her private moment had become suddenly public, then her holidays would be complete. She imagined herself flipping through the glossy pages of a tell-all magazine as she basked in the sun on the private beach that stretched for miles at Aldo's sanctuary.

The result of her plan was nothing more than a lecherous traveler copping a feel as his wife snapped grainy photos on a cell phone. Melissa's anxiety was rising. No paparazzi were in sight and no little Max.

About to hang up and try another number, she heard her soon-to-be ex-husband's voice answer, "Hello?"

Typical Max. With all his money he could afford the most current technology to tell him who was calling; probably her exact location; maybe her recent three-pound weight loss off her already-stunning five-eleven, one-hundred-fifteen-pound frame; and possibly even what brand and color of pumps she was wearing, except he didn't bother to look at the caller ID on the display.

"Where is he? Is this some kind of a power play or something?"

"Missy?" His hesitation concerned her. Normally he was quick with a witty comeback. Even when his mind was muddled by her calls, when they interrupted his latest conquest, he never answered with such hesitation. Experience told her the number of rings it took Max to answer his phone was directly proportional with the number of years younger the tramp between his silk sheets was. And this one was quite young.

"I don't have time for your games. Aldo and I were planning on leaving for Papeete in the morning." Melissa watched as the BlueSky employee behind the customer service desk pretended to act busy with other important matters, rather than let her know he recognized her behind those large sunglasses. Who wouldn't, she thought.

"I didn't give you permission to take little Max out of the country," Max said.

She imagined Maximillian Bennett Williams II wrapping a slippery sheet around his thin waist, beads of sweat dripping down his six-pack abs as he ran his fingers through his dark, wavy locks. And her practiced hatred for him was suddenly overshadowed by her desire to be that conquest tangled in the heap of silk sheets in his Manhattan high-rise apartment.

Only the BlueSky employee's gaze pulled her from her fantasy back to the situation at hand.

She leaned her hip against the counter and drummed her fingernails on top, realizing that several other people had also recognized her and she would need to mind her manners. She didn't want to draw the paparazzi's attention. Not right now. Not while she was so upset with Max. She never looked much like a supermodel when cameras captured anger on her face.

"So that's what this is about?"

"What are talking about?" Max sighed.

"You didn't put little Max on the plane because you were pissed that we were taking him to Papeete with us? For Christmas? You're punishing me?" she whispered, although she managed to inject a hiss and a curse into her hushed tone.

There was another pause. It unsettled her. Normally when they argued, there were no pauses, no lost opportunities for either to deliver a verbal blow. Yet Max was still on the other end.

"Max?"

"Missy, I did put little Max on the plane." His voice sounded small and unsure, completely unlike his usual self—the megadeveloper millionaire who was never short on confidence.

"Max?" She made no attempt to hide her shock.

The BlueSky employee openly stared at her.

She heard Max reason, "Maybe the plane is just delayed."

Melissa hated when Max talked to her like she was stupid. But she appreciated that he still cared enough about her to try to calm the fear that was swelling in her gut.

She attempted to steady her shaky voice and said, "I'm standing here at customer service by the baggage claim with a BlueSky employee named Darrel and we're both watching the Denver flight 1212 passengers getting their bags now. Max isn't here."

"What about the escort?"

Melissa tucked the phone against her neck and asked Darrel, "He was an unaccompanied minor. He had an escort. Could you check on that?"

Darrel nodded once, while still typing on the keyboard, and lifted the phone's handset, asking for crew members, gate employees, or anyone who might have seen the boy or his BlueSky escort.

"What's he saying?" Max asked.

"Nothing yet. He's checking on the computer and asking around about Max."

"How old is he?" Darrel asked.

"Five," Melissa answered, noting the alarm in his eyes at her answer.

She heard him mumble, "Couldn't be. He's only five. Yes, I'll hold."

He looked apologetically at her as his fingers flew furiously across the keyboard. Fixing his eyes on the screen, he explained, "This happens from time to time when teens rebel because their parents forced them to have escorts."

"But little Max is not a teen."

"What? What?" Max was asking.

"He said this happens from time to time. Teens ditching their escorts."

Max said nothing. Something inside her stirred.

"He was on that plane, Missy." His tone had softened.

Melissa glanced up at Darrel, who offered her a smile, but it wasn't kindness she saw in his eyes. She pointed at the crowd around the carousel. "That's the flight from Denver? Flight 1212, right?"

He nodded.

With her cell phone jammed against her ear, she stomped off toward the carousel, pushing her way through the straggle of travelers left standing around to retrieve their bags. Then she saw it. The blue bag with a yellow puppy imprinted on the canvas, a dark brown bear wearing a Yankees baseball cap strapped to the handle.

"Missy?"

"Max?" Her knees had grown weak. Her head was spinning and a gray fog began to swirl near the edges of her vision as if the airport was closing in around her.

"Missy, what is it?"

She drew a breath.

"His bag is here." Her words were barely audible.

She watched the bag draw nearer to her but made no attempt to retrieve it. Something told her to find little Max first, then have him identify his bag. His bear. She watched it round the corner on the belt and saw his name, Maximillian Bennett Williams III, written on the tag in big bold letters. The handwriting was not hers and it was not Max's. Probably Nanny Judy's, she thought, realizing it was easier to focus on that small detail rather than the scope of what was happening. She let the tiny blue bag slide past her and beyond the black strips of plastic that kept travelers from seeing what went on in the baggage handler area on the other side of the wall.

Out of sight.

Gone.

She could hear Max barking orders in the background, hollering to people to get BlueSky on the phone, reciting the ticket number and invoice number for the escort he'd paid to accompany little Max from New York City to Los Angeles for the Christmas holidays.

She saw Darrel, the BlueSky customer service employee, turn his back to her, but not before she saw the dread in his eyes.

She looked toward the escalator, hoping with everything she had to see a delayed BlueSky employee escorting little Max down the stairs toward her, yet she saw nothing.

And she stared at the single bag on the carousel as it came around again before the belt was stopped. The bag was taunting her to pick it up, the bear staring at her with judgment in its beady little marble eyes.

"Missy? Missy?"

The burden was too much for her to carry any longer, and she felt her legs buckle, her body crumple to the ground.

CHAPTER 5

Noah

CRITICAL MASS. THAT'S WHAT my mom and Auntie Elizabeth call Auntie Liv.

Ever since the end of last summer, Auntie Elizabeth and Uncle Michael have been gone for months at a time rebuilding the cabin in Rochford that was destroyed when Auntie Liv tried to protect the Hansons. My mom and dad think I'm too young to know what's going on. But I'm not. They also don't know Auntie Liv has been training me to be a spy. She's the one who told me the secret of the vents. I can hear just about any conversation my parents have through my floor vent, if I manage to roll close enough to listen.

Luckily, I heard the whole story of what happened at the Hanson cabin when my mom told my dad about a call from Auntie Elizabeth last summer. She had asked Mom to keep a special eye on Auntie Liv, who was traveling home from the Black Hills of South Dakota to Fort Collins with a wounded dog named Beulah. I almost blew my spy cover by letting loose a screech, since I'd never been around a dog before and knew Auntie Liv would let me play with her. But I stayed quiet and listened. My mom tried to whisper as she told my dad that Auntie Liv had killed a man and that not only had the FBI approved of what she'd done, but they also had asked her to become one of them.

Then I did blow it. A squeal raced through my throat before I could catch it. It must have echoed down the vent, because my parents stopped talking. When they opened my door to check on me. I pretended to be laughing at something outside my window, but really I was just so excited that Auntie Liv was going to be an FBI agent.

I've dreamed of being a spy, which I know would be a perfect job for me considering my superpowers of being invisible, having bionic ears, owning a bionic eye (as long as I don't lose my contact lens), and being a human lie detector. That's what Auntie Liv calls my ability to sense other peoples' feelings and truths. People, especially grownups, tend to say things to me that they won't share with others.

Auntie Liv's not Critical Mass. She's cool. Auntie Elizabeth says Auntie Liv is the epicenter for everything crazy, which doesn't sound like Auntie Liv to me. But I don't know what an epicenter is. I just know she isn't crazy. She's funny. And kind and gentle. And real. Most of all, she knows about my secret life as a spy. And we solve mysteries together.

She said she had something to talk with me about, but Mom made her and Auntie Elizabeth do last-minute grocery shopping before the stores close. They're trying to get Christmas Eve dinner ready. Dad's downstairs talking to Uncle Michael and I'm struggling to hear Uncle Michael's story about what happened today over the constant blowing of hot air through the vents. It's so snowy and cold today that Emma's afraid Santa won't come. I told her he will. He always does. No matter how cold it gets.

Uncle Michael asked where I was and Dad said I was upstairs napping. Then he asked my dad about Emma. Dad said she was downstairs playing Barbies. But I really wasn't paying attention until Uncle Michael told my dad not to tell my mom. So I had to find out what it was that he wanted to keep secret. He said Auntie Liv got injured today when they were up in the woods west of town working with Beulah on trailing in the Rocky Mountains. And apparently stuff had happened. Like always.

I strained to hear every word through the heater working overtime. Beulah, the big red bloodhound, lay next to me in the sunlight streaming through my window, fast asleep, snoring away, which made it even harder to hear. Whatever Uncle Michael was telling Dad had affected Auntie Liv a lot more than it had Beulah.

For a moment, the hot air stopped blowing and Beulah's snoring settled into a breathing pattern of deep sleep. I heard my mom's voice, dashing all hopes that I would hear what happened. Bodies moved about and chitchat began as groceries were unloaded and the holiday cooking began.

I heard Auntie Liv's muffled voice as she approached my door. "Just a minute. Frances asked me to check on Noah and then I'll tell you what happened. I've got to find somewhere quiet where I can talk. I'll call you right back."

My door creaked open and I heard her tiptoe toward where I lay. The big picture window Dad installed special for me that reaches all the way from floor to ceiling was my window to the world. I spend a lot of time here, and anyone who knows me knows that. But Auntie Liv also knows that I prefer being by the window because of the vent. With my face turned toward the sun, I closed my eyes. I pretended to sleep so Auntie Liv would stay with me. Then I could listen in on her conversation, a trick I'd learned so I could make myself invisible. A spy like me understands that adults who don't have kids, like Auntie Liv, think eyes closed is the same as asleep. Asleep is the same as invisible. Kids like me play possum all the time. Pretend to be asleep just to avoid talking with some other kid or in hopes of overhearing adults talking. Like maybe what they got me for Christmas.

I heard her knees crack when she bent down to pet Beulah sleeping next to me. "Good girl. Are you keeping guard on Noah for me? Protecting him?"

Protecting me? From what? I snorted in surprise but kept my eyes shut, which Auntie Liv must have taken as noises of deep sleep since I heard her slip into my bathroom and quietly close the door behind her as she tapped in numbers on her phone.

"I'm sorry. I just haven't had a minute alone to call. Do you miss me?"

Her voice was clear and easy to hear.

"She did her job. I just didn't do mine. I did a face-plant instead. Quit laughing." There was a pause as she listened to whoever was on the other end of the line. I don't know who she was talking to, but I could tell she had been instructed to talk slowly and include every detail, which was unlike

Auntie Liv. "You said never let go of the lead." Another pause. I kept an ear on Auntie Liv. This was getting good. "Typical? What do you mean I care more about that damn dog than myself? I care about you."

At first, I thought she was talking to Gramma Bergen because whoever it was knew Auntie Liv really well. She did care about everyone more than herself. But then I thought it couldn't be Gramma Bergen because Auntie Liv repeated whatever was said and Gramma Bergen would never say "damn." Whoops, did I just swear?

"I must have looked ridiculous. Like I was belly surfing on pine needles." Pause. "Ah, thanks. You always say the nicest things to me. I could comb my hair with firecrackers and you'd say I was beautiful."

Yuck! She's talking to a boyfriend. Probably the new guy. Jack. I heard Mom talking about him.

Her chuckle made me smile and with effort, I rolled toward Beulah so I could touch her soft fur that had been warmed by the sunlight streaming through my big window. I imagined Auntie Liv being dragged about the woods like a ragdoll as she tried to get back on her feet and muttered awful names at Beulah. And I couldn't control my laugh. I buried my face in Beulah's neck to hide the sound and I heard Auntie Liv get quiet in my bathroom. I could imagine her sitting on the bench leaning against the long, shallow bathing table that was my special tub, wondering if she'd awakened me. I heard the bathroom door open briefly and then close again. I'd managed to stop laughing and go still, fooling Auntie Liv again.

"So anyway, Beulah ignored my commands and started baying at something farther up the hill. I hadn't seen her behave like that."

I heard an eruption of laughter from somewhere downstairs and worried that the adults would notice Auntie Liv was gone, that they'd come looking for her. I hoped it wasn't until after I heard the story of today's events in the woods.

"But wait, let me tell you what she was howling at."

I heard her pause and heard the smile in her voice as she continued.

"I know you do. Thanks for that. I'm ready if Streeter ever asks. And Beulah's as good as ever."

I heard my mom call for Auntie Liv. Then I heard Auntie Elizabeth laughing and teasing Emma. Thank God for Emma. With her distracting them, I could focus on Auntie Liv's call.

"She didn't seem upset at all. But when I saw it, I was both excited and scared to death."

I stiffened at the change in her tone.

"Those green eyes. Just staring at me."

Green eyes? What had green eyes? I strained to listen.

"Well, you and me both. Scared and excited because how often in your life do you get to come face-to-face with a mountain lion and live to tell about it?"

A mountain lion!

I've always dreamed of seeing a mountain lion. On a hike. In the yard. Outside my window. It could happen. Auntie Liv has always been my hero, but now she survived a lion. How cool is that? I wonder what she did to survive. Wrestled it to the ground? Lassoed its hind legs and roped it like a calf in a rodeo? Karate chopped it in the throat? Chased it around a tree until it turned to butter? Outstared it like Davy Crockett did the bear?

I better pay attention so I'll know what to do if I ever face a mountain lion.

CHAPTER 6

I LOVED THE WAY Jack laughed. It was rare and rich, like a fine wine. I had grown to enjoy his laughter more than any of his other good qualities and it's what I'd missed the most while I was at Quantico. His gentle touch, his exotic good looks, his soul-searching gaze, the incredible way he thinks—Jack was everything I'd ever dreamed of in a boyfriend.

Although we met for the first time only four and a half months ago—but who's counting?—I feel in some ways like we've known each other for years, yet in other ways as if we're constantly on a first date. Jack Linwood's mysterious nature keeps me off balance, which may just be my best position.

Jack was one of the special agents brought in by Streeter Pierce, the temporary special agent in charge on the case in the Black Hills that led to the incident at the Hanson cabin. Streeter had asked Jack to teach me how to work with Beulah as her new handler. And from the moment I set eyes on Jack, I felt like I'd dropped into the end of that Disney movie where the jungle boy Mowgli watched the girl fetch water, only we were both grown adults—Mowgli a tall, dark FBI agent and me quite eager to let him help me carry water or help me with anything.

I had found out a lot about Jack, not from Jack himself, since I'd started as a first office agent in the Denver field office. Jack Linwood, a year older than Streeter, had only been with the FBI for five years. He had been accepted just before turning thirty-five, which bumped him up against the age limit for new candidates. Although he had only been with the FBI for a relatively short time compared to other agents his age, Jack was extremely capable and proficient at his job in the investigative unit. He had rapidly been promoted and was named supervisor of the Investigative Control Operations in the Denver Bureau.

I thought his face, although intelligently handsome, had a haunting, intense appearance, which was intensified by his large, dark brown eyes and nut-brown skin. Jack was a no-nonsense agent and was nothing but professional when it came to his work habits. Just as with Streeter, no one in the Denver Bureau knew much about Jack Linwood, except for his work performance, which everyone agreed was exceptional.

Jack's best feature, besides his exquisite body, was his boyish grin when he shared a rare moment of laughter, which he seemed to save just for me and me alone. He rarely smiled around others and I couldn't recall ever hearing him laugh at work. I could almost hear him smiling through the phone.

Leaning against the bathroom counter, avoiding the mirror, I propped my feet against the bathing table that Gabriel had installed for Noah. It's a long, narrow, contoured table with drains along all four sides. Frances tells me it's more like the new rain-massage tables they have at expensive spas, but I haven't seen the inside of many spas lately. I wondered if Noah felt like a turkey being basted when his parents sprayed him clean with the shower-like nozzle attached to the hose. But I had to admit it looked like a decadent spa treatment to me and I felt a bit envious of Noah, especially as sore as I was right now. I wouldn't mind if someone treated me to a warm raindrop massage as I slept on Noah's bathing table.

"A mountain lion? As in, cougar?" Jack said. My feet slipped to the ground, sending a jolt through my sore ribs.

"Ooh."

"Sweetheart? You okay?"

Although Jack was a kind and giving man, his joy was scarce; he was so serious all the time. The only other time I'd noticed him sporting a hint of a genuine smile was when he spent time with Streeter; they clearly shared a kind of mutual admiration. Or respect. I wouldn't go so far as describing their relationship as a bromance, since I doubt either one would have a clue what I was talking about and both would smack me for saying so if they did.

"Did you just call me sweetheart?"

After dating—and I use the term rather loosely—for nearly five months, I'd never heard any such term of endearment from Jack. That was since August, since the Hanson incident up at Rochford in South Dakota. I say "loosely" because I really hadn't seen Jack much when I was at Quantico. We'd gone out on a few dates before I left for Virginia in September and several more since I returned to Denver three weeks ago, but our relationship is still quite new. He even visited me one weekend while I was at Quantico. Said he was on business, but I'm not so sure. That's probably because I'd rather believe he flew all the way to the DC area just to see me. Something besides my insecurities made me doubt it.

"Yes," he said, his voice sounding unusually playful. "Is that a problem?"

Truth is, I'm not even sure if what was developing between us could be considered dating. It was more like the stirrings of a strong friendship. But it came with an occasional undercurrent of physical attraction so strong it would sweep us away like a riptide, and neither of us wanted to fight it.

"Nothing you say or do could ever be a problem for me. Except that you have other plans for Christmas and can't come for dinner."

I get tired of being a friend to so many men like Jack, especially when I find myself attracted to them. If I'd chosen specialties at Quantico more in line with the technician's expertise, I suppose I would be able to work with Jack Linwood more often than with Streeter Pierce. But I gravitated toward being a field agent, like Streeter, whereas Jack has crazy hours in the lab. Plus he always seems to be out of town on one case or another and I can never keep track of where he goes.

"I told you. I can't. I'm working."

Illusiveness about how time is spent tends to stunt a budding relationship, regardless of how trusting I am by nature. And I had to admit that I had a tendency to downplay how much time I'd been spending with Streeter, knowing it would only make Jack jealous. Even though Jack would never admit it or let it show.

"On what?" I asked.

I hadn't planned on telling Streeter or anyone at work about my little incident with the mountain lion until I got back to work after Christmas. Mostly because I was trying to impress Streeter with my skills, not make him wonder about my ability to make decisions under pressure, which he might if he heard about me trying to outrun a mountain lion. But I couldn't wait to tell Jack all about what had happened. Mostly because I knew I'd get to hear him laugh. And of course, I had him laughing in all the right places, once I established I was alive and unharmed.

"Tsk, tsk. I told you that some things at work must stay confidential, my dear."

I'd tried to draw out Jack's plans for the holidays, curious if he would be spending it with a family I knew nothing about or if he had travel plans. I had hoped to hear he had none, so I could invite him to Frances's house for the Christmas festivities. But my not-so-subtle attempts were unsuccessful. In fact, I was starting to wonder if Jack might be Jewish or Muslim or some other religion that didn't recognize Christmas and that I'd somehow offended him, 'cause I wasn't buying this secretive work shit. I'd never know, since Jack was so difficult to read and information from him was meted out to me like captured raindrops in a desert.

"Dear? Sweetheart and dear in the same conversation? You're getting all soft on me, Mr. Linwood," I said. Thirsty for more, I asked, "You going to keep me guessing?"

Since it was Christmas Eve, I thought I'd try one more time to see if Jack would want to spend the holidays with me, but he had texted earlier that he already had plans and was sorry to miss out. He did ask me to call him later with details about today's training exercise, considering we were facing a tough search in the snow today for Beulah. And for me.

"What's to guess? I'm working. You're not. It's Christmas. You're with your family. I'm not with you. End of story."

After the incident at the Hanson cabin in August, I'd gone to Quantico at Streeter's urging. My injured, man-trailing bloodhound, Beulah, had stayed behind in Denver with Jack. Beulah needed time to heal and Jack said he knew the exact veterinarian who could properly care for her. Once she recovered, Jack had been incorporating Beulah into the Investigative

Control Operations team so she would stay fit and be ready to trail. He'd even taken her out on some tracking exercises in the field a few times.

Since my return to Colorado, I'd been out every day with Beulah, building up from short, easy trailing exercises to today's more difficult trail in the woods with cold, heavy, drifting snows. Trust was a big part of our ability to find the target and I had to reestablish that trust after being gone so long. Today, with Beulah having been knocked off track by the mountain lion's scent, she would either bond more tightly with me as her handler or lose confidence in me completely.

"I want to hear a better story. It's Christmas, Jack."

I decided to bring Beulah here to Frances's home, fill her belly with a holiday feast, and let her sleep. Next to Noah. I wanted us both to spend time with Noah. Beulah could rest and recharge and forget all about today's exercise in the Rocky Mountain backwoods. I could reconnect, get grounded, and reenergize. My nephew, Noah, had that effect on everyone around him. He had a calming nature, one of peace, wisdom, and acceptance that I can only characterize as being . . . well I know this sounds stupid, but . . . transcending.

"And for some reason, the bad guys never take a holiday. Have you noticed?" Jack said, his words feeling as smooth and warm to my ears as my feet felt propped against the electric baseboard.

I opened the door to the bathroom and peered into Noah's bedroom to check on him. He seemed to be sleeping. I know that when I need a boost, I come see Noah. And right about now, I needed a boost, considering there was no talking Jack into spending the holidays with me. So Noah would once again be my rock.

My nephew has a positive outlook on life. I always walk away after my time with him feeling more inspired than when I arrived. I know he's only twelve, but he has a very old soul and a positive aura that draws me in and makes me forget about everything negative. He's like a human dream catcher. He's my secret weapon, a little charger where I can dock my life batteries for a renewed energy. And from the looks of my big red bloodhound, relaxed and snoring in the sunlight by the window next to my sleeping nephew, Beulah sensed the same peace that I did—that so many others did—in Noah's presence.

As I pulled the door closed to Noah's bathroom, I wanted more than ever for Jack to meet Noah and whispered into my cell phone, "At least join us for dinner tonight?"

"Wish I could," Jack said, his wistful words carrying a hint of sorrow.

I sighed, knowing there was no point in asking again. I noticed my frightful reflection in the bathroom mirror. My chestnut hair was a tangled mess falling long past my shoulders, since I hadn't had time to go to a salon for months. My face and neck had some superficial scratches from all the face-plants and scrub brush, as did my hands and forearms. My palms were scraped raw and my ribs ached, which made me stand hunched like an old woman. My green eyes looked like two angry seas rimmed in fire.

I wondered what Jack saw in me and whether his family would approve. That is, if he had a family and if they were still alive. He had told me he was raised in New York City in a penthouse apartment and that his mother was from Sri Lanka and his father was the son of Italian immigrants. But he quickly changed the subject when I asked about them. I would like to think they wouldn't disapprove of their refined, citified son dating a Western girl like me. But as I stared at my image in the mirror, I had to wonder. I leaned in to take a closer look. My toned arms were sore from holding back Beulah's weight. My freckled skin appeared healthy, save for the scratches that would heal in a couple days and could be easily concealed with makeup. And the redness around my eyes wasn't serious; it looked to me like a small allergy flare-up, probably spawned by dredging up molds and pollens as I plowed through pine needles. I'd be fine after a hot shower. Or a rain massage on Noah's bathing table, I thought, glancing wistfully over my shoulder to the porcelain bed.

He added, "So are you going to leave me hanging? About the mountain lion?"

"Are you going to leave me hanging on what's so important to make you work over Christmas?" Staring at my damaged appearance in the mirror's reflection seemed answer enough. I'd run scared too, if I were Jack.

I sensed a bit of irritation in his voice when he said, "Liv? The mountain lion?"

And I decided to finish my story.

CHAPTER 7

Noah

I TENSED AND FELT a change deep inside my muscles, the type of tension that tends to launch my skinny body like a rocket into outer space, into the vast darkness of seizures. Inside, it feels like a giant's rough fingertips strumming the taut strings of a pixie's delicate harp. I focused on my limbs and willed myself away from the edge of a seizure. Oddly, thinking about Auntie Liv's storytelling did the trick to relax me.

As she told her story of the mountain lion, I realized that knowing even the worst news or the scariest stories was less stressful than not knowing or leaving it to my imagination. I drew in a breath and tilted my nose toward Beulah's warm coat. She smelled clean and good, like a dog should. I was glad Beulah was here with me. She made me feel safe.

Was it wrong of me to pray that someone buys Auntie Liv's Fort Collins house she has for sale and that she never finds an apartment in Denver so that she can live with us forever?

As Auntie Liv told whoever was on the phone about squatting down to grab her knife, I remembered hearing about how dangerous cats had become to people. I had heard on the local news that people should watch out for mountain lions because they had become fearless of humans. The news had said the mountain lions were sneaking into our neighborhoods, hunting the irrigation ditches for easy prey like yappy dogs or loose cats. Some people jogging in the woods had gotten attacked by the cougars. Cougar. I liked that word better than mountain lion or cat. Sounds scarier. I don't know if I believe all the talk that there are more cougars attacking humans because we don't carry and shoot guns like they used to in the West. I think the cats are just mad that a bunch of us people moved in closer to their home in the woods near Denver and they don't like sharing their room. I don't like sharing my room with Emma when my aunts and uncles come to visit. I don't attack anyone, but I've been known to snarl at Emma a time or two.

But I like sharing my room with Beulah.

And I like watching out my window every morning and every evening, hoping to see a mountain lion. How exciting would that be? I know Mom would scold me for wishing something so dangerous and I wouldn't dare share my secret with Emma or she'd never go in the backyard again, but I still hoped to see a mountain lion in our neighborhood someday.

I couldn't wait to tell Emma how Auntie Liv fought off a cougar. It's such a crazy story that Emma's going to call me a liar. Then she'll tell me I should quit letting my imagination get in the way of reality. She is funny that way, using such big words she learned on Nickelodeon. She should be an actress.

Auntie Liv's tone changed. I felt Beulah shift beside me. She was getting to the good part where the cougar leapt from the tree and attacked her. I felt my own muscles bunch and I had to focus hard to tell them to relax. My arms started to relax and the dog settled back down as Auntie Liv grew quiet. She was listening to whatever her boyfriend was saying. I wanted to hear Auntie Liv tell more of her story.

I quit pretending to be asleep, hoping she'd notice and come spend time with me. I shifted my weight and studied the door as if I needed to see for myself how Auntie Liv had made it out of her pickle unharmed. I hadn't seen her when she came in, after all. And now my mind's eye imagined she was missing an arm or had a gaping wound in her side or an eyeball dangling down her cheek like a zombie or something.

I held my breath, wanting to see my aunt, wanting to know she was okay, head to toe. I was glad I had my bionic contact in today. I could see for miles and miles, but not through bathroom doors. It wasn't that good of a contact lens. But wouldn't that be cool if Santa brought a secret spy contact lens that could do that?

"Auntie Liv!" Emma called from downstairs, her intrusion causing my body to jerk.

I heard Auntie Liv open the door, tiptoe out the bedroom door and close it again, then call softly down, "I'll be down in a minute, Em."

Before she retreated back into my bathroom to finish her call, I had the chance to see for myself she had no wounds, no missing limbs. Okey dokey. Auntie Liv was fine, despite her scary story, other than a bunch of scratches on her face and hands. And she was kind of walking funny. She must not have noticed I was wide awake or she would have ended her call immediately.

She said goodbye in a syrupy girly voice. Yuck! I don't know if I really wanted to meet this guy or not. Especially the way he changed my Auntie Liv from funny and tough to squishy.

The bathroom door opened.

"Hey, cowboy," she said as she came closer to me. I was glad she noticed I was awake. "Nice view into your neighbor's house. How much of my phone conversation did you hear?" I smiled. "Spying on me again?"

She's onto me. I heard her crouch beside me, moaning with pain as she did. She lay down beside me, sandwiching me between her and Beulah. I love being sandwiched.

"I hurt my side today. That's why I grunted just now." She must have noticed my smile disappear and my frown when I heard her groan with pain. "And listen, about that phone call. The trick to being a good spy is not to share any of your secrets. So do you think you can keep all this between you and me?" I didn't smile. "Oh, is that how it's going to be?" I felt her fingers tickle my neck and sides. "Then I'll force you to keep it a secret. Tickle torture!"

I laughed, drawing my knees up to my stomach and curling into a protective ball. She only tickled me for a few seconds but it felt like hours. Torture.

"So, truth or you get more of the tickle torture." I let the laughter fade and my smile remain. Auntie Liv said, "Okay, so here's the deal. I did land hard on the ground and bruised a rib or two. But I'm fine. And I don't want your mom or Auntie Elizabeth to find out because they'll worry. And if they find out about the mountain lion, they'll flip out."

I started laughing again.

"You know the drill. Pinky swear. You won't tell anyone?"

I felt her hook her pinky around mine and I refused to smile.

"You're telling Emma, aren't you?" I smiled. "Compromise. Pinky swear you won't tell anyone but Emma?" I smiled. "Deal. She won't believe you anyway."

Auntie Liv always knew what to say. She never treated me like I was stupid, just because I was a kid. That's what I loved most about her. And she paid attention. To all of us kids. She knew Emma as well as she knew me.

"Okay, so the most important part of my morning was not that I saw a mountain lion and not that I fell down and hurt myself, but what I found while I was in the woods."

My excitement grew. I could feel my limbs growing stiff and I couldn't relax. I'd been waiting for this ever since Auntie Liv got back today.

"I found a kid's backpack. Stuffed in a bush. It looks like some kid lost his schoolwork on a hike or something. Won't that be a good Christmas gift for the kid it belongs to?" I smiled. "Want to help me figure out whose it might be?"

I flashed a smile and raised my eyes.

"I looked through the backpack and it looks like the books belong to Pennington Elementary School." I sucked in a squeal. "You know that school? Is that where you go?" I smiled. "Great! This is going to be easier than I first thought. Have you heard of any kid losing a backpack?"

I didn't smile. I had heard of a girl losing her new coat on the playground and a little boy in first grade losing the remote-control tank he had brought for show-and-tell, but nothing about a backpack being lost.

"Okay, if it helps, it looks like it belongs to a boy. I found Milky Way candy wrappers, bite-sized, and two Matchbox cars, one white with blue racing stripes and one midnight blue with orange racing stripes."

I grinned. Sounded like the kid was pretty cool to me. I'd like having those cars to play with.

"The cars have been played with a lot. I can tell. Probably his favorites. How old would you guess him to be? Younger than you?"

I didn't think so and kept my face blank.

"Your grade?" My smile was quick. "Maybe in a higher grade?" I grinned. "So around your age and maybe in fourth, fifth, or sixth grade?" I smiled and sucked in another squeal. "One book was *Everyday Mathematics.* Does that help?"

We had *Everyday Mathematics* in almost every grade, so I didn't smile.

"There was a note about a December field trip pass to—" She stopped, noticing I'd smiled. "Does that help? Is there only one grade that takes a field trip in December?"

Every grade took field trips, but only the fifth graders took one in December.

"Fourth?" No smile. Auntie Liv always forgets what grade I'm in. Emma and I are in fourth. I told her the kid was probably in a higher grade already. "Fifth? So the kid who lost this backpack is a fifth grader? Great! You've narrowed this down a lot. What else?"

My eyes wandered and my smile disappeared. She started fiddling with her fingers and knuckles. I laughed.

"First finger A through F?" I didn't smile. "Damn, I wish I knew the five-finger method. You could probably tell me a lot more if I did. Do you want me to call Emma?"

I would not smile. No way. This was our game. Mine and Auntie Liv's. A secret. I was the spy, not Emma.

"Okay. Just between us, then. So I'll have to use yes and no questions only. You can help me figure this out. I won't tell anyone else." I smiled. "Besides, you're great at this. Remember last year when we were at Gramma Bergen's house? The beeping sound no one could figure out?" I did. I heard it. It was annoying. "It took us a while, but we figured it out. Remember? It was a dying battery in a smoke detector back in a closet in the basement, the sound muffled and faint coming through the insulated floor. You figured that out all because of your bionic ears. I always knew you'd make a good spy."

Thanks to Auntie Liv, I was getting better and better all the time. Especially when she gave me puzzles to figure out, like the lost backpack.

It was fun to wonder whose it might be and I'd think hard about what I remembered before the holiday break and would listen closely to all the kids after.

"So, I got you a Christmas present, but I can't give it to you tomorrow morning or everyone will know your secret. That you're a spy."

I saw her fish a small package from her pocket. In my excitement, I forgot all about the earlier signs that a seizure might be coming on. Now, I knew nothing—not even a grand mal—could take me away from this special moment.

"At Quantico, I lived in the dormitory closest to the store. Did you know I ate for free the whole time I was there?"

I smiled. I loved to eat. Auntie Liv did, too. Not only did we have our love of mysteries in common, we also shared our love of food. She'd take me to McDonald's and buy me the Big Mac meal with a shake. I'd eat and eat and eat until I thought my stomach would burst like an overfilled balloon. Like I said, Auntie Liv never treated me like a little kid, buying me tiny Happy Meals just because I only weighed forty pounds. Instead, she treated me like I was twelve.

"Anyway, I found this really cool pin," she said, unwrapping the tiny gift for me. "I think you'll like it, but I'm not sure. Maybe I've read all the signs wrong." I stopped smiling, studying her face and the pin she pulled from the box with my bionic eye. "The signs that you'd make a great spy are that you're smart, you pay attention, and you notice everything. And you're great at pretending to be asleep." I groaned. "I think you would make a great spy. Unless you're afraid of danger, which I highly doubt."

I grinned, feeling happy that she understood and appreciated my talents and that we shared this secret of my life as a spy.

"See this? It's a goalpost with a football flying through it. Manly." I laughed. She did, too. "The football is really an activation button. The tiny cameraman videotaping the field goal is really a microphone nested in the pin. Even though this pin is the size of a quarter, the memory card can hold up to two hours of audio. A spy needs equipment like this, don't you think?"

I sucked in a long breath, feeling more excited about this gift than the flashlight she'd given me last year. It was a luminescent flashlight that detected things like bloodstains. Cool! It had a purplish glow and a big switch the size of a salad plate. But Mom and Dad took that away after the neighbor complained about the light flashing on and off on nights I couldn't sleep and was bored. I don't know where they put it, but I'd bet it's on the top shelf of my closet where Emma can't reach.

I wasn't sure if I could activate the pin because the button was so tiny, but so what? How cool was this that I could spy for real? As she held the pin close to my good eye, I could see that the brown football, about the size of a dime, was the largest part of the pin. I hoped I could reach up with my arms and at least tap the button with my crooked fingers or wrist bone.

"Now before I pin this on your shirt, you have to promise me you won't use this to get your sister in trouble or to record your parents. If you do, we'll both get in trouble. It's just for secret missions. Like to find the owner of the lost backpack. The case of the mysterious backpack. Agreed?"

I was so excited I couldn't force my mouth's wide opening to form a smile so I moved my eyes upward and kicked my legs.

Auntie Liv said, "Okay, then pinky swear."

My kicking continued and Beulah squirmed beside me. I hadn't heard Emma come into my room over my own laughing, but I heard Auntie Liv's groan when my sister jumped on her back. "Ow."

"I've got her, Noah! Two against one."

I heard Auntie Liv grunt. "Oh no!"

"Surrender. We have you surrounded."

I felt Beulah stir beside me. In all my excitement, I hadn't noticed until now the fresh scabs on Auntie Liv's hands. And Emma's roughhousing had caused Auntie Liv to wince in pain. I could tell she was hurting.

"Okay, I surrender. Stop, please," Auntie Liv begged.

Critical Mass. Stuff happens to Auntie Liv. My mom and Auntie Elizabeth were right. But now that I'm a spy, maybe cool stuff will start happening to me and they'll start calling me CM Junior.

CHAPTER 8

"WHAT DO YOU MEAN, they lost him?"

Denver Police Chief Tony Gates had found the quietest area he could, which was no small feat considering seven of his relatives and thirteen of his wife's family members had joined his family of eight for a Christmas Eve feast. But he'd managed to steal himself away to the back porch where he could be alone. It was too cold outside to entice any of his six kids to play in the backyard with their cousins. Plus the sun was already setting behind the Rocky Mountains.

After Gates had answered the phone, his best friend Streeter Pierce had followed him out on the porch, probably recognizing the expression on his face. The glare of the setting sun reflecting off the crusted snow was bright. Squinting didn't seem to help lessen the blinding brilliance of ice crystals that wouldn't last for long. So Gates turned his back to the yard and leaned against the wooden railing on the covered porch, staring into the window of his cheerful home. Streeter rested against the railing beside him. Their side-by-side reflections in the windowpane made him think of salt and pepper; Streeter's hair was as white as cotton and his was black with silver streaks at the temples.

He put the phone on speaker, now that the two of them were alone.

The voice of the deputy on the other end of the call could be heard, " . . . says the boy was put on a plane at LaGuardia by his father to be picked up at LAX by his mother, with one stop at Denver."

"How old a kid are we talking?" Gates asked, shifting his gaze toward his friend. At the word "kid," he noticed the weariness around Streeter's eyes. That coupled with his colorless hair made him appear much older than his late thirties.

"Five."

"Damn it, what the hell were they thinking? Didn't anyone notice the kid didn't make it on the Denver to LAX flight for God's sake?" Gates asked, a dread draining what little energy he had mustered for the holiday festivities. He wasn't much older than Streeter, but he felt like an old man himself after too many of these horrifying cases involving missing, exploited, or abused children.

"They did. Apparently paged the kid's name *and* the airline escort who was responsible for the unaccompanied minor. Airline rules."

"And?"

"Nothing. The boy was supposed to be in LA an hour and a half ago. His mother waited for a half hour after the Denver flight landed in LA before calling her ex in New York, which is when they figured out that the kid had disappeared somewhere between when he got off the plane at DIA and when he was supposed to arrive at LAX."

Gates exchanged a look with Streeter, both men shaking their heads.

"What the hell? How does someone lose a kid? What's wrong with these people?" Gates saw an always-prepared Streeter fish a pad of paper and pen from his pocket and gave him a nod of encouragement, asking, "Timeline?"

"The father took the kid to the airport for a flight from LaGuardia to DIA that left at 10:20 a.m. EST and landed at 12:40 p.m. MST."

"Four hours and twenty minutes. And the airline confirmed the boy was on that flight?"

"Yes. And that he arrived in Denver. Then the kid was supposed to get on flight 1212 to LAX, leaving Denver at 1:55 p.m. MST and arriving in LA at 3:20 p.m. PST. Like I said, the gate agent claims she noticed the kid and the escort never made it on the flight but assumed the kid got sick or something and the escort was attending to him. Figured they'd rebook after holding up the flight as long as they could. She said that happens all the time. The mother claims to have waited until a quarter to four her time before calling her ex. Then everything started rocking and rolling from there."

Gates looked at his watch and calculated. "It's 5:45 p.m. now and the boy's been missing since somewhere between 12:40 p.m. and 1:55 p.m., four or five hours ago."

The silence that followed was heavy. Gates knew that a four or five hour jump on the police was a huge advantage for whoever had abducted the child.

"Why wasn't this reported by BlueSky hours ago?"

"They said this was news to them. The gate agent said the system clearly showed they hadn't checked in so it wasn't her fault. The BlueSky brass claims they don't check the records of those not checking in for a flight until day's end. They found out when the parents called. An hour ago. The employee escorting the kid never reported it."

"Who the hell is this loser?"

"Guy's name is Kevin Benson. He's a Denver-based BlueSky employee."

"Where is Benson now?" Gates growled.

"No one seems to know. No one has seen him since he got off the plane in Denver with the boy."

Gates exchanged a glance with Pierce, who stood with his arms folded across his broad chest, the muscles in his arms bulging against the fabric of his button-down shirt. Although Streeter's white hair and worried eyes aged him, his rugged features and fit body made him look as if he'd just tackled the Crucible in boot camp at Parris Island. Ever the Marine, Gates thought.

Streeter's eyebrow arched, which is exactly how Gates felt. Curious. Suspicious.

"We have to find him. Now," Gates said.

"BlueSky said they're doing everything they can to locate him."

"And the parents?" Gates asked.

"Like I said, they're the ones who contacted the airline. BlueSky didn't even know the escort hadn't made it back on the plane at Denver until the father called. Then they checked the system—a no-show, for both, on any flights out of Denver. Said the father was irate. Threatened to sue, threatened to have people's jobs. Apparently, he's some big shot from Manhattan who can make good on his threats. All I can tell you is that it has made our job even tougher. The BlueSky group is completely lawyered up."

"It just keeps getting worse. When did the call come in, Eddie?"

"A few minutes ago. Literally."

Gates looked at the clock hanging on the wall in his kitchen that read 5:46 p.m. Christmas Eve dinner—the one his wife had been planning for weeks and that he would surely have to miss—was scheduled to be served at 6:00 p.m. Yet he knew his wife would understand that it was more important for him to do everything he could to make sure the young boy had a chance to enjoy a holiday meal in the future with his family. Gates felt his friend's eyes studying him and his worry became focused.

His deputy said, "The kid was supposed to arrive at LAX an hour and a half ago—4:20 p.m. our time. When they got the call from the father forty-five minutes, an hour ago, BlueSky tried locating the escort and decided to call the police when they couldn't."

"What took them so long to call us? We've lost so much precious time on this already."

"My sense of this? BlueSky is doing nothing but ass-covering," the deputy answered.

"Which means we need to get people out to the airport. Pronto. Who else knows?" Gates shot a look at Streeter, who nodded.

"Just you, Chief. And dispatch. They called me and I called you. What do you want me to do?"

"Where are you now?"

"Downtown. At the station."

"Round up a dozen and head to the airport. I'm on my way too, so don't do anything until I get there. Alert anyone we've got working out there about the situation. Get an APB and Amber Alert out ASAP. I'll bring the FBI into this immediately and they'll have someone out there with me. We should be there within fifteen minutes."

"Geez, Chief. You're taking this serious."

"He's five. This is serious. Deadly serious."

"I know, I know. I'm just saying—"

"You tell the BlueSky brass to get their asses out to DIA and meet us as soon as possible. We need some answers. Now."

"Might be hard, being Christmas Eve and all."

Gates ended the call and stared at his friend, worried about dragging Streeter Pierce into yet another high-profile case. They'd been together on so many of these emotionally charged cases over the years. And they'd solved nearly all of them, sometimes with not so happy endings. Like the case involving Streeter's wife, Paula. A horrible story.

Gates couldn't imagine a more tragic set of circumstances, unable to comprehend what he'd do if something so gruesome had happened to his beloved Lenora. He stared at her through the kitchen window, catching her eye. She was carving a ham and stopped midslice. And the outer edges of her eyes sagged, and the sad smile on her beautiful lips assured him she understood. He must go. And she knew that. Without a word, their silent exchange spoke volumes. Work. It was always work. But she supported him because it supported them. And of course, she knew he loved his work.

Gates offered his wife a smile in return.

"Want to join me, friend?" Gates said, stepping off the porch to walk around the house to his car.

"Let's roll. Aren't you going to tell Lenora?"

"I just did."

"Of course."

The sun was low behind the Rocky Mountains as the two men walked through the snow. Gates chastised himself for not finding the time this week to shovel the sidewalks in the backyard, worried Lenora would feel compelled to shovel the walks herself tomorrow morning before the kids woke up for Christmas, a moment he already sensed he'd miss entirely. Somberly, he led Streeter through the wooden gate to the front.

Gates's oldest boy bolted out the front door, looking exactly as he had at fourteen. His son was his duplicate—strong, lean, gangly limbed, with short hair, dark skin, and black eyes filled with wonder and worry.

The teen said, "Dinner is almost on the table."

Gates nodded at the boy, saying, "And make sure you tell your mother how good it is."

"Dad, it's Christmas Eve." The disappointment in his son's eyes was unmistakable.

"Which means you will lead the dinner prayer, son. You're the man of the house." Lenora came through the front door and stood beside her son, her demeanor stoic.

His son's eyes grew sadder than Lenora's. And his smile, although shaky, was meant to be reassuring and supportive. "Okay, Dad. Come home soon or Boyd will have picked the ham bone clean."

Gates smiled. "Love you, Robbie."

"Love you, too." And the teen ducked back inside, swiping at his eyes with the back of his hand.

Gates stepped onto the front porch and kissed his wife. "A missing boy. From the airport. He's five."

"You need to find him. And bring him home to his mama," she said, a tear sliding down her brown cheek.

Gates wiped it away with his thumb. "I'm sorry, dear."

She nodded and turned back to go inside without another word.

Gates stood a moment staring at the closed door, wondering when he'd ever find a life of peace. As if falling back into formation after being called up by a general, Gates took a step back and spun abruptly on his toes, fists at his side, shoulders back, and he walked crisply toward Streeter as if prepared for battle.

Before Streeter went to his truck, he said to Gates, "The boy needs us."

Gates nodded, appreciating his friend's reassurance that he was doing the right thing by leaving his family on Christmas Eve. But as always, he used humor to mask his sorrow. "I hate involving you guys. You're always so pushy and demanding, always standing in the shadows until it's time to take the bows. Probably don't have much of a choice, though, considering the child might have been taken on another flight across state lines."

"Consider us the dynamic duo. Local police and the feds."

Gates heard Streeter's cell phone buzzing. Before answering, Streeter offered Gates a sad smile. Gates recognized the expression on his friend's face, a sign that Streeter didn't think this case would have a happy ending. And Gates couldn't argue with his intuition. Missing children cases rarely did.

"And on Christmas Eve. Damn it, anyway."

CHAPTER 9

"**WE TOLD YOU, WE** don't know where he is. What do you want us to say?" BlueSky regional manager Toby Freytag asked. "And I'm not supposed to talk with anyone until the lawyers get here from Chicago."

Gates shot out of his chair in the manager's small office. Streeter was quick to follow, if only to hold his friend back from pummeling this policy-spewing suit. Wiry, but with the deadly accuracy of a professional flyweight boxer, Gates stepped toward Freytag and leaned over the cheap desk, gripping the edges until his normally dark-skinned knuckles turned light brown.

Freytag leaned back in his chair as Gates growled, "I don't give a rat's ass about what any lawyer said. What I want you to say is that you actually give a damn that a child's missing. That you and your company were responsible for the child's safety. That your missing employee, Kevin Benson, was responsible for escorting the boy from the New York City flight to his Los Angeles connection. That you are doing everything humanly possible to find Benson and the boy. That's what I want you to say."

Streeter noticed the muscles in Gates's neck bulge and ripple with every word. He hadn't seen his friend this angry in years.

"Chief Gates, we are working on it. I assure you," said Freytag, his hands patting the air, perhaps in an effort to calm Gates's anger. Or perhaps they were held up in defense as Freytag sensed how close Gates was to the edge.

"Don't you dare tell me you're working on this when I know for a fact that you only arrived a few minutes before me, hours after the boy disappeared. No one seemed to care that the kid missed his flight to LAX, and airport pages for the escort to report aren't enough. Neither was the feeble attempt to call his contact numbers. Someone should have screamed bloody murder hours ago that the boy was unaccounted for."

"But the gate check did," Freytag insisted. "They flagged the passenger as a no-show, and like I told you, the procedures for a passenger missing the flight—"

"I don't give two shits about your procedures," Gates spat, the dark lines on his forehead deepening between his furrowed black brows. "And this is a child, a little boy, not just any passenger who missed his flight. What the hell are you thinking? What's wrong with your employees that they wouldn't follow up on an unaccompanied minor, a child, who missed his scheduled flight?"

"At the risk of angering you further, let me say, it happens all the time. You just don't understand," Freytag said, bracing himself for Gates's fury.

"Oh, I understand. You probably just didn't want to be bothered on Christmas Eve. Right?"

"I don't get many holidays, Chief."

Gates took a step toward Freytag. Streeter put a hand on Gates's shoulder and eased him back. Gates pointed a long finger at Freytag and warned, "You get Kevin Benson in here in the next half hour or I'll tear this place apart looking for him, starting with your asshole."

Freytag blinked, glancing around his tiny space as if imagining what it would look like after Gates was through with it, trying not to picture the police chief climbing up his rectum, which Streeter knew Gates would do if it meant finding the boy.

Streeter touched Gates's elbow. Gates pointed menacingly at Freytag and repeated, "Half an hour."

Streeter followed Gates out of Freytag's private office, through the BlueSky complex, and into the long hall that led to the down escalator and the main level of the terminal.

The Jeppesen Terminal was an immense space with a ticketing area just inside the doors on either side, a multitude of commerce ringing the main terminal just below the halls of the upper level, and travelers herded to the center through security clearance just above the down escalators to the underground trains. Streeter observed the stores, restaurants, art galleries, coffee shops, and newsstands that encircled the security screening area one level down from Toby Freytag's office and realized that the BlueSky office complex was situated directly above the ticketing counters. Then he noticed the other airlines' arrangements were similar—office complexes were mostly above the ticketing areas, each probably having internal stairs for their employees to use. The doors to public transportation and to the mirror-image parking structures were just beyond the ticketing counters.

Streeter saw that if a BlueSky employee wandered into an unsecured area of Jeppesen Terminal, no one would take notice of him, even if he had a child in tow. Hopefully, the cameras Streeter spotted hanging all over the walls had captured something.

"We're setting up headquarters on Concourse B on the level just above where the boy was supposed to board the plane to LAX. Gate B51."

"Where did he arrive?" Streeter asked.

"Gate B31 was where the boy was last seen," Gates said to Streeter as they walked toward security. "They said your guy is already there, pulling data for us."

"Must be Kelleher," Streeter said.

Gates nodded. "I have Eddie—the deputy who called me—and the other officers canvassing the BlueSky employees throughout the airport to find out who knows what and where everyone was earlier today. It's been nearly six hours since the LaGuardia plane landed. That means many of the employees are probably off shift already. But Eddie will do what he can. Take names and numbers."

Streeter's eyes never stopped moving. His gaze skipped from face to face, scanning the area and taking it all in: the lights, the barricades, the stores, the restaurants, the hordes of travelers, and the vast space. The infinite places a little boy could be hidden from view—multilevels; unmarked doors, some locked, some not; countless merchants; dozens and dozens of bathrooms; and far too many exits on either side of Jeppesen Terminal. It would be a daunting task to locate the child if he had decided to play hide-and-seek in this place.

Streeter drew in a long breath and looked up at the steel structure supporting the peaks of white canvas overhead that emulated the snowcapped Rocky Mountains, and he could think of nothing but haystacks. Mumbling to himself, he said, "Like finding a needle."

As they bypassed the hundreds of travelers snaking through the roped-off lines and approached the police officers and TSA employees at security, Gates flipped open his badge, as did Streeter.

One of the senior officers said, "Chief Gates, we just heard."

"Cheryl, how are you?"

Streeter studied the police officer who reminded him of an adult version of Little Lotta the comic book character. The female officer was short and stout, had freckles spattered on her round face, and her blond hair, except for her bangs, was cropped at chin level.

"Not so good. Knowing there's been a boy missing for over five hours and we're just now hearing about it? So much valuable time's been lost."

"You're telling me," Gates said, looking at his watch.

Streeter noted that it was approaching 6:30 p.m. and they had gotten very little out of BlueSky manager Freytag, who didn't seem to know much at all.

All the officers waited for Gates to say something. He studied each of their faces in the silence, looking each in the eyes and then moving on. Streeter knew his routine, knew Gates had to assess their involvement for himself. After a long moment, he introduced himself to each of the officers and asked Cheryl for an introduction to each of the TSA employees.

He gathered as many of them as he could in the tiny glass-enclosed viewing room nearby and introduced Streeter. "Special Agent Streeter Pierce is with the FBI and is the regional expert on hostage negotiations."

Everyone mumbled a greeting, eyeing him. Streeter knew he was as approachable as a hungry pit bull—his shoulders were wide and bulky, his face as hard as Washington's on Mt. Rushmore, and his voice sounded as if he'd swallowed barbed wire for breakfast, as Liv Bergen had once told him. He kept his eyes fixed on each face in front of him, sure to reveal nothing about himself other than his formidability.

Gates added, "As Chief of the Denver Police, this is my investigation, which I fully intend to turn over to Special Agent Pierce and the FBI in short order, depending on the facts. But the first task is to find out what you all know, saw, or heard that might be out of the ordinary, particularly between noon and two, roughly. How many of you were on shift at that time?"

Most of them raised their hands.

One man called out, "Some of us started on the one o'clock shift."

Several nodded.

"Then all of you will be important to this case. Chief Deputy Ed Heisinger, who you may have already met, will be taking your statements. We know it's the holidays, but we have a child missing and we'd appreciate if you'd stick around until after Eddie and his team have had a chance to interview you and get your contact information."

"What about the earlier shift? Do you want their names?" another TSA agent asked.

"Absolutely. Anything you can do to help us out. Here's a photograph of the missing BlueSky employee, Kevin Benson, along with a snapshot of the missing boy. We've sent it out electronically to your official contacts. Print and forward copies to everyone you think needs to see these the second you get them. We've issued an APD on Benson and an Amber Alert on the boy. We have verified that a boy fitting his description passed through LaGuardia's security and the boarding gate to the plane, which brought him here. And the BlueSky management team has assured us that they have spoken to the gate agent who witnessed the escort deplaning with the boy at gate 31 in Concourse B."

"Show us the picture," one officer in the back shouted. "I never forget a face."

Gates passed back the photo of the boy with long, blond hair cropped in a pageboy haircut. "The boy's five," Gates shouted back. "The photo's working its way back to you. But I'll need it back."

"His hair looks like mine," Officer Cheryl, the Little Lotta look-alike, said, handing the photo to the person next to her. "Only blonder."

Streeter was thankful for the example.

The original TSA agent who bragged he never forgot a face said, "No one's been through here today looking like that. But check with her." He jerked his thumb at the TSA agent posted at the top of the up escalators. "I was stuck over here and I doubt whoever took the boy would risk coming back through security."

"What's her job there?" Streeter asked.

"Mainly to make sure no one goes down the wrong way on the escalator or into the elevator bypassing security to board the trains to the concourses. That's where travelers coming into Denver depart the terminals."

Gates nodded. "Sounds reasonable. I don't want to rule anything out at this point."

The TSA agent was persistent, pointing at the up escalators across the main concourse in the distance. "They either left the airport over there— which is where we post two of our TSA agents at all times—or they hopped a plane elsewhere without having to go back through security."

Streeter had already come to the same conclusion, but he could see how getting the employees to talk would help stimulate recall and discussion of earlier "odd" events.

"There've been only two TSA employees working security on the discharge end of that escalator since the child's flight landed in DIA. She's one of them," the TSA shift supervisor said. "Best bet is to grill her. She'd be the most likely one to see a snatcher with a kid, unless they hopped on a plane headed somewhere else. I'm telling you, that's how I'd do it."

Gates looked at Cheryl and said, "This guy's starting to think like a criminal." Then to the TSA shift supervisor, Gates said, "Did someone screen you before they hired you or what?"

The mood lightened slightly.

Streeter said, "We've already lost six hours so we need to move."

"Tell her we'll want to talk with her before she leaves work and after you get through with her," the TSA shift supervisor said.

As the photos worked their way through the crowd of TSA employees and officers and back to Gates, he said, "Case headquarters is being set up on the mezzanine level above the customer service desk near gate 56 on Concourse B. We'll be directly above and across from gate B31, where the boy was last seen."

"Who's cleared to go through security for this operation?"

Streeter was pleased with the TSA senior shift supervisor, understanding quickly how he had earned his position.

Gates turned to Streeter, a question in his eyes.

Streeter said, "No one. Call Gates or me on every individual who claims to be working with this case. Even if they have a badge or credentials. Direct them immediately to case headquarters once we clear them."

"Clear my officers who are already here now." Gates gave them a list of twelve officers who were on-site with Eddie.

"Got it," Cheryl said. "I know most of them."

"And Eddie. Chief Deputy Eddie Heisinger."

Streeter heard the buzzing of Gates's cell phone and watched as he fished for his phone and looked at the display. "They found Kevin Benson. He came in on his own. BlueSky will be taking him up to our case headquarters. Let's go."

CHAPTER 10

"WHILE ELIZABETH AND I finish preparing dinner, will you let Noah stretch out a bit in the living room?" my sister Frances asked.

"Sure."

I didn't get to spend enough time with Frances these days. Not like I used to. We were inseparable. Best friends. In school, we were so close in age—nine months and a day, my dad always says—we were in the same grade. I was the jock, and she was the natural beauty men wanted to date and all women wanted to befriend. All of us Bergen siblings were close, but Frances and I were tight. Or used to be. Now she was so busy with everything—with work, with the kids, with Gabriel. With life. As a Hogarty.

I unbuckled Noah from his blue, Styrofoam chair that was propped in the frame of the wheelchair and scooped him up in my arms, careful not to let Frances or Elizabeth see me flinch with pain.

Damn, my rib hurt.

With dinner nearly ready, Frances and Elizabeth made last-minute preparations while their husbands, Gabriel and Michael, worked on assembling the contraption my mom and dad had sent Emma. The bike depicted on the box looked like a police motorcycle with a sidecar that was big enough to slide Noah's blue chair in it. Emma couldn't wait to try it out.

My sisters and I knew the drill well. The men kept sending Emma on missions to retrieve different tools because they didn't want young ears hearing them swear every time they had to assemble and disassemble parts when they misread the instructions. And consuming vast quantities of spiked eggnog had not dulled their ability to come up with some colorful new word combinations. I truly hoped Noah wasn't recording them with his new pin.

Elizabeth stepped aside, watching me struggle with Noah. As I passed through the opening, careful not to hit his head or feet against the doorframe, Elizabeth commented, "That was a cool gift from Mom and Dad."

"Perfect," I said, trying not to wince.

"Emma's going to love racing around the neighborhood in that thing."

"She'll be the envy of the local kids," Frances said.

Emma was a good sister to Noah. A great sister, in fact. She had always been there for him. She understood him better than anyone did. She knew exactly what to say to him. She never treated Noah like a baby even though Frances sometimes made her change his diapers. Around her friends, he was Emma's big brother and she expected them to treat him with respect. All they saw was how different he was. And when Noah took an occasional hike to the top of Mount Pity Pod, it was Emma who knocked him off it. Just as a sister should.

"Heard you guys saw a mountain lion this morning," Frances said as she and Elizabeth closed in behind me.

Elizabeth was tiny, like my mom. Although Frances was shorter than me, taller than Elizabeth, she had all Mom's beauty and grace. Even the scolding tone in her polite question was exactly like something Mom would say to me. She looked relaxed, with her arms folded loosely at her thin waste, her eyes soft with compassion and absent any judgment. Her hair was the soft brown of pine trees and smelled of woodsy vanilla, fresh and natural. Which suited her life as Gabriel's wife, since he reminded me of the lumberjack character on the Brawny commercials.

"And you got hurt?" Frances added.

I groaned as I realized her request for me to move Noah was a test. Elizabeth unfolded the blanket in front of the television in the living room for me to set Noah down.

Noah laughed.

"You? Traitor," I whispered to Noah, who stopped laughing. "Tickle torture for whoever told on me."

"Don't blame him," Frances scolded.

"Elizabeth?" I asked.

"Yep," Elizabeth said, as I lowered Noah onto the blanket with a few expletives of my own. "Michael told me about how you slipped on some ice and broke a rib."

I paused, glad Michael hadn't ratted me out. Completely. Noah giggled, knowing everyone was bending the truth.

"But that sounded too convenient," Elizabeth said. "So I forced the truth out of him."

"See? Tickle torture works," I said to Noah, who laughed again.

I noticed that both my sisters were now standing with arms folded, glaring down at me as they watched me struggle with Noah. They had allowed me to move Noah to test the extent of damage from my alleged broken rib.

I stood up and took a bow and said, "See? Not broken. I wouldn't have been able to do that. Bruised, is all." Noah moaned. Leveling my gaze at Frances, I added, "I'm okay. Really. What else did Elizabeth tell you?"

"That's it," Frances said.

"Traitor," I said to Elizabeth. "As is your hubby."

"Speaking of hubby, what did Michael leave out of the story, CM?" Elizabeth said, her elfish stance as menacing as ever. The bright yellow and brown spikes of her hair were vibrating, which indicated her underlying excitement. Or anger at Michael for not telling her the whole story. I decided to cover for him, since he'd covered for me, by telling them we'd seen a mountain lion, but not the whole story about almost getting killed by the mountain lion.

"Apparently he told you more than he should have. It's not like I need a mother, so stop treating me like a kid. I was doing fieldwork, training exercises, and a mountain lion spooked Beulah, who got startled and pulled me off my feet. I landed wrong, my ribs are bruised, and I scraped my hands. That's all. End of story."

Elizabeth jerked her chin at me with her arms still folded. "By the looks of your mug, CM, the cat used you as a scratching post."

"Pine needles. And quit calling me CM. I am not Critical Mass. Shit happens to everyone. Not just me."

Over the sound of Noah's laughter, Frances scolded me, "How many times have I told you not to swear around the kids?"

"Don't worry. New Year's is just around the corner and CM will undoubtedly pretend to work on that flaw of hers with her notorious resolution to stop swearing," Elizabeth said.

"Again? How many years has that been, CM?" Frances added.

"Quit calling me CM or you'll both really hear some swearing. I've finally gotten the family to stop calling me Boots and now you're starting in on CM. What's wrong with calling me Liv?"

"Too easy," Elizabeth said.

"And what's wrong with Boots? You are the proverbial 'boots on the ground' sort of person and I would think you'd take that as a compliment," Frances said.

"We'll stop calling you CM if you quit yelling at us for calling you Boots," Elizabeth offered.

That seemed fair to me. I nodded.

"And Michael's cheek? The scratches? Are those from pine needles too?"

I ignored Elizabeth.

The roast in the oven smelled divine. I loved Christmas Eve dinner. And Frances was almost as good a cook as Mom. The screen door slammed in the other room. Noah's body jerked, his uncooperative limbs pulling toward his core, his lips curling into a giggle.

"Don't slam the door!" Frances, Elizabeth, and I said in unison.

Noah laughed. Within seconds the screen door slammed again and Emma ran back downstairs through the kitchen after retrieving yet another tool.

We scolded Noah again. He never seemed to tire of Frances or anyone pretending to yell at him, as if he had just returned from outside, climbing a tree, or riding his bike, slamming the door behind him. These are things he can never do, only dream about. He's all boy.

He was still giggling as Frances stooped to wipe the drool from his mouth. Her knees cracked when she stood, which, for some strange reason, made him laugh even harder. Boys. Boys and noises.

"What've you been eating, Noah? Is Auntie Liv sneaking you midnight snacks again? You must weigh at least forty pounds. That's why your mom's knees are cracking," Elizabeth said.

Noah was still. His mood had shifted. It appeared he took his aunt's comment too seriously. I knew Elizabeth was joking but we all wondered how long Frances could handle Noah as he grew. Frances was nothing like me. I must have had at least forty pounds and three inches on her. If it weren't for the Irish optimism and Norwegian stubbornness we shared, you'd never know we were sisters. Those two traits were instrumental in Frances's steadfast decision to keep Noah at home, despite the experts' unanimous recommendation to put him in an institutionalized home. Not a chance, according to Frances.

And Noah worried about it. Worried about his mom. I had seen it firsthand. Like the time that lady in the grocery store had asked Frances if Noah was retarded. Frances had smiled and Noah had felt bad for her. It had been written all over his face and I had asked him later about it. He had always been an expressive boy. I, on the other hand, didn't take the comment so graciously, remarking to the lady, "Not as retarded as you for asking such a stupid question," which made Noah smile and Frances blush.

Then there was the time that idiot substitute teacher at school asked Frances what she was going to do when Noah got too big for her to carry. What was she thinking, saying something like that right in front of Noah? She acted like deafness accompanied severe cerebral palsy or something. I was so mad. Noah was crushed and worried, refusing to eat for days after that, thinking if he didn't eat, he wouldn't gain weight. Instead, not eating caused his blood sugar to drop, triggering yet more seizures. Some of his worst seizures. The grand mal seizures. His reaction to the comment only made things worse.

Noah concentrated and rolled his eyes up to find his mom. I knew that look, the look of concern he had for his mom. He was struggling to bring Frances's gray, shadowy shape into better focus with his good eye. He must have lost his contact already. Sometime between being upstairs with me earlier and now. Probably when Emma and I were roughhousing with him, during the tickle torture.

I stepped in front of him and patted my belly. "Noah, tell Auntie

Elizabeth that when you get as big as me from all my midnight snacking, then maybe your mom will have something to *really* complain about." And I added a belch for good measure.

The tension in his face drained and relief led to a wide smile. A squeal of delight escaped his lips. One down, one to go.

"Nice, Auntie Liv," Frances said, shaking her head in disgust.

Elizabeth mouthed "Sorry" to me and Frances.

There. The mood shifted back. All was good. Not a shining example of how I'd like my sisters or my nephew to remember me should I get struck by lightning at this moment, but at least it kept Noah's mood light.

"Come on," Frances said to Elizabeth. "Dinner's almost ready."

"I thought you said we were having cookies and eggnog for dinner?" I asked.

"I changed my mind."

"Figures," I said, plopping down on the blanket beside Noah. "Probably something gross like a rare roast beef, fresh vegetables, homemade mashed potatoes and gravy. That junk."

Elizabeth called from the kitchen, "And when are you going to settle down and get married?"

"What the hell does that have to do with anything?" I protested. "And how the hell do you two always manage to slip that into any conversation we're having?"

"Don't swear in front of the children."

Noah giggled at our bantering.

I leaned down and whispered, "If I took you downstairs, I bet you could hear your dad and Uncle Michael swear up a storm. They probably won't be done with your police motorcycle until next Christmas. If Gramma Bergen were here, she would have it done already."

Noah smiled.

My redheaded niece had bounced back up the stairs and slid onto the blanket beside me, hugging me tight.

"Ow," was all I managed.

Emma's face fell. "Sorry."

I smiled. "No problem, Princess."

That got a rise out of Noah.

"Shut up," Emma said to Noah. "At least she doesn't call me Peanut."

"Don't swear," Frances called from the kitchen.

I whispered to Emma, "'Peanut' is a swear word?"

Emma whispered back, "No, 'shut up' is."

"Whatever. Emma, is your motorcycle done?" I asked.

"Not yet, but almost."

Frances called, "Emma, come set the table. Water for everyone, too, please."

"Cinderelly, Cinderelly," Emma mumbled only loud enough for Noah and me to hear.

Headlights swept across the living room wall from an oncoming car. Emma sprinted to the front door and bounded outside into the cold.

I got up to shut the door she'd left open as the cold blast swept across the living room floor, chilling Noah. I saw a car pull into the driveway next door.

Frances had stepped up beside me and said, "That's our neighbor."

"And?" I asked.

"He's creepy."

"Well, Emma just bolted out the front door and headed in his direction."

Frances's eyes widened and she ran out into the dark. Barefoot.

CHAPTER 11

I FOLLOWED FRANCES AS far as the driveway, bringing boots for her to step into. It was below freezing.

I could see the man in the glow of the dashboard lights and assumed he would roll down his window and talk with Emma since she stood on the other edge of the driveway waving at him. I thought I saw something move in the backseat, someone wave back, but I wasn't sure. The windows were tinted and it was dark. The neighbor's house and yard were dark, with no outdoor lights on yet.

I was surprised he didn't roll down his window and at least offer a holiday greeting to my niece. I was sure he would when my sister walked up behind Emma and stood with her. He didn't. Nor did he turn off the car's engine, or open the garage door with an automatic opener. Instead, he just sat in his car.

Staring at Emma.

All I heard was the engine idling. Then I heard Frances say, "No, let it go, Emma. Come inside. It's getting too dark."

When we were back inside, Frances closed the front door and threw the dead bolt. "Em, finish up your chores for me."

"What chores?"

"I told you. Setting the table and filling the water glasses."

As Emma stomped off to the kitchen, I asked, "What was that all about? The guy just sitting there."

"He just sat there?" Elizabeth asked.

"And stared at Emma," Frances added. "She said she ran out when she saw the lights of the neighbor's car, hoping to see the girl again, find out her name."

"What girl?"

"There is no girl," Frances said. "Sometimes Emma creates imaginary friends. She told me earlier that she'd seen a girl her age with Mr. Fletcher, our neighbor. Emma said the girl had waved at her earlier."

"And there was no girl?" I asked, thinking I had seen something move in the backseat, but I know I wasn't as close as Frances had been.

Frances shook her head. "I worry about Emma. She's always making up imaginary friends. I thought she'd grown out of that by now. Maybe I expect too much of her around here."

I clearly noticed her eyes move toward Noah and knew what she meant.

"Did you see anything move in the backseat?" I asked.

"I didn't see anything. No one was in the front. I wasn't about to make the guy prove he was alone, just because Emma thought she saw something. You haven't seen anyone, have you Noah?" Frances turned to Noah, who remained still. "Didn't think so. And believe me, if I had seen something, I'd probably call the cops. Fletcher gives me the creeps. What guy pulls up and just sits in his car, staring at little girls?"

"Creepy guys, just like you said," Elizabeth confirmed.

A cold chill skipped along my spine because I know very well where a creepy stare leads. I didn't want to go there. "What's his story?"

"Don't know. Gabriel and I tried to properly welcome the man to the neighborhood when he moved in last year. Baked him a cake."

"That's right neighborly of you," I mocked. "And?"

"The first week he moved in, I waited until he arrived home from work, but he wouldn't answer the door. I know he was in there."

We all froze when we heard the kitchen door open and close.

"Emma?" Frances called.

My redheaded niece poked her head around the wall and said, "That was Daddy, not me. He's going into the garage to get something."

All three of us drew in a breath of relief.

"Well, that's just weird that he wouldn't answer the door," I said, getting us back on topic.

"We'd heard he's a native Coloradoan, used to live in an apartment until he bought the house next door. Anyway, I finally gave up trying to get him to come to the door. So one night I left him a plate of homemade cinnamon rolls with a note of welcome attached."

"Did you get your plate back?"

Frances shook her head.

"Does he live alone?" I asked, popping a piece of chocolate in my mouth from the candy dish.

"No dog. No cat. No family. No visitors."

"Ever?"

"Ever. Gabriel said he's talked with him a couple of times. Says he's simpleminded but an okay guy."

"Gabriel would tell you if he thought you were in any danger, Frances. This Fletcher guy, he didn't have anyone stop by today? I mean, after all, it's Christmas Eve." I ate a second piece of chocolate, earning a look from Frances.

"No visitors. Not for Thanksgiving, either. But he was gone for several hours earlier and again just now. He comes and goes often. Maybe he has relatives in town."

"Weird," Elizabeth said.

"Yep," Frances said, holding out her hand like mothers do with kids to retrieve the wrappers I was about to stuff in my pocket.

"No, I meant you knowing so much about the creepy guy's comings and goings. You're turning into Mrs. Kravitz." Elizabeth and I laughed.

"Who?"

"*Bewitched*. Nosey neighbor. Remember? 'Abner, come quick. You've got to see this.'" Elizabeth had the impersonation down to a science.

"Thanks. You're both such big help," Frances said and frowned. "Mind hanging out with Noah while we finish making dinner?" she asked me.

"My pleasure," I said, flopping down on the blanket again and pretending to use Noah as my pillow, mimicking the patting and punching motions of fluffing him. "What's for dessert, Noah? Did your mom say?"

Noah rolled his eyes upward.

"Yeah? Is it done?"

Another upward eye roll.

"Where? In the fridge?"

Noah concentrated on doing nothing.

"Oven?"

Nothing.

"Freezer?"

Noah smiled and rolled his eyes again. I jumped up and headed to the kitchen. After checking in the freezer, I came back into the living room and lay next to Noah on the floor. "Custard? Really? What kind of holiday dessert is custard? And knowing Frances, it's probably lemon. Yuck."

Noah giggled.

I leaned into him. "And it's okay for you to use your secret pin to record your mom the next time she makes her famous cheesecake. She won't share her recipe with me."

I hadn't paid much attention to what was on TV and was just enjoying being next to Noah. Something about a small ostrich farm west of Louisville, Colorado. That was where Elizabeth and Michael lived, although they frequently traveled back and forth to Rochford, South Dakota, these days, now that construction on the Lost Boys campus for at-risk youths had begun. Frances and Gabriel lived south of Louisville in Wheat Ridge and I had lived in Fort Collins, with intention of splitting my time between the quarry and the Denver Bureau. But now my house in Fort Collins was up for sale and I was looking for an apartment in Denver, staying with Frances and her family from time to time when I needed to crash for a few hours. I didn't realize how hard it would be to find an apartment that took dogs, especially the size of a full-grown bloodhound. But Frances and Gabriel didn't seem to mind. And Noah loved sleeping with Beulah. The best part about getting an apartment in Denver is that the three of us sisters would all live less than an hour apart from each other. At least three of the nine of us siblings were close.

I'd zoned out for a minute and noticed how still Noah had gotten. He had his head turned toward the TV, his good eye fixed on the screen. I'd forgotten to mention to Frances that I'd noticed Noah had lost his contact lens again. He strained to see the screen, even though he was less than two feet from it. The beautiful Native American anchorwoman was reporting something about the Denver International Airport. As she spoke, images of the Denver airport terminal rolled on the screen behind her.

" . . .but the authorities have not released any more information on this tragic story. Again, repeating Channel 9's top story tonight, Maximillian Bennett Williams III, five-year-old son of New York property developer and multimillionaire Maximillian Bennett Williams II, has apparently disappeared."

My mouth dropped open. I knew Max well. He had almost married my youngest sister, Ida, seven or eight years ago. Over our dead bodies. Especially Mom's, since Ida was only seventeen at the time.

"Frances! Elizabeth! Come quick." My shouting startled Noah. "Sorry, Noah."

"What?" Frances said, wiping her hands on a dish towel.

"It's Max."

"Max? As in Ida's Max?" Elizabeth asked.

"Yeah," I answered, hushing her.

The anchorwoman's voice could still be heard as a picture of the blond-haired child flashed, spanning the entire screen, saying, "Mr. Williams could not be reached for comment at this time, but we have learned that the child was scheduled to make a connecting flight to Los Angeles, California, this afternoon, and instead disappeared from the airline escort's care. Authorities have not confirmed whether they suspect foul play. However, they have released this photograph of the boy in an Amber Alert and are asking for anyone who has seen this child or may have any information on his whereabouts to please call them immediately. The number is . . ."

The recently taken picture showed a grinning five-year-old Maximillian with his thick, blond hair parted to one side and slicked back with gel, a stylish purple silk bow tie under his chin, and a perfectly fitted custom-made three-piece suit covering his small frame. The boy's face faded from the screen and the face of the anchorwoman reappeared on the

Hogarty television just as Gabriel came in through the kitchen door holding a socket wrench and a set of sockets.

He must have noticed the sullen expressions on our faces. "What's up?"

"A story about Ida's old boyfriend was on the news," I said. "His son was abducted from DIA earlier today. It's breaking news."

"On Christmas Eve?" Gabriel said. "That's horrible."

Frances leaned her head against his shoulder as he wrapped his arms around her in a comforting embrace. Elizabeth and I just stared at the TV in shock.

Frances asked, "Do you think one of us should call Ida?"

My mind was focused entirely on the story of the missing boy, wondering if Streeter had been called in to investigate and if he had, why he hadn't called me.

My cell phone rang.

CHAPTER 12

PHIL KELLEHER OFFERED STREETER a tight smile as they entered the nearly bare room. Along the walls were several chairs and a folding table with a coffee pot, stacks of cups, sugar, and creamer. In the center of the room were two pods of folding tables. One had been set up in a large square with two computers, two printers, a video camera and recording equipment, and partitions to separate four distinct working areas with separate phones. Office space. The second grouping, the interview area, consisted of two folding tables lined with chairs, and it also included more video and recording equipment.

Streeter was amazed at how quickly Kelleher worked and how resourceful he could be at getting all of this equipment past security. He'd called Calvin, his boss and Denver Bureau SAC, the second he had closed the door to his truck at Gates's house. Then Streeter called fellow agents Kelleher and Liv—in that order—despite Calvin's unsettling news about assigning first office agent Bergen as lead on this case. On a follow-up call to Calvin, Streeter convinced Calvin to let him lead the case and, instead, to mentor Liv on her first assignment. The phone call nearly consumed the entire trip from Gates's house to DIA. Once he arrived at the airport, Streeter spent only twenty minutes or so in the BlueSky office before heading straight over to the makeshift headquarters Kelleher had already set up for them.

Streeter couldn't help but notice that Liv Bergen hadn't even arrived yet.

Streeter said, "Thanks for coming, Kelleher, for leaving your family to help us."

Kelleher nodded imperceptibly and got down to business. "Here are two computer systems. This one is secure, the other, not so much. Not yet, anyway. We're working on it. We have a video and still camera set up on both so we can capture all images from interviews, review airport security videos, whatever you need. So be careful until we can figure out how to secure this beast."

Every time he was around Phil Kelleher, Streeter thought of Felix from the *Odd Couple*, only Kelleher probably would have been offended by the comparison, considering the fictional Felix Unger was not quite as fastidious as Kelleher was.

"Here is the information we've pulled on the boy and the escort." Kelleher indicated the smaller of the two piles of files stacked on the bare interview tables.

Streeter pointed at the other, thicker pile. "And these?"

"The parents," Kelleher said with a scowl, his thin face folding like a crumpled paper.

Streeter whistled. The pile of documents was massive, indicating the parents were going to be trouble. He introduced Gates to Kelleher.

"Heard about you," Chief Tony Gates said. "If you ever want a real job, come see me."

Streeter noticed a rare smile on Special Agent Phil Kelleher's face.

Gates's phone buzzed. He looked at the text. "They're here. BlueSky. They'll be bringing Benson up to us."

"When?" Streeter asked.

"A minute, maybe two. They're headed up the escalator to the mezzanine as we speak."

"While we're waiting, tell me something, Kelleher," Streeter said. "What's up with the parents?"

"Maximillian Bennett Williams II is a developer in Manhattan. A multi-millionaire. Melissa Williams is a supermodel. Famous. They're separated, waiting for the divorce to be finalized, and the child—Maximillian III or little Max—is the product of their brief marriage," Kelleher explained.

"Ransom?"

"Possibly," Kelleher answered. "It's all speculation at this point."

"No calls to the parents reported yet?"

Kelleher answered, "Not that I've heard. I left that up to you to decide."

"Get the New York Bureau up to speed and have them contact the father, same with the LA Bureau and the mother. We'll need our people involved if there's a ransom call."

"That won't work."

"Why not?"

"They're on their way here."

"Who's on their way? Where?"

Kelleher cleared his throat. "The mother and father. They're both flying here to Denver in private jets as we speak."

"Who told you that?"

Kelleher nodded over Streeter's shoulder at the incoming entourage.

Gates and Streeter turned in time to see two men come through the door. Streeter only recognized the older, heavier man in the suit and mumbled, "Toby Freytag."

Gates asked, "Freytag told you the parents were incoming?"

Kelleher nodded.

"Nice to know."

Streeter leaned in closer to Gates and grumbled, "Especially after we just spent a half hour grilling him and he never mentioned it to us."

"Chief Gates? This is Kevin Benson," Toby Freytag announced as the door bumped closed.

The man beside Freytag was morose looking. He was young, tall, and lean with a long face and horsey teeth. His bangs were too long and his shirttails were loose. He looked drunk or stoned, if Streeter had to guess.

"So you're the flight attendant who escorted the missing boy?" Gates asked.

The lanky man nodded, his glance bouncing between Gates and Streeter.

Benson looked at Freytag. "You said I shouldn't say anything until the lawyers get here."

"I did, but—"

"Mr. Benson?" Streeter asked, cutting off Freytag and noticing that Kelleher had expertly faded into the background to help observe.

Kevin Benson fixed his blurry eyes on Streeter and said, "Call me Kevin. My dad's Mr. Benson."

"Okay, Kevin," Gates sniped. Streeter detected a note of agitation in his friend's tone. "I'm Police Chief Tony Gates and this is Special Agent Streeter Pierce. Have a seat."

Streeter extended his hand and Benson gave him a limp handshake. Streeter wondered if this was his normal greeting or if his hands were sore from a recent activity, like restraining the boy or digging a shallow grave in the frozen ground.

As Benson slumped into the chair, Streeter noticed Liv slip into the room, wearing an apologetic expression under her Rockies baseball cap. She looked beautiful and frightful; angry red scratches marked her cheeks and neck. Streeter offered her a flickering glance that he hoped she'd notice and no one else would. He made a mental note to ask her about the injuries later, as well as to remind her of the Bureau's expectation that agents dress more professionally when on assignment or working a case. He tried to ignore how the tight blue jeans and white T-shirt she wore beneath her unzipped hoodie made her look like a college coed and made him feel ancient in comparison. At least the standard Bureau dark suit she should have worn would have made their ten-year age difference feel a bit less cavernous than her apparel did at this moment.

From the corner of his eye, Streeter watched as Liv gave Kelleher a hug, noticing the big smile on Kelleher's otherwise tight lips. Streeter resisted a sigh, imagining his discussion with her about not only dressing appropriately, but also how PDAs were not typically warranted or expressed by professional agents. Especially first office agents. Then again, Liv Bergen was anything but typical.

As the BlueSky employees whispered to one another, Gates was settling into the chair beside Streeter across from the two men. Gates cleared his throat and leaned across the table toward Benson and Toby Freytag and said, "Half hour with you and you forget to mention the Williamses are on their way here?"

Toby Freytag's eyes grew wide as he stammered, "I . . . uh."

"When do they arrive?" Streeter asked.

"I . . . how would I know that?"

"Find out. You get your hands on their flight plans, the ETA, the name of their pilots, the time they left, the mechanic's shoe size, everything you can on those two private jets," Gates demanded.

"But I need to stay with Kevin or I'll—"

"Now!" Gates interrupted, seeing a smile touch Streeter's lips. "And make sure the instant their wheels touch down, you escort them to the room right next door to us and make sure we have plenty of seats for everyone. Immediately."

"How can I do that? I don't have the authority to—"

Gates was punching numbers on his phone. "My deputy is on his way. Deputy Eddie Heisinger. You'll have the authority to do whatever you need to accommodate my requests. Now do what I said."

Toby Freytag slunk out of the room with Kelleher, who Streeter knew would stick like glue to the BlueSky manager every minute until Deputy Heisinger was with him. Liv, still unnoticed by the distraught flight attendant at the table, closed the door. Streeter offered Liv a flicker of a once-over, not intended to mask the worry etched on his face. He made a mental note to personally throttle Linwood if he was responsible for her wounds.

Streeter cleared his throat, pushing away any thoughts of Liv or Linwood for later. Streeter clicked a couple buttons on the keyboard and started the video recording, announcing the time, date, location, and all persons present for the official FBI interview. Benson glanced over his shoulder at Special Agent Liv Bergen as Streeter announced her presence. His eyes grew wide at the announcement that this was an official FBI interview. Streeter might have let his glance linger a bit too long on Liv, who appeared impressively formidable even though this was her first time in an interview and he hadn't had time to instruct her. She stood in front of the door. Her stony-faced expression, wide stance, lowered chin, and crossed arms made her look like a seasoned guard in a maximum-security prison. And the cuts along her cheek highlighted with dried blood made the effect all the more convincing.

"State your full name, date of birth, and today's date, please."

"Oh crap. Oh no. Oh no, no, no." Benson buried his head in his hands, propping his elbows on the folding table.

"Mr. Benson?" Streeter asked.

"I want a lawyer," he mumbled, making no more comments about being called "Mr. Benson."

"And I want to be home with my family," Gates said. "But I'm stuck with you and you're not under arrest, so can we get on with the interview, please?"

Benson dropped his hands on the table. The heavy slap of skin against plastic echoed in the metal and tile room. "Great, just great. I'm not under arrest, but I am in trouble, aren't I?"

"Not as much trouble as you're going to be in if you don't start talking," Gates barked.

After working with his best friend for years, Streeter knew that Tony Gates had a cloudy perspective when dealing with cases involving children. He had a tendency to lose his temper, bully witnesses, and become agitated and impatient ever since the murder of the pageant girl about Max's age had gone cold—remained unsolved—a couple of years ago. Streeter had learned Tony's second oldest son, his godson, had gone to school with the murdered girl. Too close to home for the father of six, Streeter supposed.

"Where's the boy?" Gates asked.

"I don't know."

Gates shot a glance Streeter's way as Benson's gaze dropped to the floor.

"What happened to him?" Streeter asked.

Kevin Benson lifted his eyes, first toward Liv, then between Gates and Streeter. He drew in a long, ragged breath before blowing it out again.

"I took my eyes off him for a split second and the kid was gone. That's it. That's my story. That's when my world went to shit."

CHAPTER 13

"WHERE DID YOU LAST have the child in your care?" Streeter pressed.

"Between gates. On Concourse B."

"Here in Denver, then?"

Benson nodded. "We got off the plane at gate B31 and went to B51. We had some extra time so we came back to get ice cream. I stopped to use the restroom and he disappeared."

"You left him in the concourse alone?" Gates asked.

"No, I took him into the bathroom with me. Put him in the stall next to me."

"Which bathroom?" Streeter asked.

"The . . . I don't know, I don't know." Benson cradled his head, shaking it from side to side like he might rattle the truth loose or something.

"What do you mean, you don't know?" Gates asked. "You're a Denver-based flight attendant. You probably know every square inch of this airport."

"I know, I know. I mean, I can't think," Benson said. Lifting his face from his hands and narrowing his eyes at Chief Gates, his gaze slid occasionally over to where Liv was standing. "You're freaking me out."

"Freaking you out? I'll show you freaking—" Gates started.

Streeter interrupted, "Where've you been? You must know we've been looking for you."

Benson's horsey face looked even more ridiculous with his mouth hanging open as he gawked at the two men interviewing him. "I was looking for the kid."

Streeter glanced at his watch, saying nothing but implying it had been hours since the boy went missing.

"At first, I mean. I looked all over. Walked this entire airport. Twice. Which accounted for the first two hours. Then, I headed out to the taxi stand, the bus lines, asking if anyone had seen a little blond boy wandering around. I asked everyone. So by 4:20 p.m., about the time when the kid was supposed to be landing in LA, I panicked and took off."

"To the bar," Streeter said.

"No. Well, yes. See?" He buried his fingers in his mop of hair. "You're getting me all confused."

"Take your time," Streeter offered, his inflection even, his tone rough.

"Yes, I ended up at the bar. Eventually. First, I went to my apartment. My girlfriend kicked me out. Then, I went to the bar. Been there ever since."

"You lose a kid, drink yourself stupid, and at no time did you ever think to mention to anyone at BlueSky or to the police that you'd lost a five-year-old boy?" Gates pressed.

"I told you. I got scared."

The perspiration that beaded on his forehead appeared to be genuine to Streeter.

"Benson, I know you've had a long day. You're probably getting tired and you just want to go home," Streeter noted.

Benson didn't let him finish. "Home? I don't have a home anymore. And I'll be fired before I ever leave this room. Freytag's probably already cutting my final checks to hand to me the second that scary chick over there opens the door."

"She's not a chick." Streeter glared at Benson. "That's Special Agent Liv Bergen."

Gates added, "But you're right about her being scary, so watch your mouth or we'll let her show you just how scary she can get."

Streeter noticed a slight arch to Liv's eyebrow. He could tell she'd liked that. "And I have no sympathy for whether you have a home or a job, so get back to the story about the child."

Benson held up his hands and shrugged. "What do you want me to say? This is the story. I took my eye off of him for one bloody second so I could take a leak, and the kid bolts. By the time you're done grilling me about it, I'm without a job. I'm already without my apartment. Do you know how much an apartment costs these days? A fortune."

"Where's the boy?" Streeter asked.

"I told you. I have no clue." Benson looked at Streeter, then at Gates. "I misplaced him. Okay?"

"Not okay!" Gates shifted as if he were winding up a punch for the guy and barked, "He's a child. Not a set of keys, you piece of—"

Streeter interrupted, "When's the last time you saw him?"

Benson didn't seem to notice the danger he was in by inflaming Gates, the father of six kids, two about the age of the missing child. Streeter could see how inattentive the man could be, unaware of dangers around him. It would have been easy for someone to lure a child from his not-so-watchful care.

"I told you already. Just after we arrived. We were in the bathroom. Between B31 and B51. He went in one stall and I went in another. He was gone when I came out."

Streeter believed Benson was lying, about something. But he didn't think Benson had the ability to actually plan an abduction or was capable of any other menace, besides neglect. He simply wasn't aware enough for such a broad undertaking. He wasn't present enough to have carried off an abduction without someone noticing or without losing his composure during this interview. Streeter's focus shifted quickly to Benson as a witness.

Streeter decided to turn up the heat to confirm his speculation and to find out what Kevin Benson actually knew. "Which bathroom, exactly? And what time, exactly?"

Benson answered, "Around 1:00, 1:30."

"That's the best you can do? Are you kidding me?" Gates asked.

Benson plowed his long, thin fingers through his mop of dark hair and blew out his cheeks. "Okay, the plane landed at 12:40 p.m. We were off the plane and away from the gate within ten minutes. The boy and I took off for the gate of our next flight, which was only a few gates away. At B51. We landed at B31. So we were there before 1:00."

"And then?" Streeter asked, noticing Liv shift near the door, her expression as agitated as he felt.

"I took him back to the shops above the underground trains so he could get an ice cream. He whined about passing it the first time. Said he had to have it. So I took him back, went to the bathroom nearby, and the kid took off before I could finish my business in the stall next to him. I looked for him for hours."

"Before you gave up and headed for the bar," Gates sniped.

Streeter had noticed the alcohol on Benson's breath when he first shook his hand, but wouldn't have thought Benson was drunk. "Go back. Tell us from the beginning what happened," Streeter coaxed. "Where exactly in the airport were you? Which bathroom? Who else was in the bathroom with you? What did you hear? What did you see? Give us every detail."

Benson sighed and slumped, his elongated frame folding like a misshapen jackknife, as if Streeter had asked him the impossible.

"Do you have a problem recalling what happened?" Streeter asked.

"No," Benson said. "I have a problem recalling the details. Maybe it's because I drank too much. Maybe it's because you're freaking me out. It's all just too upsetting to me."

"Upsetting to you?" Gates asked.

"Give me a break, will you?" Benson whined. "That kid ditched me. He's the one to blame for all this. I'm the victim here."

Gates stood up so suddenly that his chair toppled backward. Within four quick steps with his long legs, Gates had rounded the table where Benson sat, too fast for Streeter to react in time. Gates had already grabbed the shirtfront of Benson's BlueSky uniform under the sniveling man's chin and was pulling him out of his chair.

CHAPTER 14

I WAS CURIOUS ABOUT why Kevin Benson wasn't seeing what I was seeing. I mean, I could chalk it up to it being his first time meeting the chief, but this was my first time seeing DPD Chief Tony Gates in action, too, and it seemed overly obvious to me that Benson was about to get his teeth knocked out if he wasn't careful.

I couldn't believe Benson had actually implied—in so many words—that the missing boy deserved whatever he got. Clearly Chief Gates had the same thought, since he was rounding the table to clobber Benson. I decided to abandon my post at the door and ready myself to be wedged between the two tall men, given I was the scary chick, the badass agent. I wasn't quite feeling that way, but I had to make Benson and others believe it. I'd been in a few near-brawls during emotional permit hearings, but nothing like this.

"*You* are not the victim here, you piece of shit. There is a little boy who's the victim. Stop the bullshit and tell us where he is!" Gates spat at Benson.

I wasn't sure if Chief Gates was going to punch Kevin Benson. But I sure hoped he would. I knew by the look in Streeter's eye that he was irritated, but he hadn't yet been pushed to the brink of punching anyone.

I wasn't so sure about Gates. All I knew is that Streeter adored the chief. Talked about him all the time.

"Whoa, whoa, now," Benson was saying, "I told you the truth. I don't know where the kid is."

Streeter was at Gates's side and I moved instantly behind Benson, ready to take him down just in case a full-out fight erupted. I kind of figured Gates didn't get to be chief of police by being a hothead or a street fighter, but I was there just in case. Gates was rumored to have killed a Lucifer's Lot member once when the motorcycle club had suggested that a young thug rape Gates's elderly mother as an initiation, but I also heard no one could ever prove that Gates did anything wrong or that the kid was dead. But no one had ever heard from him again. Can't say that I blamed Gates for stepping over that thin, blue line. In fact, I could see myself doing the same if anyone ever threatened my family. The easiest part of knowing whose side I'm on is when my family's gathered, regardless of who's standing on the other side.

All I know is that Chief Gates was notorious for getting information from the tightest-lipped witnesses and for using his street sense to extract it. Quickly. So I was looking forward to watching him work his magic tonight.

Gates pulled Benson's face closer to his, still gripping the man's collar in his fist, and said, "We're not buying your poor-pitiful-me story. So what aren't you telling us? Because sure as I'm standing here, you're lying, you piece of crap."

"This . . . this is police brutality," Benson stuttered, leaning away from Gates's snarl as far as humanly possible.

From my angle behind Benson, I could see the angry expression on the chief's face—a live and in-person image of someone "spitting nails"—and my knees almost started knocking.

Gates breathed out a long, low growl, pulling Benson's face so close that I imagined he could tell what flavor toothpaste the chief used. "You've already wasted precious time in our recovery of the boy. His safety, not yours, is my primary concern. I really don't give a rat's ass if we toss you out on the tarmac this very second and let a 747 use your ass crack as a parking guide."

I muffled my laughter and stepped back to my post at the door.

Up to this point, I'd been scared to death to utter a peep. I really had no clue what to do since this was my first official case. Given Streeter's initial expression when I had slipped into the room, I could tell tensions were already over the top and if I didn't know better, I would swear he was pissed at me for some reason. Especially from his clipped tone on the call I had received an hour ago. But this is my first time on a case with him, and I really can't tell if this is just how he responds in interviews. Thanks to Chief Gates, I could speak vicariously through him to this nut job since he was saying what I was thinking. And I appreciated Gates's unfiltered candor.

"And I promise you that if one hair on the boy's head has been harmed, you'll lose a helluva lot more than your job, Benson." The man begged for Gates to let him go, openly and quite pitifully, if you ask me. Gates pushed Benson back down into his chair and pointed a finger at him. "If you so much as think about lying or whining again, I'll have you removed from this room and thrown in a cell downtown until I'm good and ready to talk with you again. Hurry it up, nancy," Gates said to Benson. "We don't have time for blubbering. Talk. About the boy. Not about you."

In his unique gargled-with-a-chainsaw voice, Streeter added, "Try starting from the beginning and explaining step by step what happened."

Through stutters and sputters, Benson told his story. "The first time I met the boy was at the gate at LaGuardia in New York City, after we'd prepared the plane for our return trip to Denver. He was sitting near the gate attendant, who had somehow managed to make the kid appear to be well behaved. Which he was not. But I didn't know that at the time. My first impression was wrong. I thought he looked adorable. Once she turned him over to me, I situated the boy in the front row of the airplane near the galley so I could keep an eye on him during the flight."

Benson drew in a deep breath and cleared his throat, swiping at his face in an effort to regain his composure, eyeing Gates each time he mentioned the boy's bad behavior.

"Our plane left New York on time."

I was trying to memorize the order and wording of every question Streeter asked. With over fifteen years of experience with the FBI, Streeter

Pierce was one of the best field agents who hadn't either taken a promotion or retired from the Denver-based branch. Streeter had been appointed as case agent on so many critical and high-profile cases that it was no surprise when he was named case agent of the Williams disappearance. And even though he might not be as thrilled to work with me, based on his curt call, I was thrilled by the honor and opportunity to work with him.

"And what did the boy look like?" Streeter asked, his words reminding me of brandy—smooth and warm but with a bite.

"He had thick, blond hair. Long, but cut in a page-boy style."

I couldn't help but notice Streeter brushing his hand over his buzz haircut at the mention of the boy's hair, which made his white hair stand at attention. I wondered if Streeter had been blond as a boy.

Benson added, "He was dressed in green velvet knickers and a matching vest and beret."

"Tell me about the boy during the flight. Anything out of the ordinary happen?" Streeter asked, settling back in his chair across the table from Benson.

I caught Streeter's eye and I knew I needed to pay attention to what was being said because he wanted to talk about it later. Streeter was signaling me.

"I don't remember."

"Try," Gates pressed.

Benson's lips pursed. I could tell he did not like Chief Gates. Not one bit. The way he pursed his lips meant resentment. I had learned a lot about body language in Quantico.

"BlueSky hates it when our planes are late. Our jobs as attendants are to do anything to keep the planes on schedule. I was in the galley talking to the girls, who were clearing up and preparing the passengers for landing. I had the mic and was going through my routine about leaving items stowed and seat belts fastened until the plane came to a complete stop when Brat Boy unbuckled his seat belt and walked right up to me, taking the mic away."

"Brat Boy?" Gates asked, exchanging a glance with Streeter.

"The Williams boy," Benson answered. As the men stared, Benson explained, "The other flight attendants and I nicknamed him Brat Boy before we ever took off from LaGuardia. I am sick that he's missing, but that kid was a brat. Totally out of control. Didn't listen to anyone. Spoiled rotten."

"He's a five-year-old, Mr. Benson," Streeter said.

Gates added, "And if you call him Brat Boy one more time, I'm going to rip your lips off your face. Got it?"

Benson's eyes widened. "You told me to tell you the details from the beginning. I was trying to explain the trip with this kid."

Streeter asked, "Where do you live, Mr. Benson?"

"Excuse me?" I could see that Streeter's line of questioning had taken Kevin Benson completely off guard, which is clearly what Streeter wanted.

"You said you lost your apartment. Where is it? The address?"

"Well, I . . . I don't know where I live at the moment. Out of my car, I guess. It's why I resorted to drinking at the bar. I don't have a place to live after today."

"And why is that?" Streeter pressed.

Benson actually curled his lip. "I told you that. That's why I lost the boy. My girlfriend and I were arguing." His eyes widened at his own mistake. Then he swallowed hard as the room went still. Streeter and the chief were waiting for his explanations.

When it didn't come, Streeter said, "Actually, you never told us that. Mind filling us in on that little detail?"

"She . . . she said she had to talk with me about something." He was fidgeting with his long fingers in his lap.

"This was after you landed? Did she call you or something?"

Benson smoothed his forehead with the pads of his fingers, his eyes darting upward to the right. "She'd sent me a text. I saw it when we landed at DIA. She wanted to meet me in between flights."

He looked down at his hands, his fingers working a crease in his uniform pants.

"I returned a text telling her that I was escorting a child and couldn't meet her. So we talked on the phone."

I noticed Streeter's attempt to hold his gaze, but Benson kept looking down at his hands. I could tell he was lying and that Streeter and Gates knew it, too. I wondered why they didn't just tell him that we could subpoena the cell phone records, see what calls had been made, what texts were exchanged, so we could get to the bottom of this quickly. I figured they must have a plan that included seeing how far he spun the story, letting him trap himself in his own web of lies.

"She . . . she broke up with me and told me she dumped all my stuff on the lawn. She said she changed the locks and that I better not call her or she'd file for a restraining order."

He blew out a long breath and stared at the ceiling.

"Get to the part about the child."

"I don't know exactly when the Bra—"Benson's gaze slid toward Gates. "The boy. I don't know when the boy slipped away from me. I was only on the phone for fifteen, maybe twenty minutes."

"You were never in the bathroom. Never went back for ice cream." Streeter speculated.

Benson slowly shook his head.

"So where were you? When you were on the phone? And don't lie this time."

"At gate 51 on Concourse B. Right below where we are right now." Again, his eyes shot skyward to his right. He bit his lip. He was still lying.

"And this was when?" Streeter asked.

He shrugged and unfolded his arms. "I told you, we landed around 12:40 p.m. at B31 and we were only minutes from walking down to B51. Probably around 1:00 p.m. or so? I don't know precisely to the minute because time wasn't exactly the most important thing on my mind at the moment."

"And you never took the boy anywhere else. To the bathroom? To a store, a restaurant, the bar, out of security to the main terminal or out of the airport?" Streeter leaned forward in his chair and I knew he was studying every single twitching muscle in Benson's eyes and on his face.

Benson shook his head and lowered his eyes.

"Nowhere except straight from B31 to B51?"

He shook his head again. "That's it."

"Did you see anyone suspicious following you? Anything at all out of the ordinary?" Gates asked.

"Just a lot of holiday travelers. I didn't notice anything out of the ordinary."

"What's your girlfriend's name and what's the address of the apartment?" Gates asked.

"I told you, I don't live there anymore." Benson cradled his head, clearly frustrated by Gates.

Streeter said, "We need to talk with your girlfriend to corroborate your story so—"

"She'll lie!" Benson shouted. To Streeter, he said, "He's not listening to me. She'll tell some wild story that I took the boy and dumped his body somewhere, that she saw me do it. She's just that way. The bitch just kicked me out of my home, dumped my sorry ass, and threw all my belongings into a snow bank over a couple of text messages. You don't need to talk to her. She'll just lie about everything. She'll try to get me in more trouble. That's what she told me she'd do if I ever called her again. She said she'd say anything, do anything, to get a restraining order. Don't you get it?"

"Oh we get it," Streeter said, leaning back in his chair. "And we'll keep that in mind when we talk with her. I think we're done for now, but we don't want you leaving the airport for a bit. Are you okay with that?"

"Why not?" Benson threw his hands in the air and let them drop to his sides.

"We might have some more questions."

"Mind if I ask him a question?" I asked Streeter.

He nodded. "Go ahead, Agent Bergen."

"What did he say?" I asked Benson.

"Who?" Benson asked.

"The boy. When he grabbed the mic on the plane."

Benson paused and sat staring at me, as if the air had gone out of his balloon. Resigned he answered, "He . . . he didn't say anything. He just . . . started singing." And his eyes did not flick up and to the right this time.

"Singing what?" I asked.

"I don't know. Does it matter? Everybody was laughing."

"Why?" I asked.

"Because he was . . . cute. Singing Merry Christmas in Spanish."

"'Feliz Navidad'?" I asked, wondering why that song mattered enough to little Max to make him want to sing it to a plane full of people.

CHAPTER 15

"WHAT'S HE LYING ABOUT?" Gates asked as they replayed the video of Benson's interview.

The headquarters that Kelleher had constructed above B56 had cleared, leaving only me, Chief Gates, and Streeter. I was still totally in the dark as to my role in all of this and had no clue what the chief or Streeter expected me to do. So I simply did my best, staying fairly quiet and out from under foot.

Unless I thought something had to be said.

"He's clearly lying here when he was talking about going to the bathroom. Look at how his eyes kept darting up and to the right," I said, pointing twice at the footage where Benson's expression clearly showed what I had seen earlier. "Classic tell, according to the behavioral psychologist at Quantico."

"It's certainly an indication that he's lying," Streeter agreed. "But we can't really jump to conclusions."

I arched an eyebrow, definitely detecting the chill in Streeter's fire-swallowing voice.

"Thanks for providing Mr. Benson with a personal escort, Chief," Streeter said to Gates.

"My deputy's still tied up with Freytag, so I put Officer Michaels on Benson and he won't let him out of his sight until I say so," Chief Gates explained.

"We'll need to interview him again. After we talk with the girlfriend. Let him sweat for an hour or so before we do," Streeter said.

I was still bothered by some of the things Kevin Benson said and did. "He went into great detail about the gates, the flight numbers, the times, everything leading up to the child being missing, but then breezed through the actual disappearance, the search, and everything leading to now. Did you notice that?"

Both men nodded.

"And he used descriptions like 'the boy' and not the child's name. As if to distance himself from being familiar. That concerns me," I added. "What if Benson kidnapped the boy and stashed him somewhere? He would have had the time. He's from Denver. He could have left the airport."

"Right," Streeter said. "We'll bring the girlfriend in to corroborate his story."

"Even though he insisted she'd lie to get him in trouble?" I asked.

"It's what we would do as a natural next step and we'll do it *because* of his urgency that we not talk to her. I have a sneaking suspicion that her story will more accurately reflect the truth about what happened than Kevin Benson's. But I won't know that until I am face-to-face with her. I think it's worth flushing out the untruths, don't you?"

Gates nodded and punched some buttons on his cell phone. "Officers are on their way to the address BlueSky gave us for Benson. His emergency contact on file was listed as Bonita Smith, at the same address. They'll confirm whether the girlfriend and Bonita are one and the same."

"In the meanwhile, let's find Danica," Streeter said, rising from the computer.

"Who's Danica?" I asked, feeling a flush of envy.

Her name conjured up the dark-haired, car-racing beauty with the same name. And imagining Streeter alone with a woman like that irked me for some reason.

Streeter was of average height, maybe five-eleven or six foot, with a boxy build, and broad shouldered. I considered him sturdy looking. Not the least bit fat. Just fit. Streeter's hair was cropped short and stark white, too white for his age. And his blue eyes were alive with a fire that made people believe in him, especially when they seemed to turn green. To me, he would always be Agent Adonis.

"Danica Bradsky was the airport security employee assigned to the escalator from the underground trains to the main terminal, where passengers exit the concourses."

The stubble that grew on Streeter's tanned cheeks looked as rough as his voice sounded. Although he was not a smoker, Streeter's voice reminded me of hearing the lawn mower on Saturday mornings as a child. It had sounded rough and effective, cutting across the chirping of early birds. His voice was to the point, not to be ignored. He was driven to accomplish the task before him.

"Can I come along?" I asked.

"I don't think I have a choice," Streeter said, his tone cranky.

"What does that mean?" I asked, feeling the bite in his comment and realizing I hadn't imagined his irritation with me on the phone earlier.

Turning to Gates, Streeter added, "And I want this airport searched end to end, garbage gathered, secured, and examined as soon as possible. I want anything and everything suspicious bagged and tagged."

Gates cleared his throat. "Are you sure? The sheer magnitude of trash discarded in one hour here is overwhelming."

"Secure it all. Everything since this morning until noon tomorrow."

As he was leaving, fingers hovering above his cell phone, Gates paused as he passed me and asked, "What happened to your face? Are you okay?"

At least Chief Gates noticed my scratched up cheeks. I opened my mouth to explain when Streeter interrupted, "Gates, how many men can you have searching this place? We'll need an army to search every hiding place."

I simply nodded at the chief. He smiled, his eyes tenderly studying my injuries as he answered Streeter, "I can get the National Guard out here. Let me step out and get my team moving on the garbage retrieval and airport lockdown and get started on a more thorough search."

Streeter nodded. As Gates left the room, Streeter turned his back to me and started punching numbers on his phone. I waited.

"This is Pierce again. I need your help. This is the third message I've left so I assume you're in an area with no coverage or have your cell phone turned off. We have a situation. Call my cell as soon as you get these messages." The thick fingers of one hand flipped the phone off and slid it into his pocket while his other hand brushed through his short crop of white hair. He stood in front of the window facing the tarmac, staring into the darkness beyond. I could see the worry etched in his face in the reflection of the glass.

"Where is he?"

"Little Max?" I asked.

"Linwood."

I hesitated. "I . . . I have no clue. Is that why you're angry?"

"He wasn't with you for the holidays? At your sister's house?"

"No. Not that it's any of your business," I said, walking up beside him and staring out the same window. "Is that what this is about?"

Streeter ignored me. "And you have no idea where Linwood might be?"

"I told you, no. Streeter, if you're angry about me dating Jack I think we should—"

He spun to face me, his blue eyes blazing. "I'm angry that you're acting as if this is no big deal."

"What are you talking about? Little Max's disappearance is a very big deal," I said, folding my arms across my chest, my anger elevating to meet his.

"We have a child, a young boy, who's disappeared. But somehow, you know his name is little Max. And somehow you're mixed up in all this."

"What? I'm mixed up in all this? I've never even met the boy," I stammered.

"Little Max? Where'd you learn that nickname?"

"From Phil. During your interview earlier with—"

"But you know who little Max is, don't you?"

Hesitating, I nodded.

"And you know his father."

I nodded again, realizing where he was going now.

"The billionaire."

"Millionaire," I corrected, taking a few steps away from Streeter to give him room to cool off. I could actually feel the heat rising from his skin, could smell his scent blended with something clean and spicy. "I wouldn't give him any more credit than he deserves. Which ain't much."

He turned and stared at me as if he might explode. "This isn't a joke."

His dark mood concerned me. I'd never seen Streeter like this. Serious yes, dark no. Normally he was so calm. This response confused me and I wasn't sure why he was so worked up, other than that I was dressed like a vagabond, which I could see would be upsetting. I took a few steps toward him, holding his glare, and said, "I know that, Streeter. What's gotten into you?"

"I need to know you'll take this seriously, no matter what your personal connection with this guy." The darkness in his eyes faded to an expression of concern.

He had it all wrong. Max was nothing personal to me. Not one bit. "What in the hell are you talking about?"

"Are you? Going to take this seriously and professionally?"

What did he mean by that? Maybe he assumed I wasn't taking it seriously enough because it took me so long to get to DIA. But I was staying at Frances's house, clear over in Wheat Ridge, and I drove as fast as I could without breaking the law, not even taking time to change clothes. Based on how he was giving me the once-over, maybe it's the clothes. Not very professional, I'll admit. Maybe I'd embarrassed him in front of the chief.

Contrite, I answered, "Yes, of course."

"And not take matters into your own hands because this is personal?"

"If you think I'm compromised, why did you involve me at all? You called me, remember?" I said, the frustration beginning to build in my throat and gut, frustrated that in my excitement to prove to Streeter I could do this job, I'd missed the fact that for some reason, he didn't want me doing my job.

"Because I had to."

"Says who?" I shot back.

"Chandler, that's who," he shot back.

My eyes grew wide and my jaw went slack. I eventually managed, "John Chandler? The John Chandler? The Director of the Federal Bureau of Investigation? From Washington DC? You got your orders from him?"

Streeter scowled. "And I'm not too happy about it. Neither is Tony."

"I'm confused. Why is John Chandler telling you how to run this case?" I asked, dumbfounded.

"Maximillian Bennett Williams II apparently has a lot of money and a lot of pull. But you already knew that. You say millionaire. Whatever he's worth, apparently when he wants something, he gets it. And with his son's disappearance, he did not want the locals on the case. He wanted the FBI."

"So Max asked for us?" I asked.

"Actually, he didn't ask anything. He *told* Chandler he wanted *you*," Streeter corrected.

With everything hanging on that final word, he eyed me. Not so pleasantly, I might add. I'd even say he was a wee bit pissed. I could understand that. I'm just out of Quantico and some guy with money has John Chandler's ear and insists that I be assigned a high-profile case involving abduction. I would be pissed too if I were Streeter or Chief Gates. Or Calvin, for that matter; first chance I got, I'd call him and explain. But why the hell had Max asked for me?

My response to Streeter's questioning expression was lame. "Max and I knew each other some time ago. Seven or eight years ago."

His eyebrow rose.

"And it was nothing personal. I mean, with me. He was dating my youngest sister, Ida."

The long pause preceding Streeter's response told me he was weighing the validity of his anger with me. This was not my fault.

"The sister you're staying with in Denver?"

"No, that's my sister Frances. And she lives in Wheat Ridge, not Denver. Which is why it took me so long to get here. I made it as quickly as I could. And I'm sorry I didn't change first. I didn't think there was time." There, maybe now he'd be a bit less surly with me.

The tiny lines around his mouth softened a bit. "And Elizabeth's the one I met in Rochford?"

"Right. I have six sisters and two brothers. Remember the funeral for my brother Jens's fiancée that you and the other FBI agents were casing in Rapid City? I don't think you met Ida, but you probably saw her. She was the tallest, the model." Although your eyes seemed to be glued to FBI Agent Jenna Tate that day, I wanted to say, but didn't. I was apparently in enough trouble as it was.

His scowl became more pronounced. "Ida was the one with long, dark hair and green eyes, wearing the expensive-looking pink dress? Looks like she stepped off a Victoria's Secret runway?"

"You did notice." His attention to detail from months ago caused me a twinge of jealousy, and an acute awareness of how shabbily I was dressed. "She met Max in the Big Apple. As a teenager. She was a protégée at the Juilliard School of Music, an opera singer, before being discovered as a model. She has a fabulous voice, but Max seemed more interested in everything south of Ida's vocal chords."

Streeter cleared his throat and turned back to the window. "Well, that's how we ended up on the case. Maximillian Bennett Williams II requested you."

"How the hell does he even know I'm with the FBI?" I wondered aloud. "It's not like any of us Bergens have stayed in touch with the asshole, and certainly Ida wouldn't have talked with him. I doubt if she's ever talked with him again after walking out on him seven years ago." Then it dawned on me. "Which is why you're so angry. Max requested me, which translates to, you have to work with me."

He turned back to me, standing inches from my nose, looking down at my intense expression, and whispered, "All I know is that Williams demanded you be on the case. And I convinced Calvin to ignore Chandler and to let me be in charge of the case instead. And Calvin backed my decision. At the risk of getting us both fired."

I took a step closer to Streeter and stared into his eyes, "What? Are you saying Calvin was going to let me lead? That's crazy! No wonder you're pissed. I'd be pissed, too."

I could smell his cologne. He wasn't budging.

"Calvin's job is on the line, but he listened to me. I'm lead, as long as I work with you."

I stood staring up at him. Our faces were so close we didn't dare move.

I felt his hot breath against my face when he said, "We've got a job to do and we better do it right, or Williams will make sure John Chandler has us chucked curbside like yesterday's garbage."

I didn't move. I didn't want to. The heat felt good. Streeter wasn't about to move, either. After a few intimate seconds, I smirked, leaned back, and crossed my arms across my chest, matching his posture. "Then we better get busy and solve this case."

In the short six months that I'd known him, to say our relationship was complicated would be an understatement. One moment he's kissing me, convincing me a relationship beyond friendship is not only possible but also promising, and then the next moment it's like he doesn't even acknowledge my existence. We'd developed a strong friendship the instant we met earlier in the summer. His kiss this fall, at Storybook Island of all places, left me undeniably weak-kneed. And it was damn near love at first sight for me, but I'd shoot anyone who repeated that to Streeter.

Then, he did a one-eighty as if he'd made a terrible mistake and wanted to forget all about me. He's never talked about it. I convinced myself that maybe Streeter's just not ready, having lost his wife. More likely, his disinterest in me has something to do with the rumor that he and the lovely Jenna Tate are an item.

"Not before you look me in the eye and answer two questions," Streeter demanded.

But there's no denying the chemistry between Streeter and me. He's the single reason I chose to leave the family business in limestone mining for a life with the FBI. And although I asked to spend part time with the Bureau, it quickly turned to full time, and I haven't looked back. My days and nights since September are occupied nearly 24-7 with Bureau business, which means I get to spend a lot of hours working with Streeter Pierce and occasionally with the ICO team, which includes Jack.

"All right," I said, unnerved by how much he smelled like the inside of an Abercrombie & Fitch store, which was wildly erotic compared to his usual Old Spice scent. For the first time he smelled less like my dad and more like the young thirty-nine-year-old he was, closer to my age.

"Were you and Maximillian ever involved?"

I shook my head. "Not my type."

"Rich isn't your type?"

"Complete asshole isn't my type."

When the hint of a smile played in the corner of his lips, I uncrossed my arms and stood tall, hoping he'd notice I was unafraid of his closeness, until he asked his second question.

"And you have no clue where your boyfriend is?"

"Max isn't my boyfriend."

"I meant Linwood." His blue eyes were as intense as I'd ever seen them. Emotion stirred and roiled within me, smothering all that was logical.

"Streeter, I—"

He interrupted me before I could answer. "You brought Beulah?"

I nodded at the sudden change of topic.

"Where is she?"

I stuttered, "Next door in the room where they're setting up for the Williams interrogation."

"Work the airport. Start around gate B31 and see where the trail leads."

I was not disturbed by his directness. Or by how he barked orders. What bothered me was the way he tore his intimate gaze from me and turned abruptly away. Because I was dating Jack? Clearly, he was upset at Chandler's demand that I lead the case. That would have offended me, too, if I were Streeter. So I had to do whatever I could to make him look good on this case. To prove myself worthy.

"I'll need a scent for her to track." My voice sounded weak.

Streeter nodded toward the tiny backpack in the corner of the room. "Benson said that's the child's. He was traveling with it and Benson has been holding it for him since they deplaned."

I tried not to let Streeter's changed attitude toward me get under my skin. But it did. Tucked in the corner of the room, the tiny blue backpack with yellow puppies running and jumping and circling the fabric made me realize I had a lot of work to do and more important things to worry about than Streeter's mood.

"At least little Max likes dogs," I mumbled.

Approaching the inconsequential backpack made me suddenly aware of the enormous weight of what was at stake if I didn't do my job correctly. There was no time for screwups. I'd get no second chances. Time was of the essence and I absolutely needed to believe in Beulah and pray to God she believed in me enough to perform our first official search together. Alone.

I bent to retrieve the bag, noting it was lighter than I'd imagined it to be. Maybe it was because I had a fifth grader's backpack to compare it to from just hours earlier. "Anyone check the contents?"

Streeter simply stared. So I unzipped the bag, took inventory, and said,

"Two granola bars, a Transformer thingy, three shiny new Matchbox cars, and a jacket."

I pulled out the jacket and pinched the shoulders with each hand, demonstrating the size of the boy. "Tiny."

"Do you have enough to get started?"

I nodded. "If he's worn this jacket recently, it will help. It looks new. So does the backpack, but it might be my best bet. Still, if Kevin Benson carried it for the boy, maybe it won't help either."

Streeter's words were clipped. "Do your best."

CHAPTER 16

Noah

"NOW I LAY ME down to sleep, I pray the Lord my soul to keep . . ."

Emma was kneeling against my bed with Mom. They were reciting the bedtime prayer together followed by the Lord's Prayer, like always. But I'd stopped listening. For some reason, the words "I pray the Lord my soul to keep" hit me wrong.

I know I'm not supposed to think bad thoughts, especially about God, but what does He mean by keeping my soul? I want to keep my own soul. I'm not ready to give that up. So does it mean that I'm lying when I say the prayer in my head along with Mom and Emma every night? Or does it mean I'm a bad person if I'm not willing to just give away my soul to God? I'm just not ready yet.

I'd almost missed the fact that Mom and Emma had ended the prayers and were about to leave, when I looked at Emma. She understood.

"What?"

I lifted my eyes to the headboard.

"Me or Mom? Mom?" I did nothing. "Me?" I smiled.

"Mom, Noah wants to talk with me. Can we have a minute before I go to bed?"

"Don't take long. Santa won't come if you're still awake. You know the rules." I felt Mom's lips press against my forehead and her fingers muss my hair. "Sleep tight."

Emma added, "And don't let the bed bugs bite."

Mom and Emma chimed in together, "And if they do, I'll take my shoe and beat them 'til they're black and blue."

I giggled.

Mom shut off the light and said, "Em, shut Noah's door when you're done, please."

And I could hear Mom walk down the stairs, grateful she had found the contact I had lost earlier and also that she let me sleep with my football pin despite her protests that I might get stuck by it in my sleep. I wanted to record Santa and prove he exists, once and for all.

"What's up, buttercup?" Emma asked.

She held up fingers in the dark, and the light from the hallway was enough for me to make out which one. Emma had designed what my mom tells doctors is the five-finger method of communicating with me. They've actually videotaped us communicating and I kind of felt like one of Jane Goodall's chimpanzees, but if it would help someone else, I decided to let them do all the videotaping they wanted. One doctor told us that other CPs—that's short for cerebral palsy victims—like me have used the same method for communicating, but they called it something else.

Mom says the doctors don't believe I'm actually talking, just that it's Emma's active imagination and I only smile because I'm amused by her. But they don't know what they're talking about. Mom says they're skeptical because Emma doesn't let me finish hardly any words and finishes them for me, but that's because we know each other well.

They're wrong. We talk all the time. Mom's tried it but Emma isn't very patient with her. And the truth is, neither am I. Mom wants to spell out every single word and needs every word in the sentence and still doesn't remember what finger or knuckle goes with which letter.

It's so easy. Emma's told her a hundred times. The pointer finger is A through G. The middle finger is H through N. Ring finger is O through U. And the pinky finger is V through Z. Knuckles and valleys starting with the knuckle of the pointer finger are the rest of the letters. Emma and I figured out our own system after watching a TV interview once when Team Hoyt, the Ironman father-and-son team, were in Denver running a marathon. The dad was saying that Rick, his son, who had severe cerebral palsy like me, learned how to communicate through a computer later in life by tapping a headpiece with his head. But when he was young, Rick used a method that was similar to Emma's, using the five vowels to communicate with his brother, Russell. They call their communication the Russell Method. But vowels were too hard for Emma. She said it was like Old McDonald's farm—E-I-E-I-O—and it confused her, so she used five fingers instead.

The doctors don't believe us, but the Hoyts would. I don't know if we're doing it right, but Emma and I came up with a system that works for us, thanks to Rick and his brother.

Emma held up her pointer finger. I made sure not to smile or raise my eyes.

She held up her middle finger. I did nothing.

Ring finger. Nothing.

Pinky. I gave her a quick smile.

First knuckle.

Emma said, "Not a V. I hate Vs." I didn't respond.

Valley between first knuckle and second. I gave her a quick smile.

"W. Who? What? Where? When? Why?" she asked.

I flashed a smile.

"You have a question. What's going on? Where's Auntie Liv? When's she coming home?" she guessed.

No, but those were good questions.

"Okay, but just in case you're wondering, Mom says Auntie Liv's still looking for the little boy who got lost at the airport. Probably will be all night, even if they find him. She may not make it home for Christmas morning at all, bud. Mom said we shouldn't worry. I won't because you want to know a secret?"

I smiled.

"They keep forgetting that Santa Claus is coming tonight. He'll find the little boy. And he'll take him back to his home. Right?"

I smiled and moaned, grateful for her positive attitude. It would make me sleep better tonight. I hoped she was right.

Then I frowned.

"Okay, okay. Back to your question. "Is it a 'Who' question?"

I remained still.

"A 'What' question?"

I smiled.

"What do I want for Christmas? I want a princess dress, a blond wig like Rapunzel, and clothes for my doll."

I frowned.

"Well, I didn't think that's what you were asking. But I wanted to tell you anyway. What did I do with your gift for Mom and Dad? I put it under the tree."

I did nothing for a long time. Then I smiled.

"You're welcome. Okay, a 'What' question. Main word." She flipped through her fingers. I smiled on finger three, third knuckle.

"S!" she shouted. "Santa, right? What's Santa bringing you?"

I didn't smile.

"You're no fun. Second letter." I smiled on finger three again, first knuckle.

"O." I smiled. "Is it 'So'?" I did nothing.

Her fingers flew up again and I smiled for a third time on finger three, smiled again on last knuckle.

"U?" I smiled. "S-O-U—ooh, I don't know this word. Fourth letter."

I smiled on her second finger, fourth knuckle.

"L? S-O-U-L" she repeated. "Is it 'soul'?"

I smiled.

"What's a soul?" she asked.

I did nothing.

"Well then maybe some time when we have more time, you can explain it to me. 'Cause I don't know what a soul is. But that's not your question. Okay, more words."

She quickly worked through the rest of my question.

Third finger, valley between third and fourth knuckles. "T."

Third finger, first knuckle. "O. To?"

I smiled.

Second finger, valley between second and third knuckle. "K."

First finger, third knuckle. "E."

First finger, third knuckle. "E again?"

I smiled.

"K-E-E. Keeb, Keef, Keen?"

Nothing.

"Keep?"

I smiled.

"What's soul to keep? What does it mean, soul to keep?" I smiled. She flopped down on the bed beside me and said, "Oh, the bedtime prayer. Now I lay me down to sleep, I pray the Lord my soul to keep. What does that mean?"

I smiled and studied her face as she grew still.

"I don't have a clue. Maybe it just means our souls are in good hands with God, since it's Him we're praying to." She fluffed the pillow beside me, her soft red curls brushing against my cheek as she did. I laughed. "But now that you mention it, God keeping my soul does kinda sound creepy, like he's coming for me in my sleep. Like the grim reaper or something."

I smiled.

"That's what you were thinking?"

I smiled again.

She glanced toward the hallway, I assume to make sure Mom or Dad weren't coming. She whispered, "Remember Casey? At school?"

I screeched with excitement, my muscles bunching and my stiff arm accidentally punching her.

"I told you he's not my boyfriend. I don't even like the kid."

I chuckled, which helped me relax. I got excited because I knew Emma did like Casey and she brought home crazy-wild stories from him and they always made me laugh. I was in the other fourth-grade class at school so I didn't get to hear or see everything Casey did. The stories were great.

"He said the principals all across the world made the parents change the bedtime prayer. He said it was like illegal for them to let us say it the old way. He said that the grim reaper was using that prayer to hypnotize little kids and stealing their souls at night, even though God didn't want them. He said the old version used to be 'Now I lay me down to sleep, I pray the Lord my soul to keep. If I should die before I wake, I pray the Lord my soul to take.'"

I laughed until my gut ached.

"What? It's not funny. It's scary, Noah. Kids were praying about dying in their sleep. What kind of world was that?"

I laughed so hard all the sound disappeared.

"I'm going to bed. I hope Santa gives you a lump of coal for laughing at me." She stomped off and slammed my door.

I laughed for a long time even after she was gone.

She was right, though. The old version was scary. And there was no way that Casey was telling the truth about that. But her story did explain why such a strange yet protective line remained in the popular prayer about God keeping my soul. Kind of like, we're praying He remembers to tell the grim reaper, "Hey bud! That soul's mine, so back off!"

It might also explain why parents always say, "The Lord works in mysterious ways." Who knows?

All I know is I'm excited that Christmas is almost here, but I'm sad for the little boy on the TV, too. If Auntie Liv is still looking for him, that probably means they haven't found him. I'll know when she gets home because I'll have Beulah back in my bed with me. Auntie Liv took Beulah with her, which means they're not counting on Santa to find him. They're counting on Beulah. I'm sad for the little boy, since he won't be able to see what's in his stocking in the morning, smell the coffee on his mom's breath with her morning kiss, or hear his dad's yummy noises as he eats fresh cinnamon rolls.

I worry about him.

He is younger than Emma. I think by what the TV lady said he'd be in kindergarten. Emma's fourth-grade classroom is across from mine and right next to us between our rooms and the bathrooms are the kindergarten classes. Those kids were really excited about Christmas this year and some of them still cry when their moms drop them off at school. That's what has me sad. I think about that. The little lost boy is out there somewhere tonight.

He's probably crying.

And I wish I could help him.

I thought I wanted a swing for Christmas. But really all I want is for the little boy to be found and to get to go home so he can be with his mom and dad.

I hope Auntie Liv finds him.

I wish Beulah was in my bed so I could feel her warm fur.

I hope if they don't have any luck that Santa brings him home.

I hope the boy is warm.

Wherever he is.

CHAPTER 17

AT FIRST, I WAS excited to get started. It was my first official trailing assignment on my own. Streeter told me to begin where the boy was last seen—not the bathroom Benson vaguely described, but the location where others confirmed the last sighting of the boy—arriving at gate B31 when his plane from New York had landed. We'd trail the boy's scent through the airport from there.

When I first arrived at DIA, I was in such a hurry to report on my first official case as an agent that I hadn't noticed everyone staring. But I never could have imagined the attention Beulah and I would garner walking through DIA as we headed toward the other end of the concourse from the makeshift headquarters. We avoided the moving walkways and hugged the walls as we walked west toward the other end of the concourse. We were headed toward the center of the concourse where mobs of travelers flocked to the shops and restaurants around the perimeter.

By the time we'd arrived at gate B31, an area thick with passengers waiting to depart, I noticed that Beulah was acting as if every single movement distracted her. I felt hundreds of eyes on me; I never felt more self-conscious in all my life. Some curious travelers actually followed us. Everyone who noticed us openly stared. Even the travelers sitting in the rows of seats facing the windows had turned to watch what we were doing. People were watching us from both sides of the long moving walkways that hurried passengers down the 3,500-foot concourse.

Skepticism soured my mood.

The hundreds of travelers rushing past me fueled my anxiety and my desire to be useful on this case, to help find Max's son as fast as humanly possible. I wanted to please Streeter, to prove to him that his choosing me as a special agent wasn't wasted. As if the masses of people weren't bad enough, those who slowed and gawked made it worse. I slid the harness over Beulah's head, easing her front paws through the straps and fixing the clasps snugly around her chest and back.

Beulah became as calm as ever, seemingly undisturbed by the strange surroundings, the volume of people. It was as if her harness erased any distractions for her. She was ready to work. Most of our training and many of our actual trails were in wooded areas or fields. If I hadn't known better, I would have thought judging by her calm disposition that this dog had a regular job searching airports. Her confidence eased my apprehension and whittled away my skepticism. She was a pro.

"No mountain lions here, Beulah," I said, coaxing her to make me feel more confident.

I wondered if Beulah could actually track a scent trail from seven hours earlier in an airport where thousands of travelers had since trampled. I scratched behind her ears and she lifted her nose toward me, the folds of skin on her face sliding back and revealing her wide, bright eyes. I knew that if any dog could do this impossible task, it would be her. I'd learned over the last six months just how amazing bloodhounds were, especially Beulah. She'd practically saved my life while risking her own at the Hanson place. She'd suffered injuries, and although she'd taken time off to heal while I was at Quantico, she was back on track the instant the wheels of my plane touched down at DIA three weeks ago. Both of us were excited to reacquaint ourselves with the business of trailing.

Beulah's sense of smell is incredible and if I wasn't careful, I could indicate the wrong scent for her to follow. The backpack and the items inside it were the only articles I had from the child, and I was concerned about how many people had or may have touched or handled the bag. The boy's backpack would include his scent if the bag was actually worn or used by the child. But I had my doubts. The bag appeared to be new, as did the jacket inside. And both felt expensive. Knowing Max, this boy was showered with gifts, clothes, and toys. It would be far easier to indicate a scent for Beulah to follow from a familiar, well-worn item than from something that little Max barely touched or wore. The conflicting, inconsequential scents mingled with the one I wanted to highlight could be a significant hurdle for us in this search.

I cursed under my breath, wishing I had an article of the boy's clothing, something he might have worn more recently and more often than the new jacket stuffed into a backpack. A jacket I wasn't sure the kid had ever even tried on before.

As I hitched the lead onto the harness, Beulah set herself in a ready position. I led her to the counter next to gate B31. Passengers were moving away from the counter area and cramming into the row of chairs on either side of us as if we were repelling magnets. The crowd was waiting to board the next flight out of the gate and the marquee above the counter read "Des Moines." I explained to the BlueSky employee what I was trying to do, who I was working for, and that I hoped not to delay the boarding. She had made an announcement for passengers to clear the area and to please be patient as the authorities started a search.

Beulah leaned against my leg. While passengers stared, I nodded my thanks to the BlueSky gate attendant and told her I hoped Beulah would only spend a few minutes at the gate. Concerned about the many different scents that could be lingering on the bag, I carefully extracted the tiny, new jacket and laid it on the ground at Beulah's paws and said, "Find."

Beulah dropped her eyes to the jacket and the folds of skin on her head and ears billowed over her eyes.

I repeated, "Find."

Everyone was ogling us. No pressure there. Beulah looked up at me, circled the jacket, walked toward the gate, then back to the jacket, toward an older woman sitting closest the gate, and then back to the jacket.

"Find." Beulah stood over the jacket, and then looked up at me and down at the jacket. And sat down at my feet. She wasn't budging. I assumed that meant I was right. There was no scent on the jacket worth trailing. I ignored the mumbles and whispering from the Des Moines crowd and retrieved the jacket, stuffed it back into the child's backpack, and placed the entire bag on the ground at Beulah's paws.

"Find!" I commanded. She rose to her feet and stood above the backpack.

I was sure the boy's scent would be on the bag since he had worn it getting on the plane earlier that day. I just didn't know how strong his scent would be. I hoped the signal from the jacket allowed Beulah to isolate the boy's scent from everything else—from the scent of Kevin Benson, who wore a heavy, musky cologne, from the TSA agents in NYC, possibly from a bellhop or a taxi driver, from a staff member at Max's penthouse or the mansion he undoubtedly owned, and possibly even from Streeter's scent if he had touched the bag and left behind a whiff of that incredibly sexy new cologne he was wearing. A Christmas gift? From Jenna?

I barely managed another "Find" before Beulah circled once toward the gate and then took off hot on a scent through the concourse. I scooped up the backpack and shouted my thanks over my shoulder as Beulah pushed her way through the hordes of people toward the center of the concourse, which led us past more moving walkways as we headed toward B51, where the boy should have departed for LA, just as Kevin Benson had suggested.

If Benson was telling the truth, Beulah would head down the length of the concourse through the crowded center to B51, double back to the center of Concourse B where most of the shops and restaurants were located, and head to whichever bathroom Benson had last gone to with the boy. With five levels on each concourse, most not accessible by the public, I questioned for the first time where BlueSky employees might have access that others didn't.

But before I could formulate my thoughts around areas where a young boy might hide, Beulah lurched to the left down a nearby escalator that led to the underground train.

"Benson, you liar," I mumbled, trying to think back, to remember Benson's specific eye movements that suggested he was lying. "What were you doing down here?"

Keeping the lead short, I excused Beulah's bad manners as she pushed her way through the crowds on the escalators, in the waiting area below, and to the door for boarding the trains. The mechanical voice sounding over the PA system was announcing train arrivals and warning people to keep clear of the doors so arriving passengers could get off, but I could not budge Beulah from her post at the closed doors. Once on the train, Beulah seemed confused. I let her follow people off at the next stop, but she seemed to have lost the scent entirely.

I loaded Beulah back on the train and headed toward B31, starting the search again. She bolted from the gate directly to the same down escalator heading to the underground trams; she went to the same door and again seemed lost when she got on the tram. This time, we stayed put on the train until the second and last stop, which was at the main terminal. Beulah tentatively stepped off the train, hesitated briefly, and then bolted through the foot traffic to the escalators, nearly knocking a few passengers over. Beulah didn't trail the scent up the escalator. Instead, she broke toward a quiet area to the right, underneath the escalators, which I finally recognized as the elevators. I pushed the button and when the doors opened, Beulah pulled me on, confidently and surely.

The scent on the bag led us to this route, I thought. I couldn't believe it. Kevin Benson had lied. Worse, he took the child out of the secure area to the main terminal. Or someone did. Directly out of the secure area as the boy deplaned. What did it mean?

Maybe I hadn't trailed the scent correctly. Surely Kevin Benson would not have taken a child out of the secure area, would he? Isn't that against the law or something? To take an unaccompanied minor away from airport security? Okay, maybe not illegal, but certainly ill advised. Surely it broke some code of ethics with the airlines.

And what if I missed a signal? Beulah had only been confused when *on* the train, which may make sense given the boy likely stood in one place and didn't wander about as the train traveled. The likelihood of getting on the exact train was slim to none; surely these trains ran every few seconds. That was my speculation based on similar behavior Beulah was demonstrating in the elevator. Again, the boy likely stood in one spot, waiting for the elevator to go up to the main terminal.

The doors to the elevator opened and I saw familiar faces from the underground train exiting the escalator into the main terminal. Ticketing was around the corner to my right with the security checkpoint ahead. The down escalators to the underground train were on my left and stores brimming with shoppers rimmed the edges of a large open area beneath white canvas peaks overhead that emulated the snowcapped mountains. Beulah trotted toward a nearby bar called the Buckhorn Bar and Grill, circled, and then bolted straight for the restrooms. She pulled up short at a particular door between the men's and women's restrooms. The sign on the door read "Family" above the picture of two stick figures, one wearing a skirt. I tried the knob. The bathroom was not in use; its door was not locked. I let Beulah continue into the roomy stall. The room was a single bathroom with one seat. It had a changing table that dropped from the wall, one sink, and a large garbage can.

Beulah pulled me all the way into the Family room, and the door bumped shut as Beulah circled, went to the toilet seat, then hesitated. Beulah stood near the sink for a long moment, decided to circle, went back to the toilet seat briefly, and then to the sink. She planted herself on the bathroom floor and looked back at me over her shoulder.

"Find," I said but knew she wouldn't. The trail seemed to stop here.

I let out some slack in her lead so I could reach the door, opened it, and repeated the command. Beulah just sat there, staring at the sink, and then at me. She didn't howl. She didn't bolt back out the door. She didn't whine. She just sat there near the sink and stared at me.

I propped a rubber wedge beneath the Family door to keep it open, walked back over to Beulah, laid the backpack at her feet, and repeated the command.

She didn't move. This was the end of the trail. I didn't understand what it meant, but I certainly had confidence in what Beulah was telling me. The scent simply ended. Right here. I squatted down and rubbed Beulah's ears and sides, offered her a handful of dog treats, telling her she was a good dog and giving her lots of praise. I decided to verify the trail from B31 to the main concourse bathroom again, to confirm my results.

When I led Beulah back through security to the underground trains to Concourse B to start over, I noticed a familiar face, one I'd seen a few times before on my trail with Beulah. Twice on the trains at different times during my search earlier and now a third time on the train heading back. Maybe the woman was simply riding the trains back and forth, a bored passenger with nothing to do on her layover but ride. I turned to smile at her, catch her eye. Her face was blanched, her expression weary. And when her eyes landed on mine, she turned her face quickly away and pretended she hadn't noticed me. Odd, I thought. I assumed she was either embarrassed that I noticed her riding the trains again or that I realized she was one of the curious travelers who'd followed us to watch an official investigation in action. But I didn't mind if she was. I was proud of Beulah's exceptional skills.

Back at gate B31, the Des Moines passengers were lined up to board the plane, and I decided to give Beulah a rest and another treat as I sank into the stiff row of chairs to wait until the area was cleared. This time around, all the travelers who had earlier gawked and whispered offered me wary smiles, worried glances, and suggested "good luck," one passenger glancing up to the television monitor above my head. My eyes followed hers and I realized most of them had probably noticed the national news story announcing the missing child at DIA.

As I watched Beulah drool over her dog treat, I thought about Kevin Benson lying to Streeter and the chief earlier, knowing now that the kid had gone straight off the plane and out of the security area. No gate B51. No ice cream. No bathroom. No way. Benson had lied about all that. But I had to verify the trail one more time to be sure.

As the travelers shuffled past me, I glanced up to see how fast the line was moving. I noticed a familiar face across the concourse at gate B30. A guy who looked a lot like Jack Linwood was coming off the plane, sandwiched between a bespectacled man who appeared to have been traveling for several lifetimes and a heavy lady who seemed unsteady with every step. Jack, on the other hand, looked crisp, handsome, as always. He was punching buttons on his cell phone with the pads of his thumbs, and just as I was about to call out his name, tell him what I was doing, and ask what he was doing on the plane, my cell phone chirped. I had a message.

I fished the cell phone quickly from my pocket and saw that the text was from Jack. The idea of watching him text me without him knowing it made me smile. But the message confused me. I looked from my phone to

Jack as he slipped his phone into his pocket, quickly stepped around the weary traveler ahead of him, and walked away from gate B30 toward FBI's makeshift headquarters on the other end of the concourse.

My mouth opened in protest, then closed again. I stared at the text message that read, "On my way. At Concourse B. Be there in a few minutes."

Hoping to learn where he had just come from and why he was on that plane—maybe searching it or something?—I texted, "Where've you been? We've been looking for you."

His reply was, "Don't laugh, but I fell asleep—the sleep of the dead— and didn't notice everyone trying to call me. That never happens. But I'm awake now. And I'm here."

"Searching for the boy?" I asked.

"Not yet. Just got here. Headed to see what Streeter needs me to do."

So he was not searching the plane for the missing boy. He really had just deplaned this arriving flight as I first thought. I walked over to gate B30 and asked the BlueSky gate attendant, "Where did this flight just come from?"

The woman said, "Kansas City."

I'd never heard Jack mention Kansas City before. And I'd been to his apartment. He lived in downtown Denver. His bed was amazingly comfortable and I knew what he meant by the sleep of the dead. His bedroom was cool and dark and smelled of lavender and spice. In Denver. Not in Kansas City. I went back to prepare Beulah for the final verification of the little boy's scent trail, to prove to Streeter that Kevin Benson had lied to him, not admitting to myself that Jack Linwood had just lied to me.

CHAPTER 18

"IT'S LIKE HE JUST disappeared into thin air," Gates said as he threw himself back into a chair behind a makeshift desk, rubbing his tired eyes.

"That child could be anywhere," Streeter said, echoing his frustration.

I had missed all the excitement in the past hour. Streeter and Gates had interviewed Danica Bradsky, the airport security guard who worked the escalators for departing travelers leaving the secure area. Before they let her go home, she had said she didn't recall seeing anyone resembling the boy. Photos had been plastered all over the airport employee lunchrooms and the case headquarters in Concourse B, and broadcast to the TSA, the police, and the press.

What had been accomplished while I had been tracking the scent trail was nothing short of amazing. The interrogation center Kelleher had pulled together in addition to keeping watch on Kevin Benson showed his adeptness at multitasking. Even Benson hadn't noticed how much Phil Kelleher had altered the room, probably because Benson had spent the time pouting about not having a job, not having a home to go to, but yet complaining that he wanted to be released to enjoy Christmas.

Along this second-floor corridor above Concourse B, directly above where the boy had supposedly last been seen—although now I had my doubts—was case headquarters. It was bare but not empty. Several agents and support techs were working among the buzzing, beeping laptops, phones, printers, and a plethora of peripherals only an IT geek could appreciate that lined the walls of the room on plastic folding tables that were similar to the ones Gates and Streeter claimed as desks.

For the moment, Streeter, Gates, Jack, Beulah, and I had HQ to ourselves. Phil Kelleher was in the room next door, babysitting Kevin Benson. I had trouble making eye contact with Jack. I needed him to explain why he had lied to me.

"I just can't understand why we haven't heard anything from the kidnapper by now," Jack said.

"If that's really why the boy was abducted," Streeter corrected.

"I have a sick feeling about this one, Streeter," Gates said.

With hands planted on my athletic hips, I paced in front of the glass windows, lights from the tarmac traffic slicing the walls and ceiling of the large empty room. Tugging on the baseball cap that made me look more like a teenager than my actual age of almost thirty, I wondered what Jack saw in me. I should have taken the time to do more than simply tuck my oversized gray T-shirt into my faded blue jeans when Streeter called. I could have changed at Frances's house, but I didn't even think about it. I'm surprised they let me through security. Luckily, I had my credentials with me. I was certainly going to have to step up my game a bit, now that I was an agent. I had learned to wear dark suits, but I hadn't really worn them during my field training with Beulah and it was a holiday.

I noticed Streeter studying Gates, then me. I wondered if he was waiting for me to weigh in or if he sensed my unease about Jack.

As I was about to explain what I had learned with Beulah, Streeter asked, "What happened to your hands? And your face?"

I had long forgotten about the mountain lion thing. That seemed like eons ago. It took me forever to explain to Emma earlier in the day that Auntie Liv fell down and went boom but wasn't really hurt. I doubted if Gates would buy that explanation. I knew Streeter wouldn't. And Jack already knew.

"Uh, I fell when I was hiking with my brother-in-law."

Their skeptical expressions were like the one Emma had displayed that screamed "liar." Jack lowered his head, amused. I rubbed my palms on my worn blue jeans as if I could wipe away the scabby remains of Christmas Eve morning. I adjusted the ball cap's bill lower on my forehead to hide the bruises and scratches, which of course were superficial in comparison to what could have happened. That was something Streeter didn't need to know.

My entire focus since returning from Quantico was to impress Streeter, prove to him that I was worthy of his belief in me. I didn't want him to think for one minute I couldn't physically handle Beulah when she was intent on marking her target. I was getting stronger, better at reading her unique signals in her communication with me.

"We were in the mountains taking Beulah for a walk."

I would have given him more. His gaze volleyed between mine and Jack's. I was about to explain the whole story but I didn't need to.

"What about Beulah, Liv?" Streeter asked. "What'd she find?"

"That Kevin Benson is a liar." I sighed, staring out at the Boeing 747 pushing away from the skywalk. For some reason, the large planes reminded me of whales. "I didn't think she'd ever be able to pick up the scent here. Hundreds, thousands of people have walked through this place since noon today." I glanced at my watch. "Anyway, we tracked the same trail three times with no variance."

"Not to gate 51?"

I shook my head. "Benson was lying. Beulah tracked from gate B31, where the boy arrived, down the escalator to the underground trams. I took her on the train three times and each time she took me up the elevator, to—"

"Out of the secure area?" Streeter interrupted.

I nodded. "Up the elevator out of the secure area—right past Danica Bradsky at the top of the escalator—to the Buckhorn Bar and Grill in the main concourse, and over to a family bathroom nearby."

"To a bathroom?"

I nodded. "Inside, near the sink."

"On the elevator. Off the train," Streeter repeated, walking next to me and staring at the same blackness beyond the windows. "Out of the secure area."

Gates said, "You thinking what I'm thinking?"

"Did you happen to see a TSA employee at the bottom of the escalator when you got off the trains?"

I shook my head. "No, but the crowds always push their way to the escalators, closer to where the TSA employees sit. I don't know if any of them even knew about the elevators. I didn't. Beulah cut across traffic all three times to get there."

"Danica was at the base of the escalator for part of her shift, at the top for the other part," Gates said.

"From below, she wouldn't have been in a position to see little Max from where Beulah indicated he'd walked."

"Right," Streeter said. "If someone took the boy from the gate to the main terminal and was intentionally trying to avoid being seen, the elevator would be a good choice."

"Exactly," I said.

"But Benson said he took the boy directly to B51, the departure gate," Gates said.

"He lied," I said.

"Let's get him in here and see if he changes his story."

"Streeter, I was thinking," I said, turning toward him and nearly forgetting Jack was in the room. "Maybe there's video? There are cameras all over this airport. They must have something."

Gates cleared his throat.

"First thing we did when we arrived on the scene was to ask airport security for video footage. There are hundreds of cameras throughout this place, so for every hour, we have to look through hundreds of hours. They gathered it up and started on footage from the cameras between gates, focusing first on where the boy was last seen deplaning his flight from New York City at gate B31."

"According to Benson," Gates said.

"He lied," I repeated.

They offered me a smile.

"Seriously, I believe in Beulah. The boy was taken directly from the arriving gate to the main concourse. Out of security. Easily out the door in no time."

"'Like casting a stone into the ocean," Streeter mumbled.

"But at least Beulah narrowed down the target area and the time. I doubt if much time passed from when they disembarked from the NYC flight to when little Max was hustled into the main terminal," I offered, eager for acknowledgment from Streeter, which he paid me with the hint of a smile as his eyes locked with mine.

"Who's reviewing the video footage?" Jack asked, leaning against the doorframe, his long arms crossed over his chest.

"Dodson, at the moment, back at your office." Streeter was curt with Jack. "I was hoping you would do it. Where've you been?"

"Sorry. I was at home, but I had forgotten to turn on my cell after charging."

Jack avoided Streeter's eyes. And mine.

"I tried your home number, too," Streeter said, folding his arms across his chest and eyeing Jack.

"Must have had the TV on too loud," Jack said with a shrug.

Jack had told me he fell asleep, the sleep of the dead. And I knew for a fact he never slept with his television on because he told me he needed absolute quiet and even then was often robbed of sleep.

I could tell from the slightest narrowing of Streeter's eyes that he was as convinced as I was by Jack's lame explanation. Jack's eyes were locked on Streeter's, as if daring him to challenge him. It looked like a modern day showdown, and I for one wanted to know the outcome.

In the end, Streeter's reply suggested it was not the time. "Well, touch base with Dodson and then I'll need you to work the garbage detail that Gates has set up."

"Garbage?"

The DPD chief walked over to the table near Streeter, picked up a sheet of paper, and handed it to Jack. Gates said, "We gathered all the garbage receptacles and spread the contents in grids. We plowed the snow off of one of the outer parking lots and taped off the grids so we could keep track of where the receptacles came from in the airport."

I suspected the sheet Jack was studying was a footprint of the parking lot grids where his team had spread the garbage.

"What are we looking for?"

Streeter answered, "Anything."

"And you want me to work whatever I find? Out there?" Jack asked. "It's only five degrees."

"No, I want you to work whatever Gates's team bags and tags in here. You're just out there to check on them, make sure the procedures work for you. Not to help pick." Streeter pointed toward one wall. "Kelleher set up your equipment over there. It's crude, but it will help us get started. Time is of the essence and we've already lost a lot of it."

"How long has it been?" Jack asked.

Streeter looked at his watch, as did the rest of us. "Nine hours. Give or take a half hour."

Jack's mouth puckered. I looked at my watch. It was 9:30 p.m. I glanced over at Beulah, glad she was sound asleep on her pallet in the corner.

"The videos are critical," Jack said. "I'll check on Dodson's progress, but we'll need to narrow down the footage, Streeter."

"Like Liv says, narrow it to the arrival gate, to the main concourse near the Buckhorn Bar and Grill, and the family bathroom."

"What about Benson's story from arrival gate to departure gate?" Gates asked.

"I trust Liv's findings," Streeter repeated. I grinned, happy to know I had finally proved something, at least. I just hoped Jack would find little Max on that footage and further validate Streeter's belief in me.

"We'll study the cameras where the train unloads beneath the main concourse as a priority. Near the elevators. And the arrival gate, which is what?"

I answered, "Same concourse, gate B31. Directly across from B30."

Jack's eyes flicked over to mine and I held his gaze fast.

CHAPTER 19

I PRETENDED NOT TO notice Jack's concern. "It's at the end of the last moving walkway on this side of the escalators leading down to the trains."

"The trail for the boy leads from B31, the gate where his flight from New York City arrived, straight down the escalators to the underground trams, up the elevator to the main concourse, over to the bar and bathroom, and then disappears," Streeter summarized. "Which means the boy was taken from the secure area by Benson. That's what you're saying?"

"He was taken out of the secure area, yes. By someone. I didn't trail Benson's scent. What I'm saying is the trail of the boy's scent conflicts with the story Kevin Benson gave us earlier," I added. "He was emphatic that he and the boy went directly from B31 to B51 and that they were at the departing gate for Los Angeles by 1:00 p.m. or a few minutes before. Then he said they doubled back and went into the bathroom. Then he recanted that story and said he was on the phone with his girlfriend at gate B51. That's not what Beulah is telling me. Neither story is true."

"You think the boy went directly from gate B31 to the main terminal?" Jack studied my face, but only because I was looking at Beulah and not at him.

I nodded. "Benson definitely lied. I believe Beulah."

"Could Benson have taken the boy from B31 to B51 and then someone else snatched the boy from B51 and backtracked toward the escalators to the underground train? Could Beulah simply have taken the freshest trail from B31 down, rather than backtrack?" Gates asked.

I shook my head. "With some dogs, that may be true. But that's not how Beulah trails a scent. She would track the scent for the entire path where the boy went, doubling back as many times as the boy did. It's just how she works."

"And you found no scent in the main terminal beyond the bathroom?" Streeter asked.

I shook my head.

"Did you try the other concourses?" Gates asked.

"I did. Concourse A—nothing. Concourse C is in the other direction. I could try that, if you want."

"He has to be somewhere." Gates was getting irritated.

"The abductor only had five options for escape from the airport," Streeter said. "By foot, plane, car, public transportation, or . . . without the child. Right?"

"We've scoured the place over the past three and a half hours," Gates said. "Every level of each concourse. Each level, every room, bathroom, restaurant, store, airline club, and smoking lounge—one and a half million square feet of this place. That kid could hide in this place for months and never be found, if that's what he wanted. We haven't had any report or discovery of a body, discarded clothing, or bodily fluids, not even a stench."

"Isn't it too soon for a stench?" I asked.

"And too cold," Streeter added, somehow frustrated by my question.

"It seems unlikely we missed a dead body. There's got to be four dozen DPD officers and half that many agents, not to mention the DIA security, which is what? Twenty or so? You tell me how we missed a dead body," Gates said.

"What about the bathroom where the trail ended in the main terminal?" Streeter asked. "Let's get someone from Investigative Control Ops on that, Jack. Cordon off the area, see if we can lift prints, check the traps, and use luminal to see if we find something."

"It looked spotless in there," I said, feeling both relieved and discouraged, not wanting to think about why the scent ended there.

"Gates, you and I need to put the screws on Benson and get to the bottom of what he knows," Streeter said.

"I have a thought."

All three men looked my way.

"Maybe what Benson's lying about is that he went to the bathroom without the boy, told him to wait, and someone took off with him. That would make some sense, wouldn't it?"

"It would imply a traveler in the secure area took a huge chance to snatch a child in broad daylight and left the airport with him or something," Gates said. "It's not likely, but not impossible. I would agree with you if it hadn't happened in a secure area that requires a passenger with airplane tickets."

Streeter added, "We'll ask BlueSky for the list of all passengers who might have missed their flight leaving Denver after the boy arrived. Anyway, it could be an arriving passenger to Denver who was leaving the secure area."

"Or an employee," I added.

"Which would imply the abductor lives locally," Gates said.

I asked, "Didn't you say you laid out a grid and mapped where the garbage came from?" Gates nodded. "What if I took Beulah out to the grid with the contents of the bathroom? See if she finds anything?"

"Good idea," Streeter said. "That would be a fast check on the contents, but we also need to isolate that bathroom's garbage and bag and tag it. Let's put a priority on that, Linwood."

He nodded.

"Have you found anything yet?" Jack asked.

Streeter shook his head. "But we didn't have it narrowed down."

Gates explained, "I instructed the pickers to be looking for a corpse."

Streeter instructed me, "Take Beulah out there and see if she can find anything in the outer parking lot. Gates will tell you who to talk to about the grid pattern. See if she can find something our handpicking crews haven't so far."

"It's going to be cold for Beulah."

"Do the best you can without endangering her. Or yourself," Streeter said, eyeing me. Then, with a frown he instructed Jack, "Go with her. Make sure they're being thorough out there and that every garbage can and storage bin used to collect the waste for the entire travel day is being analyzed. Dumped and spread. Every inch of it is being searched for throwaways. Pay particular attention to the grid containing the bathroom where Beulah led Liv."

"And if they find nothing?" Gates asked. I got the sense he already knew that was the answer Beulah and I would deliver.

Streeter said, "Either the snatcher took the kid directly to a connecting flight, unnoticed, which is highly unlikely in my opinion, or he left the airport with the kid."

"But one thing is for sure. That boy is definitely not still in the airport. Dead or alive," Gates said. "I trust the results of my team."

"You're probably right," Streeter said. "But something tells me this is not a typical kidnapping." He picked up the report and said, "We received most of the reports from the airlines with lists of last-minute reservations between the hours of noon and two today that would involve a boy. There are less than six so far. Gates's team is following up on those."

"What if whoever did this made reservations long ago, planned this ahead of time? Like the nanny or one of the parents? Didn't you say they were divorced?" I asked.

Again, all three men looked my way.

"Great thought. Is that something Max would do?" Streeter asked.

I shrugged. "I wouldn't think so, but maybe the divorce is an ugly one, a desperate custody battle. Do we know that yet?"

Streeter shook his head.

Jack said, "Parental abduction accounts for the lion's share of kidnapping cases and about one-fourth of the total missing children in America. If it's one of the parents, then we'll probably get an indication when Streeter interviews them."

Streeter asked, "Where are they, anyway?"

Gates said, "According to Eddie, Freytag pulled their flight plans and estimates that both planes should arrive sometime within the hour."

"If it's not one of the parents responsible for little Max's disappearance, then God help us," Streeter said, appearing annoyed by Jack, who was now sitting at a computer and clacking on the keyboard. "At least in that case, the child may still be alive. If it isn't one of the parents, then maybe this was a kidnapping for money. What are you doing, Linwood?"

"Sending a request for my team to get the list of BlueSky passengers who might have missed flights after 12:40 p.m. I've also told them to get us the list of other airline passengers who meet the same criteria. At least we can narrow down the suspects if this is a random abduction. They'll pull employee time sheets too."

"I don't know how we will get through all the outgoing passengers traveling on Christmas Eve with children without spending a lot of time researching each one and verifying each child's identity," Gates admitted.

"But you will," Streeter assured his friend.

He hadn't told the others about the directive from John Chandler that I be assigned to the case because Maximillian Bennett Williams II said so. At least, I didn't think he had.

"We need to find this guy and quick," Streeter said, crossing his arms.

"Why do you think it's a guy?" I asked, fantasizing about one of our guys down there drawing his weapon and arresting the perp so we could all go home and enjoy the holidays.

"Most abductors are. That's all," he said, glancing my way. "Why would you think it isn't?"

I raised an eyebrow. "I agree with you. That's why I asked you. It's definitely a man."

"Because . . ." he asked.

I shrugged. "It's Christmas. Women don't abduct kids on Christmas."

Jack made a noise that sounded a bit like a muffled laugh.

Gates scoffed, "Well that's about the most sexist thing I've heard in a long time. What kind of logic is that?"

I felt like I'd just said "shit" in church. Or, reminded of my earlier days, I heard a sea of plaid-clad grade-schoolers giggling after I'd just asked the bishop at Friday mass why women weren't allowed to be priests. "It's speculation, not logic. Probably flawed, on second thought. A woman might be driven to such an act if she's emotionally distraught with the holidays bearing down on her like nails in a coffin. Or another way of looking at it, a woman might kidnap a child, even on Christmas, if it meant protecting the child from something more ominous."

"Uh-huh," Gates said.

The judgment in the men's eyes grew heavier.

"And you don't think it's a kidnapping?" I challenged.

"Nope," Gates said.

"Come on, Chief. I don't want to be the only one in the confessional. I poked holes in my logic, let's hear yours."

"I told you. My guys are digging through the garbage for a corpse. I'm assuming homicide. Just speculating. Because just as you can't imagine a woman abducting a child on Christmas Eve, I can't imagine a traveler or employee changing holiday plans in a moment of opportunity without changing his mind just as quickly and deciding to cover up his momentary lapse in good judgment."

"By killing his victim?"

Gates nodded, holding my gaze. "And I can only hope my logic is flawed."

"Me too," I said, dread weighing heavily in my gut and replacing the optimism I earlier felt at finding some answers with Beulah.

"Want to clue me in on the basics, so I'm up to speed and can join the debate?" Jack asked. "I feel like I'm watching a movie in reverse."

"Next time maybe you'll remember to charge your phone," Streeter said, rising to his feet and pacing near the windows. "The missing boy is Maximillian Bennett Williams III, son of Maximillian Williams II and his wife Melissa. The kid sometimes goes by little Max. As far as we know, the five-year-old boy was put on a plane in New York City by his father. The father paid a BlueSky Airlines escort, Kevin Benson, to take the kid to his mother in California. Los Angeles. The kid and escort were supposed to change planes here at DIA. Benson got distracted for a moment and the kid's gone."

Jack nodded. "So what distracted the guy?"

"A call from his girlfriend who lives in Denver. It's a Denver-based crew," Streeter answered. "At least that's what he tells us."

"You believe that story?" Jack asked.

We all answered at once.

Streeter said, "No."

Gates said, "Definitely not."

I said, "Not anymore."

"Why not?"

"Too many holes," Streeter said. "And Kevin Benson isn't a good liar."

CHAPTER 20

"WHY CAN'T I LEAVE? Haven't I gone through enough in one day? It's almost ten o'clock and I've been up since—"

"Sit down," Gates interrupted. "And shut that mouth of yours."

Kevin Benson's mouth gaped. Apparently he was unaccustomed to such directness. I noticed a tiny curve to Phil Kelleher's lips as he escorted Benson to the makeshift conference table opposite Chief Gates and Streeter. I was relieved that Streeter allowed me to hang back so I could participate in the second interview with Benson. I was even more relieved that I didn't have to go with Jack to the outer parking lot. If I had, we would have been alone, forced to talk, and I hadn't decided how to handle the lie that Jack wedged between us. Not yet.

I had convinced Streeter to let me linger so I could hear Benson's follow-up interview, in case he continued to lie about where he went after deplaning at DIA and Streeter needed me to confirm Benson's movements by using Beulah to trail his scent through the airport. With my decision to stay at case headquarters a bit longer, not only could I help Streeter dig the truth out of Benson but also I could avoid one-on-one time with Jack Linwood. Jack would go alone to the outer parking lot, get to work on organizing the collection of evidence from the priority grid, and then be on his way back to the office downtown to view video footage with Dodson. Before I arrived with Beulah to search the isolated grid, I hoped Jack would be long gone and I wouldn't have to pretend that I didn't see him come off the Kansas City plane at B30.

Benson asked Streeter, "Why is he being such a jerk?" indicating Chief Gates.

"Where's the boy?" Gates demanded.

"What? I don't know."

"Where is he?" Gates repeated.

"I told you before, I don't know."

"You told us a lot. Most of it lies," replied Gates.

"What do you mean? What lies?" Benson looked from Gates to Streeter and back to Gates.

Both men glared at Benson.

"Where did you take the boy?"

"I told you, I didn't take him anywhere. He took off, got lost, and—"

"Zip it," Gates said, suddenly on his feet. He lunged across the table and gathered Benson's shirt collar in his fist. "Remember me? The only time you speak is when we ask you a question, got it? And the only kind of answer you give us better be the truth. I swear if you . . ." his words trailed.

I didn't blame him for not finishing that thought. Judging by the look in his eye, Gates might have knocked Benson's teeth in before he ever had a chance to finish that sentence.

"We know you lied about taking the boy from gate B31 to B51," Streeter said.

A knock on the door forced Gates to let go and Benson shrank back in his chair as I opened the door. A police officer handed me a file. "From the airlines. The tickets bought today, including those traveling with a minor. There's an email address if you want the electronic file sent."

I said, "Thank you."

"Thanks, Lou," Gates called out as the officer left.

"You're welcome, Chief," the officer called back before I closed the door.

In response to Streeter's nearly undetectable head motion, I laid the file on the table between Gates and Benson.

"What's this about?" Benson looked over at Streeter, studied him, and then leaned back in his chair. It appeared that Benson was sizing up which menacing man he'd rather deal with, and I could have told him neither option was good.

Streeter explained, "You didn't take the boy from gate B31 to gate B51."

I could see the Adam's apple of Benson's throat bob as he swallowed.

"And if you're assessing how much trouble you're in for lying to a federal agent, let me save you the trouble and tell you. Deep. So deep, your nostrils are plugged with excrement," added Gates, his words measured. "If you start digging your way out now, you just might have a snowball's chance. Tell us where the boy is."

"Honestly, I don't know," Benson said, shaking his head.

"But you do know something," Streeter said. "You know what happened from the instant you exited the plane from New York City to when you no longer had the child in your possession here in Denver."

"I . . ." Benson closed his gaping mouth and lowered his face into his hands, his elbows propped on the table.

I thought he was about to spill his guts, but then he seemed to reconsider.

The long silence was finally broken by Streeter. "Chief Gates, your offer to go easy on Benson—if he tells us what he knows—is quite generous, considering you were planning on hanging him by his scrotum from the scoreboard in Bronco stadium," Streeter said, without a hint of sarcasm. He stood up, rounded the table, and leaned on the table next to Benson. Close enough that I knew Benson could smell his cologne, although it was more likely Streeter who was detecting the smell of fear on Benson.

Benson's face grew white. "He really did? What's wrong with him? You're serious."

"I am," Streeter said.

I hadn't seen this side of Streeter. He was growing as impatient as Gates and neither man would hesitate to cross the line if it meant getting to the boy sooner.

"We are," Gates added, commanding Benson to look his way.

"Talk," Streeter growled.

The man blew out a long breath, a prelude to a decision he hadn't wanted to make. "You're right. I lied. I didn't argue with my girlfriend on the cell phone. We argued in person."

"You met up with her?"

He nodded.

"The same woman who kicked you out of your apartment?" Gates asked.

He nodded. "Threw me out. I didn't lie about that."

"Then what did you lie about? And be quick about it," Gates snapped.

"She sent me a text. She told me to meet her. At a bar on the main concourse."

"The Buckhorn Bar and Grill," Streeter said.

Benson's eyes widened. I saw recognition on his face, which meant he finally fully believed the FBI and Denver Police knew the truth and that he'd better come clean.

"How did you . . ." Benson alternated looks from Streeter's face to Gates's, both too stony for him to find purchase in his climb out of the deep hole he was in. "You saw the text messages. Well, then you know. She gave me no choice. I had to meet her." I knew Streeter and Gates probably hadn't received any records from the cell phone company yet, but every text message would eventually be ours to review. "I had a decision to make. She left me no choice. I had to take the boy with me and meet her."

"So the boy was with you."

He nodded.

"Start over," Streeter commanded. "Tell us what happened step by step, from the moment you and the boy stepped off the plane from New York City here at DIA."

"Be specific this time. Were you holding his hand? Carrying his backpack? Buying him ice cream cones?" I thought Gates's tone was far calmer than his body language would suggest. But I'd only met him today.

Benson was shaking his head. "We arrived on time. Normally, we would wait until all other passengers got off the plane, but I told my fellow flight attendants that the boy had a tight connection and I wanted to get him some food. So they let us off first.

"Within minutes of landing, I'd say no later than 12:45 p.m., we were off the jetway and in the concourse. I was carrying the backpack and told him to hurry. At first he was running beside me, but when he started to fall back, I grabbed his hand. We went straight from the gate to the escalators."

"Which one?" I asked, wanting to know if Beulah had tracked it correctly.

"The one on the left."

"And which door of the train?" I asked.

"I can't remember."

Gates stood up and Benson leaned back with his hands up in surrender. "Okay, okay. The one in the middle because it's the least crowded."

"And you were carrying the backpack?" I asked.

"And the boy." With everyone staring at him, Benson asked, "What?"

"When did you go from holding his hand to carrying him?" asked Streeter.

"I left that part out by accident," Benson whined. "You guys are freaking me out with all these questions. It's not like I'm lying. I just forget steps."

"You get off the plane first, you tell the boy you're in a hurry and that he should keep up, and you're carrying his backpack for him. Take it from there," Gates instructed.

Streeter walked around the table and sat by Gates, which made Benson relax.

"I told him to hurry, but he couldn't keep up. His legs were tiny. He was running. I grabbed his hand, but people started staring at us because I was practically dragging the kid. My legs were so much longer than his and we didn't have a lot of time. I knew we'd have to go back through security."

"So you picked the kid up at what point?"

"By the newsstand, where they sell magazines, books, candy, that stuff. Just before the escalator. I remember because Brat Boy—I mean, the boy—stopped and asked me for candy. I picked him up and told him if he behaved, I'd buy him candy in a few minutes but that I had to meet a lady first."

"Before you reached the escalator down to the trains," I confirmed. Streeter shot me a look that told me not to interrupt again. I was only trying to confirm Beulah's results.

Benson nodded. "Once I started carrying the boy, we made it through the crowd onto the train and then to the main terminal and the Buck-horn Bar quickly. And people stopped giving me dirty looks for dragging him. My girlfriend was waiting at the bar. Her arms were crossed and she looked pissed."

"About you bringing the boy? Being late? What?" Gates asked.

"No, nothing like that. She was still pissed over a text message another flight attendant sent me. She said she saw it on my cell, broke into my Facebook account, and said I was flirting with her, which I wasn't. Anyway, I told her I didn't have much time because I had to get the boy to his next flight, and she told me what she had to say wouldn't take much time."

"And did it? Take much time?" Gates asked.

"Five, ten minutes tops." Benson's mind was working the timeline. "She told me our relationship was over and shoved a piece of paper in my hand that I later saw was an application for a restraining order to be served on me here at work, which would mean I'd lose my job. We started arguing. She said she threw all my stuff out the apartment window and that I better go get it before the snow buried it; that is, what was left after neighbors had picked through the good stuff. I was so angry at her I could have . . ."

We all stared at him, wondering.

"You could have what? Killed somebody?" asked Gates, the calmness in his voice more unsettling to me than his earlier gruffness.

"No, I didn't mean . . . I wouldn't . . . I didn't touch that kid."

"Where was he? While you and your girlfriend where fighting?" asked Gates.

"Arguing, not fighting."

Streeter reminded, "Step by step, as you arrived at the bar carrying the boy."

Benson drew a breath. "As soon as I got there I put the kid down right next to me. All three of us were standing near the empty chairs at the bar, kind of not really in the bar but more like in the main concourse. The bar-tender was busy helping the waitress serve the people at the tables and the kid started watching the TV hanging above the bar. I told him to stay there and I'd get him some candy if he did."

"And when did you notice he wasn't standing there anymore?" Streeter pressed.

"After my girlfriend and I finished arguing. Like I said, maybe five or ten minutes after that." Benson drew in a deep breath and admitted, "By the time my girlfriend stomped off, the boy was gone."

CHAPTER 21

THE ODOR THAT WAFTED from the refrigerator as he opened the door reminded him of how neglectful he'd become in the past few months. His spirits buoyed now by a renewed sense of purpose, he was motivated and eager to scrub every square inch of his home. To cleanse himself of the past and prepare for a better future. He wanted to get started immediately. But first, he wanted a bite to eat.

So many choices.

He had bought turkey and ham and hot dogs and apples and carrots—he hated vegetables, but the boy had asked specifically for them—and cookies and bread and peanut butter and lots and lots of boxes of macaroni and cheese. His refrigerator was packed with goodies and his mind filled with memories of shopping for groceries and the joy of seeing the world again through a child's eyes.

"Beautiful daughter, you have," one shopper had commented to him as the child ran about the store, pulling item after item from the shelves.

The compliment made his chest swell with pride, and the memories of such a simple moment tasted sweet on his tongue.

It would be the best Christmas ever.

He pushed aside the box filled with packages of peanut M&M's so he could reach the deli sandwich and the jar of dill pickles that had been shoved to the back of the refrigerator. He bumped the door closed with his hip, feeling his buttocks jiggle from the motion, bringing another smile. It had been too long since he felt like moving again, dancing again, living again, which only confirmed that his decision this morning had been right.

Without the light from the refrigerator, he was standing in the darkness of his kitchen, not wanting his neighbors to study his movements. He moved toward the cupboard, felt for a plate, unwrapped the meatball sandwich, and slipped the meal into the microwave. As the light shone over the food turning in the oven, his mind floated back to the lightbulb in the closet and the voice of his father demanding that he think about what he had done wrong. He recalled the terror of knowing what would follow his answer and the feeling that he would never measure up to whatever it was his parents wanted of him. Snap! The sound of his father's leather belt sounded in his childhood's mind. And he remembered screaming.

The beep of the microwave yanked him from his long-ago nightmarish life and alerted him to the seconds remaining before he was once again left in his pitch-black kitchen.

Wrapping his hands around the warm bread of the sandwich, he leaned against the tile counter and took a bite. As he chewed, he fished out a spear of pickle and munched it to a nub. The food was satisfying, necessary.

He needed to clean, needed to scrub the house. Needed to erase any memories of the horrid past and prepare for the beautiful future that he had always deserved.

Although his intentions of bringing joy to a sad child's life were pure and good, his execution had always fallen short of his goals. That, he knew, was his parents' fault for not providing him with better role models on proper parenting. But unlike his parents, he refused to throw the children in a closet until they complied. Instead, he was more kind and benevolent. When any of his kids violated rules, disobeyed, or fell short of his expectations, he chose instead to free the little creatures in the woods, turn them back to the wild lives they insisted on living rather than to tame them by forcing them into a closet for days at a time. What good was it to cage the poor creatures when they were born to run wild?

But this child was different. The wildness had been tamed almost the instant he'd held out the package of peanut M&M's.

This time, it would work.

He wouldn't cry, or scream, or bite, or run away.

This time, he had chosen wisely.

With his sandwich gone, he reached under the sink, snapped on the rubber gloves, and grabbed the bucket and bottle of bleach.

CHAPTER 22

"HE'S NOT IN ON the abduction in any way?" I asked.

"I don't think so," said Gates. "You?"

Streeter shook his head. "Not knowingly. But he may have been used as a pawn by the girlfriend. Or someone else. The distraction of the argument he had with his girlfriend may have been calculated."

Gates leaned back, lacing his long, dark fingers behind his head. "Good thought. And makes sense. He insists the text was real, but the rumor she'd heard about him having an affair with another flight attendant was untrue and the girlfriend refused to tell Benson where she heard it. Could play either way. She set up the distraction or whoever told her about the alleged affair did."

"A stretch, but it's worth pursuing," Streeter added. "Let's get the girlfriend in here. Did your officers pick her up yet?"

"Done. Let me see where they are," Gates said, unfolding himself from the tiny plastic chair and punching in numbers on his cell phone.

"And before Benson came in, you guys started to tell me about a witness to the boy's disappearance?" I asked.

Streeter answered, "I wanted to see if Benson's story matched up. A guy with a long layover was in the bar at the main terminal where Benson stopped with the kid."

"The Buckhorn?"

Streeter nodded. "The guy says he was having a beer, said the BlueSky employee was in some kind of quarrel with his girlfriend and the kid took off, unnoticed. The guy said it couldn't have been more than a few minutes from when the child was there. Then he was gone. He didn't think anything of it. Thought the mother or someone had him. But when he got home and saw the news, he called it in."

"That corroborates Benson's version," Gates said, returning from his quick call.

"So little Max ran away," I concluded. "To where? He's five."

"To the bathroom, according to you," Streeter said.

"Maybe little Max walked in on someone in there. Saw something," I imagined.

"Since the guy says it was shortly after the two started arguing, it makes some sense that the distraction was set up, that someone was waiting for that specific moment to nab the child," Gates speculated. "Which is why we need to grill the girlfriend. They have Bonita Smith but she's making every excuse under the sun not to come back to the airport. I told the officer to look around the apartment for signs of the boy, ask to use the bathroom, and make note of her reactions for us but to bring her here in cuffs if he had to."

"If little Max was targeted for who he is," I concluded, "it would be some serious set of coincidences that Benson received a text, broke all the airline rules by taking the child out of the secure area, and then decided to risk losing his job just to see his girlfriend."

"Which would suggest either one or the other is involved, knowingly or as a pawn in a planned abduction of this particular boy," Gates said.

"Or that it was simply coincidence. That this was a random abduction," Streeter added.

"And if it was a planned abduction, this file of ticketed passengers with minors may not do us any good," Gates said, picking up the file from the table and riffling through the pages.

"Why do you say that?" I asked.

Gates said, "Because if this abduction of this particular boy was planned that far in advance, then the abductors would buy tickets under assumed names, not risk drawing more attention to themselves by buying last-minute tickets on Christmas Eve when the police are searching for a missing child in the airport."

"Unless a last-minute purchase was done as a misdirect," Streeter added.

"Makes sense," I said. "But will this list be helpful if this was a random abduction?"

"Doubt it," Streeter said. "Random abductions don't usually involve predators traveling long distances, especially with no cover and no control, like a passenger on a very public plane."

Gates said, "And if this was a planned abduction, by a parent or someone trying to ransom the child considering the parents' celebrity status, they would have to know who the escort would be and research the escort's background to know a girlfriend was involved and that she could be used to distract him. That's pretty complicated."

"Didn't you or someone say the father hired the escort?" I asked, wondering if the Max I knew would be capable of abducting his own child.

"That's what the deputy told us in the original phone call about the missing child. But hiring an escort means when a child is dropped off by the parent to fly, the airline assigns an employee on duty to stay with that child until he's delivered to the responsible party at the other end, according to BlueSky's Toby Freytag," Gates explained. "It's not like the father would dictate who escorted the boy to LA from NYC."

Streeter and I exchanged a glance. Max dictated who would be working this case. So it certainly wasn't out of the question that he'd dictate who would escort the boy from the airline.

"What? What'd I miss?"

Streeter said, "The father has connections. Although you called me in to this case, my boss also called."

"The call you took when we were getting in our cars outside my house?"

Streeter nodded.

An unexpected flutter tickled my stomach. I was relieved to know that Streeter had been spending Christmas Eve at Chief Gates's home rather than holed up alone. Or with someone else. Who'd bought him cologne.

"If the parents are flying in here on private jets, why do you suppose they stick their five-year-old on a commercial airplane with an escort?" Gates asked. "Would you take that risk, if you were little Max's uber-rich parents?"

Streeter shrugged. "Maybe their private jets were busy. Maybe they were concerned about limited pilot air time. Maybe they didn't want to risk seeing one another."

"Or maybe Max is simply the cheapest son of a bitch you'll ever meet," I said.

"Max? You know this guy?" Gates asked.

My cheeks burned. "That's what Streeter was trying to say. He muscled our bosses into me working the case. Look, I don't know what Max's game is here, but we need to grill the shit out of him to find out. All he's done is given me more reason to believe he had something to do with this abduction, the kidnapping of his own child, and that this was planned, calculated."

Gates and Streeter continued to stare at me.

"Why do you say that?"

"Cause he didn't ask for the best to be assigned to his son's abduction. He asked for me, a brand-spanking-new Quantico puke," I admitted.

"How do you know the richest man in Manhattan?" Gates's eyebrow arched, an unspoken accusation in his tone.

"Not me, my sister. They almost married. Years ago."

Gates rested an elbow on the arm that wrapped around his thin waist, his hand rubbing his mouth. "So why you?"

"That's what I'd like to know. Why pick the least-experienced agent in the country?"

"Maybe he trusts you," Gates said.

"Doubt it," I said. "It's not like there was any love lost between the two of us."

"We'll ask when Melissa and Max Williams arrive," Streeter said reassuringly. "Kelleher is setting up next door and preparing a list of pertinent facts to help us with our interrogation of both the father and mother. We'll add the private jet question to the long list we already have."

"He's cheap. Bottom line," I repeated.

Gates cued up the short videos of the boy; Streeter and I gathered behind him to watch.

The child had thick blond hair, brilliantly green eyes, and a smile that was almost as infectious as his laugh. Even if someone wasn't fond of children, he or she would notice this one. He was a beautiful boy, full of life—running, jumping, mugging for the camera, talking and laughing at the videographer. His voice was high-pitched, but not tiny. He spoke with conviction and confidence, with the power of innocence.

"Little Max," Gates said in a sad tone.

They stared at the screen until the last video went black.

"No matter who's behind this, how could little Max just disappear?" I started to pace again, feeling the soreness in my ribs with every step.

"The guy at the bar said he had watched the child for several seconds before he disappeared, and said the boy was precocious, energetic. I think he used the words 'a handful.' The witness has kids of his own and said with that boy's energy, he could see the boy slipping away from anyone," Streeter explained, walking toward the cold, dark windows.

"And no one saw little Max," I said puzzled, walking toward Streeter and standing a few steps behind him. "It's Christmas Eve. Is it possible the airport was less crowded earlier and—"

"No," Streeter interrupted. "On the contrary. DIA has been swarming with people all day long. The airport security said it's one of the busiest travel days of the year."

"Christmas Eve? Don't these people have families?" I asked, remembering the crowd Beulah had maneuvered through, just to follow the scent trail.

Gates lifted his hands in surrender. "Okay. So, it's Christmas Eve. Little Max is all decked out. He must stand out, even in a crowd. He's got a white shirt, little hunter-green velvet beret, matching bow tie, knickers and little black suspenders, thick blond hair in a page-boy-style haircut, and a big grin. How could anyone not notice this kid? I would have noticed a cute kid like that, alone in the airport."

"Was he alone?" Streeter challenged.

Rising to the challenge, I theorized, "And if he wasn't alone, would people notice if he was with his mother or with Max? Even the witness said he just assumed the mother had him. Is this some wild publicity stunt, a pathetic grab for headlines and sympathy? Maybe about money?"

"You know him. Is he that kind of person?" Gates asked.

I shrugged.

There was another knock on the door. Gates shouted, "What!"

"Chief? The Williams parties are here," the officer named Lou said, offering me an apologetic smile.

"Parties?"

The officer said, "There're a bunch of them. Toss in a football and whistle, and you've got yourself a game. Agent Kelleher is getting them set up next door. Give him a few minutes and he'll be ready."

Gates nodded and Officer Lou stepped out, closing the door. Gates and I both turned our attention on Streeter.

"Let's make them wait. We'll get the cameras rolling in there and have Phil stall for us. Getting them onto our schedule may make them a bit more forthcoming. Liv, take Beulah out to the priority grid and see what you can find. Tony and I will go through the ticketed passenger list and interview Benson's girlfriend. When you get back, then we'll interview the Williams party next door."

"Kindling to see if sparks fly?" Gates asked.

"I want to send a strong message that this is my investigation. Making them wait won't kill them," Streeter said. "See what you can find, Liv."

"Cross your fingers," I said. I walked to the corner where Beulah slept. "It was nice to get confirmation that Beulah had tracked the exact scent trail Kevin Benson described, although I'm not sure if she was tracking Benson or the boy, given that Benson was carrying the backpack. So I hope that Max and Melissa Williams brought something more personal we can use."

"Or that you find something in the priority grid from the bathroom where Beulah stopped tracking," Streeter suggested.

I crouched to pet Beulah, and she stretched and yawned. "And Chief Gates?"

"Tony, please."

"To your earlier question on whether I think Max is capable of kidnapping his own son? I don't know him that well. But what I do know about Max is that he's an asshole. I can't say that knowing Max is an asshole makes me believe he's capable of kidnapping his own son."

Streeter raised a single brow of encouragement. "Let's find out when you get back."

CHAPTER 23

Noah

IT'S CHRISTMAS EVE!

I can't wait for Santa to come. I'm staying awake all night to see Santa, hopefully to see an elf, and definitely to find out what Auntie Liv and Beulah have been up to. I'm sure Mom will make coffee for Auntie Liv no matter what time she comes home. I've practiced hitting the football button a couple of times to make sure I can record Santa's movements. I hope I can get him to talk to me. It takes me a few seconds but when I concentrate, I can land my fist or wrist against the pin.

I'm so glad Auntie Liv bought this for me. And that she gave it to me while we were alone today. I love her. She gets me. And she believes in me. I know Beulah and I are both going to be sad when Auntie Liv finds an apartment in Denver, but it's been like a big sleepover party every night since she's been home from Quantico.

Special Agent Liv Bergen.

So exciting!

I've been lying here all night thinking about the fifth grader who lost his backpack at school. The case of the missing backpack is what Auntie Liv called it. For the life of me, I can't remember ever hearing about anyone at Pennington Grade School losing a backpack this year. Well, except once early in the year when some kid left it on the bus. I forgot to ask Auntie Liv the color of the backpack. Maybe that would jog my memory.

I want to ask Emma about it, but I don't want to tell her why I'm asking. And I don't like to lie. Lying makes my stomach hurt. The only time I lie is when I'm trying not to worry my mom. Like when she asks me if I slept through having a dirty diaper in the middle of the night, I lie. If I tell her the truth—I don't want her to lose any more sleep at night than she already does—she'd tell me I was being silly and then force herself awake to check on me throughout the night. She'd never get a good night's sleep. And I think that's silly.

Besides, why would I want her to learn how good I've gotten at spying, like how I've gotten so good at pretending to be asleep? CIA agents have to be good liars and even better at pretending. I bet they taught Auntie Liv that as an FBI agent sometimes you have to pretend, like they will teach me when I work for the CIA. I have to start somewhere. And thanks to Auntie Liv, I have this new football pin. So cool! Best Christmas ever! Almost makes me forget that I have CP. And definitely makes nighttime a lot less scary.

Nighttime is my favorite because when I sleep, I dream. And in my dreams, I run. I chase bad people, like spies from other countries. And I run away fast when they're chasing me. Then in my dreams, I sit back in my wheelchair and pretend I can't walk. It makes me the best spy ever because when you live in a wheelchair it's like an invisibility cloak.

Dreaming is the best part of sleeping and there's something else I like about the nighttime. At night I sleep deep. Not like naps during the day. And when I sleep so soundly that my dreams come alive, I can't feel the constant pain in my arms, legs, hands, and feet from bunched up muscles. At least, not as much. The deep-in-my-bones pain is always there, like an annoying sister, constantly reminding me of who I really am, but it's still pain, all the same.

Even when I can't sleep—pain being a best friend and keeping me awake—I love the night because it's so quiet and I can think.

But nighttime can also be the scariest time, too. Like waking up after a nightmare and having to lie in the dark trying to figure out what's real and what's pretend and not having someone to talk to about it. Or feeling a seizure coming on and knowing I'm all alone.

It's not always scary when I lie awake at night. Sometimes it's just lonely. And I hate being lonely. In the daytime, I'm rarely alone. I don't mind being alone, though. A lot of times when I'm alone, I never find the time to be lonely. I'm busy spying, listening hard to all the activities that are happening in the nearby halls at school, the gossip between friends at the next table during school lunch, or the secrets that float around the playground.

I should write a book.

Just because I can't talk doesn't mean I don't listen. So I know way too much and could really tell some crazy stories if Emma ever agreed to be my five-finger interpreter. Until then, the secrets are safe with me. Alone time affords me that special time to actively listen.

To everything.

Everyone around me is interesting and funny. I never tire of listening to Emma play her make-believe games with her dolls. I get excited about being a spy and listening through the vent to adults talking over coffee in the kitchen. I listen close to the tone of my father's whistle while he fixes a broken screen or replaces a lightbulb, to guess how frustrated he is. I'm usually hoping he'll curse, which makes me laugh. I sing along in my head with my mother as she sings songs when she's doing the laundry or baking cookies and bread. I strain to hear the sounds in the neighborhood—the dogs barking, the cars creeping by, the kids in far off yards hollering as they play—and to guess what all the neighbors might be doing in their houses.

But at night, everyone's asleep. And it can get lonely waiting for the sun to come up or scary on the nights I think I hear things I shouldn't. When I can't sleep, I try to lie in bed and think about the day to come and not about my empty stomach or my dirty diaper.

My parents keep the monitor so close to my bed that I know if I breathe too loud or make a noise, they'll be by my side in a flash. I hate to wake them. They both work so hard and need their sleep. Even on the scariest of nights. Sometimes when I get really, really bored I make a noise on purpose but I always feel guilty when I hear my mom's groggy voice asking if I'm all right or when I feel my dad's rough hands slide beneath me and hold me close to his neck, rocking me back to sleep.

The older I get, the less I want to wake them. I know how being awakened feels and it's not fun. It's annoying. All the times I've spent in the hospital when things haven't worked out so great with my body, those hospital people are like vampires. Never sleeping, keeping the lights on all night long, and waking me up over and over to check my pulse and take more blood.

For some reason, nurses with needles aren't fooled like most adults are by my pretending to be asleep. And my invisibility never works with them, even though it works with most adults. Maybe it's because when I'm in the hospital, I'm not in my wheelchair. So maybe my wheelchair really is my invisibility cloak. When I am out with my family at Elitches, at the Denver Zoo, or at the Cherry Creek Mall, some people openly stare at me, study my body top to bottom. Mostly other kids, younger kids. But nearly everyone else either refuses to look at me or gives "pity glances" to my parents.

Hello! I'm not stupid! And I'm not blind . . . well, not in one eye. Not entirely, anyway. I can see people who stare over my head, pretending they don't see me. I see it all with my bionic eye, when I have my contact in. Like tonight. But they don't see me.

Maybe I am invisible in that chair?

Except to children. Children—especially little ones—always see me, stare at my twisted limbs. I don't mind at all. At least kids are honest. The funniest thing I ever heard was from a tiny tot a few years ago. The kid was wearing a cowboy hat and Levi jeans tucked into his cowboy boots. With his thumbs looped into his front pockets, the kid stepped up to me at the circus and asked his mom, "What's the matter with this kid? Did he get kicked in the head by a horse or something?" His mom looked like she'd seen a ghost or something. I laughed until I got the hiccups. It was the funniest—and most honest—thing I'd ever heard a kid say. He'd probably seen an uncle or ranch hand all laid up and dazed looking just like I did, after a spill from a horse or from an accident during branding.

I wish more grownups were that direct. Not all grownups ignore me. Some actually look me in the eye, smile, or offer a greeting like, "Great day, isn't it?" or "Cool chair, bud" or "Nice haircut." Those people don't pretend I'm invisible.

I wonder if people like that have seen Santa Claus?

Tonight's a good night to see Santa Claus. It's cold outside, but it's not snowing or windy. It's quiet. I think I could hear the hooves of reindeer on the roof and the jingle of Santa's bells. My room's on the second floor, right under the roof where they'd land.

I wonder if he's already been here, because I can feel the sheets heavy near my feet, like a filled stocking was left at the foot of my bed. Santa always does that. Maybe I dozed off for a few minutes. Or maybe he put a spell on me. I think I missed him again.

Every year Emma hangs our stockings over the fireplace and by morning—poof!—the stockings end up filled with candy and lying at the foot of our beds. I love the sound, smell, and feel of the candy when Emma grabs the stocking with the big letters NOAH running the length of it, then dumps everything out of the stocking on my bed. She describes every piece of candy and every toy Santa gave me while we wait for Mom and Dad to wake up on Christmas morning. She even holds the tangerine—Santa always sticks one in the stocking's toe for me—close to my nose so I can smell it. Yum!

I must have stayed awake hundreds of times trying to see him, only to fall asleep. Well, not hundreds. I'm only twelve. But a bunch. My mom says he's magic and knows when I'm pretending to sleep and uses his magic to make my eyes heavy. Emma says Santa puts those thick, white gloves over kids' mouths and noses like he's squeezing the life out of the ones who try to trick him. She's twisted like that and tries to scare younger kids. It just makes me laugh. I have proof that Emma's version isn't true, 'cause I'm alive to talk about all the times I've tried. But I can't argue with my mom, since all those times I've tried, I haven't seen him yet. I always fall asleep.

Tonight's different. I can just feel it.

I agree with Emma, though, that although Santa Claus must be real, we're not so sure about the elves. The way Emma figures it, no matter what drawing or picture or cartoon is created of Santa Claus, he's the same—big belly, red clothes, and white beard. But the elves? Never the same. By everyone's guess, they seem to be little people, but that's where agreement stops. Especially with kids. Some drawings show elves with pointy ears, like aliens; some show them with big noses like Snow White's dwarfs; and some show them as people just like us only smaller. So Emma guesses that there are no such things as elves and Santa does all this stuff by himself. She makes me laugh every time she says, "No elves, just Santa and the Mrs."

Maybe Santa was just here and he's over at the neighbor's house. If I turned my head just so, I could spot the sleigh and reindeer on his roof-top. Luckily, although Mom and Dad shut my door each night to give me peace and quiet, they leave the curtains open so I can watch outside. They used to shut them so it would stay dark in my room, hoping I'd sleep bet-ter. But I told Emma to tell them to please keep the curtains open. They listened to her that time and ever since, my curtains stay open.

I'm glad my contact lens is still in place, my vision in one eye crystal clear. The snow is falling outside and the moonlight is bright. The stars aren't so clear yet since too many people still have their lights on in the Denver area. Only on occasion can I see the sky filled with stars twinkling against the blackness. In these winter months, the times I do see stars seem to be really, really early in the morning when most people are tucked in their beds with their lights out. Dad tells me the more lights that are turned on, the less chance I have of seeing the stars. Just the brightest ones.

Tonight I see a few.

No sleigh or reindeer on the neighbor's roof. But I doubt if Santa visits our neighbor Mr. Fletcher very much anyway. No one else seems to. He never talks with anyone. Keeps to himself, mostly. Mrs. Parrent, the neigh-bor on the other side of Mr. Fletcher, said that he's grumpy. I believe Mrs. Parrent because she'd never lie to me. And I've never been invisible to Mrs. Parrent. I wish I could see Mrs. Parrent's house, because I bet Santa Claus is on her roof. They're probably good friends, Santa and she. Or maybe she's friends with Mrs. Claus? That would make sense. I wonder if they bake cookies together?

The light that flicked on in the window across from mine startled me. I had never seen anyone in that room at night before; it was a room Mr. Fletcher never used. Or at least I didn't think so. But tonight, there was a light. And a shadow. Oh, wait! Maybe the shadow behind the thin blinds would be Santa Claus sneaking around in Mr. Fletcher's house and I'd finally get to see him live and in person. He couldn't magic-dust me from here, could he? At first I reached for my football pin to record Santa, but then I remembered it only picked up audio. That wouldn't do any good. So I just watched. And waited.

Fingers poked between the blinds and the shadow peered outside into our backyard or off to the mountains in the west. I wasn't sure. The fingers weren't gloved in white. They were bare. And tiny. The face studied the surroundings, looked around at everything in the neighborhood. The gap in the blinds slammed shut as the fingers pulled free. Before I could be sad that that was my only glimpse of Santa, the blinds flew open, the light of the room becoming a perfect halo around the black-haired person standing in the window.

It wasn't Santa.

Nope, too tiny.

It was a child.

CHAPTER 24

SNOW WAS FALLING, THE big flakes melting almost as quickly as they landed under the bright lights surrounding the outer parking lot. I stood in the cold air, flakes sticking to my eyelashes and chilling the tip of my nose, as I drank in the surreal scene around me. I'd guess the lot was a mile long and a half-mile wide. The snow had been plowed into a wall of snow toward the east and must have been at least twelve feet high the entire length of the lot. A row of light plants, presumably brought in by Chief Gates, dotted the edges of the blacktop to augment the parking area street lamps. Barricades were placed at all eight roads leading in and out of the remote lot from the west, and several police cars—some with their blue and red lights flashing in the dark skies— were parked on the busy street leading to and beyond the lot. No cars were parked in the outer lot and the only thing I could see, well into the darkness beyond, covering every square inch of the asphalt lot, was an ocean of garbage.

The police escort moved the barricade for me and told me to follow a second officer in my car to the priority grid I'd been asked to search. We had driven on a single lane skirting the far edge of the lot where garbage hadn't been strewn, and as we approached the area, I noticed a half-dozen people handpicking through trash in an area that was cordoned off with yellow crime scene tape, approximately one hundred by two hundred feet.

The priority grid.

I was amazed by how organized and efficient the search had become, suddenly realizing the similarities shared by Streeter and Chief Gates. Tony. That would take some getting used to. Anyway, both men were dedicated, persistent, relentless experts in their jobs. Both had deep-rooted ethics and a strong sense of justice. No wonder they were close friends. Close enough to share the holidays.

I glanced around to see if Jack was still out here and didn't think so. I was admittedly avoiding him. I didn't want to talk about his claim that the television was too loud, or his lie to me about sleeping through it. He most certainly hadn't fallen asleep at home and missed the calls as he told Streeter. Unless he had a home in Kansas City I knew nothing about. Which was entirely possible. Maybe he wasn't lying. To me or to Streeter.

But why would he have a home in Denver and a home in Kansas City?

Then it hit me, like the cold blast of winter to my face as I stepped out of my car. Maybe Jack had a family I didn't know about. It would explain his mysterious absences and his infrequent visits while I was at Quantico. If he did have a family in Kansas City, did the home belong to his parents? That would make sense. Or did the home belong to a wife? That would make me the other woman.

But why else would he have a home in Kansas City?

"Well, this is it," said the young officer approaching in the cold wind, shrugging into his padded police jacket and zipping it up to his chin.

I wanted to ask him if he'd graduated from high school yet, his face was so boyish looking.

Instead, I asked, "All this came from one bathroom?"

He shook his head. "All this came from one section of the main terminal that we were told should take priority."

I thought about that, noticing for the first time the beer bottles, the discarded paper plates, the plastic utensils, and the empty plastic soda and water bottles. This was much, much more than a single bathroom's garbage. This likely represented an entire chunk of the expansive main terminal's trash.

I sighed, my resolve slipping just a bit.

"When you leave, back your car onto the field rather than jeopardize the integrity of the evidence," the officer said, motioning toward the strewn garbage.

"Evidence, of course," I said, still amazed at how much garbage had been gathered in one day at DIA.

I watched as the officer maneuvered the police cruiser in a two-point turn, reversing between two light plants onto the snow-covered field, and then forward in a tight curve back to the single lane of blacktop toward the barricade.

I put on my winter coat, pulled on my boots, and put my ugly, winter-lined, red-and-black-checked hat on my head. Yes, fully equipped with earflaps. I unloaded Beulah, who seemed reluctant to be in the cold weather; she was shivering from the first moment I strapped on her harness. I ruffled her fur and told her how much I believed in her before putting on my gloves. I walked her to one corner of the priority grid and set the child's backpack—the blue one with the yellow puppies, not the fifth grader's camouflaged backpack I'd also thrown in the back of my vehicle—on the empty blacktop nearby. Beulah perked up, forgetting how cold she was.

With the command, she went to work. Since we weren't technically trailing a scent, but rather trying to find evidence that might be linked to the missing boy, I led Beulah up and down the grid, walking on the strewn garbage, repeating the single command, "Find."

The four leather dog boots that my brother Ole had loaned me during the last family pheasant hunt this fall fit Beulah perfectly and protected the pads of her paws from broken glass, discarded needles, anything sharp in the garbage. Beulah did as she was told, allowing me to walk her in a back and forth, crisscross motion over the grid, each time turning at the wall of snow and back to the strip of empty blacktop where I'd place the backpack in front of her again and repeat what I wanted her to do.

I felt bad as we passed an occasional picker in the grid, knowing that Beulah and I were taking few precautions as we walked on top of the garbage, trampling the evidence. But it was part of the decision to use Beulah for faster results, knowing we may destroy something in the process.

Weaving back and forth in about three- to four-foot-wide swaths allowed Beulah to search for a similar scent in the garbage, to determine if little Max's belongings—or little Max—could be among the refuse.

At what I estimated was near the halfway point of the grid's length, I started to lose confidence that we'd find something. We'd already trampled on half the potential evidence from the priority grid, passing four of the six pickers, with no indication from Beulah that she was even working the scene any longer. Her nose, as always, was not on the ground, but instead high in the air where it always was when she trotted along, whether she was working or not.

The difference when she was trailing a scent was that she charged with all her strength toward the target, pulling me along. Here, I simply hoped she'd recognize something that resembled the scent of the backpack as I led her along, amid rows and rows and rows of garbage, smelly, stinky garbage that thankfully had its stench muted by the freezing temperatures.

I felt worried because Beulah's thin coat was not designed to withstand the cold. Her breed was more accustomed to a warm climate and I found it difficult enough to get her to go outside to relieve herself. Instead, on the days it had been cold over the last couple of weeks, she had held it for as long as she could. I had requested an insulated, canine flak jacket for her, but it hadn't been approved yet. She could sure use it tonight in this cold weather in the dangerous heap she was searching.

When I'd done research at Quantico, I found that most search dogs in the mountain states were trained German shepherds or Malinois with thick coats to withstand the cold. But a bloodhound's sense of smell was estimated to be sixty times greater than that of a German shepherd. I also discovered that bloodhounds were known to be the most docile and least likely to bite, which utterly confounded me every time I thought about Beulah at the Hanson cabin attacking the killer. Bloodhounds didn't have that attack instinct or propensity to bite. Especially Beulah. I'd always wondered what sent her into attack mode during that moment. She had saved my life.

Beulah's loyalty to me had earned her special favors. I would search for the perfect apartment where she could have the indoor comforts and the ability to duck outside if need be. Until then, we'd enjoy the accommodations at the Hogarty house.

After the fourteenth pass, I was trying to decide if we should continue or abandon the search and head back to Concourse B for the interviews with the Williamses. I glanced at my watch. Eleven o'clock. I'd only been out searching for a half hour. I'd finish up the priority grid, admit the search was a bust, and head back. On the sixteenth pass, just as we were nearing the end of the first hundred-foot length before hitting the twelve-foot snow wall and doubling back, Beulah lurched to my left, pulling me into the new area of garbage that hadn't been searched. She lowered her nose a bit and stopped, looking back over her shoulder at me.

"Beulah?" I asked, looking around the area to find what it was she'd detected.

Luckily, a light plant stood at the edge of this side of the outer lot and the area was easy to scan. I looked around at my feet, around either side of Beulah and in front of her, digging in the garbage with the toe of my boot. Beulah shivered, her body trembling from the cold. For a minute while I poked and prodded through paper towels and discarded coffee cups and chunks of wasted, rotting food, I wondered if Beulah had simply bolted off course in defiance of this silly exercise I had her doing. After all, I'd felt the same way a few passes back, until I saw the corner of green poking up from beneath the layer of strewn garbage.

Right in front of Beulah.

"Way to go, girl," I said, sensing immediately that this is what we were hoping to find.

Just as I bent to pick up the green cloth, a voice called, "What'd she find?"

I was so startled that I nearly fell on the layer of garbage we'd been searching. A hand grabbed me under my arm and kept me hovering until I regained my footing. I rose to a standing position, finding myself face-to-face with Jack Linwood.

I said nothing.

He smiled.

"What did you two find?"

I realized then that he was the sixth picker I hadn't yet passed on my search with Beulah. He was dressed like the others—same blue parka, same navy stocking cap, and black gloves. He had been picking through the garbage, a task well beneath his pay grade, off by himself on a remote part of the priority grid. Helping out to speed up the investigation? Or waiting for me?

"I . . . We . . ." I couldn't find my words.

For an instant, my mind said I shouldn't answer him.

After all, here he is out in the priority grid, picking through garbage on his own, blatantly disregarding Streeter's instructions to oversee the operations for the priority grid, gather key evidence already collected, and help Dodson review videos.

"What are you doing out here?" I managed.

My breath hung in the cold air near his chest.

He looked down at me. "Searching. Like you."

"But you were supposed to oversee the search efforts, not become a part of it."

His smile wavered as he looked over his shoulder toward the other pickers. "It's Christmas Eve and five degrees out here. I don't have a lot of people helping." Something came over his face that I would have to describe as a grave seriousness. "We have to find the boy. We're running out of time. And it's very cold. He won't survive in this cold if he is out there."

I looked away from his stern face and at the ocean of garbage. "You . . . you think he's here?"

"I believe in you. And Beulah. She found the trail to the bathroom. The end of the line?" His smile was soft and genuine. It was an offering.

The green corner of fabric in front of Beulah no longer held the victorious aura it had only moments earlier. Now it was something much more ominous to me.

I looked back at Jack, realizing that my earlier compulsion to stay quiet and not answer him had nothing to do with my concern for little Max. It had been purely out of jealousy. I saw him fly in from Kansas City tonight around 8:30 p.m. and then he'd lied to me—to all of us—about where he'd been. Maybe he had a second home in Kansas City. So what? And what business of it was mine? After dating him, I was starting to fall in love with this man, and my jealousy didn't need to be the reason I stopped trusting him now. I simply had to ask.

"I saw you."

His smile faded. "You saw me?"

"Tonight. I saw you get off that plane."

His face became guarded.

"From Kansas City."

He averted his eyes from mine.

"Are you married, Jack?"

He closed his eyes and took a deep breath. "I was."

That answer took me by surprise. I really hadn't thought my delusions—that somehow Jack flying to Kansas City meant I was dating a married man or that I had reason to be jealous—would turn out to be real.

"Does she live in Kansas City?"

He shook his head, still avoiding my eyes.

"Do you have kids?"

It took him many moments to answer. His liquid black gaze slid back to mine and the distance in them indicated his thoughts were a million miles away. In the stillness that followed, I could see my breath linger in the cold air, which gave me a chill.

His words were small. "I did."

CHAPTER 25

A PIT OF REGRET—MORE like sorrow—grew in my gut hearing the formality of the past tense he used. He'd said "I did," not "I do." I sensed this wasn't going to turn out well for either of us.

Jack's gaze returned to me, first with an expression of hurt, and then he tightened his jaw and raised his chin in defiance.

"My son died. It was tragic. My wife and I couldn't cope. We divorced, many years ago. I should have told you. I haven't seen her since. And no, she doesn't live in Kansas City."

I stared at him.

"Then why did you lie?"

"You know how Calvin is, my boss. How Streeter is, my peer. I'm on call 24-7. I'm supposed to let them know my every movement, anytime I travel. In case they need me."

I did understand that. Work at the Bureau was all consuming. It was almost unnatural.

"I went to Kansas City to see an old college buddy of mine. I flew out yesterday and back in today. In case you wanted to spend time with me tomorrow. That's why I couldn't come to your sister's house tonight."

I must have looked skeptical, because he pulled off one glove and fished for something in his jeans pocket. He pulled out some slick pieces of paper I recognized as e-tickets. "Here. Believe me now?"

I saw from the itinerary that he'd left on December 23 at 3:46 p.m. for Kansas City, returning at 8:29 p.m. December 24.

"I left work early. Ask Dodson. Or Noreen. Anyone, really."

I shoved the tickets back at him. I watched as he stuffed the e-tickets back in his pocket and demanded, "And your college buddy, male or female?"

He grinned and kissed my forehead. His lips were warm. "Male, you silly girl."

"When are you going to let me meet your parents?" I asked, wrapping my arms around his waist and resting my cheek against his chest.

He gave me a squeeze. "They are both gone. I never had siblings. You are all I have."

The idea broke my heart. "I'm sorry. I really would have liked to meet them. Would they have approved of me? For you?"

"Absolutely not," he said, chuckling, and held me closer.

I laughed. "Sorry I didn't mention the Kansas City thing until now. I was just . . . jealous. And I'm on edge."

"Me, too. This is personally very hard for me." He let me go and stared down at me. "A boy missing, I mean."

"I'm so sorry about your son. How did he die?"

He shook his head. "I think we need to focus on finding this boy. Whatever it takes. Even if it means you stay out here and pick with me."

My mood brightened, suspecting what Beulah had already found.

I turned from him and bent down near Beulah who by this time was shivering like a leaf in a windstorm. I fished out the green fabric with my gloved hand and tugged until a tiny beret appeared.

"It's the boy's," said Jack.

"Little Max. His name is little Max."

As Jack gathered the other five pickers and directed them to the area where we'd found little Max's beret, I took Beulah back to my car. Loading her into her kennel wasn't comfort enough for me. I turned the key and let the engine warm up, set the heater to seventy-five, hoping the car would reach a comfortable temperature quickly. I gave Beulah water and food, removed her leather boots, and ruffled her fur to show her how proud I was of her search, waiting to make sure the heat would rise before turning it to a steady seventy and heading back to the picking area.

All seven us picked through an area that Jack had outlined, what he thought would capture more than items from the single-stall bathroom. Mostly, the mess was paper towels and discarded toilet paper, with candy wrappers, used feminine products, and dirty diapers. Not a pleasant pick for sure.

As we picked, I said, "The Williamses made it."

"Streeter's interviewing them now?"

I shook my head. "Waiting for me to get back. He was going to interview Benson's girlfriend first."

The more we picked the more relaxed I became, overjoyed that we hadn't found a body part or a discarded corpse. Small talk was welcome and reviewing the points of the case was productive small talk.

"Do Chief Gates and Streeter think Benson might have something to do with all of this?"

"Maybe," I said under my breath. I didn't know the other pickers and didn't want to discuss the case with them if they weren't Bureau.

Jack recognized my reluctance and moved to the farthest reaches of the area, closest to the beret I'd found. He instructed the others to move out to the edges and work toward us.

"Do you think Benson had something to do with this?" whispered Jack.

"I'm not sure. Wouldn't be surprised." Streeter and Tony had mentioned the difference between planned and random abductions. Was all this coincidence? Benson and his girlfriend's involvement felt like a stretch to me.

"Why?"

I shrugged. "Maybe he's a pedophile. Maybe he abducted little Max for attention. Maybe he wanted an excuse for his girlfriend to feel sorry for him."

"So he snatched a little boy?"

I shrugged again, resisting the powerful urge to yack from the sight of the trash I was picking through. I tried to stay focused on the case. "What are the alternatives?"

The wind died and it was quiet for a moment. Snowflakes fell but quickly turned to dots of wet under the lights. I could hear gloves scraping against piles of debris and sliding along evidence bags; the pickers were talking amongst themselves about planned Christmas activities and holiday feasts.

I'd almost forgotten I'd asked a question when Jack answered, "Someone might have paid Benson to derail the child's travels or to get rid of him. Like the father or mother?"

"Maybe. I know little Max's dad. I just can't believe that would be possible."

"You know Maximillian Bennett Williams II? The richest man in NYC?" Jack had stopped picking and was staring at me.

"Why does everyone keep sounding so surprised?"

Jack grew quiet.

"What?" I asked.

"Is he a former boyfriend of yours or something?"

"And why does everyone keep jumping to that conclusion? No. I did not, would not, ever date Max. He's not my type. Max is my sister's ex-fiancé."

That seemed to please him.

"What time is it?" I asked, finding nothing of interest and growing worried about missing the interview.

"A quarter to midnight."

I'd been out there for an hour and fifteen minutes. Benson's girlfriend had probably been retrieved and taken to headquarters already, and their interview was either already over or just finishing up.

Jack must have read my mind. "You thinking about cutting out?"

I nodded. "Doesn't seem to be much here except a lot of DNA for you and your team to analyze."

"Looks like it. At least that means he might still be alive."

We exchanged a worried glance. How could I have ever entertained the idea that Jack would cheat on me? Or on his wife? How paranoid could I possibly get? How ridiculous? I rose to my feet, surprised that Jack did the same.

I asked, "You cutting out, too?"

"No, we're almost done here. I'll head back to the lab downtown with all this and line out the protocol. Mind if I keep the beret?"

I shook my head. "I want to use it to do another search at the airport. Just in case the Williamses didn't bring any of little Max's personal belongings. But I'll give you his backpack. I promise I'll give you the beret when I'm done. To analyze. Time is of the essence and all."

Something seemed to be weighing on his mind. Maybe it was the beret. "Liv?"

"What?" I noticed we'd walked out of earshot of the other pickers.

His voice was still in a whisper. "Don't tell Streeter. Please."

"About you picking out here instead of reviewing videos?"

"No, about me lying. He won't trust me."

"That's what happens when you tell lies, Jack. People don't trust you."

"Do you?"

I studied his face a long time, wondering what it was I saw behind his shiny black eyes. Sadness, desperation? The only thing I could think to say in response was, "Does it matter to you if I do?"

"A great deal," he said. "More than you could ever imagine."

"Then of course I do."

I believed that Jack went to Kansas City yesterday and returned today. I believed he was divorced and had lost a son. I believed he did not want me to tell Streeter about him lying about where he'd been. I believed all he had in the world was me. So why wouldn't I trust him, even if he had been reluctant up until now to share such important parts of his past? He had been married. He'd lost a child. His parents had died. He had no siblings. He was a man unwilling to trust just anyone and yet he trusted me. And wanted me to trust him.

I walked slowly across the sea of garbage toward the car, hoping Beulah had warmed up and was fast asleep. Only a few feet away from the pick area, Jack called, "Liv!"

I turned back and saw him holding something up in the night for me to see. I couldn't make it out, but I hurried back to the picking area, wobbling and twisting ankles as I worked my way over the unstable surface in response to his urgency. "What is it?"

"Shoe polish."

"So?"

He shook the large bottle. "Empty."

"I don't get it."

"If you were a businessman who needed to spiffy up your shoes, you might buy some shoe polish at the sundries store, right?"

I nodded, still not seeing his point.

"But a bottle of shoe polish this size would last for months. Years, really. No one could use this up in one buff."

"Maybe the businessman brought the nearly empty bottle with him. From home."

"Why? Wouldn't he just polish his shoes before he left?"

"Maybe the bottle is from one of the airport shoe shiners."

"Just one bottle? I was thinking something a little different." He squatted down and scooped up a handful of used paper towels smattered with black. "See?"

He held the papers closer for me to inspect.

"What is that?"

"Paper towels with black shoe polish on them."

"So? They used the paper towels to polish their shoes in the bathroom."

He shook his head. "Look closer."

I did. And I saw it. "Hair."

"Black hair. Maybe it's actually blond hair dyed black. With shoe polish." He grabbed the evidence bag from my hand, examining the beret carefully until he found what he was looking for. He pointed. "There!"

I leaned in and peered through the plastic bag at the tiny cap inside. "What?"

"Shoe polish. A spot inside the beret."

I saw it. Definitely a smudge of black. "Like a partial thumbprint."

"Right," Jack said, grinning. "It means we have hope."

"He's not dead," I said, feeling buoyed by this newly found evidence.

"Why bother dyeing a boy's hair if you're going to kill him?"

I stood on my tiptoes, kissed Jack hard on the lips, and headed back to the car.

A few paces away, I heard Jack call after me. "He was six!"

I knew he meant the son he'd lost.

CHAPTER 26

I WALKED INTO CASE headquarters, just as Streeter keyed his radio. Heads turned our way as I walked side by side with my big red bloodhound. I led Beulah to her pallet in the corner and she quickly curled up and went back to sleep, happy to be left alone for a while. It was warm in the makeshift office space, her corner far from the cold windows and the blackness beyond. And it was well past her bedtime—12:30 a.m.— Christmas morning, technically.

"Search it again. Tell them all to be looking for hiding places. It's a long shot, but maybe the child hid somewhere, got stuck or fell asleep. Look through a five-year-old's eyes, think playing hide and seek. Go!" Gates put the radio back on the folding table.

"How did you do?" Streeter asked.

I held up the beret.

"Good work!" Streeter said, moving quickly toward me to inspect the bagged evidence. "Are you sure it's his?"

I nodded. "I brought Beulah back and did a search one last time from gate B31, using the beret. She took the same route, led me to the same bathroom stall and stopped. But this time the bathroom was cordoned off and the pipes to the sink and toilet were missing."

"Control Ops removed the catch basin for the sink and the curve of the commode pipe to check for any blood or tissue that might have been flushed down the toilet or washed down the sink. Luminal showed nothing in the bathroom out of the ordinary," Streeter explained.

I let out a sigh. "That's great news. I don't think you'll find anything."

In reaction to the smile plastered on my face, Streeter pointed and asked, "What's up with that?"

"Guess what else Jack found."

Streeter scowled. "Jack? I thought he was downtown with Dodson reviewing videos?"

I shook my head. "He's still out there with the pickers. But he found something that might have explained why Beulah lost the scent at the sink."

"What?" Gates asked, approaching me, taking the bagged beret from Streeter's hand and turning it over to inspect it.

"Shoe polish. See the smear inside the lining of the beret?"

Gates asked, "What does that have to do with—"

Streeter interrupted. "Quick and easy hair dye when you're on the run."

"Exactly! And the odor would likely be overpowering to Beulah if a child was drenched in it. At least, that's what I'm speculating at this point," I said. "Beulah's trained to scent people. Sometimes animal scents distract her because their scent is more like ours. But not items like shoe polish. In fact, she's trained to ignore them. Like the formaldehyde we use to preserve tissue. So I can't find the trail beyond the damned bathroom."

"And you're smiling because to you that means little Max is still alive," Streeter added.

"Of course. Why take the time to dye a kid's hair if you're only planning to kill him?" Gates asked.

"That's what Jack said." I noticed Streeter looked away at the mention of Jack's name. "He found some paper towels with some shoe polish and some straight hair stuck to it. He's taking it back to the lab."

"He'll need the beret," Streeter said.

I nodded.

Gates handed the bag to Streeter, who pulled a desk lamp over to inspect the cap more closely. He poked his head over the dividers to see which of the technicians were still with us. Streeter called, "Taylor?"

A man came over to where we were working.

"See this?"

Taylor nodded.

"See if you can lift a print. Looks like a partial thumb to me."

"Did to me, too," I said.

"When you're done with it, upload it to AFIS and tell Linwood. Then run this down to the field office."

"Uh, Streeter, do you mind if I search the parking structures before we send the beret back to Jack?"

He nodded. Taylor took the beret over to his tiny lab area against one of the walls.

Streeter turned back to me and I said, "I also worked Beulah on a second scent from gate B31."

Both men stared at me.

I held up Kevin Benson's sweater that he'd left behind accidentally after the interview.

"Beulah followed the exact same path, only once we got the Buckhorn Bar and Grill, she circled the area several times, wandered about the main concourse, and eventually came back through security, back to Concourse B. I stopped trailing at that point, realizing she was following his scent when he was frantically searching for little Max in those first hours. I'd have been there all night."

"So he's telling the truth," Gates said. "He's not our guy."

"Appears that way to me. What about the girlfriend?" I asked.

Gates and I had joined Streeter at the table.

"She most definitely is not a fan of Kevin Benson. And although he apparently told the truth about losing the boy at the Buckhorn and then looking for him, I'm not convinced that there isn't a greater force at work here, a plan to deceive and distract." Streeter added, "The shoe polish would be a strong indication that the abduction was planned, whether it was a random or specific victim."

The door opened and in came Phil Kelleher.

"Are they ready?" Streeter asked.

"They've been ready for nearly two hours and are getting snippy. East conference room," Kelleher said.

"Both of them?" I asked.

"All of them," he said, his tight smile revealing something that looked like disgust.

When we approached the closed door on the other side of HQ, Streeter whispered in my ear, "Go on. You know the guy."

"Crap," I mumbled. "Can't I go downstairs and look for little Max instead?"

Gates laughed. Streeter shook his head and motioned toward the door.

I opened it. To all of them. Officer Lou was right. Throw in a football and a whistle and we've got ourselves a game. There must have been twenty people in the room, half sitting along the wall on one side, half sitting along the wall on the other. His and hers. I felt like it was a mutual firing squad. I walked over to a man at the end of the table, sticking my hand out, saying, "Max."

His black hair was still thick and wavy. A dimple punctuated his white, toothy smile, brilliant as a game-show host's. And his suit was tailored to hug the biceps and pectorals he worked so hard to build. Ever the charmer, Max hadn't aged one bit.

"Agent Bergen," Max responded.

No one had ever called me that before. My cheeks burned. I felt silly dressed in grubby jeans and a baseball cap surrounded by an entourage of custom-tailored suits and couture purses. Until we shook hands, that is. His grip was painful against my raw palm. And his expression was vacant, as if I were a total stranger. I figured he was just being an asshole as usual and nodded at the dozen suits crowded around him.

I was tempted to announce to Max where my hands had just been a half hour earlier, picking through miles of garbage, but why spoil the surprise for the rest of these beautiful people? So instead, I asked, "Who are all these folks?"

"Business associates," Max said, looking past me and shaking Streeter's hand.

"This is Special Agent Streeter Pierce and Denver Police Chief Tony Gates. Chief Gates, Agent Pierce, this is Max Williams and his business associates."

"Maximillian Bennett Williams II," he said, correcting me before releasing Streeter's hand and grabbing Tony's.

"Oh, excuse me. Maximillian Bennett Williams II and his business associates." I nodded with exaggeration toward Streeter. He suppressed a smile. I bit my tongue and zipped my lip so I wouldn't add "the asshole to whom I was referring earlier" to my introduction. Instead, I walked down to the other end of the room, meeting each member of his entourage and then hers. I ended up face-to-face with the only woman in the room who could possibly be Max's wife and shook her hand.

"I'm Special Agent Liv Bergen. And you are Mrs. Williams?"

The Barbie-doll blonde extended a limp-fish handshake, not unlike flight attendant Kevin Benson's earlier. I didn't squeeze it hard, though, because I was pleased that it was her hand, not Ida's, that Max had taken to be his. She was Mrs. Asshole.

Her teeth were equally as perfect as Max's; their dentist surely spent most of his winter months in the Bahamas after all the work he must do for them. Her eyes were wide and bright, the makeup she wore perfectly applied. I wondered if it had been painted on, knowing she'd been crying. Or maybe it was reapplied over and over. I just didn't understand makeup all that much. Being the closest I'd ever been to a supermodel—my sister Ida excluded— I must say Melissa Williams was absolutely gorgeous. I imagined she was always that way, even without makeup. She had a killer body, sculpted taut and smooth, and her eyes commanded my full attention.

"Melissa," she said. Shooting a quick dagger of a look in Max's direction, she added, "And these are my friends."

Point taken. Max had business associates. Melissa had friends. And there you have it, the continental divide that might otherwise be known as the Williams party.

"I'm so, so sorry for the strain you both must be under tonight, and we appreciate you flying into Denver to answer some questions," Streeter said to everyone in the room after introducing himself to Melissa. "Let me start by thanking all of you for wanting to help us find Mr. and Mrs. Williams's son. We're going to need everyone's cooperation and time is of the essence."

"Then why did you keep us waiting so long," whined the man with long hair on Melissa's side of the divide. I think he was the one she called her publicist, but he could have been her hair-and-makeup artist.

"Because we were in critical interviews that will hopefully lead to the recovery of little Max," Streeter said. His voice was sugary, yet firm. "We have rooms set up for everyone. We will lead you to your assigned rooms where individual interviews will occur, and we have other agents who will be helping us gather information."

"From us? What kind of information?" The man was on Max's side of the divide and I think he said he was one of the attorneys. Max brought several.

Streeter added evenly, "Information that may help us find little Max."

Separate and conquer. Well done, Streeter. The seventeen people in the room who were friends and business associates were rumbling. The Williamses said nothing. Standing midway in the room, careful not to choose sides by my position, I felt like firing the starting gun for the battle at Gettysburg.

"For the record, the interviews are being recorded and we'll need to have you speak your names clearly, please," Streeter stated the date, location, and names of the officials present for the interview including himself, Tony, Phil, and me.

"Wait," Max interrupted. "Isn't Agent Bergen going to conduct the interviews?"

Streeter looked to me to answer, knowing this was about who was lead. To avoid further delays, I simply said, "No, Agent Pierce will."

Max's eyes slowly moved from my face to Streeter's as he calculated his next move.

Streeter continued, "Mrs. Williams, can you please introduce each of your friends to me and tell me his or her relationship to little Max so I know what room to assign them to?"

Melissa looked like a deer caught in the headlights. Her perfectly lined lips parted and then closed. She started again with a hug to the woman sitting next to her. "This is my publicity agent." Then she pointed. "My hairdresser. My makeup artist. That's my attorney. Those two are bodyguards. And that's my pilot and copilot."

No one moved. They all just sat there. Streeter stared. So did I. Not one name. Maybe Melissa didn't know their names. Streeter addressed the first woman. "Your name and relationship with little Max?"

And the eight people stated their names for the record, all of them indicating how they knew little Max. Most had met him, but none of them stated anything more than that, except one bodyguard who admitted he had to babysit the child once and the hairdresser who indicated he'd cut the boy's hair on a couple of occasions.

Streeter turned to the other end of the room, saying, "Mr. Williams?"

"Following my brilliant wife's lead—"

"Ex-wife," Melissa corrected.

"Not yet, dear," Max added, his smile forced. "To be brief: pilot, copilot, attorney, attorney, attorney, bodyguard, bodyguard, assistant, and personal assistant."

Streeter repeated his line of questions, asking for each person to state his or her name and indicate how he or she knew little Max. Most had met the boy but had little interaction with him.

"And the nanny? The child's caregiver? You mentioned her on the phone." Streeter asked, "Judy Manning, is it? Did she come with either of you?"

Melissa jerked her head in Max's direction. Streeter, Tony, Phil, and I looked to him for an answer.

"No, I did not bring her. It's Christmas. She had the week off. She was planning to go back to England for the holidays," Max answered.

"Who took little Max to the airport?"

"Nanny Judy."

CHAPTER 27

STREETER REFRAINED FROM COMMENT and stood. "I am going to check on the rooms and agents assigned to each of you so we can get started. Mr. and Mrs. Williams, I want you to stay here so Chief Gates, Agent Bergen, and I can talk with you. Alone."

"Very good. But I want one of my attorneys to stay," Max said.

"Me too," Melissa piped in.

Streeter smiled. "Then that changes things."

He left the room and indicated that I follow. Outside, he stepped toward Kelleher and said, "Set up the room for Mr. Williams and his attorney. I want cameras rolling in there, if they give us their consent. I'm going to leave Mrs. Williams and her attorney in here. We'll put them together after we've interviewed them separately."

I went back inside the room with Melissa and her attorney until everyone was situated. Gates was helping Streeter with the arrangements and with what I assumed would be a plan for the interview.

As she sat next to her preoccupied attorney, who was busy with his smartphone, I couldn't help but stare at Melissa, whose eyes were staring at the windows. She had an intoxicating beauty. I decided to make small talk with her until the men returned. "I don't suppose there's such a thing as a white Christmas in LA," I mused, staring at the snow falling in the blackness beyond the windows.

Melissa shook her head. The room grew silent. So much for small talk. After a long moment, she said, "It's what I miss the most about New York. Aldo said he'll buy me snow. All the snow I can stand. After we move to Papeete. Is that even possible?"

"Where's Papeete?" I asked.

"Oh, it's on Tahiti, an island in French Polynesia. Aldo owns a whole bunch of real estate there. But it's so hot," Melissa admitted with a sigh. "And I told him I'd miss the snow."

"Well, have you ever heard of Ski Dubai?"

She turned to face me, really studying me for the first time, her eyes settling on the scratches on my face. She shook her head, loosening a blond lock that tumbled down from a fashionable pile at the nape of her neck and bounced against her cheek.

"It's a ski park in the Middle East."

"In the desert?"

I nodded. "Anything can be done with enough money."

"That's what Aldo says."

"Who's Aldo?"

"My boyfriend. We're going to get married as soon as—"

"Melissa," the attorney said, placing his hand on her arm.

It was a signal to stop talking. I could tell by the apologetic look in her eye. I offered her a sympathetic smile and gazed off at the snow. The attorney went back to tapping cryptically on his smartphone. She motioned for me to follow her and she eased away from the table and walked toward the windows.

"I didn't think I'd like you," she said almost wistfully, staring out at the snow racing through the black night.

"Me? Why?" I asked.

"Max told me about you. About your sister. I thought I'd be jealous." Her eyes went up to my baseball cap, lingered on the scratches across my cheek, and moved quickly down to my grubby shirt and jeans. "But I'm not."

"Thank you, I think." She had no idea how jealous she should be since Ida was drop-dead gorgeous, not like me. But I had to say, both Ida and Melissa were striking. I just didn't see what either of them saw in Max, other than that he was easy on the eyes. Too perfect looking for my taste, though.

"Why'd he pick me?" I asked.

"To be assigned the case?"

I nodded.

She shrugged. "He told me he didn't. He said he had no idea you were with the FBI here. But I knew he did the second you introduced yourself to me. He does that. Exercises his muscle now and again. He hadn't put Chandler on the spot in years. No need for the FBI, I guess. Until now." She stared in silence for a long moment and whispered, "Or it was to piss me off? Who knows?"

"Are you pissed? That I was assigned the case?"

"Like I said, I thought I'd be jealous," she answered, giving me the once-over again. "But I'm not. You're okay."

"I'm okay, but Agent Pierce is the best."

As if I'd conjured him, in walked Streeter. He was the kind of man who suited my taste.

Not someone like Max. Streeter was not as tall or as lean as Max, and his white buzz was nothing like Max's full head of black, wavy hair. The play of a boyish grin on the corner of Streeter's manly mouth was much more appealing to me than Max's commanding presence. But it was Max's eyes that unsettled me, always shifting from a wary cunning and then back to charm.

Melissa's attorney looked up from his smartphone, just noticing Melissa and me returning to the table. "About time. Do you have any idea how late it is on the West Coast?"

"An hour earlier than here, Mr. Sinclair," Streeter said, coming around the table with Gates and taking a seat next to me. "And it's two hours earlier here than on the East Coast, where the other Williams party came from, so shouldn't we be starting with them, based on the late hour?"

"I apologize. It's been a long day. We're just edgy, eager to locate the boy."

"So are we," Streeter replied. "Mind if we get started? Videotaping? I'll need verbal confirmation from both of you."

They both said it was okay.

"Mrs. Williams, when did you discover your son was missing?"

She looked at me before answering. "When I went to pick him up at the airport today."

Streeter said, "Let the time reflect that it's 1:17 a.m. December 25. You mean yesterday, the 24th?"

"Yes. My driver took me out to LAX. Aldo was busy with last-minute planning for our trip to Papeete. We were scheduled to leave today, on Christmas, for a week away with little Max."

"Aldo is who?" Streeter asked.

"Aldo Giottani. He's a billionaire. He lives in Papeete but has a second home in Hollywood. That's how we met. At a director's party."

"When was this?"

"Does it matter?" the attorney asked. "We do have a pending divorce case and unless this is relevant, I'm going to have to instruct my client not to answer."

"I heard Mr. Williams make reference to that a few minutes ago." Streeter cleared his throat. "Both Mr. and Mrs. Williams referred to themselves earlier as divorced, not separated. So the divorce is not yet final?"

The attorney answered, "We're waiting for the final hearing on distribution of assets."

Streeter nodded and made a note.

Melissa blinked and then stared at Sinclair. It appeared to me that she didn't understand why he was being difficult with Streeter. I wondered if it was because she cared so much about her son that she didn't expect anyone on her team to be an obstacle, or if it was because she didn't fully grasp the exchange. But maybe I was judging her too harshly.

"Then a point of clarification, Mrs. Williams. Aldo is a billionaire with land in and around Papeete in Tahiti and a home in Hollywood, but what relationship is he to you and your son?"

"We're getting married and we—"

Mr. Sinclair put his hand on her arm. "As I said, the divorce is not final and I'd appreciate some discretion when asking these questions."

"Mr. Sinclair, I really don't give a flying fig about the divorce. What I care about is finding Mrs. Williams's son. And unless and until I identify all the people in little Max's life who may have an interest in his well-being, I really am ill equipped to find him."

Gates added, "So forget about your job of protecting her assets for the time being and focus on protecting her ass."

"My ass? Am I in trouble here?"

"You have insisted on having a lawyer during an interview about your missing son. Innocent people don't choose that," Gates said.

"I only chose it because Max insisted on having his lawyer there. Go. Step outside. I have nothing to hide." She was shooing away her attorney.

Sinclair's eyes widened. "Melissa, I would advise—"

"Go. I'll be fine."

Sinclair eyed each of us before slowly pushing himself away from the table and walking toward the door, letting himself out.

Gates called after him, "Turn left, three doors down on your left. Go on in. They'll take care of you."

"Thank you," Streeter said to Melissa. "You know, you're within your rights to have an attorney with you."

She smiled and nodded. "I know. But I don't need a lawyer to protect my ass. I need to get my son back."

CHAPTER 28

"OKAY, MRS. WILLIAMS," STREETER continued. "You arrived at LAX at what time?"

"Around 3:00 p.m. I wanted to make sure I was there for little Max. He'd be worried if no one was there to pick him up."

"And his flight was scheduled to arrive at 3:20 p.m.?" Gates asked.

She nodded. The muscles around her eyes sagged. She looked as if she was about to cry.

"And then what?"

I could tell by the change in Streeter's tone that he noticed it, too.

"I . . . my driver said he'd circle in a pattern and to wait for him on the curb right where he dropped me off. I never made it back out there." She started crying; her attorney wasn't there to pat her arm. She said. "My driver eventually parked the car and came looking for me. He found me inside with airport security. They were trying to help me locate my son."

"How did you know he was missing?"

"I waited twenty minutes at the security exit at the bottom of the escalator to baggage claim and I saw that nearly everyone from that flight had already passed me, retrieved their bags from the carousel, and were leaving. So I called Max."

"What time was that?" Streeter asked.

She looked at me for reassurance, her eyes wide when the answer didn't come to her right away. I offered her a tiny smile of encouragement. She was thinking. I was studying her face; she had mascara smudges under her eyes from crying. She drew a breath, wiped away the black, and finally said, "I'm pretty sure it was around 3:45 p.m."

"That's Pacific standard time," Streeter clarified for the record. "And what did he say?"

"He said he put little Max on the plane."

"And you believed him?"

"Not at first. I thought he was messing with me, punishing me for demanding that little Max come to my house on Christmas Eve. He had wanted to keep him until the day after Christmas. He didn't want Aldo and me taking little Max to Papeete. Max is jealous. We argued over it earlier in the week, so I thought he'd decided to exercise his muscle in his usual way and keep little Max."

"What eventually made you believe him? That he'd put little Max on the plane?"

"When I noticed little Max's bag on the carousel and his Yankees bear on the handle, I . . . I lost it."

"What do you mean, lost it?" Gates pressed her.

She unceremoniously lifted her arm, shrugging out of her faux mink coat to show the early signs of bruising. "I fainted. I hit my arm on the carousel on the way down. Airport medics took care of me until I was alert enough to tell my story."

"Which was?"

Melissa's eyes welled with tears again. "That little Max was missing and that someone better find him for me or I was going to start taking names and filing lawsuits."

My question startled Streeter and Tony as much as it did Melissa. "And what is Aldo planning to buy for little Max?"

"What?" she said, sniffling, confusion etched on her otherwise perfect forehead.

Streeter swung his gaze toward me, probably thinking me quite insane for asking. But I had a purpose.

"What do you mean?"

"Well, Aldo loves you, right? Plans to marry you as soon as the divorce is final?"

She nodded, looking perplexed.

"Loves you enough to buy you snow on a tropical island, because you said you'd miss it when you move there, right?"

She nodded again, lowering the tissue she had been using to dab away any flawed makeup.

"And Aldo certainly loves little Max, doesn't he?"

She didn't nod at first, hesitated, then blinked, and said, "Of course."

"What did Aldo tell you he was planning to buy for little Max once you moved to Papeete? Once you were married?" I asked my questions with just enough casualness, forcing a smile to my eyes to comfort her. "What did you talk about that little Max would miss the most?"

"A nanny," she answered without hesitation. "Aldo said he was working on arrangements for someone to take care of the boy."

"What about Nanny Judy? Wouldn't she go with you?"

Melissa shook her head. "She wouldn't be needed in Papeete. Aldo and I don't like the way she's raising little Max. It's unnatural the way she treats him. We've talked about it. As soon as the divorce is final, little Max will spend half of his time with us. Mostly in Papeete, but sometimes in Hollywood, and half of his time with Max, in New York City. That part of the divorce is already approved."

"And have you told Nanny Judy?"

Melissa nodded. "That was part of the argument Max and I had. He hadn't told Nanny Judy. We argued about it. I know she hates me, but I'm little Max's mother. And I don't agree with how she keeps worming into his life, delusional and acting like she's his mother. She's his nanny and she never seemed to get that concept through her head from day one. She loves the boy and I knew it would devastate her when she learned of our plans. But Max hadn't told her."

"Told her what?" I asked.

"That she would no longer be needed full time," Melissa answered. "That Aldo and I would be hiring our own nanny and that she would only be needed by Max for half the year. Or maybe not at all. He hadn't decided."

"And when was he planning to tell her?" I asked.

"The last I knew, he was planning on suggesting she take a week's vacation to England to decide if she wanted to continue with her employment seasonally, part time, whatever you'd call it, while little Max was with us in Papeete."

"Did he ever tell her?"

"I assume he told her yesterday. On Christmas Eve morning, before she took little Max to the airport." She fished for her cell phone, her long fingernails scratching across the screen. I assumed she was looking for something.

"Here," she said as she handed her cell to me. I read the text aloud: "A text from J. Manning 12/24 at 4:45 a.m. PST. 'Five years. Every day of his life. And now this? Unbelievable, you heartless bitch. You won't get away with this.'"

CHAPTER 29

EVERYONE ELSE IN THE Williams party was scattered among the rooms at mezzanine level above gate B51 where little Max was supposed to leave for LA. Melissa was led down to the third door on the left where we'd sent Sinclair, leaving the interview room next door to our makeshift headquarters empty. Her attorney, Sinclair, was probably grilling her about what she had told us, likely still fuming about her dismissing him. The interview room on the opposite side was much smaller by comparison and I noticed the sliding dividers had been pulled tight. When I opened the door, I noticed Max and his attorney sitting at the far table by the windows. They had their backs to me and must not have heard me slip into the room. They thought they were alone. They were wrong.

The gorilla-sized attorney was saying to Max, "Agents Elmer and Fudd suggested that you two just don't seem sincerely concerned about the fact that your only son is missing."

"Agent Pierce and Chief Gates," Max corrected. "And FYI, the one you want to watch out for is the scary-looking brick of a man who acts like he's in charge—Agent Streeter Pierce. He's the one who can cut us a deal if we need it."

"Max, I thought you said you knew that bitch Bergen? Had this all sewn up? She looked as if she'd been in a bar brawl or something."

I couldn't disagree there. Max smiled, probably thinking the same about me. Scratches and bruises on my face, walking tenderly, and dressed like a vagabond. "I know her well. And I advise you not to underestimate her."

He was probably referring to the time Ida and I were in NYC at her opera debut and a pickpocket took Max's wallet and tried to take Ida's clutch. I had kneed the guy in the groin just long enough to retrieve both Ida and her purse and hustle everyone off the subway, grabbing the suit coattails of a stunned Max just to get him to move. He had warned me all through Ida's performance that we weren't in the Wild West and the guy could have stabbed or shot me—although he actually mentioned himself, not me or Ida—and told me to refrain from brawling in the future. My response at the time was simply, "I think what you meant to say is thank you," and I swore I'd never go back to the Big Apple as long as I lived. I thanked God that this asshole was not my brother-in-law and then asked for forgiveness for using the word "asshole" in my prayer, promising a renewed effort in this coming year's resolution.

"I recognize Pierce from the news. He gets a lot of coverage. One of the FBI's hotshots," the attorney explained. "The point is you and Melissa had better convince everyone that you are terribly upset."

I saw Max turn toward his attorney, his expression wounded, which surprised me. His words surprised me even more. "I *am* upset, Gil. My son is missing. Or did you miss that?"

The gorilla, otherwise known as Gilbert Alderman, didn't seem to hear. "If you are convincing, these agents will start looking for the real kidnapper, abductor, or murderer. Capeesh?"

"I understand, Gil," Max answered confidently. "Wait, what? Murderer?"

From the horrified expression on his face, I'd say it might very well have been the first time he'd even considered this outcome. I was starting to wonder if maybe my overwhelming dislike of Max might warrant a little reconsideration, given that he seemed to have softened over the years. After all, no one had ever accused Max of not loving Ida, just that he'd seemed hell-bent on changing her to match his ideal version of Mrs. Williams. It was something he and I had exchanged words over at one point with Ida begging us to get along. Which we pretended to do after that since Max wasn't the only one who loved Ida.

Alderman shot a look at Max. "I don't need any surprises. Are either of you behind this?"

Max didn't answer.

"Or aware of who might be?"

Good question, I thought. And exactly what we wanted to know, too.

Max drew in a ragged breath, the rawness in his reaction and words again a surprise to me. "I wish I did. I love that kid. And whoever's behind this is going to pay for scaring him like this."

Scaring him? Max was in serious denial here. A lot worse could be and is likely happening to the poor boy by now. I was thrilled to hear his concern for little Max was genuine, heartfelt. The look in his eye reminded me of the time he flew to Rapid City, begging me to convince Ida to reconsider her decision to leave him. His pain was real. His promises to change were not. And I didn't. And neither did Ida. What he had never quite grasped was that she was stronger than both of us ever hoped to be and if he had only seen that in her, she probably would have stayed with him.

"I just need to find whoever it is before the FBI does. Before they screw it up and the guy goes scot-free."

As heartfelt as his belief in our ineptness sounded, he was at it again. Not recognizing Streeter's talent and conviction, or mine.

"Max, they may never even find these people. They didn't even know your kid was missing for hours."

"Any time now, I'm going to receive a phone call from some jackass demanding money from me. I'll pay it. That's it," Max said. "How fast I pay depends on how much they want. Anyway, they'll get their money and I'll get little Max. Those imbecilic FBI agents are so busy investigating us that they're going to miss the jackass who's responsible for this crime. I hate incompetence."

"They won't find anything, will they?" Alderman pressed Max. "That you're involved in this somehow?"

I wasn't convinced that Alderman really wanted an answer from Max by his wishful tone.

"Of course I'm involved," Max rumbled. "Some asshole kidnapped my boy, my flesh and blood. And I intend to pay whatever they want to get him back unharmed."

Alderman grabbed Max's elbow. "How much money can you get your hands on?"

Something made Max glance toward the door. He saw me and I shut the door as if I'd just opened it and was coming in, unaware.

"Time to play musical rooms again," I called in a voice too loud for the small room. Nerves. For a moment, all they could do was stare, until I said, "Chop chop."

I observed his attorney gather his papers while Max walked straight to the windows.

At first, I wondered what he was doing until I figured out he was angling to get the best reflection of himself. Max stood before the windows and adjusted his blood-red, French silk tie and matching kerchief that protruded from the breast pocket of his Italian, custom-fitted, charcoal gray pinstriped suit. He smoothed his perfectly coifed, wavy black hair and leaned into the window, sneering. Flashing his porcelain veneers, he picked away any food remnants, real or imagined, which suggested any imperfection. Wiping the rheum from the corner of his eyes, he patted his cheeks. Giving them a rosy glow? For the interview cameras? Bizarre. Turning from side to side, he reviewed his appearance for a final time. And he liked what he saw.

"Are you about finished?" I said, crossing my arms and tapping my foot.

Both men said nothing and followed me to the interview room where Melissa had been only moments ago.

Max and his attorney Gil Alderman sat at one side of the table, Streeter, Gates, and I on the other.

"We know your time is precious," Streeter began. "And we know you're anxious to answer questions from the media, based on this written statement provided by your staff during the other interviews. But we ask that you refrain from holding a press conference. We have a case to solve and we'd prefer certain aspects not be leaked to the press. So we'd appreciate your cooperation on this."

"Absolutely," Max said. "Cut to the chase."

"Did you put little Max on the plane yesterday morning?" Gates asked.

He shook his head. "I did not. I kissed little Max goodbye around 8:00 a.m. yesterday morning. The boy's au pair, Judy Manning, took him to the airport and she safely transferred his custody to BlueSky Airlines around 9:00 a.m. The flight boarded sometime after 10:00 a.m. and the flight departed LaGuardia at 10:20 a.m. This is all Eastern time, mind you. And my lovely ex-wife phoned me at 3:45 p.m., which is the first I'd heard of my son's disappearance."

Precise, succinct, and practiced. Typical Max.

"And what did you pack?" Streeter asked.

"What?" His practiced, controlled smile faltered.

"For your son. What did you pack in his suitcase?"

He shrugged, looking uncertain.

"Did you pack his suitcase?"

"What does this have to do with anything?" Max's attorney asked.

"Mr. Williams told me to cut to the chase, so I am," Streeter grumbled. "Who packed the boy's suitcase?"

"The au pair, I suppose."

"But you don't know?" Gates asked.

"I work, Chief Gates. Do you know what it's like to have a kid at home when you're trying to work?"

"I think I might. Considering I have six of my own. And I'd know exactly who packs their suitcases and what's in it every time they travel."

"What's your point?" Max asked.

"Why didn't you bring the au pair tonight?" Streeter asked.

Max reached into his pocket, extracted a gold monogrammed box, and plucked out an expensive cigarette, flipping it between his lips. He was struggling to regain his composure from what I could see.

"I believe smoking isn't allowed in the airport," Gates said, leaning forward.

Without words and with only a slight nod, Max ignored Chief Gates and offered a cigarette to the rest of us, but there were no takers. He lifted a gold lighter to the stick between his lips. Cool, very cool, I thought. And practiced. I had seen Max do this a hundred times before in tense situations, mostly at family events. He used it as a stall tactic to give him time to collect his thoughts. Our family scared the shit out of him for some reason.

One time he told me if our family had been born in Italy, we'd be dangerous. I think it's because one of my siblings had just taken Max aside and warned him about verbally abusing Ida. We do have a tendency to cover each other's backs.

Max sucked the nicotine in long, hungry draws for many moments as he assessed us. His attorney seemed bored. Gates's face was stony, scary, pissed.

In what could only be described as the most uncomfortably long silence I had experienced since third grade when the kid sitting next to me had passed gas so loudly that Sister Delilah lost her place in catechism, I noticed Streeter studying the man's techniques, not the least bit tempted to shatter the silence and hand Max his first concession. I followed suit and kept my lip zipped.

Finally, Max asked, "So you think Nanny Judy had something to do with little Max's disappearance?"

"I didn't say that," Streeter said, leaning toward Max and leveling a look at him that I could only categorize as menacing.

Max said, "I told her she could have the week off. I assume she went back to Manchester. Who knows?"

"So you haven't contacted her about little Max's disappearance?" I asked, appalled at his insensitivity.

Streeter shot me a sideways glance before asking, "Do you think she had something to do with the boy's disappearance?"

"No. I don't know. It doesn't matter," Max said, acting defeated from my perspective. Then in classic Max style, he morphed into a pitiful character intending to evoke sympathy. "I assume someone is squeezing us for money. Of course, Nanny Judy came to mind. However, others who are much more ruthless, vindictive, and greedy shoot to the top of my list ahead of Judy Manning. And whether it's Judy or whoever, I have every intention of paying whatever it is they ask."

"Anything?" I asked.

Max looked toward me. "Why? Are you the one blackmailing me, Agent Bergen?"

"I think you mean kidnap, Max," I said, pointing out that he had just shared an important detail he might not have intended to. "Or do you want to talk about who might be wanting to blackmail you?"

Alderman interrupted, saying, "Where's this going? Is this an interview or an interrogation? Because I haven't heard you read my client his rights or anything. And to remind all three of you, my client's the victim here, not the suspect."

Gates leaned back, lacing his fingers behind his head. His expression made me think of a young Morgan Freeman during his PBS *Electric Company* years—cool, collected, and nailing the scene no matter how silly the skit. "The interesting thing is that when a child is abducted, chances are overwhelming that it's a parental abduction. Like eighty percent or something. And the balance is normally a nonfamily member abducting the child on behalf of a parent, one with money. Maybe one whose asset distribution case is bearing down on him like a freight train. Don't you find that interesting, counselor?"

Alderman glared at Gates and said, "I find it biased and patently unfair to my client."

"But you can see my point," Gates said. "And you told us to cut to the chase. From where I'm sitting, if I had a freight train bearing down on me, I might be tempted to stage a kidnapping and throw 'anything' at a ransom demand so I could tell the judge I had a lot fewer assets to distribute to my ex-wife."

Alderman pushed away from the table, his chair screeching against the tile. "Enough. Max, we're leaving."

Max's eyes landed on me and we shared a look that I knew to be a deciding moment for Max. I'd seen that look before. I'd pinned him with the same accusatory stare the last time I'd seen him with Ida, his fist cocked and ready to punch her. My stare had warned him that if he touched my sister ever again, he'd be very sorry. Just from my look, he could tell I would unleash the beast within me and fight him to the death, if he so much as harmed one hair on her head. He saw that the look in my eyes confirmed I would keep that promise. He knew I was making him the same promise if I found out he had touched one hair on little Max's head.

"No Gil, we're not. They're right."

CHAPTER 30

GIL ALDERMAN STOOD OVER his client with his mouth open and his hands lifted in exasperation. "What do you mean, they're right? Don't tell me you had any responsibility in little Max's disappearance?"

"No, no," Max countered. "Nothing as nefarious or as cunning. I'm saying that's what I'd be thinking if I were them. Now sit down, Gil. Or get out. We have work to do here. I wanted great minds like theirs on this case. That's why I asked for Agent Bergen. She has a great bullshit meter and cuts to the core quicker than any professional I've ever worked with."

"Thank you, I think?" I said, as all eyes turned my way.

As Gil slunk down in the chair next to him, Max looked at me and added, "Plus I know if she finds whoever did this, she'll rip them to shreds like a hungry pit bull."

I thought I noticed the tiniest hint of a smile on Streeter's lips.

I asked, "But isn't it true that your hope is to get to whoever did this first, because you're afraid we'll 'screw this up'?" I made sure he saw me making air quotes, eyeing him as I did it to let him know that I had indeed overheard much of his conversation with Gil.

He held my gaze, offered a grin that had "touché" written all over it, and said, "I meant it when I said cut to the chase. You have. You are. So let me cut to the chase myself. I most definitely want to get my hands on whoever did this before you get to him, before he's safely behind bars. I did not stage this abduction as a phony kidnap to hide assets, and I hope you don't waste time following that line of thinking. Because you'd be wrong. I really do want you to find little Max."

"So do we," Streeter said.

"And I'm not afraid to go to prison for destroying the person who took him, gentlemen," Max said, tapping ashes off his cigarette and waving his hands in surrender. "And lady, sorry Liv."

It was the first time he'd called me by my first name. A chink in his veneer?

"If I get to who did this before you do, you may very well be locking the cuffs on me and I will get what I deserve. And I will be happy with that outcome. But don't put the cuffs on too quickly for the wrong reason. If the odds are that this is a parental abduction, look on the other side of the ledger. Aldo Giottani hates my kid. Little Max is the only thing standing in his way to have a supermodel to himself. Think about it."

He took another long drag on what I could only imagine was a very expensive cigarette. "With Melissa and me being wealthy, high-profile celebrities, I suggest you broaden your scope a bit beyond the obvious to consider kidnapping for ransom."

"But there has been no ransom call," Streeter reminded him.

"And it's been less than twenty-four hours. And this is early Christmas Day. If I were taking little Max for ransom, I'd force the purse to suffer through Christmas morning without him before I made the call. Wouldn't you, Agent Pierce?"

I never said Max was stupid. I just said he was an asshole.

"That's fair," Streeter said. "So let's start there. Who would stand to benefit from kidnapping your son?"

"Besides Aldo Giottani? Just about anyone who knows me knows I'll pay anything to get my boy back."

"Anything?" I asked.

Max turned to me. "Why do you keep asking me that?"

I shrugged and answered honestly, "Because I always thought you were stingy with your money."

Alderman actually laughed out loud, which earned a reproachful look from Max. "You have me there. I do pinch every penny. But you knew me before I had a child. Children change things, don't they, Chief Gates?"

A chill ran up my spine the way he asked that of Tony. I was probably overthinking this, but Max seemed to be threatening him.

"They do," Gates growled. "But I'm confounded that any parent able to afford a private jet on both coasts would be willing to send a five-year-old off in the hands of a complete stranger to fly commercial. That doesn't strike me as a parent who cares much at all for the well-being and safety of his kid. What am I missing?"

Max smiled. "Agent Bergen?"

"What?"

"Well, you said it best. I'm stingy. That would have been an unnecessary cost. I prefer being called tight, but let's not quibble over semantics. And I believed since hundreds of thousands of children are escorted across this country each year with no incident, that little Max was quite safe in BlueSky's care. What parent wouldn't believe the same?"

Gates's expression hardened. "You seem to have an answer for everything."

"Tell me something, Max," I said. "If you'd give anything to get little Max back, how do you suppose Judy Manning will feel when she finds out little Max is gone? Hasn't she been the one raising him since birth?"

He shrugged. "She's a nanny. Nannies come and go. She'll move on to the next child needing a nanny."

"Is that what you told her? To move on to the next child who needs her?"

"Little Max starts school in the fall. Preschool after Christmas. Melissa wants him for summers and holidays and school breaks. Judy Manning has served her purpose. Things change. Life goes on."

"So you fired her?"

"Not exactly." Max smiled. "I cut her hours. To part time. Why pay more than you need to? You're right, Agent Bergen. I am a tightwad. That's why I'm a billionaire."

"Multimillionaire," I countered. "That's what I'd heard."

He raised an eyebrow. "With Judy Manning, I made it clear that she would no longer have a full-time job when the holidays were over, suggested she spend a week in England considering her options, and told her we'd talk when she returned."

"When was this?"

"Yesterday morning," Max said. "When little Max was getting ready to go to his mom's for Christmas. He was upstairs and Nanny Judy was waiting at the door for him. And no, Chief, I still don't know who actually packed my son's bag. All I know is that I didn't."

Streeter said, "How did she take the news?"

"Not well."

"Yet you sent your son, the one you care so much about, to the airport with a woman you just fired?" I asked.

"Not fired. I just cut her hours. And why wouldn't I send my son with her? That's what I pay her for."

"And it never once crossed your mind that she might be so upset that she'd do something stupid?"

Max was annoyed with me. "Again, I believe there are dozens of people who climb my suspect list over her. She's angry, not ruthless or greedy. Or stupid. She'd know better than most that I'd go after her with a vengeance. She knows what I'd do to her, if I ever found her."

The thought of her taking the child to another country popped into my mind until his eyes met mine again. Clearly, he meant what he said. And I was sure Nanny Judy would be fearful he'd make good on any threats. For the first time, I found an ounce of respect for his resolution to defend his son.

Max added, "So you think Nanny Judy might have kidnapped little Max to squeeze me for more money?"

Streeter shook his head, "Not any more than I think you planned it yourself. I'm trying to gather all the facts, Mr. Williams. That's how this works on our end. First priority, to find the boy. Quickly. Every passing minute makes the odds of us finding him that much more difficult."

"Then you shouldn't be wasting any more time with me." He crushed out the last of his second cigarette and stood to go, his attorney standing alongside him. We stayed seated. He added, "Nanny Judy told me this was Melissa's fault. That Melissa had always hated her and now she'd poisoned me, too. She said she had cared for little Max every day of his life for five years and didn't like being cut back to part time, that she should have the option of going with little Max to LA when he visited his mother. She asked me to talk with Melissa. To try to change her mind."

The whir of computers was the only noise in the quiet room. Max stood over us, his attorney by his side. Max's eyes were staring at something a long way off, something he was seeing in his head, not in the room.

His voice was nearly a whisper when he said, "She cried when she told me she had taught little Max a cute Christmas song to sing for Aldo. She told my son that if he was nice to Aldo then Aldo would tell Melissa to be nice to Nanny Judy, so she could come live with little Max in LA."

That explained why little Max had practiced singing "Feliz Navidad" in front of the attentive audience on the plane.

Max blinked, lowering his eyes to the table. Finally, he turned back to Tony. "Do you have any idea, Chief Gates, what it feels like to have someone you pay, someone you bring into your home to care for your fragile, impressionable child, tell you how successfully they've manipulated your child to get what they want?"

Gates stared at him. "No, I can't say that I have."

"Well then, please don't judge me when I tell you that I didn't fire her. But I do admit there was nothing more I wanted to do at that moment than to throttle her."

CHAPTER 31

THE MULTIPLE INTERVIEWS THAT followed lasted until well past two o'clock in the morning even though Streeter cut the interviews short after nearly an hour when he realized none besides the one with the Williamses would amount to anything. Losing precious time, Streeter told Max and Melissa they were dismissed, and the Williamses wasted no time whisking their friends and associates off to the private airport for all who needed rides home. Mr. and Mrs. Williams opted to stay in a local hotel. In two different rooms, I assumed.

After dismissing the impromptu debrief of agents and officers who had been involved in the interviews, Streeter, Tony, and I were once again left alone.

"Well, they sincerely seemed to know nothing about what happened to little Max," Gates summarized. "From my perspective."

Streeter put his hand over his mouth and rubbed either side of his jaw with his fingers and thumb. I couldn't get a read on whether he agreed with Tony or not.

"Maybe. But the way I see it, although they both love the child, I don't think either one really knew much about little Max," I said.

"Your Maximillian also pretended to know little about you, as well," Streeter added.

"Yeah, that was weird. And he's not *my* Maximillian."

"And their entourages—servants, attorneys, bodyguards? Hell, we should have rented the Bronco stadium," Tony said.

"Image is everything for people like them, I imagine," Streeter offered.

"I remember now why we all pleaded with Ida not to marry him," I said. "I know Melissa is a famous model and all. She is gorgeous and her compassion for little Max seemed genuine. She didn't strike me as someone who would risk her son in a feigned kidnapping just to get back at Max. What do you think, Chief? You've got kids."

"She didn't know much more about the boy than Max did. But I have to say, their love for the child seemed genuine."

"They seemed interested in finding out what we'd learned so far in our investigation. And although everyone loaded up on their private jets and flew back to LA and New York City, they both chose to stay here in Denver, neither one with a single assistant or bodyguard or anything. Does that strike anyone as odd? Or is it just me?" I asked.

"It made me believe they are both sincere in wanting to find their child," Streeter said. "But the jury is out, depending on if they heed my warning not to involve the press in any way. I have a sneaking suspicion Max has something up his sleeve with the media tomorrow."

"Why do you say that?"

"Just a hunch. What do you think, Tony?"

Streeter and I looked to Tony for confirmation.

"Either they were both in serious denial about the potential fate of their child or I'm afraid that the proverbial saying applies: Nobody's hands are clean."

I had to think about that. Thinking required pacing. If something had happened to their son, how did I expect them to react? Not realizing it, I had started to think out loud. "I'd be pissed, too, if the airlines misplaced my son. I'd probably blame my ex for not taking better precautions, for not flying with him, for not sending the private jet. Who am I to say they didn't care about their son? If my son ended up missing, I'd probably immerse myself in denial, too. Probably end up drowning in it."

I sat down on the edge of the table and in the process I knocked a cold cup of coffee over. Scurrying about case headquarters, I grabbed as many fistfuls of paper towels as I could and started dabbing. Putting one fistful of brown paper on the spill on the table, I dropped to my knees—groaning from the tug in my ribs when I did—and mopped up the mess on the floor.

Gates got busy mopping up the spill on the table.

"Thanks, Tony. Sorry, Streeter. How embarrassing. Did I ruin any of your papers? Anything?"

"No," he comforted. Reaching down and touching my shoulder, Streeter said, "Come on. Leave that. You were on a roll."

I looked up, staring at him from beneath my lowered baseball cap. "I get a little worked up sometimes," I said as I grabbed his extended hand, stood beside him, wiped my damp hands on my worn blue jeans, and straightened my cap.

"I didn't notice," he said with a grin, his breath warm and minty against my face.

I blushed and sidestepped his closeness. "I know Max well enough that he was manipulating the situation in there, but I have to tell you, I believe he has no clue who's behind the abduction and he has every intention of finding the person who did this before we do. And if he does, we will never have the opportunity to press charges or interrogate because we'll never find the body. Seriously. My sense is that Max is desperate to get little Max back and kill whoever's behind this." I wiped my palms on my jeans and paced. "But I have to admit, his love for his son is genuine and I'd listen to his instincts about the nanny, who would have been at the top of my suspect list right behind Max and Melissa before the interviews."

"And now?" Streeter asked. I knew he was testing me, trying to figure out if his influence in my becoming an agent was a worthy one. Up until now, I'd forgotten all about my desire to impress him and was just doing what came naturally. Now, I was wondering if I'd said anything I shouldn't have. Doubting myself.

I decided to just say what was on my mind. "Unless Max has become a better actor, I think he has a few suspects in mind who might end up wearing some concrete shoes before the sun rises and we'll never know about them. That's my belief."

"You really think so?" Gates asked.

I nodded. "He's an asshole, but I forgot to mention, he's also quite connected."

Streeter pursed his lips. "You don't have to tell me that."

I'd forgotten. After all, Max was able to get me assigned to the case.

"We need to talk with the nanny as soon as possible," Gates suggested.

"We're already on it. We've got people headed to her family's house in Manchester as we speak," Streeter assured him.

"What was your gut feel about those two?" I asked him.

Streeter cleared his throat. "People respond in these situations very differently each time, rarely how you would expect. My experience is that the worse the circumstance, the less predictable the response by loved ones of a victim."

Tony added, "But I agree with your assessment of the Williamses, Liv. They both seemed genuinely concerned."

"I hate to say this, but I had wondered whether Max had staged this whole event for some self-serving purpose," I mused. "Now I just don't know."

"Why? To what end? For money?" Gates asked.

I shrugged. "I don't know. At first I thought he might have staged this to hide assets in the divorce. After eavesdropping, I think he really is concerned about what happened to little Max. But then I started wondering again. I guess it was the way he decided to fly everyone back to New York in such a hurry. My mind went somewhere slippery. Like what if he had staged the abduction. And little Max is somewhere here in town. Max wouldn't want any witnesses to whatever he plans to do tonight. Maybe he plans to collect little Max. To make sure he's safe."

Both men stared at me.

"Well, for one thing, the nanny and Max may be in cahoots here, Streeter. The Max I knew wouldn't hesitate to hire the nanny to get little Max out of the country and blame it on someone else, just to save himself a few bucks on child support in the divorce. No matter what he's saying. Although my read is that it would be a long shot and wishful thinking, since that would mean the boy is alive and well somewhere. That would explain why Max sent everyone back to NYC."

Streeter said nothing. I couldn't tell if he thought I was crazy or if I was proving myself worthy and helpful on this case as I'd hoped.

"Or another option is that Max paid someone else to abduct little Max. Okay, say a kidnapper calls demanding ransom. Max pays it, gets his son back, and all of a sudden the divorce settlement owed Melissa goes down considerably, since his net worth drops by that sum of cash. The fact that he so adamantly denied that would be his intent is exactly why it made me want to look at it from that angle."

Tony stared at me like I was crazy. "Remind me to warn the poor bastard you decide to marry not to cross you."

Streeter chuckled.

"Am I missing something?"

Streeter wrapped an arm around my shoulder, still laughing. "Not a thing, Liv. What Tony's trying to tell you is that you have a fertile mind."

"Fertile as in bullshit?"

I might have enjoyed the feel of Streeter's arm around me if it weren't for the fact that I'd just noticed Jack was in the room. He must have come in while we had our backs to the door mopping up the mess.

He wasn't smiling and I suppose my smile appeared a bit guilty.

I slid out from under Streeter's arm. "Jack, did you get the beret?" Awkward. Noticing what he was holding, I said, "You brought food? For us? Thanks!"

I took the bags of burgers from him and set them on the table.

Gates said, "I'm famished."

Jack took a step toward the table, eyeing Streeter. "You were talking about the boy's father?"

Streeter nodded, taking a bite from one of the sandwiches Jack had brought. "Thanks, Linwood."

I said, "We were talking about the interviews of him and the mother. We were speculating about either the father or mother's involvement in little Max's abduction."

"I heard your speculation about the creative way he might hide money in a divorce."

"He already has more money than he knows what to do with, so I'll start getting suspicious if there's a call for an inordinate amount of ransom," I said, glad Jack had picked up a sandwich and joined the conversation.

"Kidnappers tend to keep demands reasonable to improve the odds of getting paid," Jack said.

"Exactly. Which is why I said I'll really start wondering if the amount is super high."

"You're forgetting one thing," Streeter said. "No ransom call."

"Yet," I said. "Like Max said, maybe the kidnapper wants them to go through Christmas morning without their son, to make them more apt to pay the ransom."

Jack said, "Statistics support what Liv's saying. Eight hundred thousand kids under the age of eighteen are reported missing every year and a quarter of them are abducted by family members. A fraction of those who end up missing, like only a hundred or a hundred twenty, are abducted by the stereotypical kidnapper asking for ransom or intending to keep the child for themselves. Or to kill."

"How do you remember all this? The statistics?" I asked, chomping another bite from the burger.

"He's a walking encyclopedia," Tony added.

Jack shook his head, grabbed his sandwich, and walked over to the windows.

I grabbed mine and followed him. "And the shoe polish? How does that fit in?"

"I think it means whoever has the child doesn't intend to kill him. Right away, at least."

"I agree," Streeter added. "Did you find any prints?"

"Dodson and Michelle are working on it. Our top priorities are to test the bottle of shoe polish, the smudge print on the beret, and the paper towels with the black dye and hair."

I leaned into Jack and whispered, "You okay with all this?"

He nodded once.

"I didn't say anything. About earlier," I whispered, hoping that would make up for the compromising position I'd found myself in with Streeter when Jack found us.

"Thanks," he said, kissing me on top of my head.

His kiss made me feel warm and I knew he held no grudge.

"What about Melissa? What motive would she have for little Max to be taken?" Gates asked, unwrapping a second burger.

"Publicity? Freedom?" I asked. "Or more likely, to torture Max."

"You told them we advised that they both sit tight and wait for some information, any information, before they started talking with the press," Tony said to Streeter. "You made yourself perfectly clear what the Bureau recommended. So publicity is out of the question."

"And wouldn't freedom for Melissa require that the child disappear forever?" Streeter asked.

I noticed the pain in Jack's face and wanted to say something comforting, knowing I should wait until later. In private. His authentic expression of torture made my mind's eye flash to the strange woman riding the underground trains earlier. The woman—riding the trains back and forth, back and forth, who avoided my eyes when I recognized her—seemed to have the same expression on her face. Haunted. Tortured.

Streeter answered his own question, "That just doesn't sound right for some reason. No mother thinks like that, unless she's psychologically twisted. I didn't sense that about Melissa."

"Aldo?" I asked.

"Maybe, but even Max said although he'd like to believe Aldo was behind this, he didn't really think him capable of it."

"Odd that Melissa didn't bring Aldo Giottani," I commented. "Do we have the list of passengers on the plane from New York? Aldo wasn't on that same plane, was he?"

I was thinking of the distraught woman on the underground train, the one I first thought of as a bag lady until I realized she must have a plane ticket since she was on the secure side of the airport. Had she turned away from me embarrassed because I'd caught her following me watching Beulah work?

Streeter moved to his computer and hit a key, the printer whirring to life. He handed me a single sheet. "I haven't looked at it yet, but the team didn't see his name or any other they recognized, but knock yourself out. Maybe a name will jump out at you because you knew Max in the past."

I scanned the list.

"What do you make of their request to hold a press conference?" Tony asked.

Streeter explained, "It may not make sense to us. But it does to them. Maybe the cameras are their comfort zone, the only way for them to regain control over this situation. During the interviews with us, they had no control."

"Speculating isn't getting us anywhere," Tony said. "Who's on our short list of suspects right now—Kevin Benson, his girlfriend, Max Williams, Melissa Williams, Aldo Giottani, and Nanny Judy. Who else might have had either motive or opportunity?"

My eyes went to the bottom of the list, to little Max's name, and worked backward from W for Williams. "You've ruled out Benson and I'd bet it's not the mother. Or Max, if I was being truthful."

"And you forgot it could be a stranger," Streeter said. "The nanny seems the most likely, which is why I initiated a search for her hours ago. She seems to have the most to lose by not being in the boy's life. The question I want answered is if one of these people *is* responsible for the child's abduction, then where is he? Who has little Max? What are they covering up? And who's lying?"

My eyes flicked toward Jack, then back to the list of passengers on the same plane as little Max from NYC, when my eyes landed on a name near the top of the list. A name I knew well. My fingers fished for my cell phone and with shaky fingers I punched in numbers.

"What is it? Liv, are you okay?"

I ignored Streeter, listening as the phone rang. She'd been sleeping. "Where are you?"

"Boots? What's wrong?"

"Just tell me, where are you?" I asked.

"In bed. At Mom and Dad's. Why? Is this about Max's son?"

"Yes. Max is here in Denver now. We're working on it. We'll find the little guy," I said, relieved to know she was nowhere near Denver. "Since when have you been home?"

"Uh . . . since last Friday. It's like four in the morning, right? What's going on?"

"Have you traveled anywhere since last Friday?"

"No, why?"

"I just wanted to know if you had heard about Max's son. And to tell you I was working the case. That's all," I lied.

"We'll keep praying for that little guy. No one deserves that worry, not even Max."

"Good. Go back to sleep. Merry Christmas." I hung up and stared at Streeter, shoving the list toward him, pointing near the top of the list.

"Ingrid Bergen," Streeter's voice rumbled.

"The famous actress? The one in *Murder on the Orient Express?*" Gates asked.

"Not Bergman. Bergen. My sister Ida. Ida Ingrid Bergen. She uses Ingrid as her stage name. She's an actress, model, and opera singer. I just called her and she's been in Rapid City, South Dakota, all week. Someone rode on the same plane using my sister's name. Or it's one helluva coincidence that someone has the same name."

Streeter said, "I don't believe in coincidences."

CHAPTER 32

I SNUCK BEULAH INTO Noah's room, hoping he'd be sound asleep. But I found Noah in bed staring out the window. Wide awake. I reached over to his bedside monitor and flicked it off. I felt his forehead to see if he had a fever and checked his diaper to see if he needed changing. His eyes were tracking, not listless, so I didn't think he'd had a seizure, but he seemed wiped.

I was exhausted, my mind racing with everything that had happened and with the idea that someone had posed as my little sister on a flight with her ex-fiancé's son. Again, it was too close to home, too close to my family. I climbed into Noah's bed under the covers with him and held him as we faced the window.

"What are you doing, Peanut? It's six o'clock in the morning."

He moaned softly and smiled in the fading moonlight.

"Waiting to see Santa?"

He didn't smile. I noticed his full stocking at the foot of the bed. "Oh, he already came. Did you catch him with your secret spy recorder?" Noah didn't smile. "Did you try?"

He smiled. Then I watched as his face grew still.

"Something's up. Are you okay?"

He still didn't smile. I noticed him staring out the window.

"You're not. Is it something you saw?"

Noah's smile flickered.

"What did you see out there? A mountain lion? Did I scare you with my story yesterday?"

Nothing.

"Of course not. You're brave. Or is it what you didn't see out there? Are you upset you didn't see Santa Claus?"

Still nothing. I stared in the same direction. He was staring at the window across from his, the only room of the neighbor's house with no window covering, the darkness within yawning.

"Did you see something at the neighbor's house tonight? Santa putting a lump a coal in the creepy guy's stocking?"

That made him smile, but it quickly faded.

"Seriously, did something happen over there last night? Something that's bothering you?"

Noah smiled. I stared at the house. It was dark, the shades drawn on all windows except the one across from Noah's room. No movement. "I wish I had night-vision goggles." He smiled. "Then I could see what you saw." He smiled again. "Did he scowl at you or something like he did last year when I gave you that flashlight? Asshole."

Noah's sigh was a mixture of elation and sadness, but the smile was there. Relief. I leaned my head against the headboard, my chin resting against his forehead. His skin felt warm. I was finally relaxed. Relieved. Noah always seemed to have a way of calming my nerves while reenergizing me. I loved being with him.

"Well, don't let him bug you. He's not the boss of you, kiddo."

Noah's laugh was weak, his bony shoulders jerking beneath the covers. I studied him and brushed the strands of brown hair from his forehead. Emma told me once that Noah hated when people touched his head, felt his hair, sometimes long and silky, sometimes cut short like Streeter's. A military flat-top. Noah turned his face toward mine and studied me.

"Have you been lying here thinking about the case of the missing backpack?"

Noah smiled.

"I wish I was as good at the five-finger method as your sister. Seriously, do you have a question about the backpack?"

Noah smiled.

"Let's see, have I figured anything out yet? No, because I've been working on that case at the airport. Did you?"

Noah didn't smile.

"Oh, sweet pea, you've got to get some sleep. Today's a big day. It's Christmas."

Noah's eyes searched my face.

"No, I have to go back to work. We still haven't found the boy yet. But we're all trying. I just wanted to bring Beulah back home so she could get some sleep. She did great last night. Found a lot of answers for us."

Noah rolled toward Beulah on the bed, poked her side with his stiff arms. She groaned and went right back to sleep.

"Oh, wait. I did learn something about the case of the missing backpack. Guess what? I found a name in the boy's backpack on some old homework stuck in one of the books. Well, at least a first name. Clint. Does that ring a bell?"

Noah looked perplexed. His eyes flicked up and his mouth moved to an "o" shape. I wasn't sure what that meant. "Thirsty?" No, that was when he poked his tongue out. He kicked his leg and his bony heel struck the top of my thigh. "Do you want me to get the stocking off the bed?" Nothing. His eyes found mine. "Something about the backpack I found?"

Noah smiled.

"Let's see. I told you the contents of the backpack. I told you about the two cars that appeared to be well worn, played with a lot; the candy wrappers, Milky Way. You figured out he was in the fifth grade because of the December field trip to the Baugh House."

Noah flung his arm toward me, smacking me in the arm. "What? You did, too. You figured that out. You told me the fifth graders went on field trips in December."

Noah smiled.

"And I found the notice in his backpack that the field trip was to the Baugh House at Historical Park."

Noah did not smile. What did that mean?

"You didn't know that they went to the Baugh House? I hadn't told you."

His face stayed hard and blank.

"Something more? Something different? Didn't the fifth graders go to the Baugh House?"

Again, no smile. No mistaking Noah's growing frustration with me.

"Did they go somewhere else?"

Noah flashed a quick smile.

"Hmm. That's strange. Better do some more homework."

Noah smacked my arm again.

"What? Is there something I left out? Did you figure out who it is already?"

No smile.

"Um, let's see. *Everyday Mathematics*. Fifth grade. Clint. Do you know him?"

No smile.

"Have you heard of a Clint at Pennington Elementary?"

No smile.

"That's weird. Small school. Do you know that there's not a Clint in the fifth grade?"

Noah smiled.

"There's not?"

He smiled wider and his arms stiffened, his legs crossed.

"It's a kid from Pennington named Clint, probably a fifth grader who likes playing with cars, who was planning to go on a field trip to Wheat Ridge Historical Park's Baugh House. But you say the fifth graders didn't go to Baugh House this month and that there is no one at your school named Clint. Is that where we are with this mystery?"

Noah smiled.

"Then whose cool camo backpack do I have in the back of my Explorer?"

Noah smiled and sucked in a loud, gleeful sound.

"Shh, you'll wake up the whole house. I've got to go back to work. You think about it and let me know if you figure out whose backpack I have. You should come with me to return it, don't you think?"

Noah smiled and then grew serious again, staring off at the neighbor's house.

"And I'll make sure to tell the creepy guy next door to quit scowling at you or whatever he's been doing at all hours of the night that's keeping you awake. Or maybe I'll rustle up some night-vision goggles and we'll spy on him tomorrow night. See what he's up to."

Noah smiled and closed his eyes, his lids growing heavy. I stayed a few more minutes until he fell asleep, his face precious and innocent, his breathing as soft and sweet as a baby's.

I stroked his soft cheek, wishing I could stay with him all morning. But I couldn't. I kissed his cheek and smiled.

CHAPTER 33

THIS WAS THE FIRST time all night that the boy hadn't trembled as he slept. The first three times he awoke, he tried to assure the child his parents would come for him. Someday. That didn't seem to bring any comfort to the boy. He wasn't sure the tot believed his story at all about how the boy's father had asked him to collect him at the airport. But he seemed to believe his mother had gotten too busy to pick him up—good guess on his part that she might be self-absorbed, like so many mothers were these days—and would be here soon. He seemed to like the idea that in the meantime they'd play some fun games together until she arrived. But it was the endless supply of M&M's that seemed to calm the boy the best. Parents underestimate the power of candy when they raise their kids totally deprived of having regular treats. Rewarding a well-behaved child with his favorite candies had always been the quickest way to allay a child's fear, from his experience. Up to a point. Older children took a bit more convincing.

When they'd first arrived home last night, the child had cried for the first time when he first saw his reflection in the mirror, until he learned the shoe polish he'd put on the boy's hair was only temporary, just pretend. He'd stopped crying once he saw how easily the color came off between rolled fingertips. He demonstrated this to the boy over and over, pinching the long locks of hair well after the boy had fallen asleep, the pads of his fingertips covered in bluish black stain, not unlike the ink at the one-hour photo shop where he worked. No one would even notice his smudged fingers, since he had stained fingers all the time. He lay beside the child in the dark, feeling him trembling for hours, sure the boy was too afraid to make so much as a whimper.

In dawn's first light, the boy looked calm, relaxed, and rested in his effortless sleep. The morning rays stroked the boy's flawless cheek. He looked angelic, innocent. Yummy. The flash of his bulb did not awaken the boy. He lay nestled against the pillow, his black locks of hair splayed this way and that, his bare shoulder in the well-heated room poking out from beneath the covers.

A cherub, he thought. A tasty cherub.

His camera flashed again and the boy stirred. He stood motionless above the boy's bed, willing him to sleep undisturbed by his activities. He studied the child's worry-free face and wondered how the young boy so easily and readily swallowed the whale of a tale he had told him, about his mother not getting all her Christmas shopping done and wanting to be ready by the time the boy saw her, and his father requesting the child stay with him until his mother finished finding exactly what this little tike wanted.

He wondered what miserable kind of life this poor tot had before he had saved him from all of it. How could he so eagerly believe his parents had asked this man to pick him up at the airport because they were too busy to spend any time with him anymore? On Christmas Eve, no less? How long would this child stay so naïve, so fresh? How long would he have before the boy would begin to ask more questions? How long before it was no longer too good to be true?

The cherub snorted in his sleep, which brought a smile to his lips.

He saw himself in this boy's hauntingly beautiful eyes. Mother, always gone, working. Father, a worthless drunk, predictable only in that he routinely beat his kids. A loveless home where the beatings were the only attention, and a rough shove into a dark closet the only human contact he had ever had. He became morose at the thought and his soft cheeks drooped to a sorrowful scowl. He had been so lonely since his mother's death seven years ago. So incredibly lonely.

Until this Christmas. It was a great Christmas. With Sammy. Not lonely. The best Christmas since his mother died. No. The best Christmas ever. Sammy was the best thing that had ever happened to him. Oh, he had hosted little visitors before, but not for very long. Sammy was different. He understood him. He'd obey. He'd stay.

He reached down and brushed a strand of the black hair from the boy's ear, dragging his finger against the tiny, bare shoulder. The sleeping child shivered and he pulled the covers up over him.

Sammy. My Sammy.

Ah, the gullibility of pampered five-year-olds, he thought. How easily the tot believed his explanation that whenever a child moves to a new home, he must receive a new name and his hair must match his new parent's, even if it was temporary. Black hair had become easy for the boy formerly known as Max, now his precious little Sammy, after two bags of peanut M&M's. And when he asked the boy about his grandparents, he was delighted when the boy told him he had none except one named Papa whom he'd never met before.

The boy was just like him!

No grandparents, except a man his mother called Papa now and again, when she sat staring at the living room couch and the sprawling form of his father, reeking as if he'd soaked in rubbing alcohol all day. She was too tired to care. He never remembered meeting his Papa, either. So he decided to let the boy call him Papa, even though he wasn't old enough to have a grandson yet. Papa could double for Dad, which he would become. In time. The boy needed space for now, to learn to trust him. He would treat Sammy as his own. Give him the care and attention he never learned from his own parents, may they rest in bloody peace. He would be different from them. He would protect the child from harm. He would never raise a hand to the boy. Never beat him. Never.

He was so grateful to have found Sammy. He had spent his entire adult life scanning pictures of kids—kids who had loving parents, kids who had lots of attention at home, kids with childhood riches that can't be bought with money. He could see it in their eyes. Smiling eyes. Only a few had smiles on their faces and sadness in their eyes. A sadness so dark and omniscient it could only be born of lousy parents. Absent parents. A sadness he understood. A sadness that he spent a lifetime trying to reveal in the darkroom at work in the photos he would develop of that child, hoping someone would notice. But they never seemed to. He cursed those parents along with his own and longed for an opportunity to make a difference in one sad child's life.

Sammy could be that child, he thought. He could make a difference in Sammy's life. This could be his opportunity. He would care for Sammy. Be tender to Sammy. Love Sammy. Sammy would soon forget all about his once-blond hair, his parents living on both coasts. The child had described having homes "in the Big Apple and in the Big Orange," which he understood meant NYC and LA. They were probably divorced, or very rich—bicoastal parents to contend with, and a troublesome nanny.

The nanny.

Nanny Judy is the only person the boy seemed to talk about. To care much about. The trembling must be attributable somehow to him missing her. He wondered if the nanny had the same attachment to this lost child as the boy seemed to have for her. If so, she would be looking for him. She would not give up until she found him.

He would need to work fast.

He touched the boy's head one last time as he decided it was time to make breakfast for the two of them. As he turned from Sammy's bed, something caught his eye. He peered out the window above the bed and saw the neighbor boy lying along the second story bay window in the house across from Sammy's room. It was as if the older boy's gray eyes were staring at him, watching him, boring through him like a piercing hot poker.

He studied the boy in the picture window and could see his arms pulled into his chest, his body lying supine, bent and unwieldy. He had seen the older boy before—maybe a teenager—sitting in the driveway in his wheelchair, grunting noises that were beyond recognition. He couldn't speak. At least he didn't think so. He was retarded or something. Yet he was lying there staring across at him like he knew something, like he saw something with those dead, gray eyes.

He yanked the blinds closed, unnerved by the thought of those eyes. Too much like his mother's accusing eyes seven years ago. Before the blowflies discovered her. Then the maggots. He recalled the smell that had lingered on his clothes every day when he left for work. Eventually, he moved into an apartment. But they never found his mother with those gray, judgmental eyes. Eyes that would never land on him ever again. Or Sammy. He would make sure of it. He would protect the child from anyone who judged.

He shuddered, staring at the closed blinds.

He convinced himself that the neighbor boy in the window had no knowledge about what was going on over here and no ability to tell anyone about it, even if he did. Sammy stirred in his early morning sleep. Awareness of Papa's heavy breathing and even heavier sweating brought him stillness.

He was in the kitchen when Sammy padded down the stairs. "Morning, sleepy head. You're finally awake. You want some breakfast?"

Sammy straightened his shirt. "Coming, Papa."

He had adjusted to calling him Papa as easily as he had adjusted to the thought that his parents were simply too busy for him. Sad.

Sammy asked, "There's a little redheaded girl playing in the backyard next door. After breakfast, can I go out and play with her? Please?"

Papa smiled. So far, Sammy had obeyed every house rule. Dressed. Face washed. Hair combed. Never leave the house without asking first.

"Did you make your bed?"

"Yes," Sammy said smiling. "Can I go outside?"

Papa's grin superseded a pat to his knee, encouraging the boy to come sit on his lap. Happy to see the boy's willingness to please him and be compliant, Papa knew the boy was ready for the next step. He lifted the boy onto his lap and held him close, stroking his small back, and whispering into Sammy's ear. "Not today. Today's special. It's Christmas!"

"Did Santa Claus come?"

The smile on the cherub's face was everything he hoped for. Santa had most certainly paid a visit.

He nodded. "Santa left a surprise for Papa's little Sammy. Do you want to see?"

The boy rubbed the sleep from his wide, green eyes as he ducked around the stairs to peer into the living room and kitchen. "Where?"

"In the basement."

CHAPTER 34

I WAS SURPRISED BY how quickly we arrived at the Federal Building on Stout Street downtown. Must be because no one in his right mind would be out at 8:30 in the morning on Christmas. Not even in Denver. Streeter punched in his security code and held open the door marked "FBI—Investigative Control Operations" on the seventeenth floor, directly below our offices.

"Thanks for waiting for me. And thanks for letting me take Beulah home."

"No problem. You could have grabbed some shut-eye and a shower before coming back."

"And miss all the excitement? Never." I wondered aloud, "By the way, have we found Judy Manning?"

Streeter raised an eyebrow. "No, the New York Bureau is on it. They haven't found her."

"Didn't Max say she went to Manchester, England, for the holidays?"

"Supposedly. But her family said she didn't come home for the holidays. She wasn't at her NYC apartment either. I know Jerome Schuffler at the NYC Bureau and he'll find her. He said once he does, we can video conference with him, if we'd prefer."

"Can we do that?"

"We can do whatever we want. Chandler's cleared the way for us." The derisive tone suggested Streeter wasn't at all grateful for the extra "help." Couldn't say that I blamed him.

The Investigative Control Operations was a maze of laboratories, computers, research units, and study cubicles. Jack Linwood's office was directly below Streeter's. When we entered, Jack surfaced from the ocean of files splayed on his desk and floor.

"Linwood," Streeter greeted.

"Streeter, Liv," Jack said, his eyes lingering on me. "Either of you get any sleep yet?"

I shook my head. Streeter did the same.

"Me neither. No time even for catnaps at this point."

Even without sleep, Jack possessed the striking good looks of an exotic prince—standing tall and lean with dark skin and hair, with powerful hands, shoulders, and eyes. He looked like he belonged on a lacrosse field, not in a research lab. I was glad we had cleared the air last night. There was no reason for me to be jealous and every reason to open my heart to this man.

"Thanks for bringing burgers and sandwiches for everyone. Thoughtful of you," Streeter said. "And most necessary, since everything was closed at DIA."

"Anytime."

"The best part about DIA between midnight and five in the morning is that there are fewer people to negotiate through and around. I worked the heck out of Beulah, validated all her findings, and searched the parking structures." I realized I was still dressed like a vagabond and I'd also worked up a sweat trotting through the miles of parking structures with Beulah, and I smelled even more frightful than I looked. I wished I had taken a shower while I was at Frances's house, but I was afraid I'd wake everyone.

"No body?" Linwood asked me.

I shook my head. The relief on his face was evident. I enjoyed the intoxication of Jack's attractiveness, could see what Bessie and the other ladies in the Bureau were talking about. How his rare expressions of contrition were even more alluring than his occasional smiles. Mostly he showed no emotion.

"But Beulah did indicate some kind of confusion or hesitancy in the short-term parking area. She may or may not have picked up little Max's scent there. Probably faint, but overpowered by the shoe polish."

"Which would make sense. Where?"

"In fairly close proximity to the exits near the Buckhorn Bar and Grill." I pointed the area out to Jack on the map.

"That helps," Jack said. "What Liv just told me confirms what we're thinking about how the boy left DIA. Which is why I called you down here."

Jack cued up several screens of airport videos captured on Christmas Eve, showing us what his team had found so far. The images were mostly in grayscale, which meant it was difficult to determine faces, since the pictures weren't really clear.

"We know the boy didn't leave the airport through the garbage. Nothing there."

"I heard you made sure of that. Personally," Streeter said.

Jack shot a look at me. I quickly confessed, "I told him you found the shoe polish."

I didn't blame him for being angry with me for ratting him out, but I wanted Jack to get credit for discovering the black dye, especially if it turned out Jack's speculation that it was used to disguise the boy turned out to be fact.

I wasn't happy that Streeter was making me regret my choice to tell him about Jack's find, until Streeter added, "Good call. We wouldn't have gotten the possible lead that we're looking for little Max with black hair if you hadn't stayed to pick."

It was as if Streeter read my mind. Jack and I both let out a breath, neither realizing how tense we'd been about Streeter's reaction.

Jack continued, "We've completed our airline record search of all listed passengers aboard connecting flights between 12:45 p.m. and 5:45 p.m., when the child was officially reported missing to the police. I added an hour to that timeframe in case the airport security or airline employees missed the APB. All passengers and their flights were confirmed as legitimate. I am comfortable ruling out that the boy left DIA via a connecting flight, unless he was checked through as baggage," Jack said unceremoniously.

I cringed at this thought, hoping Jack couldn't possibly be serious. But of course, he was. That was his job.

Streeter said, "And we have thoroughly searched the airport several times using Denver PD, focusing on potential hiding places like closets, doors, cupboards, compartments, every tiny space. Plus, we had Liv work the airport using Beulah and she's gone through every square inch, including the parking garages, using the beret as the scent target." Streeter tossed the evidence bag with the child's cap on Jack's desk. "It's all yours, depending on where you're going with all this."

"So you'd both agree there's no evidence to indicate little Max was left behind in the airport, either intentionally or accidentally?" Jack asked.

We both nodded.

"And he didn't walk. DIA covers more than fifty square miles and temperatures were near zero to subzero. Or maybe it's more accurate to say that if he did leave on foot, he wouldn't live to talk about it," Jack said.

"Unless little Max took off earlier in the day and someone picked him up, which means we're still dealing with an abduction since DPD received no calls that a five-year-old boy was found along the road or in a barren field around the airport," Streeter said.

"That's what we came up with," Jack said. "So it's improbable the boy left by plane, through the garbage, by foot, or is still in the airport. That leaves escape by car, by public transportation, or in service vehicles. Our team has completely exhausted all service vans and units that departed from the airport within fifteen minutes of the boy's arrival from LaGuardia to several hours following. Every vehicle and company checks out."

A gorgeous, tall woman in a tight skirt and thin blouse—too thin for a winter morning in the Rocky Mountains, by the looks of it—strode efficiently into Jack's office and interrupted them. "Excuse me, Jack? You said you wanted to see this right away?"

"Yes, thanks Noreen," Jack replied, reading the file as he dismissed her.

I noticed Jack had barely noticed the vixen, fixated instead on the documents she was delivering. Good to know, since it would be easy to feel insecure. Again, I took inventory of my stench, my scuzzy jeans and T-shirt beneath the oversized sweatshirt and winter jacket I had wrapped tightly around me, which caused me to sink further into my chair.

"Is she Cathy's new replacement?" Streeter asked, watching Noreen walk out of the office and back to her cubicle.

Jack nodded while he read.

I adjusted my baseball cap and grinned at Streeter's blatant wolfishness. How could people around here in good conscience spread the rumor I'd heard about Streeter Pierce my first day in the office? If the expert way he kissed me wasn't proof enough, how about the fact that he had been married before? Or the way he appreciated beautiful women like Noreen and Jenna Tate? He definitely preferred women. And how much more blatant could he be about it?

He must have noticed me watching him or heard me snicker because Streeter cleared his throat and held a finger up to his lips, hushing me as Jack read. The impish spark in his eye made it harder for me to stay quiet.

Jack dropped the file on his desk. "That's what I was afraid of. Not enough of the partial print from the beret to make a match. We'll keep trying. With the hair dye, I'm focusing my team's efforts on the belief that the boy is still alive, at least for now, and that the perp and/or the boy left DIA by car or by public transportation. Because if he's not, we have all the time in the world to find his body."

I couldn't help but notice how easily Jack distanced himself from the subjects: the perp, the boy. No names. Cold. Everyone coped in a different way. Jack coped clinically. Maybe he had to, given his history with losing a son.

"We need an image from the surveillance videos to narrow our search. I was thinking that we know the path Kevin Benson took from gate B31, down the escalators to the underground trains, coming up to the main terminal and to the Buckhorn Bar and Grill. But we've found scant video evidence of his movements, even knowing the time and path. And nothing after the bar."

He played four short clips of videos, first with untouched footage, then enhanced footage where the subject—Kevin Benson carrying little Max—was highlighted, the rest shadowed to help focus our eye.

"That's it. These four clips from the numerous cameras mounted in the airport."

"Someone can easily avoid detection if they know what they're doing," Streeter concluded.

"See? Benson carrying the boy. Clearly the child has blond hair, even though this is grayscale video. Our team's still looking. Focusing on all children in his age range."

I wouldn't have recognized Benson if Jack hadn't pointed him out. Or little Max. The video's vantage point was from above and the images were of low quality. With the enhanced, highlighted version, it was clear that Benson was carrying little Max, but I marveled at how keen their eyes were to pinpoint them in the first place amid all the distracting images.

Jack continued, "This is tedious. And we haven't gone through each video as thoroughly as I'd like. But we don't have time for thorough. We need a break. We're keying in on the exits closest to the Buckhorn Bar and Grill and watching those videos first. If we exhaust all our options with those videos but find nothing, then it becomes a bit more problematic."

"Disguise is the most successful technique used in abductions. You've been watching for black-haired boys, but make sure you watch for other changes," Streeter suggested.

"So much time between when it happened and when we found out makes the Amber Alert nearly impossible to be effective. Especially given that witnesses have traveled to other places and maybe don't even know about the missing boy. No wonder we've gotten nothing." I closed my eyes and rubbed the bridge of my nose. I was tired.

"You need some kind of physical description of the abductor or you can't narrow down the car and the license plate identifying him on the videos above the tolls," Streeter said.

"Right," Jack said.

"Or we need a witness," I said. "Beyond the man at the bar who saw Benson with little Max."

"Which is unlikely, given the first twenty-four hours in any abduction are critical," Streeter said, looking at the clock. "And we're at twenty hours since the alleged abduction now. We haven't had any credible information coming through our tip lines yet."

Jack said, "Our guys are documenting every car that went through the tolls for future reference. They're designing a special database to link with the National Automotive Altered Numbers File so we can refer to it if we need to. The information will help if we can narrow down the perp's license plate."

"Good plan," Streeter said.

"Although I think it's a waste of time, they'll also be looking at the video glimpses the cameras catch of the people in the front seat of the car as they drive through the gates."

Streeter said, "Whoever did this would more likely have thrown the child in the trunk or backseat. Probably bound and gagged him to be safe. Maybe even drugged him at some point."

"An airport camera image of who had the boy last would make it quicker for us to correlate to a license plate."

I asked, "What about public transportation? What do we have there?"

"Nothing." Jack frowned. "Except on the service vehicle end of things. The exit system for the taxicabs, hotel shuttles, and buses is totally independent from the tollgates. The public transportation goes through special automated departure lanes requiring a specially issued identification card. They do not monitor those lanes of traffic."

"And if the abductor was organized enough to have shoe polish, it is unlikely he'd risk taking public transportation. And somebody or several people would have seen the boy with his abductor. We should be able to rely on the Amber Alert to flush that out," Streeter said.

"I agree," Jack said. "And ironically, with Melissa being an international supermodel from LA and Max being the highest-profile tycoon and developer in Manhattan, they will undoubtedly grab headlines for days. The boy's picture will be all over the news. We might get lucky if someone saw something and lets us know about it, or if the kidnapper makes a ransom call soon. It's a waiting game from here on those developments. And it may be all luck."

I stared at the screen, watching different videos from airport cameras streaming on several monitors. "But we're not going to wait, are we?" I said, frustrated by the thought of doing nothing. "We can't just sit around. We have to do something."

"We have plenty to do," Streeter said. "I agree with Linwood. If we can help him narrow the search on videos, we can get a description so he can get something useful on the toll videos. If we have that, we have a name and an address."

"Unless he stole a car," I said, an image on one camera catching my eye.

The image was of a woman, her head turning right and left and peering over the heads of travelers as if she'd lost something. Or someone.

"Not likely," Streeter said. "Let's work on eliminating the most likely scenarios first and work our way out to those unlikely scenarios."

I leaned forward and watched as the woman pushed her way through the crowd, disappearing off camera, and then coming back on.

Jack added, "Our immediate goal is to get a description of the abductor or abductors."

"You have the diagram Linwood's team mapped out of the airport cameras," Streeter said to me. "Work on how the boy could have been taken out of the airport undetected from that bathroom to the short-term parking where Beulah hesitated. Linwood, continue to review the airport videos and building the tollbooth license plate database. We'll get you Liv's ideas as soon as she comes up with them to help you narrow your search. Highest priority is if you can verify little Max's hair was dyed black and if your team can match that smeared thumbprint."

Something about the woman in the video struck a chord with me. I felt a gut instinct telling me the mother had lost her child. Her desperation was palpable, relevant.

"Taylor's on it," Jack said, tapping the file Noreen had just brought him. "Nothing yet. Too smudged. Slow process trying to isolate line by line of a print. What we have is not enough to get a match. We'll keep working on it."

"Keep trying," Streeter said. "The rest of your team can look for anything or anyone even remotely suspicious in those tollbooth videos, for a mistake. As a lower priority, work on the public transit angle."

"Maybe if we try a different direction—the potential that the abduction was arranged by someone who knew little Max or the parents—we can determine the motivation and find the guy from that angle. I'll work on the possibility that this might have something to do with the nanny."

"The nanny," I repeated, wondering what she looked like, while staring at the image of the woman pushing her way past people on the escalator to the underground trains. I recognized her. It was the same woman who had been watching me and Beulah trail, the one on the trains.

"I sent Gates home for a few hours. He had six bright, smiling faces who needed him by the tree for Christmas morning," Streeter explained.

"He fought me on it, but he knew it was the right thing to do. Plus I wasn't about to disappoint Lenora again."

"Streeter. Jack," I called, realizing what I was looking at. Their eyes followed mine to the monitor I was studying. My mind was trying to compare the image of the woman I remembered on the train to the photos in the file from Max's pile. "Jack, rewind. More. Look."

The men stared at the screen, watching people mill about the down escalator to the trains at Concourse B, and saw the dark-haired woman searching the airport.

Streeter whistled.

"Right," I said. "I noticed her on the trains because she kept showing up on each of my searches with Beulah. I tried to get her attention, but she pretended not to notice and turned away. Do we know who she is?"

"That's why Jerome Schuffler couldn't find her," Streeter said.

"Find who? Who's Jerome Schuffler?" Jack asked.

"NYC Bureau. They've been looking for the nanny," Streeter said.

"That's the boy's nanny?" I yelped. "Why is she in Denver?"

"Can you improve the feed, zoom in, add pixels, or whatever it is you guys do? So I can tell for sure?" Streeter asked.

Jack's fingers flew across the keyboard. The images slowed, offering a frame-by-frame view of the desperate woman. Jack zoomed in on the frame, the nanny's face looking up to the second floor of Concourse B, offering the best image of her face. The focus sharpened.

"I'll be darned," Streeter said. "Judy Manning. We've been looking for you. Good catch, Liv."

"Streeter, look," I sat down at a computer terminal outside of Jack's office, logged on to my Bureau account. I went into my personal email account and pulled up a family photo that my oldest sister had sent. I zoomed in on one of my siblings. "Look. Long dark hair. Like Judy Manning. Similar features."

"Ida?" Streeter asked.

I nodded. "Judy's not as tall or as thin, but she could pass as Ida."

Streeter barked orders. "Check hotel reservations under Ingrid Bergen."

"And Ida lived in NYC, lived with Max. Maybe she left an old driver's license or passport behind," I speculated.

"Well, this changes everything."

CHAPTER 35

Noah

OH MY WORD!

First, I've never seen anyone in that bedroom before and now I not only saw a child in the window late last night, but this morning, too. Creepy man is lying in bed with the kid. And why is he wearing pants and a shirt instead of pajamas? Why wouldn't Mr. Fletcher sleep in his own bed? Maybe creepy man wet his bed and didn't want to change the sheets in the middle of the night. Or maybe the kid was scared, being in a new place, and creepy man crawled into bed with him so he wouldn't have nightmares. And fell asleep. Sometimes Dad does that.

I didn't like the way the man glared at me this morning, like I'd done something wrong. Or how he slammed the blinds shut. WHAM! How rude!

It's Christmas and everyone should be happy.

I'm happy because I kept my soul and didn't die before I woke up. Little victories. I've been awake for hours. I decided to roll off my bed to my window. Dangerous, since it's a long drop to the floor and my skinny bones could break so easily. But I had to. Not because I was still looking for Santa and his reindeer. I gave up hours ago. I rolled off and got closer to the window so I could search for mountain lions creeping around my backyard at dawn. I didn't see any, but maybe they're home with their families, too.

It's Christmas!

When I rolled off the bed, my toes hooked the stocking and it tumbled to the ground along with me. I had to muffle my laugh every time I inched closer to the window, since I could feel chocolates and hard candies poking my back and my ribs. They smelled good when I squished the soft ones.

I can smell the cinnamon rolls baking, which means Mom is awake. She must not have heard me thump on the ground at dawn or she would have come in to see if I was okay and changed my utility britches. I bet Auntie Liv forgot to turn on my bedside monitor again. Mom's going to be mad at her.

Even though my britches are foul, I can smell the breezy outdoors. That's what it smells like. A breeze. At first, I couldn't figure out what carpet deodorizer my mom was using lately. I appreciate Mom's efforts to make the carpet smell the best possible. She was doing it for me, since I spend so much time lying here. But I'd grown tired of the floral scent she had used for weeks since Halloween. Too . . . too flowery. Yuck. The breezy scent was better.

The smell of fresh oatmeal makes me ache for breakfast. I know Mom made that special for me, since I'm the only one who likes it. Everyone else will eat the cinnamon rolls. I'll have one of those, too, I hope.

I'm tired of staring out the window because I think the mountain lions are all home by now. And I can't see through the blinds anymore, so no chance of spotting the child. Or the creepy man again. My fanny was starting to get a little sore, since I dirtied my utility britches hours ago. I decided to take my mind off my empty stomach and my sore bottom by playing with the rubber snake that Santa Claus had brought me last year.

Maybe Mom had forgotten about it and I could scare her again. Mom hates snakes. The snake is lying between me and the window, maybe six inches from my side. It might as well be a mile.

Concentrate. If I focus on the muscles in my right arm and try real hard to reach for the snake, sometimes I can make it happen. It just takes a lot of focus. And time. All I have to do to touch the foot-long, green rubber reptile is extend my arm until my elbow, wrist, and fingers uncurl. Doesn't seem like much, but for me, it's a huge ordeal.

I grunted, focusing intently on the snake.

After several attempts of accomplishing nothing but some wild jerks with my arm, I have decided to roll over toward the snake instead. I twisted my long, skinny legs, turned my head in the same direction, and pulled my bony shoulders until I'm almost overturned from my back to my stomach. The strong muscles in my neck allow me to eventually overcome the opposing force of my bunched-up arm and leg muscles. Flipping my forty-five pound, four-foot frame onto my stomach and bent arms, I rest my head on the carpet face down to give my tired neck a break and give a moan because I'm proud of my accomplishment. I rest before continuing with my next task, snake retrieval.

Scaring my mom is almost as much fun as spying.

My mom called from the doorway. "Noah? Where'd you sneak off to?"

I raised my head to show my mom the smile, so she wouldn't worry. I was right here.

"Well, good morning, Beulah. I didn't hear Liv come home last night. And we had one little monkey jumping on the bed again. Or was this a prison break? Let's change those britches, Noah."

I moaned approvingly and said *thanks*, but what I heard myself say was nothing more than jabber. If only I could say and do what my mind was thinking.

"You'll have to be patient until your dad gets some pictures of you and Emma under the Christmas tree. Santa came and he brought lots of presents."

Although I could not control my muscles well enough to pronounce words clearly except for an occasional "I go," I have mastered the art of communicating, at least with a few people who cared to notice. My lips tighten into a small circle if I'm disgusted or don't like something. I stick my tongue out over and over when I'm thirsty. And when I poke my tongue out and leave it there, I'm full. I'm done eating. I have a lot of friends at school, at church, and in the neighborhood who all know when I like something, because I laugh or smile.

Emma says I'm popular.

I have so many friends, I can't even remember all their names or where I met them. But they all know my name. It makes me happy when people say "hi" to me, even if I don't know their name. Especially when they tell me at first they were scared of my wheelchair. Some kids are. Mostly little kids. But once they tell me that, I know they're not scared of the chair anymore. Emma said she's jealous of me at school. That bothers me, because I don't want her to feel that way.

Mom was still doing something in my bathroom when I heard Emma coming around the bed. "Mom, come quick! It looks like an elf puked in here!"

I laughed, remembering all the candy I'd spilled from my stocking when I rolled off the bed. Mom and Emma laughed with me.

Emma flung herself on the carpet beside me. "Merry Christmas, Noah!"

I lifted my eyes. *Merry Christmas to you, too, Emma*, I tried to say, but all I could hear was gurgling coming from my throat.

"Couldn't wait to see what Santa brought you, huh?"

I grinned. I made my face go serious, my eyes searched for Emma. "What?"

I flicked my eyes upward. Her fingers flew. I smiled when she lifted her pinky.

"A question?" I smiled. "Who?" I smiled. "First letter."

I quickly got her to my question about a boy named Clint at school.

"Nope, no one." That's what I thought. "Oh, wait a minute. Remember the kid from last year? When we were in third grade? It was after Thanksgiving, I think. We came back to school and everyone was talking about some kid who stuffed his food in his milk carton, now they say he's the ghost who haunts the lunchroom. Isn't his name Clint? I think he was lost in the woods, got chased by a bear or something. The grownups wouldn't talk about it. The kid was embarrassed and the parents moved him to a different school. Casey said something bad happened to him. Like the bear ate his leg or something and that the parents lied and the kid died. It's Clint, right?"

Emma was right. Not about the bear eating his leg. That was just a tall tale, gossip spread by us kids. But now I remember the kid's name was Clint and he was a fifth grader. It was all hush-hush and none of us kids ever knew the real story. I'll have to tell Auntie Liv.

"Anyway, why are you asking?"

I stayed still for a second, not wanting to share my spy secrets, then decided to distract Emma. I was lying on my stomach and decided to lift my chest and shoulders from the floor by tightening my arms while holding my head high. Tough to do, but at least I'd get Emma on a different line of thought.

"Where are you going?" Emma asked.

I heard Mom approach, but wanted to finish what I'd started. Mouth wide with determination, I worked my long, thin, crooked fingers along the carpet toward the rubber snake, inches from my curled hand.

"Oh, good one," Emma whispered.

Just as I touched the cool, rubbery skin of my toy, Mom said, "Look at you, Noah. You are just moving all over the place. Pretty soon I'll find you heading out the door on your own to visit the neighbors. Mrs. Parrent better get her house prepared, because Noah is stepping out!"

I laughed at the thought of it, a deep belly laugh. Wouldn't she be surprised! I had to lower my head to the floor to rest my tired muscles. Especially in my neck. Mom bent beside me and rolled me over on my back, exposing the rubber snake I'd gripped between two fingers in my left hand.

Mom screamed, "Noah, you scared me with that awful thing. I thought I told Santa, no snakes this year! Wait a minute. This is last year's snake."

She tickled me and then Emma. We both squealed until she was distracted.

"Honey?" Dad called. "Better come down here. Quickly."

Mom said, "Be right back."

Skipping toward her bedroom, Emma said, "Me, too."

I listened through the vent. Dad turned up the volume on the TV. I heard the headline story blaring. I could almost hear my smile shrink, like a balloon with all its air seeping out.

I couldn't see the images but I could hear the TV announcer's voice saying, " . . . a couple minutes ago at a press conference held in his office complex. His former wife, Melissa Williams, Los Angeles supermodel, also presented a brief statement about their son's disappearance."

The voice faded and a new one took its place. A confident voice that spoke with authority said, "And to whoever has our little Max, make your demands quickly and return him safely or you will have hell to pay from me. I will hunt you down like an animal. I will do what I have to and show you no mercy. And I will leave you to suffer a lingering and painful death if you so much as touch one hair on my little boy's head. But if you return him safely and soon, I will meet your demands. And I will not involve the authorities. We just want little Max to be returned safely to his mother and me."

I heard every word and wished I could see the TV.

Mom was reminding Dad how Auntie Ida had dated this man a long time ago. I don't remember meeting any man named Maximillian Bennett Williams II, but I would have only been four or five. The missing boy's age. I kind of remembered, or there was something familiar about it all. I heard the TV announcer say something about a rough home video of the young boy playing on the slide at a neighborhood or school yard playground. The lady was remarking on the red and golden leaves covering the ground and how the trees in the background were bare. All I noticed was the kid's laugh.

The lady was describing what the boy had been wearing when he disappeared but all I could hear was the voice of an excited five-year-old saying, "Nanny Judy! Nanny Judy! Watch this!"

Then I heard the voice of a woman with an English accent. "Maximillian, say hello to your mummy and daddy first."

"Yes, ma'am," the little boy compliantly agreed. "Hi, Mom! Hi, Dad! I'm having a good time, but I miss you. I love you! Bye, Mom! Bye, Dad! Nanny Judy, watch this!"

I had no idea what my mom and dad were watching the little boy do, but whatever it was, the kid was laughing. Hard. He sounded like he was running, occasionally breathless, and his laugh filled the speakers of the television and poured through my vent. His laugh reminded me of a kid I had heard in kiddie land at Six Flags last summer. A crowd had actually gathered around the mini-roller-coaster near the Ferris wheel, just to listen to the kid laugh. Even the teenagers, who never think it's cool to hang out near kiddie land or the Ferris wheel, decided to stick around to hear the kid laugh.

I heard my mom chuckle, too, and wondered if she was thinking the same thing I was thinking. I heard the lady on the TV with the English accent laugh. The boy's laughter was unique, contagious, born only from someone who was truly filled with joy. When the boy repeated his command, "Watch this!" as he laughed and laughed, my laugh became so intense my body tightened into a ball and my laugh had no sound.

And just like last summer, I felt the hot trickle of laughter tears streak down my cheek, the tickling drip in my ear making me laugh harder. I breathed deeply and made a gasping noise to catch my breath, my stomach muscles cramping.

I heard my Mom run up the stairs, concerned with my loud gasp. She patted my thin leg through my sweatpants. "Oh, good. You're laughing. I thought you were choking."

Emma ducked through the door. "On elf puke."

CHAPTER 36

I'M MISSING ALL THE Christmas morning joy right now.

Instead, here I was in Control Operations lab, showering in a tiled stall intended as an emergency wash station for flushing chemicals off skin or from eyes. Luckily, Jack had the bright idea that Streeter and I freshen up before heading back to the airport. I had taken a quick nap while Streeter showered and now it was his turn to take a nap. I decided to let him sleep. I stayed in the hot shower longer than I should have, enjoying the clean feeling and the heat massaging my sore ribs.

This time yesterday, Christmas Eve morning, I had been off to the mountains with Michael and Beulah for two hours of training that had ended in a tangle with a cougar and more scrapes and bruises. Then I was off to help Frances with Christmas dinner. I never got a morsel of that fabulous feast, as dinner was interrupted by a call from Streeter about the very case Frances and I were watching unfold on the evening news. I didn't know then that I wouldn't get to enjoy sleep for a long while, instead scouring DIA along with the rest of Denver's finest until we found the boy.

If we found the boy.

I heard something and turned off the shower. I waited for a minute, listening, hearing nothing but the drip of water. It must have been one of

Jack's team members moving around. Probably warning me my time was up. I stepped out of the shower and nearly tripped over my heap of discarded clothes.

I slipped into a change of clothes that Streeter had scavenged for me. He always had an extra set for himself. He had told me on my first day in the office to bring my own set, suggesting that once I was on a scene with a corpse, I would understand the urgency of changing into fresh clothes and possibly burning the old. Of course, I had procrastinated and hadn't heeded his good advice. So here I was wearing a set of clothes that belonged to Kelleher, who was taller and much better dressed than me on his worst day. The black T-shirt I slipped over my head was silky and thin. The gray pants were lined and tailored to hug his lean frame, which meant they were super tight on me. Or at least, tighter than I liked. I slipped into a fresh pair of socks and laced up my boots.

I scooped up my heap of dirty clothes and bounded down the short hall.

"Jack!" I said, startled when I bumped into him. It struck me as strange and wonderful at the same time to see him this close to the shower. "What are you doing here?"

Jack smirked, "Making sure you had your privacy."

"That was thoughtful," I said, shifting my dirty clothes to my other arm so they wouldn't be between us.

He breathed in my scent, wrapped his arms around my waist, and rested his chin on top of my head. "You smell clean."

"You feel amazing," I said, melting into his embrace.

"We just got word that Mr. and Mrs. Williams held a press conference here in Denver. The story has been picked up by the AP," Streeter's voice said, interrupting us.

Jack stared into my face, a longing look in his liquid eyes. He kissed the top of my head and took a step back, allowing room for me to pass him.

I stretched up on my tiptoes and pecked Jack on the cheek and whispered, "Merry Christmas."

Jack cleared his throat, his eyes holding mine, telling me all the things I wanted to hear. To Streeter, he said, "I thought you told them not to do that."

Streeter had his back turned to us, staring off into the lab, allowing us the private moment. "I did."

"What are you going to do?"

"Officers are on their way to escort them back out to DIA as we speak," Streeter said, eyeing me, his nostrils flaring ever so slightly as he scanned me from head to toe, assessing how the borrowed garb clung to my frame.

"Don't say it. Whatever you're thinking," I warned.

He grinned, handed me his oversized, rag wool sweater, which I tugged on over my wet head, self-conscious that both men might be eyeing my curves as I did.

Streeter said, "Are you ready?"

And we were off. I studied the airport security camera diagram all the way to DIA while drinking the coffee Streeter had given me.

"Did you eat something?"

I shook my head. "Not since Jack brought food last night. You?"

He said nothing.

I took a break from studying the diagram as we drew closer to the airport. I stared out the window at the high, asymmetrical peaks of fabric over DIA's main terminal and finally saw what the architect had been trying to simulate. The peaks really did look like snowcapped Rocky Mountains. Kind of. If I squinted really hard.

"What are you seeing?" he asked.

Again, I thought he could read my mind, until I realized he was talking about the diagram. "I'm seeing some possibilities. But I want to try some things out first. What did you find out about Judy Manning? Anything yet?"

"We're checking out the hotels in the area. And the flights out of Denver. We'll find her."

"And hopefully she'll lead us to little Max."

My cell phone chirped. I noticed it was Frances's phone number. "Do you mind if I answer this? It's my sister."

He said, "No."

"What's up?"

"Are you going to make it for breakfast?" Frances asked. Her voice sounded tentative and I hated to disappoint her.

"No, Frances," I answered, glancing over at Streeter who offered me a sympathetic look. "I took a quick shower at the field office and we're headed back to the airport."

There was a long pause. "Frances?"

"Is . . . everything okay? I mean, I know you can't share any details, but the boy, is he going to be okay?"

I glanced over to Streeter who could hear Frances, the volume being set to high. He blew out a deep breath.

"I hope so. If we stay on it. It's way too early to give up yet," I said, wondering if I believed it myself and finding that I truly did.

"Well, the kids were waiting to open their gifts from Santa until you came home."

"Better not."

"Okay," Frances said. "Merry Christmas, Boots."

"Merry Christmas. Give them a hug from me."

"Oh, and Emma wants to tell you something."

I smiled as her cheerful voice said, "Santa Claus came. Where are you? Are you coming home? We want to open presents."

"You do that, Princess. I'll have to miss this year. Show me everything when I get home, okay? Bye, sweetie."

"No wait! Noah wanted me to tell you something. He won't tell me why, but he said to tell you that Clint's field trip to Baugh House was last year. Do you know what he's talking about?"

God bless Noah. He was figuring out the case of the missing backpack. "I do."

"Then tell me."

"I can't. Noah and I did a pinky swear. Just like you and me when you cut your bangs last summer and I covered for you. A secret's a secret."

She hung up on me, which ended our call.

"The work can be brutal sometimes," Streeter offered. "Especially on families over the holidays."

I looked out the window at the heavy flakes sailing by my window. "Not as brutal as it would be if I pretended that the boy wasn't missing and I just went home until the next workday. I couldn't live like that."

He smiled.

"Streeter? Do you have family?" I knew little about Streeter. I wanted to learn more about him. And Jack.

He didn't answer for a long time. "Used to."

I knew he had lost his wife. She was murdered. But I didn't know anything else about him. His answer could mean they were all dead or it could mean he was estranged from them. I had no idea.

But one thing I did know.

Now wasn't the time to ask.

CHAPTER 37

STUDYING THEM, I SENSED a change between Max and Melissa this morning—a tenderness with one another I hadn't seen before.

Everyone gathered around the small folding table at airport HQ—a total count of six people with me, Streeter, Max, Melissa, Phil, Kelleher, and another police officer I hadn't met yet. Tony was still at home with his kids for Christmas. Streeter calmly said, "We do have some information about your son and will share it with you as soon as you answer a few questions for us."

That got Melissa's attention. I wasn't so sure about Max.

"Our people tell us neither of you have heard any word from the kidnappers. Is that true?"

Max furrowed his brow. "Yes, of course. Why would you think we would know something your people didn't?"

"Because you made it clear at the press conference that you had no intention of involving us," Streeter countered. "And you told us you wanted to find the guy first, remember?"

"Oh, come on. What are we supposed to say? That was for the kidnapper's sake," Max said, putting his hands up in surrender.

"You were supposed to say nothing. Agent Pierce made that clear to you last night," I said, not wanting Max to bully his way through the issues like he was used to doing.

Streeter cleared his throat. "You told us in your interview that your people were working on locating your son. Without our assistance. I just want to make sure your people are not withholding information from us. You see, that would be a federal offense. This is not intended as a civics lesson, but rather as a warning. Unequivocally."

"We'll call you the minute we're contacted," Max said with a shrug.

"Are you well versed in bugging devices? To capture a kidnapper's call? Or would you prefer our New York Bureau tap your home line?"

Max clearly knew the rules. "I am not giving permission to any federal agency to install listening devices of any kind on our phone lines or in either of our homes. Not in New York, not in Missy's LA home, and not in our hotel room here in Denver."

Did he say *our* room? Are they actually staying together?

"And yes, I am familiar with bugging devices. Corporate espionage is a reality in my line of work. I have become very successful by outsmarting my competition on development projects. I take risks and I attack opportunity. I hedge my bets by making sure no one else knows my strategy, so I have a habit of routinely sweeping my living and working spaces for bugs."

Streeter had my attention. His technique for quickly harvesting information was amazing. Max had a reputation for being impenetrable and Streeter had garnered so much already from him in the private interviews. Now he was letting Max save face and exercise some muscle with Melissa in the room.

"Makes sense. Especially since our people in the New York Bureau have shared what they've gathered about the people you deal with daily."

Max was not easily surprised and had a reputation for always being prepared to swing regardless of the curve ball thrown at him, but Streeter had caught him flat-footed with this one. I could see it in Max's eyes. I was beginning to think Max actually hated Streeter more than he hated me.

"What are you up to, Pierce?"

Streeter remained unmoved and calmly said, "Oh, I think you know exactly what I'm talking about. You have been messing with some very nasty players. And in addition to all your busy activities in the Big Apple, you have found time to line so many DC politicians' pockets with your dirty money that it looks like a one-sided tennis match—they all simply look the other way in unison when a subpoena is served anywhere near your side of the net."

Streeter had remained calm while making these allegations and now he walked slowly back to his chair. Max was shocked shitless. I could hardly contain my glee.

After a momentary tongue-tied pause, Max stuttered. "Now wait just a minute—"

Streeter did not allow him to finish. "Agent Bergen, Chief Gates, and I are not the least bit interested in your extracurricular activities. We are interested in finding little Max. I am only trying to tell you to cut the crap and tell us who your enemies are so that we can start chasing tangible leads." After a few sobering seconds, Streeter continued, "Do you under-stand me?"

Melissa jabbed a finger at Max, any tenderness between them gone. "Did you have something to do with this, you son of a bitch? Tell me where he is. Tell me or I'll cut your balls off and feed them to your guard dogs."

"Missy, calm down." Turning to Streeter, Max explained, "Obviously, she's still a little upset about our son's disappearance. She's not thinking clearly." He sliced a sideways glance at Melissa that was so precise it would have negated her next appointment with her plastic surgeon.

She scrunched her nose as if discovering a rotten, discarded washcloth in a forgotten corner of her mind. I noted that Melissa Williams was not silenced easily, but she still reluctantly obeyed Max. I also noted how she turned away from him, rolling her eyes every time he opened his mouth.

"You have our full cooperation. I'll get you a list of anyone who might want to harm me or my family, might want to exact a pound of flesh from me, if you will. And Missy will, too."

"What? I had nothing to do with this."

"Neither did I," Max assured her, "just like I told you last night. But someone who knows one of us might have little Max, and are you willing to take that chance?"

I noticed that their exchanged glare seemed to morph back into a gen-uinely tender gaze. At the mention of their time together last night? For the sake of little Max? Either way, my conclusion from yesterday that these two really did love the boy, cared for him the best way they knew how, was confirmed.

"I'll get a list," she said, never taking her eyes from Max's face.

"Good," he said, holding her stare. "You have our full cooperation."

"Thank you," Streeter said. "And contact us immediately if you hear from any kidnappers."

Streeter had told Tony and me that the LA Bureau and NYC Bureau had already ordered taps for both homes. The FBI didn't need permission in an abduction case. And of course their hotel rooms were wired, including the room with Max's attorney and with Melissa's hairstylist, the only two people from their entourages who had stayed in Denver.

"Full cooperation, except we are going to continue the press conferences," Max announced.

"Why do you insist on holding press conferences?" I asked.

"Strategy," Max responded without pause and with overwhelming confidence. "You see, this situation calls for more than your police procedures."

I was proud of myself for keeping my composure, even though I wanted to jump across the table and personally wipe the smug look from his face. Thankfully, my desire to impress Streeter was greater than my need to pummel the contempt out of my sister's ex-boyfriend.

Max continued, "We needed to formulate our own strategy with our own people that will allow us to find our son. The press releases are a big part of who we are and what we do. We are going to use that to our advantage, take opportunities every chance we get, despite your . . . uh, advice, shall we say, to the contrary."

Maybe my restraint was ingrained after the hours I had spent in Sister Maria's office, waiting to be scolded about mussing my hair, ripping my pinafore uniform, and being disciplined for my unladylike behavior, after scuffling on the playground. Actions certainly do have consequences. And right about now, I wouldn't mind being called unladylike.

Max concluded, "With all due respect, Agent Pierce, your advice is bad. We have given you ample time to find little Max."

Streeter looked at his watch—9:43 a.m.

"Sixteen and a half hours? That's ample time?"

"It's nearly twenty-one hours since little Max went missing, in fact. The first twenty-four are the most critical. And you have come up with nothing, am I right?"

"Sixteen hours thirty minutes since the FBI has been involved. Twenty-one hours since little Max was taken. Four and a half hours lost because you and the airlines decided not to involve the authorities," Streeter responded. I leveled my gaze on Max.

"You see, my original strategy was to call in the best from the Bureau to find my son. But if this is all the best can do, well then . . ."

Streeter said, "You requested Agent Bergen. Three weeks out of Quantico."

I didn't take it personally. Streeter was making a point. But it didn't make me want to pummel Max any less, the arrogant prick.

Melissa glared at Max. "I knew it. You liar. You told me she was the best. What else have you been lying to me about?"

Max paused, staring directly into Streeter Pierce's unwavering eyes. "I thought maybe Agent Bergen would have amounted to something by now. She was the most determined in the litter. But I was wrong," Max replied. The contempt he held for me was obvious; although, I found it amusing that there might be a veiled compliment hidden in all the shit he was spewing. Until he added, "More like the most pigheaded. You are a mess, Liv. You look like you've been in a back-alley brawl. And lost."

I couldn't argue there. The scratches on my face were healing, but a few bruises had surfaced since yesterday and I wasn't looking very sophisticated wearing a man's suit pants and rag wool sweater. But I wasn't about to take the bait. I was just too smart for that. I grinned, knowing this would be an unexpectedly maddening response to all his barbs.

Streeter held his gaze with Max and warned, "Keep this professional, Williams."

"Oh, Agent Pierce. Don't you understand?" I asked, uncrossing my arms and leaning back. "This is Max being 'professional.' Dominance through intimidation. And not only am I not the least bit intimidated, but I also find it quite amusing."

Melissa scoffed. I saw the flicker of anger in Max's eyes before he said, "Be amused. But I didn't become as successful as I am without backup plans or by assuming someone else could do the job that I wanted done. My son's too important to me for that. So, I implemented my backup and called for a press conference while you made me wait. Now, I am in control."

Just as I was afraid I had disappointed Streeter with my interjection—something he might view as getting too personal or emotional—Streeter rose to his feet and placed his massive hands on the flimsy, plastic folding table, thick fingers splayed. He leaned close to Max, who sat comfortably in his chair on the other side. Max appeared amused. Streeter's eyes fixed fiercely on Max. I wouldn't want to be Max. Streeter's voice was steady and commanding as he spoke. "You may have a strategy, Mr. Williams, but we have a job to do. That job is to find your son and bring him back unharmed, if at all possible. We do this for a living, and whether you two like it, we will continue to do our jobs, despite your efforts to the contrary. Do you understand me?"

"Perfectly," Max answered through his flashy smile.

"I understand your frustration and can only imagine your impatience. But you need to understand this. It's been less than twenty-four hours. We've been working around the clock. We request your continued assistance to find your son and to approach this situation with a unified strategy. Without that, there is no reason for me to keep your names from sailing to the top of our suspect list where they belong." Streeter leaned closer to Max, who stared back at him with an impish grin. Softly yet sternly, Streeter growled, "In the future we will not be making any more requests. Instead, we will give orders. And if either of you deliberately goes against the orders of the FBI again, we will consider it obstruction of justice. Which is a felony. Do you understand me now, Mr. Williams?"

Max's grin faded. "Don't threaten me, Agent Pierce. You're not even lead investigator. Agent Bergen is."

"Wrong. I am. I don't care who you know. Oh, and it's not a threat. It's a promise. And I keep my promises."

The flicker of anger I'd seen earlier in Melissa's eyes had grown into a raging wildfire. "Where is he, Max? Did they take little Max for the money? They did, didn't they?" Melissa asked Max.

"Missy, darling, how would I know?"

"You're the one surrounding yourself with a bunch of crooks and thieves."

"Unlike Aldo?"

"Aldo's not a thief."

"This is not my fault, Missy. You can't blame me for this one."

She stood up and turned on her three-inch, canary-yellow heels and slammed her fists on her waist, staring down at him. "I can and I will. My lawyer said that Christmas was my holiday and that meant little Max should have been with me no later than Christmas Eve morning. So it is most certainly your fault."

Max said, "It's not my fault if some lunatic snatched our son. And I've never dealt with a kidnapper before. But what we have to do is quit ripping each other apart and focus. I can only assume that whoever did this wants money. Why else would they want a kid?"

I added, "He's right. You have to work together on this. It might be the difference between little Max coming home alive and . . ."

"And what? What? Do you think he's dead?" Her pleading eyes were fixated on me.

When I didn't answer, Melissa shuddered, her bare, sculpted shoulders twitching, before she sat back down, wrapping herself in her thick, white fur coat and warning, "Okay. I'll cooperate. I'll try to stay focused on what's best for little Max. But if anything really has happened to that kid, I'm going to sue your ass for everything you have."

Max grinned. "You already did, dear. Don't you remember all the depositions we've given, visions of alimony plums growing bigger with every harsh word? And then who do you think will be paying for those sunny excursions to Papeete? Aldo?"

"I hate you," she hissed.

"That's not what you told me last night, dear."

"I was crazy with grief."

So they *had* reunited.

"You hate that even Aldo can't afford you. Now, why don't you be a good girl and start preparing yourself to be the distraught and grieving mother, rather than the bitter, greedy ex."

Turning to me, Melissa said, "See what I have to live with?"

I was just glad it wasn't Ida who was asking me that.

CHAPTER 38

Noah

MOM LIFTED ME INTO her arms and carried me upstairs to take a quick nap before lunch. The excitement from Christmas morning was exhausting.

I felt my hair brush against the doorframe of my room, and my legs involuntarily stiffen the more I focused on relaxing. Mom could barely maneuver me. I focused hard to relax. But the excitement of the morning—unwrapping presents, eating so much candy, listening to Christmas music—made it nearly impossible for me to relax my body. Plus every time I thought about the missing boy's laugh, I'd start laughing again, which made it almost impossible to relax. It seemed the more I tried, the worse it got.

My mom walked sideways through the door and dropped me on the bed.

I should have fallen right to sleep, since I had hardly gotten any last night. But I didn't. I daydreamed for a time about when this would end. When diapers became a thing of the past. When I could go to the bathroom by myself. When I didn't get embarrassed in a crowd, just because I had to go but couldn't get myself to the bathroom or have the privacy for pooping, like most people. I didn't like that I needed my mom or dad to notice, to act, and to change my mess.

Worse, I never saw an end to my dependence.

I decided I shouldn't be thinking about this on Christmas. So I started thinking about the missing backpack and the fifth grader named Clint from our school, the kid the adults refused to speak about. It was all hush-hush, leaving us kids to make up stories about him having his leg eaten by a bear. I tried to remember if he liked playing with cars and eating Milky Ways. And at some point, I started talking out loud. I forgot that my mom had turned the monitor back on, and I suddenly realized she'd know I wasn't napping and would come get me.

I was right.

I heard her soft footsteps on the stairs and my door open. "You just don't want to miss a thing today, do you?"

She was right. I didn't.

Mom carried me back down into the kitchen where my wheelchair waited like a faithful steed. I heard Uncle Michael say that once. I thought it sounded funny. Especially when he told me a steed was a horse. I've always wanted to ride a horse. The swing that Santa brought me makes me feel like I'm in a saddle riding a horse, or walking on the moon. I love it! That's another reason I should be exhausted and take a long nap, but I don't want to.

Mom buckled my harness and belt, placed my feet in the stirrups, and washed her hands. I heard her ask Emma, "Where's your dad?"

Emma shrugged. "He was here a minute ago."

The front door opened and closed quickly. I knew who it was before I heard my dad's voice call, "Ho, ho, ho, Merry Christmas!"

Emma stomped out and said, "Dad, that is getting so old."

"But don't I look like Santa?" He pointed to the snow that crusted his dark beard and eyebrows. He patted his large stomach. "And I've worked hard on this belly, put away a lot of groceries to try to convince you."

"I'm not," Emma sassed.

Mom called back, "Thanks for putting the breakfast dishes in the sink for me."

Dad came in, shivering. "That was Emma, not me."

Feeling Dad muss my hair, I grinned, arching my back in my excitement. I heard Dad kiss Mom and say, "The thermometer in my car said it's three below zero out there. Maybe you should put long johns on Noah, a couple of extra layers today, just in case." He removed his gloves and stocking cap before bending to kiss me on the cheek.

I smiled.

"Your appetite's been good today. You didn't eat a very good dinner last night. That's not like you. Are you getting sick or something?"

I forced my smile to disappear. I wasn't sick.

"No?" Dad asked as he removed his topcoat. "Then you just didn't like the Christmas Eve dinner that Mom fixed for us?"

I froze my face, wishing I could say, *Not it at all. Mom's a great cook.*

"Where were you?" Emma said as she sprinted into the kitchen, curly red pigtails bobbing by her ears. She jumped into Dad's arms and he dropped all of his winter clothing.

"Outside shoveling Mrs. Parrent's driveway and sidewalks." Kissing her and blowing raspberries on her neck, he paused only long enough to ask, "Miss me, Princess?"

Emma giggled.

As Dad put Emma down, Mom said, "Emma, will you please pour a glass of water for Noah?"

"Okay, Mom, but after that can we please, please, please go outside to play? Please?"

I lifted my eyes, in case Mom was wondering if I wanted to go, too. And I smiled.

"We'll see. Maybe after lunch. It's so cold. You'll both have to dress in a bunch of layers, if you do."

I squealed, wanting to go outside, too.

I heard Dad scoop up all his winter clothes and store them in the closet by the front door. After he kicked off his snow boots, he came back in and sat in the living room with Emma. I thought they'd forgotten about me until I felt Mom release my wheelchair brakes and push me out of the kitchen into the living room through all the scattered toys, boxes, and wrapping paper.

"Auntie Elizabeth is coming later this afternoon to take you two ice skating and then for a sleepover."

Emma hollered, "Yippee! You didn't tell us that. Thank you, Mommy. It's the best Christmas ever."

"So do you still want to play outside? If so you'll have to head out soon so you'll be ready to go when she and Uncle Michael get here."

"Yeah, yeah, yeah. Noah, we're going to Uncle Michael and Auntie Elizabeth's house. We're going skating and to Fizziegoobers."

"I never said anything about Fizziegoobers," Mom said.

"I know, but Auntie Elizabeth always takes us there for dinner."

"It's Christmas. It's probably closed. Even pizza joints get a day off sometime, Em. Auntie Elizabeth said she's taking you skating at the outdoor ice rink and then taking you to her house in Louisville for macaroni and cheese."

"Yeah, yeah, yeah," Emma sang.

I smiled. Mac and cheese was one of my favorites.

"Go get your long johns on first, then redress and put your snow clothes on and I'll bring Noah out in a minute. Stay in the backyard."

Emma was gone.

Mom started tugging off my shoes and stripped me bare. She pulled on two layers of long johns, my heavy sweats, and two pairs of socks before putting my heavy socks and my snow boots on me. Then, she started dressing me in my snow clothes.

Dad said, "Emma told me that Noah saw a kid next door at the neighbor's. That true, Noah?"

I smiled, not knowing Emma had told Dad already.

"She told you that? When?" Mom asked, pausing just as she lifted my left foot to fill a boot.

I could feel the fuzz of its lining against my toe through the sock.

"About five minutes before I stepped outside to shovel," Dad explained. "I didn't see any visitors. Or any little boot prints in the snow. I assume she meant Mr. Flicker and not Mr. Andrews."

"Jason Fletcher," my mom sighed. "And she told me that, too, but I told her to quit making up stories like that."

"Like what? About Fletcher?"

"About make-believe friends. She's getting too old for that. I mean, I know she's not too old to play pretend, but to believe so strongly in her imaginary friends . . . it might cause rumors to get started about others."

"Like Mr. Fletcher?" Dad asked.

I strained against the clothes she was layering on me, angry that she wasn't looking at my face. So I could tell her the truth, that there was a child next door. That Emma wasn't playing with another imaginary friend.

But she pretended I wasn't there and kept talking to Dad. "He's pretty private. No one around here knows much about him. I heard he was into photography or something. The one-hour-developer kind of store. He's not very friendly though. And I told Emma that involving Noah and Mr. Fletcher in her make-believe world wasn't right and could lead to trouble."

"Noah, did you and Emma come up with this story?"

I raised my eyes and smiled. *I saw the child. Last night and this morning.*

Mom noticed. "See? They made it up. And now Emma's got Noah in the middle of it."

My smile faded. What did I do? I meant to answer Dad that Emma and I started that story and that I actually *saw* a child, not that we made up the story as pretend. By miscommunicating my "yes" with Dad, I'd already gotten Emma in enough trouble for the day.

Dad said, "Why would Emma do that?"

I figured I better let this one go for now. Besides, I was about to go outside and had a mystery to think about. I wanted to sit in the fresh air and puzzle through the case of the missing backpack. And maybe I'd see a mountain lion.

"Maybe she was trying to get him in trouble. We call him Mr. Creepy," Mom admitted to Dad.

"Mr. Creepy? That's not nice."

He *was* kind of creepy. He kept his distance from me, but I assumed it was because the man was uncomfortable with me having cerebral palsy. Or being in a wheelchair. If I could talk, I'd tell him it isn't contagious. Then I'd laugh.

"Yeah, when I was in our driveway shoveling, I saw Fletcher walk by the front window and close the curtains. I don't think he saw me sneaking some peeks in there, but who knows. Why do you suppose Noah's saying he saw a kid?"

Because I did! Those are the words I shouted in my head, but only "Errrggh" came out of my mouth.

"Well, like I told Noah, he was probably mistaken, probably saw a shadow or Emma's reflection in his window. But let's not encourage Emma with her delusions of imaginary friends that involve others," Mom replied, wrapping a heavy winter coat around my body. "Or rumors will start spreading like wildfire."

But it's not a rumor if I saw the child over there, is it?

My mom pulled gloves on my hands, then mittens; she put a stocking cap on my head and bumped me down the stairs in my wheelchair. Dad must have followed, because I heard the basement door open to the back-yard and felt the cold air rush in on my face.

"Well, maybe we need to set up some play dates for Emma tomorrow or later this week with kids from her school. At nine, Emma really should be growing out of this imaginary world of hers," Dad said. "Before it gets out of hand."

It already had. And I was sorry I ever mentioned it.

"I bet Em would like that."

I just wanted to go outside before I missed the mountain lions sneaking around in our backyard. And if I did see one, I certainly wouldn't let Emma tell Mom or Dad. They'd never believe us.

Or maybe I'd just look for bears. Maybe I could ask one of them if they knew what happened to Clint, the kid who might be the owner of the missing backpack.

CHAPTER 39

IT DIDN'T TAKE ME long to do my analysis on the possible paths out of the airport that were out of camera range and to finish up my report to Streeter. Hopefully, that would help Jack narrow the video search.

I was hoping not to call DIA's Concourse B home for much longer and was happy to have a few moments alone, curling up on the floor to take a quick nap. Apparently, my nap wasn't all that quick, because when I awoke, it was nearly eleven in the morning, which meant I had slept for almost an hour. Groggy, I heard Streeter and Gates talking with one another in front of the computer screen.

I yawned and stretched, hopped to my feet, and rubbed my eyes.

Gates heard me approaching and turned toward me. "Merry Chri— what in the hell are you wearing?"

I looked down at my clothes. "Oh, Phil Kelleher from LoDo. And the shoes are Louis L'Amour."

The men gaped.

"You know, red carpet? Louis Vuitton? Fancy shoes? Louis L'Amour? Storyteller of the frontier? I'm wearing boots? On the red carpet, movie stars are asked, 'What are you wearing?' Never mind." I puffed out my reddened cheeks. "Okay, I borrowed these clothes from Phil."

"You're wearing Agent Kelleher's clothes?" Gates asked. "Do I want to know what happened while I was gone?"

"Mine were filthy."

"I don't want to know." Gates said, shaking his head.

"What are you guys looking at?" I asked.

"The results of the work you did earlier," Streeter said. "I'm just now reading the email you sent to Linwood at 9:45 a.m."

"Good!" I replied enthusiastically. "What do you think?"

"I think it's thorough and the best chance we have to narrow down video footage quickly," Streeter answered. "Tell us how you came to your conclusions on the best six cameras for Linwood's team to search."

For the first time, I actually felt like an equal with the chief and Streeter. "I had help. Jon Tuygen and Kyle Mills went to airport security where the videos were playing and watched my movements as I went from the family bathroom out into the main terminal. They talked me through what they saw and how to improve my movements to avoid cameras. I tried to imagine what I would do if I knew the airport as well as someone like Kevin Benson."

"Tuygen and Mills? Bureau guys?" Gates asked.

I nodded. "I'd start in the bathroom and move to the nearest doors. Trial and error. There are six cameras that are key to monitoring the exits closest to the bathroom by the Buckhorn Bar and Grill. If the abductor took little Max outside to a car or to a bus, we're guessing there's an 85 percent chance he'll be on one of those six cameras."

"But not more than one," Streeter said.

"Right," I said, noticing that Streeter was studying me as I paced, his eyes locked on mine. "The cameras are positioned above the exits and there's no way he could avoid the cameras. At least one of them. Unless he went out the door a great distance from where the boy was last seen, which is entirely possible. That's where Jon Tuygen came in."

Streeter asked, "He ran a probability analysis?"

"Statistics based on the camera diagram Jack provided," I said. "Not foolproof, but the six cameras will at least narrow Jack's search."

Gates moved near Streeter, who was reading the screen. "Based on an 85 percent probability that the perp used one of those exits."

I said, "Yeah, and on a hunch, we might want to steer Jack to the fourth and fifth cameras listed on Tuygen's six-camera list to start with, based on those doors being closest to where Beulah drew the scent in short-term parking."

"Great idea," Streeter said.

"Where'd you find the statistics guy?" Gates asked Streeter.

"Jon Tuygen? He was a new office agent last year. He's feisty and a numbers whiz," Streeter said. "I like him. He fits in well with the team."

"Kyle Mills is no slouch, either," I added. "He talked me through the main terminal as if I were on a major heist or something, stepping over, around, and through what felt like invisible sensor beams, monitoring my every movement and correcting me so I could truly avoid the cameras, while noting how difficult it was for me to do so. Don't let his offish persona fool you. Mills is meticulous."

Streeter clicked on the email and closed the screen. "Good job. Now all we can do is to wait."

I saw the two men glance at one another and sensed some bad news. "What did you guys find out about the nanny?"

Streeter pursed his lips. "We found her."

"She was at a nearby airport hotel," Gates said. "She was staying under your sister's name, just like you suspected, Liv."

"Then what's wrong?"

Streeter indicated a chair at the table, which I took. Gates and Streeter did the same. Streeter reached over and clicked the mouse. The photo I'd seen earlier of Judy Manning in Max's file appeared. A woman in her early thirties, I'd guess. Mousy hair pulled back into a tight knot, an even tighter smile, white skin, and pretty eyes. Next was a photo captured from the video at Concourse B. And finally there was a live video stream from next door. Of what appeared to be Judy Manning's mother.

"Wow, what happened to her?"

"Ask her yourself," Gates said, folding his arms. "She's next door waiting for us to interview her."

"She doesn't even look like the same person I saw on the trains last night. Looks like she's aged twenty years," I said, observing the dark circles under her eyes, the sallow skin, and the crop of wrinkles that had seemed to sprout overnight. "She looks like hell."

"That's not even what I wanted to show you." Streeter said, clicking to the next image, to something on the screen that I didn't quite understand. "These are photos sent from Jerome Schuffler of Judy Manning's living room."

"A bookshelf?" I asked. "But what is all this? These aren't books."

"They're DVDs."

"She's a movie buff?"

Streeter's gaze slid from mine to Tony's. "Sort of. They're videos of little Max. She took videos of everything he did. All the time. Since he was born."

"There must be six dozen DVDs there," Chief Gates said.

"Obsessed? That's crazy." I marveled at not only the sheer number of DVDs but also at the organization of them.

"Quite possibly," Streeter agreed. "We'll know more after we talk with her. I just wanted you to see this first. Agent Schuffler's people recorded a walk-through of Manning's apartment. The judge allowed the search warrant, believing time was of the essence, since Maximillian Bennett Williams II said Manning was the one who took the child to the airport yesterday morning."

Tony speculated, "Maybe she never did. Maybe she did a bait and switch on us?"

"The Williamses have positively identified the boy Kevin Benson was carrying as little Max," Streeter explained. "And we have confirmed Judy Manning was on the same plane as little Max, flying under an assumed name."

"As Ida. My sister. Maybe she intended to snatch little Max and pretend it was a kidnapping. Or had someone kidnap him so she could have him all to herself. No more parents?" I mused, realizing if she had, my sister's name would be all over the paper trail.

"That's what I'm wondering," Gates said.

"We'll have to be delicate," Streeter cautioned. "She's the person who knows little Max the best and could help us the most if she's not behind the abduction. We can't risk alienating her if she's not the perp."

"Wait, Streeter!" I said, staring at the screen and pointing to the shelf beneath the two with DVDs. "There's one missing. See?"

"Good catch," Streeter said after zooming in on the shelf with the missing DVD. "Maybe I can work that into my line of questioning, see what comes of it."

I studied the monitor that was trained on Judy Manning in the other room, the aged woman clutching her purse. "See if she'll show you what's in her purse." The two men turned on their heels and eyed me as they reached the door. To their questioning stares, I shrugged and said, "Call it woman's intuition."

"But you don't even carry a purse."

CHAPTER 40

Noah

BECAUSE OF MY TWISTING and turning, my winter hat had slid down my forehead and over my eyes. I kept trying to get Emma's attention so she would lift it away from my face, but it wasn't happening. What little vision I had in my right eye, I really needed. The soft contact lens Mom sometimes put in that eye helped me see a lot better. But each time she bought a new one I managed to lose it. I liked to think I lost my contacts from messing around at school, being so active, so rough and tumble and on the go. Mom teases me about the foreshadowing of me being an irresponsible teen.

The stocking cap was really starting to bug me. The temperature had finally clawed above freezing. Mom had let me out of the house for the first time in over a week. I loved being outdoors, but she said it had been too cold. The crisp, cold air on my cheeks and in my small lungs felt wonderful. If it weren't for the stupid stocking cap covering my eyes, I'd say it was starting to look like the best Christmas ever.

I groaned to get my sister's attention. Emma ignored me. Like always. My frustration quickly steamed into anger. But it didn't last long. It never did. In fact, anger was not one of my strong suits. I tended to lose it too fast. It was a wasted emotion, in my opinion. It never accomplished much.

Strapped in my chair, clad heavily in winter clothes, I hung my head, chin against my chest, in defeat. I could hear Emma laughing and talking to her snowman, Howie. And I knew all I could do was to wait for Mom to notice, *if* she noticed, because I'd like to see again and take a look around a bit, before having to go back inside. What a bummer.

Emma introduced herself to her newly built snowman. She mimicked a low, grown-up voice, "How do you do, Howie? Nice to meet you, sir. Howie you doing?"

Amused by her own wit, she giggled.

Her giggling made it difficult for me to stay mad at her. I joined in, laughing slowly at first but eventually as energetically as Emma. She bounced through the snow toward my parked wheelchair and adjusted my hat so I could see again. After adjusting my cloudy vision to the bright sun reflecting off the crusted snow, my first image was of the angelic, freckled face of my sister framed in curly, red hair. I could see that much. She had pushed her face within an inch of my nose so I could see and smell her.

I couldn't help but laugh at Emma when she demanded in her low, grown-up voice, "Give me your hat. Howie needs your hat."

She smelled like peppermint candy canes.

Snatching the winter hat from my head, Emma bounced back through the snow to see if it would fit on her friend Howie's large, round head. When it didn't, she stretched the hat in every direction to make it big enough to fit. I listened to my sister arguing with the hat and complaining to Howie.

Until something by the fence caught my attention.

I turned my head toward the fence and listened. The noise was muffled and I almost convinced myself I'd imagined it at first, but I definitely heard something. I heard the soft crunching of the crisp snow beneath cautious footsteps. Someone was there. I strained to hear more noises coming from the neighbor's fence.

"Aren't your ears cold?" a small voice asked from behind the fence.

I startled. My arms tightened against my body like the underdeveloped wings of a newborn chick and my knees jerked skyward with a spasm. The child's voice was so strong and small that it had completely surprised me.

I turned my face toward the voice and furrowed my brow with determination. Although my left eye was useless, I strained to make out a shape or figure with my bionic eye. Focusing, I could make out a small silhouette behind the spaced slats of the neighbor's fence. Given the size of the image and the sound of the voice, I'd guess it was a child younger than Emma. A lot younger. The gaps between the wooden slats were not quite wide enough for the toddler to pass through, but wide enough for me to see where the child was standing.

Pink coat. Black hair. No cap or mittens.

"Didn't you hear me?" The small voice sounded again. "I said, aren't your ears cold?"

I smiled at the child and exhaled a noise that was not quite a laugh, but sounded more like being on the verge of one.

The child replied, "Why'd that girl take your hat?"

This made me laugh. Even this kid couldn't understand my strange little sister. I could hear Emma's engrossed conversation with her frigid friend, Howie, which made me laugh even harder. I laughed so hard that I sucked air to catch my breath and instead made a squealing noise. The small child from behind the fence giggled. The giggling was intense, playful, and as contagious as the chicken pox. I couldn't stop laughing. He kept giggling.

Then, something in my gut told me to be still. To listen. Alarms sounded in my head. CLANG! CLANG! I heard the bells at Six Flags near the kiddie park roller coaster in my head. Something was wrong about that funny laugh. I forced myself to stop laughing, stop moving, stop breathing . . . and to just listen.

In a single moment, an extreme wave of anxiety flooded my chest, which made my heart beat faster, my breathing quicken, and my brow and forehead break out in nervous sweat. I had heard that giggle before just an hour ago, not last summer. It sounded like the giggle from the news program we had been watching this morning that I'd heard float up from the vent. It was on an Amber Alert about the boy who was kidnapped from the Denver Airport, the boy who kept telling his nanny to watch him. It was the same boy. I was sure of it.

Dead sure.

My body contracted like a coiled spring as I strained to listen, to confirm, to be sure. I memorized the giggling that was coming from behind the fence only two feet from me and realized I had made no mistake. This *was* the boy from the news. I pulled my arms into my chest, hoping to reach the football through all the layers of clothing, to activate the listening device so I would have proof.

The child said, "You're funny."

His voice. It was the same. This was the missing boy. I needed to get Emma. I yelled for Mom. A long, worried screech came from my lungs, which I thought would surely have Emma running over to me and my mom coming outside, but all I managed to do was make the boy laugh.

Giggling, he said, "I see you from my bedroom. I looked for you this morning when I woke up. You were lying on the floor by your window. Why do you lie next to that window so much?"

I smiled, pleased that the boy had noticed. I let out another high-pitched holler, nerves constricting my throat. I wanted to tell him I had noticed him, too. And that I saw him last night. Late. By the window. I wanted to tell him I lie by the window because I love the outdoors, the birds that sing in the trees, the wind that blows through the branches, and the rain that falls on the windowpane. I wanted to tell him I knew who he was and what was going on. I wanted to, but I couldn't. All I could do was gurgle and shriek up and down the musical scale as I tried to call for help.

"Why do you keep making those funny noises? Can't you talk?"

I knew the boy was too young to understand why I wasn't answering— why I couldn't answer—and it made me sad to think the little boy might think I'm rude or, worse, that I'm mean. I smiled and let out a quieter noise to encourage the boy to keep talking.

As I waited for the boy's response, I heard my sister's footsteps crunching in the snow behind me. The child's giggling must have caught Emma's attention and she came bounding toward the two of us to see what was happening. Perfect. Now Emma could explain to the little boy why I couldn't answer his questions and I could explain who he was. Instead, my body stiffened from the sudden chill as Emma pushed the cold, wet hat that was too small for Howie back on my head.

"Hi! My name is Emma. What's yours?"

The child from behind the fence stammered in a very small voice that faded to a whisper, "Uh . . . well . . . I'm not supposed to tell you. It's a secret."

It's Maximillian. Maximillian! the voice in my head shouted. But nothing more than a garbled mess tumbled from my stupid, lazy lips.

"Ooh," Emma squealed. "I just love secrets."

"I'm not even supposed to be out here. I snuck out while Papa was making me a sandwich."

Papa? He calls Mr. Creepy, Papa? *Emma, look at me. I have to tell you something. Emma!*

Emma faced the fence. "Can I guess what it is? Your name? Since you can't tell me?"

I could understand how Emma couldn't see it at first. I barely recognized him with that black hair since it made his green eyes look so much bigger and more brilliant. But couldn't Emma hear it in his voice?

"Sure, I guess so," the child said, shrugging his small shoulders and stuffing his bare hands deep inside the pockets of the pink coat. "But make it quick. I've gotta go before he finds me out here."

Emma tapped her temple with a gloved finger. The small figure shook his uncovered head at each name she guessed. "Megan? Patty? Ivy?"

It's Maximillian, Emma! My inner voice screamed. *Five fingers, Em. Let me explain.* Nothing. I needed to get the boy to laugh. Then Emma would understand and tell Mom and Dad.

"Those are all girls' names. I'm not a girl," scoffed the little boy.

I arched my back and stomped my feet. They ignored me.

"Then why are you wearing a pink coat?" Emma argued.

The boy giggled at her silliness. I went still. This was definitely the missing boy named Maximillian. *Emma, listen! Can't you figure it out?*

The little boy added happily, "You can call me Sammy."

And he laughed. It was *that* laugh.

"What's so funny?" Emma asked angrily. "How was I supposed to know? I'm not the funny one. You're the funny one. Only girls wear pink." She stomped her foot in the snow to show how angry she was.

This made the kid giggle even harder, which really upset Emma. "You're not my friend anymore, Sammy!"

She stomped again before running off around the corner of the house to make another snow friend for her snowman. Out of sight.

Come back, Emma! It's him. It's the missing boy on TV! I screamed after my sister. The only sounds were jumbled again. I felt my mouth tighten into a frown.

The small shape huddled on the other side of the fence. Why was the boy here? Here of all places? The child, who had been missing since Christmas Eve, the boy an entire nation was looking for, was playing in the backyard by my house. It just didn't make sense.

The small boy said sadly, "Will you be my friend?"

I turned my face to him again and forced myself to smile in response, hoping to make the boy feel better somehow.

The child was just too young to understand why I didn't answer him. "Will you? Please?"

My muscles tightened, my arms crossing, my smile broadening. When my head stiffened against the headrest of my wheelchair, I once again pushed my hat forward and over my eyes. Accidentally. Just as I lost all sight of the child's shape, I heard a door slam and felt startled by the noise. But no one yelled, "Don't slam the door!" so I knew it wasn't Mom or Dad or Emma.

I heard the crunching of large footsteps in the snow on the other side of the fence.

CHAPTER 41

JUDY MANNING LOCKED EYES with me the second we walked into the room. It was her—the woman on the train—without a doubt. She even had on the same clothes.

Chief Gates and Streeter Pierce sat opposite Judy Manning at the table and I hung back by the door, hoping the nanny would focus on the two men across from her rather than on me. But that wasn't happening.

Although yesterday I thought the woman on the train appeared less English and more Amish, Judy Manning's appearance had totally changed to be almost unrecognizable. Her long, black hair was now pulled back into a severe bun and straggles of hair tumbled loose around her face and shoulders. Her eyes were rimmed red, bloodshot.

The nanny's voice was squeaky yet firm, clawing me from my observational reverie and forcing me to listen as she answered Streeter's first question about where she lived. "If you take the first right and then take four flights of stairs. I'm in apartment 407."

"And when do you go to work?" Streeter was asking.

"I work every day for Mr. Williams at the Manhattan house. I love little Max. I am at their home by 6:20 each morning. Eastern time." Her eyes may have flitted across different areas on the table, but they seemed to always rest on mine.

"What can you tell me about little Max?" Streeter asked.

"He is a dear, dear boy. So energetic. A regular bundle of joy, he is," she said. Her accent was most certainly English; there was a note of refinement in the way she lingered on certain words. "I've been with him since he was born. Five and a half years. I've been an au pair for over twenty-five years." So much for her being around my age, as I'd speculated. Unless she had started working when she was a kid. Judy added, "No one would want to hurt him. No."

"And what makes you say that?" Streeter asked.

"Well, I . . . I just don't know," she said, refusing to meet Streeter's eyes. "I just can't imagine why someone would do this to the child."

Streeter let silence settle in the room, baiting her to fill it. But she didn't.

"Before being a nanny for the Williams family, did you work the prior twenty years as a nanny in England?" Streeter asked.

"I've only been in the US since I've been with the Williams family." Her English accent was remarkably unchanged, even after being in New York for nearly six years.

"Mr. Williams hired me out of Manchester. Took care of everything for me, my passport, transportation, work visa. Even my apartment. He discovered my name in a conversation with one of my former clients. Charming girl. All grown up and quite the young lady these days."

"Tell us about Christmas Eve, Ms. Manning," Streeter said.

Her mood visibly shifted. Tears instantly welled in her eyes and her hands instinctively went up to her hair, her fingers bunching and then smoothing the loose strands, quickly fastening the band to capture all the strands into a neat, tight bun. When she was done, she folded her hands back on top of the purse on her lap.

"It was a glorious morning. I didn't want to see little Max go. And I certainly didn't want to see him fly alone, clear across the country. I begged Mr. Williams to let me fly with him to Los Angeles. He said the Mrs. did not want me in California."

Streeter and I exchanged a quick glance.

"Did you get along with Melissa Williams?"

"Oh, no. Never. She hated me from day one. But I didn't take it personally. She hates everyone. Or almost everyone. She likes beautiful things and beautiful people, not ordinary people like myself." Her delivery was monotone with no passion or anger behind the words. She was just matter-of-fact.

I thought her observation odd, especially after meeting Melissa, whom I had found to have an average emotional maturity. I had never sensed she was holding back a raging hatred or anger for the nanny. And I didn't sense that Melissa had discounted me for not being one of the "beautiful people," which I most certainly was not. She seemed to treat me as she did most everyone else in the room. The only one I sensed she had some anger or bitterness toward was Max, which seemed a normal emotional level for an ex-spouse.

"Did that pose problems for you as the child's nanny?"

"I never found her disdain for me to be a major problem. She largely left me alone to do my work in caring for little Max."

"And on Christmas Eve? Was it an issue?" Streeter asked.

"I told Mr. Williams I would fly with the child to Los Angeles and then turn around and fly back to New York the same day. I just didn't want him flying alone."

"And why didn't he let you do that?" Streeter asked.

"Said it was an unnecessary expense," Manning said, pursing her lips. "He told me the airline had an escort that would be much cheaper. I begged him to let me pay for it with my own money and that irritated him. He wouldn't have it. I knew I'd gone too far."

"What did he do?"

"He told me to do as he'd said—take the child to the airport and use the arranged escort. Then he told me to take the week off, go back to England, and not come back to Manhattan until little Max came home."

"But you didn't," Streeter said. "You flew with little Max against your boss's orders, didn't you?"

"How did you know?" Her eyes flicked across the men's faces and landed on mine. With no one willing to answer, she answered, "No, I didn't do as Mr. Williams instructed. I was concerned. I wanted to make sure little Max was safe. Wouldn't you?"

"What made you concerned?" Streeter asked.

"He's five. Traveling alone."

"So you bought a ticket to LA for yourself when you went to the airport?" Streeter asked.

Her face drained of color and her shoulders sagged.

"Ms. Manning? It would be in your best interest to tell the truth."

She closed her eyes. "No, it wouldn't."

"Why not?"

"You don't know Mr. Williams like I do." She sighed and sat upright, folding her hands on the table, regaining her composure as quickly as she'd lost it.

"What's the worst that could happen?"

"I would lose my job and never see little Max again." Her glassy-eyed gaze met mine.

Judy Manning could have been my age or Streeter's or even older; she had one of those ageless faces. Her skin was pale and smooth, not with youth but from living an uneventful life. She was far too weak, but not too thin. Her washed-out hair might have been black at one time—maybe dark brown—and had been pulled back into a harsh knot on the back of her head. She wore a tunic of dull blues and grays, which made her face appear even paler.

"Wasn't that going to happen anyway?" Streeter asked.

Manning shot a look at Streeter. She said nothing, a quizzical look falling over her face.

"Once he started school next fall, it would be normal for parents to dismiss their nanny, wouldn't it?" Streeter expertly explained, as if it must be so.

"Not always," she said, the pitch of her voice becoming higher, belying her confidence.

Streeter asked in the calmest voice imaginable. "Had you planned to buy a ticket to Los Angeles all along or was it a spontaneous decision?"

Manning looked down at her hands; her fingers were knotted together so hard that the knuckles on her fingers bulged and whitened. I noticed that her hands also distorted her age; it was not just her eyes.

"Spontaneous," she said eventually. "Little Max was crying. I practically maxed out my credit card at the ATM on the way to the airport. The escort took him away through the security gates. I couldn't bear to see him go. So I took most of my bonus money from Mr. Williams and paid the airline employee to get me to the top of the list, used cash to purchase a round-trip ticket to LA, to make sure he made it safely."

She looked up at Streeter and took a deep breath, holding back her flood of emotion. She admitted, "But he didn't."

My cheeks were burning. I was trying to hold back my urge to grab this woman and shake her. If her story was true, why did she fly under Ida's name?

Phil Kelleher came from behind Manning over to where I stood at my post by the door, whispering, "Join them. She's fixated on you. You can help."

I nodded, squeezed his hand, and moved quietly to the table. Gates and I were flanking Streeter. I could smell his cologne. Spicy and rich. I could feel the heat rising from his neck. My peripheral vision picked up the sheer bulk of him and nothing of the chief on the other side of him.

"Special Agent Streeter Pierce?" she asked.

"You can call me Agent Pierce, Ms. Manning."

"Could you please show me your badge? And who are all these other people?"

I watched as Streeter hesitated, then pulled out his credentials and slid them across the table toward her. "Would you feel more comfortable if Special Agent Bergen and Denver Police Chief Gates showed you theirs, too?"

Manning's eyes flicked over to mine. "Bergen?"

I raised an eyebrow.

The thin woman first reviewed Streeter's and then Chief Gates's credentials. I got goose bumps the way she looked at me, as if she were staring right through me. I showed her my credentials. As she pushed my credentials back to me, Manning said, "Ida's sister. It figures. He owns everyone."

"Who?" I asked.

"Mr. Williams. Does he own you, too?" she turned to Streeter, then Gates.

"I've never even met the man until today," Streeter said. I realized he was telling the truth, since he'd met Max for the first time after midnight. "Neither has Chief Gates."

"And you?" she asked, turning those haunting eyes of hers to mine.

"I knew Max a long time ago. As you know, he dated my sister, Ida—Ingrid Bergen. Give me back her ID, by the way, before I forget."

She held my gaze for a long moment, likely measuring whether I was bluffing. A flicker in her eyes told me she had indeed used my sister's identification to fly from NYC to Denver. I wondered what else she might be up to while posing as my sister. She lifted her purse from her lap to open the clasp, and as she looked down to fish out Ida's ID, I craned to see inside.

"Thank you," I said simply, as she handed me a passport.

Streeter cleared his throat. "Ms. Manning, why did you fly under an assumed name?"

"I told you. I had to. You don't know Mr. Williams like I do. I was disobeying him. I had bribed an employee to let me on that plane. I couldn't let him find out."

"And you'd have us believe that you happened to have my sister's ID in your purse for just such an emergency?" I asked.

"Actually, yes. I would. Because it would be true. Ever since I found it under the breakfront when the entryway was retiled, I've kept it with me. Just in case."

"In case what?" Streeter asked.

"In case I . . ." Her words trailed off into silence as she looked between the two men and then at me.

I wondered what was going through her mind. Her expression changed so suddenly, I thought maybe I was looking at an entirely different person, as different as she had been yesterday in comparison to today.

"Tiny," she said, her voice small.

"Excuse me?" Streeter said. "Tiny, did you say?"

"My apartment. It's tiny."

Just like her, I thought. Tiny. I had no clue where her thought process was leading, but I knew from the drastic change in her demeanor that I'd better listen carefully. She reminded me of those shrunken heads, only her entire body had been dipped in that magical concoction. No wonder she was pushing through everyone in the airport video. She couldn't see over anyone to locate little Max. She was too short. She wasn't just a little shorter than Ida, she was a lot shorter.

"Everything in my apartment is tiny. Little Max believes I'm the little old woman who lives in a shoe. Just like in the nursery rhyme." Her smile sent chills down my spine for some reason. She held me with an eerie gaze. "What can you tell me about my boy?"

Her boy? Was she insane? For the first time, I wondered if I was experiencing my first example of split personality, something the behavioral psychologists mentioned as a rarity, difficult to diagnose. I'd argue I was staring it in the face.

"We know very little. We're hoping you can help us find him, Ms. Manning. Is it Ms. or Mrs.?" Streeter asked.

I realized he didn't want Manning to control the direction of this interview and his unspoken direction was for Chief Gates and me to stay silent, not to allow her to bait us into answering her questions.

"Ms. You've heard nothing from the kidnappers?" She was staring directly at me. I practiced my blank expression, which was harder than I'd ever imagined.

"No," Streeter said. "Will we?"

She cocked her head, quizzically.

"Do you know them?" Streeter asked.

"Who?"

"The kidnappers."

She shook her head and looked confused. "Why would you ask me that?"

Streeter shrugged. "Because you were on the plane with little Max. After you told Mr. Williams you were going to Manchester for the holidays. Yet here we are. And we don't even know if little Max has been kidnapped or not. But you seem to think he has. So wouldn't it make sense for us to ask you why you think he was?"

Her eyes widened slightly and she clutched at her hair again, pulling chunks of strands from the tight knot. She let her hands fall slowly back into her lap and said, "I just assumed. Why else would they want little Max?"

"Any ideas?"

She pondered, pulling more hair loose. It was an odd behavior at best, more like neurotic. I realized it was her eyes that made her look old. They had seen too much in her lifetime, held too much pain. On closer study, Judy Manning may have actually been younger than me, perhaps late twenties, maybe early thirties. Maybe she'd lied about being a nanny for twenty-five years. It suddenly dawned on me that the straggles of loose hair—not by design to soften her looks, but pulled from her bun as she battled whatever demons danced around in that gray matter of hers—might actually indicate the state she was in, the near frantic panic she must have felt, as she hurried through the airport yesterday. And how utterly different her demeanor appeared now compared to the calm she had exuded on the train yesterday.

"I couldn't imagine," she said, her gaze far off.

"Then why did you ask about kidnappers?" Streeter asked.

"If my Max wasn't taken because of money, then why?" Manning was staring at me again. Her stare was at once pleading and demanding.

Streeter answered, "We'll be asking the questions, Ms. Manning."

I blurted, "Maybe if you show us what's on that DVD you're carrying in your purse, we can help you find him."

Judy Manning stared at me longer than was comfortable before reaching into her purse and sliding it across the table to me. "I hope so. It's my favorite."

When Streeter placed the DVD into the computer's drive, a video of little Max popped up on the screen, his face close to the lens. With such cuteness, I could see why this was her favorite.

After all, little Max was singing a song over and over where the only lyrics were "I love Nanny Judy."

CHAPTER 42

Noah

I STRAINED TO SEE beneath my lowered cap and could barely make out the large shape of my grouchy neighbor. The child whimpered. The man was breathing heavy, like he was nervous or scared or something. His hushed tone was gruff, like he was mad.

"Sammy, what did I tell you about never leaving the house?" He sounded more scared than angry. I fumbled against my winter jacket and thick mittens, hoping to activate the football pin through all my padding.

"I was just playing—"

"Did you forget the rules?" He was still whispering, but I could hear him. Then I heard him mumble. "What have you done, what have you done?"

"Nothing. I just . . . You . . . you were busy, Papa, and I didn't want to bother you," the kid said, sounding just as scared and nervous as my neighbor, who still hadn't caught his breath.

"Who's seen you out here? Tell me," Mr. Creepy said. From the sound of him, I should have nicknamed him Mr. Scaredy Cat. I could smell him sweating, even in the ice-cold air.

"I just came over to see my friend."

Maybe he hadn't noticed me before or maybe he thought I was sleeping in my wheelchair or something. But I could tell he noticed me now. I tensed, sensing the large, angry man's eyes all over me.

The man snorted. I couldn't tell where he was standing in relationship to the boy and the fence—the hat was still covering my eyes—but I could swear I heard the snow crunch beneath his rubber boots as he took a step closer to me, the squeak of wet, rusty nails straining against wooden slats, as if he were climbing over to get me. I wanted to scream, but I was afraid Emma might hear me and then she'd be in danger, too. So I stayed really still and listened. For a long time. With no more noises than his heavy breathing, I realized he was probably just leaning against the fence, sizing me up and thinking.

"What'd you tell him?" Mr. Creepy's words sounded panicked, like I remembered my friends at school sounding once. They'd been playing with a lighter in the bathroom the week before Christmas break and were afraid Mrs. Davis would catch them and send them to the principal's office. Only Mr. Scaredy Cat's voice was deeper.

"Nothing," little Max whimpered, which made me wonder if the grouchy man was clutching the boy's arm or pinching his ear. "I tried to say 'hello,' asked him his name."

"And what'd he say?" he whispered, hushed and hurried.

"Nothing. He just sits there. I don't think he can talk."

For once, I was glad someone didn't understand me. Maybe little Max would stay safe if Mr. Creepy thought I was no threat.

"What's your name, kid?" His words were rushed and demanding. I didn't move.

"See? He won't answer. What's wrong with him, Papa? Why won't he be my friend?"

I thought little Max was about to cry and prayed he wouldn't, again worried about Emma hearing us and her curiosity leading her to come around the corner to check things out. And I prayed even harder that little Max wouldn't mention talking to Emma.

Finally, after a long time, Mr. Fletcher said, "This kid's broken. And it's a good thing. Because if you had talked to anyone else besides this vegetable, it would have been really bad."

"But Papa, I wanted a friend and I don't—"

"Shh, stop it! Let's go back inside. I'm your friend, remember? That's all you need."

Terrified, all I could do was pray that Emma stayed on the other side of the house out of view and out of earshot of this horrible man. And that my football pin was working. I didn't understand everything that was happening next door. The angry, terrified neighbor. The missing boy. I didn't even pretend to understand exactly what was going on in the backyard, right here, right now. But I knew deep in my twisted bones that Max would be in great danger if the creep discovered that he had also spoken to Emma a few minutes earlier. The neighbor would certainly know she was not a vegetable and that she could talk. Or scream!

Although normally being called a vegetable or broken might hurt my feelings, for the first time in my life, I was relieved that someone thought of me that way. I knew that if the scaredy-cat neighbor believed I couldn't think or speak—that I was nothing more than a vegetable—the little boy would stay safer somehow. I sensed this. I knew it simply by what the man had said to the boy. I went into spy mode and pretended to be a vegetable, since invisibility was out of the question.

I must have done a good job because Mr. Fat-and-Creepy was walking away. I listened to the snow groan beneath his heavy footsteps and twice as many, but much lighter, steps of the boy. When the door slammed as the two disappeared into the house, I startled.

And breathed.

Underneath the snow clothes Mom had layered on me, my chest was heaving with fear. I was proud of myself for staying brave, but it was starting to hit me how close Emma was to being taken. How close I had been. It was scary. I felt the corners of my mouth dip and my lower lip being sucked in and out of my mouth in rhythm with my heaving chest. I fought back tears. With my hat tilted over my eye, my mind still raced and my body trembled with fear, and I surrendered to the weight of it all. I let the tears come.

And I let out a single, piercingly high note of hurt.

Once I had forced all the air out of my lungs with the first wail, I snorted in more before the floodgate of tears opened, which was followed by much louder sobs.

By the grace of God, Emma hadn't heard the angry man minutes earlier. She hadn't heard Mr. Scaredy Cat whisk the child away into the dark house. But Emma had heard me crying and came running to my rescue.

"What's the matter, Noah? Is it your hat again?"

Although she quickly adjusted my hat to reveal my tear-streaked cheeks and trembling lower lip, I could not for the life of me stop crying long enough to answer her questions, her tiny five fingers flying in my face. Emma desperately tried to comfort me, but I just couldn't focus. For the first time in my life, I was scared to death. For an instant, I understood why it would be better for God to have my soul than for me to hold on to it. Concerned for the child next door and despite Emma's efforts, I wept.

"Okay, Noah," she said as she bent to release the brakes on my chair. She pushed me laboriously through the snow toward the back door of our house. "I'll get you inside. You must be cold or something, huh? Was it the hat I put back on your head? Too cold? Too wet? Don't tell Mom, Noah. She won't let us go to Auntie Elizabeth's house for our overnight."

I snorted in gasping breaths and wailed even louder as I felt my chair thumping along in the snow and breaking through the crust.

"I'll take you to Mom. She'll know what's wrong, Noah. She'll make it all better. Don't tell on me, okay? I'm sorry, Noah."

I heard Emma slide open the door just before pushing my chair into our basement playroom. Even through my wailing, I heard Mom's hastened steps on the stairway. She would know. She would understand. She would get me to calm down so I could explain and get that little boy some help.

I could feel Mom's heavy breathing on my face as her hands quickly assessed every part of my coiled body. She was expediently removing my winter clothing while interrogating Emma about what had happened. Dad was by her side in no time, helping to take my arms out of the sleeves and the boots off my feet.

Emma answered, "I don't know. Really, I don't. I was making a snow lady for Howie and—"

"Who's Howie?" Mom asked in concern, as I felt Dad pry the right snow boot off.

When he did, I felt the giant's thick finger strumming the inside of my rib cage—the early sign of an oncoming seizure

"My snowman," Emma answered in exasperation.

I could barely catch my breath in between sobs. But I had to. I had to calm down or the darkness would come. My mom was feeling all of my extremities for excessive cold, fractures, or bleeding. My dad's hands expertly ran over every inch of my body, just as Mom's had a second ago.

I'm not injured! I screamed in my head. My voice never even made it up my windpipe because the thrumming in my chest had drowned out any sound.

As Dad performed his assessment, Mom grilled Emma. "Was he tipped over somehow? Did his foot get caught under his chair or in the wheel?"

Emma shook her head. "I don't think so, Mom. But I was on the other side of the house making Howie's snow lady. I was putting on the head when I heard Noah crying. I went to see what was wrong and I found him in his chair where I'd left him. The only difference between how I left him and how I found him was that his hat had slid down over his eyes again. You know how much he hates that. Not seeing."

"This is not an angry cry, Emma," Mom snapped.

I wanted to tell Mom it wasn't Emma's fault. She didn't know. And I was glad she didn't know. I just needed to talk with Emma for a second. But first I needed to calm down and steady my breathing. I reached for my football pin and tapped it hard, hoping my mom would notice, but she didn't. Besides, she doesn't even know what it is. Maybe I could get Emma to call Auntie Liv. If I could only calm down and talk with Emma.

"Maybe it's his contact lens again. Maybe it's bunched up in his eyeball," Emma said.

Mom looked under my lid, but my contact was fine. "This is his hurt cry. You know, when his feelings are hurt, or the way he cries when he listens to opera, or when he's been frightened badly."

See, she did know. Mom always knows.

There is something wrong, Mom. The little, missing boy, little Max, is a prisoner of the creepy man in the house next door. See for yourself, my mind screamed against wracking sobs and tears spilling down my cheeks.

My dad pried open my eyelids, again, to see if somehow the hat had injured my eyes in some way. Finding the contact still in place in my right eye and finding nothing but tears in my left, he quickly unbuckled me. "He's not injured," my dad said.

Mom pulled me from my chair and heaved me up against her body. Carrying me over to the couch in the family room, she cradled my long, thin, trembling body in her arms and rocked me while Dad rubbed my back. I knew she could sense my fright.

With my tears and trembling beginning to subside, I heard Mom tell Emma, "Why don't you go on upstairs and make yourself a snack."

"All by myself?"

"All by yourself."

Emma ran up the stairs two at a time. With every bump of her feet on the carpeted stairs, I felt hope fade. *I needed Emma to explain about the boy!* And as my hope faded, my anxiety grew. I felt the drag of a thick finger on the inside of my rib cage again.

Mom called after her, "Hang up your coat first, Emma, and put your hat and mittens up to dry. Auntie Elizabeth will be here soon."

Holding me close to her chest, my mom rocked me until my wailing and tears stopped. Only the aftermath of breath-catching hiccups remained.

Dad spoke softly to me. "Noah, are you okay?"

I did not smile and did not raise my eyes. My gasps for breaths intensified and my lower lip began to tremble again.

"Were you hurt?" Dad asked. My mom was still rocking me back and forth, back and forth. Getting no response, Dad asked, "Did something happen to frighten you, Noah?"

No smile. But I arched my body by tightening my muscles, in a last attempt to explain. I rolled my eyes toward the ceiling, affirming Dad's suspicions. No more questions. They didn't understand. I had started to suck my lower lip again, in and out of my mouth, as I fought back tears. Losing the battle, a small cry had begun to seep out of my lungs.

"Were you afraid of the snow? The cold? A noise?" My mom pressed on with a battery of questions quickly before I became too upset to reply. "Of something Emma did?"

Receiving no response, my mom reiterated, "But something did happen outside to frighten you. Is that right, Noah?"

I lifted my eyes and flashed a fleeting smile amid more waves of tears and sobs. I knew my mom would have dozens of questions for me, but I sensed she knew I had grown too upset to answer them anymore. I needed to calm down first or I'd be no good to anyone, especially to the little boy next door. I tried to relax. Until exhaustion overtook me.

Then it came.

The sudden, involuntary tremble of my muscles gripped my thin frame. I imagined it was what a snake must feel like when shedding its skin. That's the first thought I always had when these came on. I hated seizures. Particularly the grand mal seizures. The big ones. The serious ones. The ones I was never quite sure I'd ever live through. The ones where I held fast to my soul so no one, including God, could take it.

My muscles rippled and buckled in waves up and down my limbs, starting small and rising like the ocean tides with an oncoming hurricane. The muscle spasm climbed up my arms and legs like a python, squeezing the consciousness out of my thin body. The last thought I had was *Not now!*

Then my world turned black and still.

CHAPTER 43

JUDY MANNING'S EYES WERE glued to the screen.

Streeter leaned toward the keyboard to shut off the video. "Why do you carry this?"

"Isn't it obvious?" Her gaze alternated between the chief and Streeter.

"Not to me," Streeter said, his voice low and easy. "Help me."

"It's Christmas. I was going to be all alone. Without little Max. I needed a reminder of how much he loved me."

Her gray eyes looked nothing like Ida's to me now, and although I had seen a resemblance, for the life of me I couldn't understand how TSA had let this woman through security using my sister's identity.

"Did you go home to pack? When you took little Max to the airport?" Streeter asked.

"What? No. There was no time for that," Judy said, her eyes dropping to the black screen where little Max's image had been playing. "Can you play it again?"

"So you packed ahead of time? Knowing you were traveling with the boy?" Streeter asked.

"Packed?"

"Don't you have luggage with you?"

"No, I . . . I grabbed a bus to the nearest hotel after spending the night looking for little Max in the airport. I saw you tracking a scent, tried to figure out where he might be, if he was hiding. I followed the officers, too, and doubled back over the entire airport on this side of security. Then I went to the main terminal and spent time searching every crevice, every store, on every level. I had just enough money to get a change in my ticket back to NYC, but I just couldn't leave without little Max. I didn't know what to do and finally decided I needed a shower to clear my head."

I actually felt sorry for her. Almost.

Streeter asked, "So if you didn't go back to your apartment yesterday, what made you think to grab that video before leaving for work?"

"Well, I knew little Max was leaving and that I was taking him to the airport. I was hoping Mr. Williams would let me go with him, and if he didn't, I suspected it would be a long holiday for me."

"I still don't understand," Streeter said. "Where did you intend to play that video once little Max was on the plane? I mean, if you had every intention of going back to your apartment at the end of the day, after work, why grab the video?"

An expression of surprise registered on her sallow face. "I always carry a video of little Max with me everywhere I go. I thought you were wondering why I chose that particular video."

Streeter's eyebrow arched and I managed to exchange a glance with the chief, telegraphing that this woman was nothing but weirdness.

"So let me get this straight. You just happened to have a video of little Max in your purse, you just happened to have a phony ID in your purse, and you just happened to have a fistful of cash, enough to bribe the airline employee to get you a seat on the plane on Christmas Eve." The rare expression of Streeter's sarcasm was totally lost on the nutty nanny.

"Agent Pierce, you have this all wrong. I always carry the passport and a video of little Max in my purse. And Mr. Williams gave the cash to me as my Christmas bonus yesterday morning. So that was unusual. I did stop at an ATM, just in case." Judy Manning shot an apologetic look my way. "I found your sister's passport. She must have lost it years ago, before Mr. Williams married the Mrs. I was going to let Mr. Williams know, but I . . . I decided against it. I didn't do anything wrong."

"What do you mean, you didn't do anything wrong? You posed as my sister. Were you planning to abduct little Max all along and pin the crime on her?" I balled my fists, ready to throw some punches at her for involving my sister. "And why in the hell were you stalking me last night?"

She buried her face in her hands, rocking side to side as she moaned. Streeter shot me a look that told me to back off. I knew I'd made a mistake the second the words left my mouth. I let my emotion—my sister's involvement—take priority over my job.

"Ms. Manning, do you know where the boy might be?" Streeter's voice was calm.

I was on the edge of my seat, staring at the woman across from me, embarrassed that I had caused her to start pulling out clumps of her own hair, the straggles a raggedy mess.

"Or who might have taken him?" Gates mumbled, but I didn't think Manning had heard him through her sobbing.

She shook her head, her face down on the table, her shoulders racked with sobs and her fingers clutching her hair.

"Where do you think Maximillian Bennett Williams III is? Ms. Manning?" Streeter pressed.

I didn't realize I'd been holding my breath until she began to shout, "I don't know! I don't know! I lost him. He was on the plane with me. He sang 'Feliz Navidad,' just as I'd taught him. And then he was gone." She was sobbing, swiping her nose with a sleeve and wiping her face on the inside of her shirt.

"What do you mean, you lost him?" Streeter asked.

"He was just gone. When I got off the plane. Normally, escorts make unaccompanied minors wait until everyone else deplanes and then take the child to the next gate. But he was already gone by the time I made it up the aisle. I was in the very back row by the bathroom. The last row. And by the time I deplaned, every seat was empty. Empty. No little Max."

She buried her face in her hands again, bending at the waist and rocking back and forth, as she wailed, sobbing and moaning. "I lost him. I lost him. My boy. My poor boy."

There she goes with calling little Max her boy again. She's totally bonkers, if you ask me.

Streeter shared a look with Tony and me and then said, "Ms. Manning. Can I be honest with you?"

She sat up, wiped her face, and stared at him—her eyes puffy and red, her nose a purplish rose color, and her hair bedraggled. She not only looked twenty years older but wasted. "Of course."

"My observation is that you love little Max dearly."

"Like he was my own flesh and blood."

"Did you ever have hopes you would raise him that way? As your own flesh and blood? As your son?"

She shook her head. "Not hopes. Reality. He was my son."

That confused me. By the looks on the others' faces, it confused them, too.

Streeter leaned forward. "You were the nanny, not the mother."

"You're wrong. I was the mother and the father to that boy. The Williamses simply owned him. They were the sperm and egg donors."

I just couldn't imagine Max entrusting his child to this *Hand that Rocks the Cradle* crazy lady or why he didn't see her neurosis.

"You clearly love little Max," Streeter said, even more calmly than before. He was starting to creep me out, too. Didn't he recognize the whack job in front of him? "What would you do if you *had* found little Max last night?"

"I would have . . ." her voice trailed off and her glance slid toward the windows. "I don't know."

"Oh, I think you do."

"I didn't have much money. But that wouldn't have mattered to little Max. We would have been fine. At least he'd be safe. With me. I could have eventually made it back to Manchester. In time."

"So you thought about it? Taking him from DIA if you found him?" Streeter coaxed.

Her eyes flicked back to his face, flitting to every square inch of his rugged, granite features. "Of course. He'd be safe."

"With you."

"With me," she said, raising her chin.

"And what would you have told the Williamses?"

"I . . ." she lowered her eyes. "I thought about it. But I doubt I would have ever found the courage to take him. I'd have called Mr. Williams. Brought little Max back home. To NYC."

I shivered, thinking of how vulnerable parents must feel about leaving their children in the care of others, people like Judy Manning who became so openly attached that she admitted to thinking about kidnapping him. Predators came from every angle for these young, naïve children. Streeter noticed me shiver and I felt his leg press against mine to comfort me. I was grateful to him for that, for allowing me to work through my emotions as I stared into the face of evil.

Streeter added, "And what would you say to me if I told you we'd found him hurt or dead?"

She pulled her hands away from her face and leveled a glare at Agent Pierce with her beady, dark gray eyes appearing positively maniacal. She jabbed a finger at Streeter's nose and warned through clenched teeth, "If someone so much as touched one hair on my boy's head, I would find them and rip them apart, limb by limb, and drag them skinless. I'd let them die a slow, painful death."

Streeter's nostrils flared. Was that a look of amusement on his face? "Who do you think was capable of doing this to your boy?"

"I have plenty of names. Bad people. Mr. Williams does business with a lot of them. And he seems to anger everyone he works with."

She started listing names; some were familiar from the list provided by Max earlier and some were new. Then she started in on names from Melissa's dealings, people who had threatened her over the years in the course of being a supermodel: stalkers, crazy people, jealous people, desperate people who might take extreme measures to make their point or extract their pound of flesh from the Williamses, as Manning put it. I found it both odd and interesting that never once did she mention either Max or Melissa's potential suspects.

When she had exhausted her list of names, Streeter said, "Well I think we're about done here, Ms. Manning. You've been quite helpful."

"You won't be sharing what I've told you with Mr. Williams, will you?" she said, suddenly realizing how much she had revealed.

"Specifically, what wouldn't you want us to share?" Streeter asked.

"That I disobeyed him," she said, as if telling us she had contemplated kidnapping the child and moving him to England wasn't the single biggest revelation, not to mention a crime. This woman truly wasn't operating on all cylinders, from what I could tell. "That I flew here. On the same plane as little Max. He has exacting standards. And I've made mistakes in the past, mistakes that nearly cost me my job."

"Do you think Mr. Williams's exacting standards had any relevance on little Max's disappearance?"

"If you're asking me if I think either Mr. Williams or the Mrs. was capable of staging the boy's disappearance, I can most assuredly tell you 'yes.'"

"Tell me about the text you sent Mrs. Williams this morning," Streeter said.

Judy Manning's expression morphed yet again. "She's horrible. And she should pay for what she's done to—"

The door flew open. Melissa Williams rushed toward Judy with Max close on her canary-yellow heels. "I thought that was you! Where is he? Where's little Max, you crazy bitch?"

Before we could stop her, Melissa had rounded the table and stood over our witness. In a flash, Judy rose to her feet and leveled a punch to Melissa's gut, screaming, "Where's my boy?"

Melissa reached out and grabbed Judy's hair, yanking with both fists. Judy's thin body was tossed to the floor like a rag doll, Melissa landing on top of the nanny in a brawl. The women went at each other, clawing and scratching, punching and shoving. It looked like a fair fight between a rabid, miniature pit bull and a giant canary. Max was trying to pull Melissa off Judy as the two women accused each other of abducting little Max.

Gates attempted to intervene and Judy Manning slugged him in the mouth. Streeter was calling for back up and I heard Phil calling on his radio. Max had his arms snaked around Melissa's shoulders. I took quick steps to do the same with Judy Manning, only I was too late.

At the instant Max restrained Melissa, Nanny Judy rose quickly to her feet. As she moved to level a powerful swing intended for Melissa's face, Max pulled Melissa back, lost his footing, and fell backward to the floor, Melissa falling on top of him. In the commotion, I hadn't noticed Manning grab the pistol from the holster clipped to my pants, leveling the barrel of my 9mm Sig Sauer at Melissa Williams's beautiful forehead.

Several other pistols were pulled and aimed in a fraction of an instant, the chief, Streeter, and Phil training their weapons on Judy Manning.

"Where is he?" Manning screamed. "My son? Where did you take him, you narcissistic witch!?"

"Don't shoot! Put it down," Streeter growled.

"What did you do? Who took him?" Nanny Judy growled at the stunned model sprawled across her ex, and she stepped closer to the pair.

"What are you talking about?" Melissa Williams whimpered, scrabbling backward so fast her feet came out of her shoes and she bumped into Max, who also crab-crawled away from Judy Manning. "He's not your son. He's our son, you crazy bitch."

"Judy, you're not helping," I said. "Give me my gun. Seriously. Before you do something stupid."

"Where is he?" Judy Manning hadn't heard a word Streeter or I had said. She had snapped. She took another step, this time twisting her foot on a yellow spike heel.

Instinct made me lunge at Judy and tackle her as if I'd been a lineman all my life. My gun discharged close to my ear as I threw my arms around the tiny lunatic, our shoulders slamming against the floor. I actually heard her head bounce against the tiles and my pistol skitter across the floor.

For several moments, nobody moved. Judy Manning lay still on the ground beside me, knocked out cold. Melissa panted as she rolled off of Max. Streeter was at my side instantly and was helping me to my feet, handing me my pistol, which I clipped back in my holster. Officers and agents poured into the room as Gates dabbed at his bloody nose and split lip.

Everything had happened so fast. An instantaneous eruption and then the room grew eerily silent. My ears were ringing, but the sounds were starting to reach through the ear-piercing shot that had deafened me.

I noticed Manning moan as she sat up, blood dripping from her head. Phil rushed to her side. In a low voice—maybe he was shouting—Phil said to Streeter, "We need medics."

Melissa's gaze slid from the hole in the drywall toward her canary yellow, spike-heeled shoe, and she froze in horror at what might have been if not for the nanny tripping. Max embraced her as she repeated, "She doesn't have little Max. She doesn't have him. Max, who does? Oh no!"

At the same time, Judy Manning was mumbling something similar. "If she doesn't have him, who does? Who has little Max?"

In the chaos, my Quantico training came rushing back with a flood of data that made me realize who it was we should be looking for, thanks to the insane obsession of Judy Manning. My mind raced for the first time with certainty toward the idea that little Max was not taken by his dad for monetary maneuvering in a bitter divorce as I had first suspected, was not taken by his mom for publicity as I had speculated, or by a kidnapper for ransom, but by someone with far worse intentions than Nanny Judy. I shuddered, fearing we might all be too late, wasting time focusing on those closest to the boy instead of on the real perpetrator. A pedophile. Or murderer.

Streeter's tender embrace—his strong, warm hand wrapping around my waist—steeled my resolve to stay focused.

"Streeter, we have to hurry. Before it's too late."

CHAPTER 44

Noah

I HEARD FOOTSTEPS APPROACH and the door swung open. They must have been startled to see my disheveled bed empty. Dad hurried around my bed. "Noah, what are you doing over by the window?"

I had rolled out of my bed and inched my way across the floor to the full-length picture window in my room again. My favorite spot. When Mom and Dad bought the home seven years ago, Dad had suggested they install a window that was all the way to the floor so that when I was lying on the floor in my room, I could see outside and enjoy the sunlight. Here I was. By the window. Only this time, it was the boy I wanted to see.

My dad and mom stood watching me tap on the window with my awkwardly contracted and contorted fist.

"You should be exhausted. You usually sleep for a day or longer after a seizure like that, Noah. Are you okay?"

I didn't smile. No, I was not okay. I was exhausted from the seizure. I heard my doctor say that every five minutes of my major seizures was the equivalent of running a marathon. Hell yes, I was tired. And hell no, I wasn't okay. Maximillian Bennett Williams II was right next door and I had to get someone to listen.

I arched my back and flipped myself over onto my stomach. Lifting my head and shoulders and propping my weight on my thin elbows, I craned my neck to see into the neighbor's yard below from my second-story window vantage point. I had been waiting for what seemed like an hour to see if the boy would come out to play again. Or come to the window. I was looking for an image, a shadow, or any movement at all in the neighbor's yard below.

I was worried about the little boy and hoped to relieve some of my concerns by seeing him again. Unfortunately, I'd seen nothing. The creepy man had warned him about not playing outside. What had he done to punish little Max?

I heard my mom bend down beside me. "Noah, do you want to tell me about it now?"

I smiled briefly.

"Emma went with Auntie Elizabeth and Uncle Michael, so I'm all you've got. I'm going to have to figure this out. Yes and no questions? Or five fingers?" My mom paused, then asked, "Questions?"

I did nothing.

"Spell it out?"

I smiled.

She sighed. "Okay, let's see. First finger. Yes?"

I flicked my eyes up.

"All right, first finger is correct. Now first knuckle? Nope? Okay it's not 'A.' The second knuckle? No wait, valley between is next. The valley? No?"

This was going to take forever. I told myself to be patient. But it was hard.

While she asked, plucking through to last knuckle "G," second finger, first valley "I," third finger, second valley "R," I finally inched my way close enough to the window to show them. On second finger, third knuckle "L," my dad finally said, "Girl?"

My eyes flicked up.

"Emma?"

I did nothing.

"Girl, but not Emma. Someone at school? No? Next word?"

I was going to look up, but then decided we might be here all day and I had already lost time, although I didn't have a clue what time it was.

In exasperation, Mom asked a question that did not have a yes or no answer. "Noah, what's the matter with you?"

I had to do something. I had to answer her question quickly and with conviction. I knew what I should do, but I still didn't want to do it. It was going to hurt and the very thought of it made my eyelashes flutter. It may cause another grand mal seizure, which I wasn't sure my body could take. I was exhausted and sore and this would only make things worse. But my mom needed an answer. Quickly.

I closed my eyes, anticipating the noise and pain and I flung my head against the window with a loud thud. The window didn't break. I had never done anything like this before, but it seemed the only thing to do.

Startled, my dad fell to his knees beside my mom. "Noah!"

I lifted my head and smiled at them, releasing a moan of happiness that I had finally gotten their attention. I squeezed my eyes shut again as I flung my head against the window a second time.

My mom rolled me over on my back and scolded me. "Noah, stop that. You could hurt yourself. What has gotten into you?"

I could feel my dimples deepen as I smiled widely and rolled my eyes upward. I had their full attention. I arched my back and flung my arm against the window, my knuckles striking the cold pane of glass with a small thud. My hand hurt. I moaned with a laugh and repeated the trick.

Confused, Dad asked, "Noah, do you want to go outside?"

I did not smile. Trying to stay focused, not to mention the head banging, was giving me a headache.

Mom spoke to Dad as if I wasn't even there or couldn't hear them. "Gabriel, Noah has never woken up this quickly after a seizure, never rolled out of his bed after a seizure. He knows how much it hurts to hit his head, yet now he's intentionally flinging himself at the window. Maybe we need to take him to a doctor."

Then I heard her grow still. I held my breath, hoping she was catching on. I really really wanted to shout, *There's a girl next door who is not a girl at all. It's the missing boy from the airport. Call Auntie Liv. The man is getting mean. Hurry!* Of course, nothing came out of my throat. Not even a gurgle. I was too tired.

"Look. That's where Emma said Noah was sitting earlier when he became so upset. See his chair tracks? Noah, is this about earlier today? What upset you?"

I squealed. I could barely contain myself. They were finally getting it. I could communicate. I kicked my legs, arched my back, and opened my mouth wide. I struggled to smile, but knew they understood. I was saying *yes*. My whole body was saying *yes*.

My mom asked, "And something happened out there today to upset you, right?"

I squealed again and arched my back even higher before relaxing back to the floor in anticipation of the next question.

Dad pointed. "Footsteps in the snow. On the other side of the fence. There are little footprints all over the yard and one large set of footprints from the back door to the fence and back again. Looks like a child was outside with our neighbor sometime since last night, since it snowed until early this morning when I shoveled Mrs. Parrent's driveway and walk."

"You're right!" My mom asked, "Noah, was the neighbor man outside today?"

I smiled.

"With a girl? The girl Emma said she saw? Was that the girl you were trying to tell me about earlier with the five-finger method?"

I smiled.

"There's a girl after all." My mom asked at the same time my dad asked, "Do you want to go play with the girl?"

I smiled and my moan no longer sounded joyous.

"Did something happen? Something bad?" Mom sounded worried.

I smiled, but it wasn't happy.

"Did the neighbor man say something mean to you, Noah?"

I vividly recalled the man calling me a vegetable, but I didn't want my dad to veer off track, so I suppressed my smile. *Of course he was mean to me, but that's not the point!* I screamed in my head.

"Did the neighbor man say or do something mean to the little girl?"

Kidnapping is mean. Keeping little Max prisoner is mean. Everything about this man was mean. Wasn't it obvious? I smiled and whimpered. I couldn't see their expressions, but I hoped they were horrified enough to call the police.

"Did he hurt the little girl, Noah?" my mom asked.

I had to think about that. I concentrated really, really hard and smiled. Weakly. It was the first lie I'd ever told my parents, which nearly broke my heart. But it had to be done.

CHAPTER 45

AFTER THE EMTs DOCTORED Chief Gates's face and strapped Judy Manning on a gurney, Tony charged her with assault with a deadly weapon and intent to murder before she was hauled off to the hospital. Max and Melissa Williams staggered out of the makeshift headquarters in retreat to their hotel room, both appearing more like whipped pups than the global superstars they were. With everyone gone, we fell into our chairs as if we'd been carrying the weight of the world.

"Could this get any worse?" I asked.

"What in the hell was that all about? Am I misunderstanding what just happened or do none of these three have a clue where the boy is?" Gates asked.

Streeter shook his head. "I don't think they do."

"That's not good, is it?" I asked.

Streeter eyed me, the shake of his head nearly imperceptible.

"I'm sorry, Streeter, for letting her get to my weapon. It will never happen again," I said.

He plowed his fingers through his short, white hair. "It appeared to me that Judy Manning was the aggressor here; she threw the first punch."

"There was a fight?" Jack asked, poking his head through the door, carrying boxes of pizzas, which instantly made my stomach growl.

"Melissa Williams stormed into the room talking smack, and Judy Manning had had enough. She snapped. Threw a few punches and got ahold of my gun," I explained. Jack set the boxes on the table.

"Your 9mm? Everybody okay?" Jack asked, studying my face.

Rubbing his bandaged jaw, Gates said, "It may hurt to eat that pizza, but okay."

"What happened to you?"

"Nanny Judy happened," Gates said.

"She hit you?"

Streeter said, "Tony, let's search the hotel where Manning was staying and confiscate everything in her room."

"You think she was lying? Staged all that to cover her tracks?" Gates asked, echoing my sentiments of incredulity.

Streeter shook his head. "I don't. But just in case."

"I don't think Nanny Judy's responsible. Or Max. Or Melissa," I said, grabbing a slice of pepperoni. "Not any more. I'm convinced after all that."

"And I don't think it's a kidnapping for ransom," Streeter said, leaning back in his chair, watching me.

"Me neither," I said. "But Manning's obsession reminded me of what they taught us at Quantico about the warped minds of abductors. It made me realize how crazy some folks are and how desperate they can become to 'protect' and 'save' children. I'm thinking the psychological profile of whoever abducted little Max might very well be a lot like what Nanny Judy just demonstrated to us. Obsessed with a child, desperate to keep him safe."

"A pedophile," Gates said.

"Or a whack job like Nanny Judy," I said.

Streeter said, "Gates, don't you keep a list of Denver's registered sex offenders?"

"And the Greater Denver area," the chief said, folding his first piece of pizza and eating half of it in one bite. Through a mouthful, he said, "Worst Christmas meal ever. No offense, Linwood."

"None taken. And agreed," answered Jack. "If your team can pull that data, can we narrow it down to a list of those sexual offenses that involve children?"

"Already on it. I'll find out what they've learned so far." Gates was punching away at his cell phone as he rose to his feet. He stuffed the last of his slice in his mouth and walked out of the room to get the data coming.

"Where do we go from here?"

Streeter said, "We need to have someone stick like glue to Melissa and to Max Williams. Something might break after what just happened. Who's on that detail now?"

I said, "Kyle's with the officers who followed Manning to the hospital, waiting until she's well enough to be booked and taken to jail. Phil followed Melissa and Max to their hotel."

"Good. Witnessing something like that shakes people up. Maybe this will get one or the other to talk if they know something more about little Max. What'd you find, Linwood?" Streeter said, lifting his eyes from the files he was studying to the video screen.

"Just watch," Jack said.

I sat beside Jack, and Streeter walked around the table and stood over my shoulder. I focused on not letting thoughts about Judy Manning grabbing my pistol and nearly blowing away the Williamses crowd my mind. But I found it difficult to stay focused as Jack queued up the video. My eyes drifted to the chunk of drywall where the bullet had lodged in the outer wall, inches from the large pane of glass that would have shattered all over the tarmac beyond.

"After reviewing eight hours of video per camera angle from the key cameras Liv selected, I think we found something. But I want you to weigh in on it before we pursue this much further."

Jack dragged the sliding bar to a certain place on the video clip and clicked play.

On the screen near the back of the crowd heading for an exit, I watched a heavy man with dark sunglasses, a long dark coat, and shiny, dark hair heading toward the camera.

"This video was taken on key camera four, at the closest exit from the bathroom near the Buckhorn Bar and Grill to the short-term parking lot."

We stood transfixed by the grayscale movement on the screen.

When I saw the images of the heavy man in a dark coat quickly escorting a small child, I felt a surge of excitement and asked, "Is that him?"

The grainy images of the man were impossible to glean an identity from, given that all we saw was the top of his head because of the angle of the camera lens. Unless at any point the man looked up directly into the camera, which I didn't expect, given how "invisible" this guy had been up until now, this was the best we were going to get.

Jack hit pause and zoomed in on the image. "I think this is the boy. See? His hair is black under that stocking cap, like the man's hair."

Jack added, "See the child's face? The eyes? Don't you think this looks like the boy?"

We studied the zoomed image of the child, a child who frequently looked up at the camera and all around. A child full of wonder and curiosity.

Tony leaned closer and said, "This looks like a little girl to me. See the flowers rimming the hat? And on the pink coat?"

I hadn't even noticed the chief coming back in the room and was glad he had made it back in time to see these video clips.

Streeter said, "The eyes. That's him."

Jack said, "We think you're both right. Watch."

The man walked toward the camera and just as they approached the glass doors visible in the bottom edge of the image, the child broke free from the man's grip and ran toward the glass door, pressing his face against the glass.

"What is she doing?" Tony asked.

"Making a slobber impression on the glass. Look, see? The kid's laughing and pointing at the masterpiece."

The fat man hurried toward the child who had broken free from his grip. As if they'd been walking across a crowded street at rush hour, the man looked panicked in his movements and reactions. When he grabbed the child by the wrist and pulled her away from the window, the child laughed and pointed at the window.

Streeter said, "A slobber face."

"Not a girl," Tony said.

"Exactly."

"What is a slobber face?" I asked.

Streeter said, "I thought you had brothers?"

"I do. Two of them. But I don't see the connection."

Jack's said, "Parents don't like having their windows messed up, so in most houses, children are forbidden to play with the glass, right?"

I nodded. I remembered that rule when I was growing up. Both at home and in the car. With nine of us, my mom was constantly washing windows.

"Little boys this age love to press their noses and mouths and tongues and grubby hands against the glass to make a funny impression. It's what boys do," Jack said.

I looked back over my shoulder from Streeter's face to Gates's face and saw that both men agreed with that categorical observation of five-year-old boys. I stole a glance toward Jack, who nodded.

"The boy in this video is doing what boys do when they're away from the watchful eye of parents. They break free from an adult's grip and do slobber faces," Jack said.

"Or wander off from an escort out of boredom," Streeter said.

"Or grab the flight attendant's mic and sing 'Feliz Navidad,'" I added.

"It's what willful, energetic, happy little boys do," Jack said.

I wished I weren't sitting beside Jack and that I was facing him instead so I could study his face. He knew this from direct experience, his son forever frozen in time at the age of six. He had probably replayed every single movement, activity, and decision related to his son over and over in his mind. He'd know. And it's probably the reason this moment caught his eye. Someone like me with no kids might not have caught the subtlety. But now that they had pointed it out to me, I remember doing the same thing. Only as my brothers stuck their tongues to the inside of the frozen windows and made slobber faces in our station wagon on the way to school, us girls were making flowers or tiny feet from the heel of our curled hands, using pinkies to dot the five toes.

"I would have expected any child on the video to be scared, upset, looking lost, or maybe crying or trying to pull free from the grip of the stranger who's taking him. But this child is happy and laughing," I said. "I wonder if he knows the man?"

"He did pull free, and see how the man reacts? He looks the other way first, around him to see if anyone notices, then hurries after the child. Definitely suspicious behavior," Gates said.

"He looks terrified," I observed. "At least judging by his body language."

Jack nodded. "Right. The man's reaction was what made us pause the first time. And if it weren't for the slobber face moment, I might not have looked closer at what I first thought was a little girl being led out of the airport by her father. On second glance and after clarifying the close-up of the child, I'm thinking this is the boy."

Jack's finger tapped the keyboard until a large image pulled in slowly on the screen.

Streeter said, "See? The eyes. It's definitely him."

Jack pulled up a picture of little Max and put the image side-by-side with the photo we'd been showing to drum up witnesses.

"Oh my," I said under my breath. "It is him. It's little Max!"

"It fits, Streeter, the time of this video with the account by Kevin Benson," Jack confirmed.

"And with the scent that caused Beulah to hesitate in the short-term parking. But why hadn't she followed little Max's trail from the bathroom out this door?" Gates asked.

Jack looked over at me and then answered, "I'm speculating, but the smell of shoe polish, especially as much of it as this guy would've used on the boy's hair, probably confused or overpowered the scent for Beulah."

I nodded. "That's what I told Streeter last night. Makes sense."

"Replay that," Streeter said. After rewinding and playing the clip several more times, Streeter told Jack, "Stop it, right there. What's that?"

Jack zoomed in on the hump on the man's back. "Oh, I see that now. I didn't before."

"It's a backpack, probably filled with the clothes he dressed him in: the light coat and stocking cap and what looks like sweatpants for little Max. See? He probably just slid those over little Max's knickers."

"And that's where he had the black shoe polish. In the backpack," Jack added.

"Oh, sure. Look how baggy the pants are on the child. And the coat is too big," Tony said. "What's he carrying?"

"Peanut M&M's," I said. I knew my candy. "That's probably how the

NOAH'S RAINY DAY   289

guy got little Max to come to him. Offered him candy. And look how happy little Max is."

"He doesn't even know what's happening," Streeter said.

"Unless he knows the guy, like Liv suggested. Unless someone hired him to do his or her dirty work," Tony said.

"I just don't think this was all part of a plan like that. I really think that sex offender list will help us, Chief. I don't think someone paid Kevin Benson's girlfriend to convince Benson to meet her in the main terminal and distract him so this guy could snatch little Max. It just doesn't fly," I said. "Besides, who in their right mind would hire this guy?" I pointed at the slovenly man on the screen.

"I agree with you, Liv," Streeter said. I noticed him studying the man on the video as closely as I was and wished I could read his mind. "And not a kidnapping."

Jack said, "And even if something tragic happened—like the boy was accidentally killed—a kidnapper would most likely go through with a ransom attempt, if that was the plan all along."

Streeter turned his wrist. "It's been more than twenty-four hours and no call. We have hourly reports from both field offices in New York City and Los Angeles, who've been monitoring the Williamses' phones. Phil is watching their every movement. Our best use of time is to find this man and worry about who hired him or his motives later. I agree with Liv. I think the list of local child sex offenders is key, Tony."

"Might be dozens. It will take time to locate each person on the list," the chief said. He hitched a hip and huffed, I assumed with exasperation, which is what we all felt.

Jack replayed the clip as we all watched the man's movements in slow motion. "We're working on the exact sequence of events on this guy and the so-called little girl once they left the airport."

Streeter said, "We have to find this guy. And fast. Before it's too late."

CHAPTER 46

Noah

MY DAD PLEADED WITH my mom. "No, no, no, Frances. If you're thinking what I think you're thinking, stop. We can't do anything about it."

"We could call the child protective services people," Mom suggested.

Yes, yes, I screamed.

"No," Dad said sternly. "No, we can't. They'll think we're crazy. Think about it, Frances. How are we going to explain that our son who cannot talk, write, or sign told us that he witnessed a young girl getting abused by our neighbor? It will never fly. They'll just think we're lunatics."

Not a girl. Not a girl. The boy. Maximillian! I kept saying, the moans tangling up with my parents' discussion.

"But Gabriel, we can't just ignore this. What about that little girl? Isn't there something we can do? Maybe we should call Liv."

I squealed. Then I heard my dad walk over to the window. Maybe he would see what I couldn't. Maybe he'd spot Sammy playing in the back-yard. Maybe the creepy neighbor photo guy would come barreling out of the house again and yank Sammy back inside. Maybe my dad would see a reason to call the police.

"Let me think about it. We'll come up with something." I felt Dad lean down to tickle my stomach, saying, "Good job, kiddo! But listen here, cowboy. I don't want to see you banging your head against the window again, you hear me? You've got a knot and a bruise the size of a golf ball."

I didn't care. It was worth it. If my parents called the authorities, they would figure out that the girl next door was actually the missing boy from television.

Dad scooped me up and carried me downstairs. "So we have Christmas dinner on our own tonight. Your mom thought maybe we should eat whatever we want."

That brought a smile to my lips.

After eating my fill of leftover roast beef, mashed potatoes and homemade gravy, and so many cookies I felt like a stuffed piñata, I shoved my thick tongue out my lips to tell my mom *Enough*. Dad lifted me from my chair and laid me on a blanket in front of the living room television while my parents did dishes. It was early and the sun was still shining, but I hadn't eaten much lunch before my seizure and almost nothing last night. I should be exhausted, but the thought of that poor kid next door missing out on Christmas kept my mind too busy to sleep.

I heard my mom ask my dad, "What do you think we should do about the girl next door?"

"I don't know," Dad answered.

"I was thinking maybe we could take a plate of Christmas cookies over there. Just be friendly? Maybe see if the girl's okay. Discreetly, of course."

"Of course," Dad said. "I wish Emma were here. So our inquiries after the little girl might not feel so intrusive. Like we've been spying on him or something."

"Well, we could say Noah saw her," Mom suggested.

I frowned, didn't smile. My lip started trembling.

"Not a great idea, huh, Noah? And Emma wouldn't have cooperated anyway, even if she were here. Maybe I can say I saw the little girl from the window."

As they finished the dishes, I heard my parents clanging plates and clinking silverware as they loaded the dishwasher. My attention was split between them and the lady on the television. I had hoped they'd finished. But they hadn't. If they didn't finish soon, they'd miss the lady altogether. I needed to do something fast.

I squealed as loud as I could to get their attention. I hated to have to do this again, but I held my breath and hurled my head like a spear, but this time my target was not the window. I heard quiet in the kitchen. They must have heard the thud of my head against the television screen. Stars circled my muddy gray vision. I was pleased.

My mom was first to run into the living room. Dad was right behind her. They stood above me and stared as they watched me push my weight onto my elbows, lift my head high, and fling myself at the television set again.

They stood, silent.

On the screen, they watched as the images of the now familiar missing boy named Maximillian Bennett Williams III flashed across the set. The volume was up high enough that they could hear the giggling boy. He called to his nanny from the top of a slide. "Nanny Judy! Nanny Judy! Watch this!" His giggling was distinct, infectious. To drive the point home, I mustered enough energy to lift myself off the floor again and to launch myself a final time at the TV. Even to me, the thud sounded like a bowling ball being dropped on a concrete driveway.

My head was pounding. WHAM, WHAM! But at least there was no giant finger plucking at the inside of my rib cage. I would be fine.

Mom knelt and scolded, "Noah! Stop doing that!"

When she rolled me over on my back, my gray eyes darted about in an effort to focus on hers and not on the circling stars. I squeezed my eyes shut to stop the throbbing.

My parents remained still. They listened to the rest of the news story as the female reporter spoke somberly into the microphone. "The authorities have not confirmed reports that kidnappers have contacted the Williamses. Mr. and Mrs. Williams insist nothing has changed since the earlier press conference, still offering a quarter-million-dollar reward for information leading to the return of their son. We will stay on top of this story as events unfold. And we here at Channel Nine News are hoping for the safe return of little Max Williams."

"Now what, Noah?" Dad asked.

Mom added, "You seem obsessed with this kid. Are you trying to tell us something about him, too?"

She got it. I knew she would. I smiled and moaned happily, which was saying a lot since my head kept pounding and throbbing.

"Do you think the missing boy is being hurt by someone just like the little girl next door?" Dad asked.

I was confused about how to answer that question. The answer was definitely *yes* but if I answered the question that way, my parents would misunderstand why I was banging my head against the television. I wanted them to notice the missing boy's giggle.

Dad had tried to figure out what I was thinking but missed the mark. What do I do now? Mom was so close and now was getting off track. Too much time had passed while I was making up my mind on how to answer, while I tried to blink the stupid stars away that kept circling and spinning. My parents assumed my answer was *no* anyway.

"Noah," my mother asked. "Do you think that there are some similarities between the girl next door and the missing boy?"

This time, I smiled and darted my eyes upward. Better that they stay alert, even if not exactly on target.

"Do you think maybe the little girl is missing from some other home? That she doesn't belong to our neighbor?"

I arched my back. My limbs jerked and stiffened as I smiled. My mom had finally understood. Sort of.

"Not good," Dad said.

She patted my tense leg to calm me. "We'll take care of it, Noah. Don't worry. But you have to stop this head banging thing, okay?"

Gladly, I thought. I heard them slip back into the kitchen for a moment, noticing the sounds of crinkling saran wrap as it zipped across the sharp blade of the box. They were fixing a plate of cookies. They believed me! Their faith in me made me so happy, I sucked in a high-pitched screech.

"Let me go, Frances," Gabriel insisted.

"Don't be silly," Frances reasoned. "Besides, if you go, it won't look as convincing. Not many fathers go over to the neighbors' to bring cookies as a gift. That would be weird."

"Then we'll go together."

"You have to stay with Noah. Why don't you call Boots, just to be on the safe side? She might want to know about this."

Yes! Yes! I screamed in my mind. I wanted to show Auntie Liv what I recorded with my football pin. If I got anything. And she'd figure out right away that the kid next door was little Max.

"You can call Liv yourself when we get back. Noah will be fine staying here by himself for a few minutes, won't you Noah?" Gabriel said.

I smiled. I liked the idea that they would both have a chance to see the little girl and hopefully recognize that she wasn't a girl at all but the boy on television. After a few seconds of the sound of coats and boots and hats being pulled on, Mom and Dad were out the front door.

And I was left alone.

CHAPTER 47

BY THE TIME SHE and Gabriel arrived at their neighbor's door, Frances's heart pounded in her chest. Nervously, she rang the doorbell. Listening to the faint noises behind the door, Frances held Gabriel's hand, trying not to look too nervous in case their neighbor was watching through the peephole or from behind the curtains.

After several seconds, she rang the bell again. No one came to the door.

"Come on, Frances," Gabriel said. "You tried."

Frances pounded on the door with the heel of her fist. Eventually, the door opened, an odor wafting from inside that reminded Frances of a hospital. Or a laundromat. She couldn't quite place the smell. Bleach maybe? The large, slovenly man on the other side of the door had a pocked face. Childhood acne, she wondered? She'd never seen her neighbor up close, only from a distance, his face always obscured. But now, here he was. His eyelids were heavy, his lips thick. His hair was black and shiny, as if it hadn't been washed for a few days. It could have been from gel used to slick the thick hair into place, but Frances didn't think so. Her bet was bad hygiene. Really bad. His sickly pale skin appeared translucent and made Frances think of what a mole would look like if it took a human form. He wore baggy khaki pants and a badly wrinkled flannel shirt that smelled musty.

His wide feet were covered with dingy sweat socks, and a few unclipped toenails poked through holes in the left sock.

Pushing the wire-rimmed glasses up the bridge of his nose, his pudgy face and wide smile greeted them. "Yes?"

"Hi, I'm Gabriel Hogarty. Your next-door neighbor?" He hooked a thumb toward their house and extended his hand. "And this is my wife, Frances."

The big man looked as if he had no choice but to grab her extended hand. But he didn't. He looked past them to the street, his eyes darting about. And Frances noticed that he looked back over his shoulder, as if worried about a pot boiling over or something. He hadn't invited them inside and the door was partially open, like the yawning mouth of a scavenger.

"Did we interrupt something?" Frances asked, noticing a trickle of sweat dripping from his hairline near his right ear down his neck.

"You did," the man answered and looked at her with a puzzled expression, studying her face.

"We . . . uh, we brought you cookies," Frances said, lowering her eyes from his unwelcome gaze. She felt the burn of embarrassment on her cheeks. "For Christmas."

He stood staring at the plate of cookies in her hands, saying nothing.

"Well," Frances swallowed hard to regain her nerve. She had noticed that he had not opened the door wide enough for her to see beyond him. His large body filled the slightly open doorway. She hoped Gabriel had a better view.

Gabriel said, "We thought the girl might like some cookies, might want to come over and play with our daughter."

"Who told you about the girl?"

"Uh . . . no one. I saw her in the backyard earlier. When I was doing dishes. Who is she?"

The man stared at Frances as if she'd dumped red ants down his pants. "My daughter. I'm divorced."

"Your daughter?" Frances asked, flustered by this revelation. "We don't mean to sound nosy, it's just I saw her playing and . . . well, I thought maybe you might not have had time to bake cookies so we thought . . . well, here."

She shoved the plate at him, unceremoniously.

He took the cookies and began to shut the door without so much as a "thank you." His antisocial behavior and nervousness were unlike those of anyone she'd ever met. She actually imagined Fletcher as one of those rare people with obsessive afflictions, like hoarders or germophobes on those reality shows who never leave their house.

Frances panicked, blurting, "Can we see her? Your daughter?"

"She's busy," Fletcher said, shutting the door.

"Well, sorry to impose," Gabriel said, trying to steer Frances away from the door.

A sudden chill gripped Frances. She hadn't much cared for the way he was brushing them off, trying to get rid of them, dripping in sweat from his twitchiness. Her maternal instincts were screaming to protect the girl inside. "Doing what?"

Fletcher opened the door again, offering her a puzzled expression.

"Your daughter is busy doing what?" Frances asked again.

She drew in a breath and told herself not to jump to conclusions and not to let her imagination run wild. If Frances were honest, she'd have to admit that although odd, Fletcher seemed like a very nervous intro-vert, possibly a shy man. Her discussions with Noah had obviously biased her opinions of Fletcher. Gabriel was probably going to point that out to her the second they got back in their warm home. Noah's self-destructive behavior of late had clearly increased her anxiety. Her nerves were raw. She drew in a deep breath and told herself to relax.

Frances cleared her throat. She was about to explain her question when she noticed that Mr. Fletcher had accidentally allowed the door to open enough for them to see past him. There she was. Walking up the stairs. The little girl. She had jet-black hair, just like her dad, but it was cut long below her ears and down the back of her neck. Her bangs nearly covered her eyebrows and she wondered why the man hadn't clipped the hair with a barrette or band, so the child wouldn't be bothered with it. Below the long bangs were brilliantly green eyes, a dimple on her right cheek, and an endearing smile. But she was fidgety and nervous just like her dad.

"Is that my mom?" the child asked, her presence startling Mr. Fletcher.

"I thought I told you to stay downstairs," Fletcher croaked, choking on the last word.

"Sorry, Papa." Her eyes widened before glancing nervously from the door to her dad. She was wearing thick sweatpants, a clown shirt, and a tiny derby on top of her head. Fletcher's forehead was covered in beads of sweat and he kept glancing at his watch.

"We were busy playing. Downstairs. It's Christmas and we don't get much time together." And again, he began to shut the door.

"Merry Christmas," Gabriel said.

The child ran to the door, the movement stirring a faint smell that reminded Frances of her own childhood and watching her dad shine his shoes.

"Are you Santa?" the girl asked Gabriel.

Fletcher ignored his daughter and started to close the door.

Gabriel flattened his hands on his belly and threw his head back. "Ho ho ho, Merry Christmas!"

The little girl started to giggle. She was holding her stomach, bent over her knees by the door beside Fletcher. The child's giggle rang out loudly and clearly. Fletcher's face blanched. His ears turned bright red and his mouth was set in a determined line.

Gabriel waved again and said, "Be a good little gi—"

And Fletcher swung the door closed. Frances heard the locks turn, the girl continue to giggle, asking about Santa Claus. Frances stood staring at the closed door, listening to the girl, hearing the man saying how they had to hurry, that the child's mother would be there soon. They stood on his front step for a beat, listening to the giggling girl until it stopped altogether. And Frances's heart ached.

"No bruises, no cuts or scrapes," Gabriel said, grabbing her hand and walking her back to their house.

"That were visible."

Frances could not shake the feeling that the girl seemed somehow familiar. As she walked back to her home with Gabriel, she sighed in exasperation at how sad that little girl's life must be. She smiled at the visual image of the beautiful young girl as she came up the stairs, completely amused by Gabriel. Her smile faded when the image returned of Jason Fletcher's expression as he stared at her when she'd challenged him about his daughter.

She shivered involuntarily and hustled indoors ahead of Gabriel.

CHAPTER 48

Noah

THE HOGARTY HOUSE WAS sure quiet for it being Christmas.

As soon as they got back from Mr. Scaredy Cat's house, Dad went to meet Auntie Elizabeth and Uncle Michael at the ice skating park so he could ask Emma some questions. He's been gone for at least an hour. Mom keeps checking on me. And she keeps checking out my window. She turned the Christmas tunes up really loud to drown out her mumbling, but I can still hear her. She's worried about the little girl next door, upset by Mr. Fletcher.

At least she knows how I feel now.

I've tried to sleep, but I can't seem to turn the video off in my head. I keep seeing little Max at the fence, the man stomping up behind him and dragging him back inside. I don't want to have nightmares. I can't live with the idea that the boy is all alone over there.

All I want is for the police to come so the boy can go home and I can get some sleep. I can't figure out why Mom hasn't called Auntie Liv. Or maybe she did.

Every time I close my eyes, I see the big man take the little boy with the heartwarming giggle away from me, retreating back into that house like a rat into its hole. I want my mom to understand. I want her to try the five-finger method again, so I can explain that the little girl is little Max. But she thinks she's already figured out what I was trying to tell her. She thinks I was concerned about the little girl's safety and now she's trying to figure out a way to involve the authorities that won't further endanger the little girl. But she keeps mumbling about needing more of a reason, more evidence, or the police will have nothing to act on.

I don't know if I'm angrier at the big man for frightening the boy or at myself for not being able to communicate with my mom about what had happened sooner and more clearly. I can't seem to even get her attention to listen to me when she keeps checking on me.

I've tried.

I cursed my useless limbs and mouth for not staying in step with my mind, and I'm determined to make her listen to me. My fear has slowly evolved throughout the day to an intense anger. I want to rip through my broken shell and emerge a perfectly normal kid. A kid who could talk. A kid who could dial 911. A kid who could tell the police about his proof with his secret football pin. Instead, I'd have to wait for Auntie Liv, tell her that the missing boy from New York City was living right next door to us in Wheat Ridge, Colorado. She'd figure it out.

My mood soured. My body was spent. My seizure earlier today was serious. My parents were worried. My sister was gone until tomorrow.

My mom came in to check on me again, just as the phone rang. It was my dad. I could hear his voice, even though my mom didn't know it.

"Emma said the girl told her that her name was Sammy. I assume as in Samantha, wouldn't you?"

Mom said, "That would make sense."

"She said she never saw Mr. Fletcher, but she did see Sammy talking with Noah."

I made myself get very serious, pursing my lips tightly. That way, if Mom looked my way, she'd think I was focused on the television.

"Where did she come from, Gabriel?"

I extended my bent arm toward the television set as I craned my neck in the same direction, hoping my mom would understand that I was answering her question.

I heard Dad say, "Just a second. Let me ask her."

The television. They were talking about the missing boy on the television. Again. *That's what I'm trying to tell you, Mom. Look at the television. I know where he is. He's right next door.*

Just when I thought my efforts to communicate with her were hopeless, Mom turned up the volume.

I smiled.

The news reporter was winding down his brief story, " . . . which was rumored to have been against the FBI's suggestions. The Williamses are serious and they want their son back. I'm Bernard Allen with Channel Nine News. The complete story at ten o'clock." The background switched quickly to the face of the beautiful blond boy with the captions underneath reading "Maximillian Bennett Williams III, Missing Since Christmas Eve".

I was still. My bent fingers and hand were wavering as I attempted unsuccessfully to stretch them into a point. A moan quietly escaped my lips just before I swallowed hard.

Mom was quiet. Still.

I heard my dad say, "Nah, she doesn't know." Pause. "Frances?" What was my mom doing? She wasn't answering my dad. "Are you there?"

My mom's voice sounded odd. "Noah, is it the missing Williams boy? That's what's been bothering you?"

I smiled weakly. *She got it!* I let another moan escape my parched lips. I was tired. No, exhausted.

My dad asked, "What? Frances?"

The clip of the boy running and laughing and sliding was playing on the big screen. "Oh my Lord!"

"Frances, what is it?"

"He wasn't wearing shoes. The smell when Sammy ran to the door. It was shoe polish."

I had no clue what my mom was talking about.

"Who wasn't wearing shoes?" my dad asked.

"Meet me down at the police station. Denver, not Wheat Ridge. I'll call Boots."

She hung up the phone and said, "That laugh. Those eyes. It's little Max, isn't it Noah? That's what you've been trying to tell me."

I smiled.

Finally.

CHAPTER 49

SAMMY WAS CONFUSED.

The surroundings were dark and scary for a moment. With his eyes barely open, he looked around the basement, trying to understand all the strange shadows around him. Oh. Now he remembered. How could he forget? He yawned deeply. Nanny Judy calls it being drowsy-wowsey-woo-woo.

He giggled.

Then came the odd-smelling dampness, its funny taste on his tongue. Yuck.

He was cold and naked. Why was he naked? Where was Nanny Judy? He tried to remember why he was here. And what happened today.

Then he remembered. Papa. And the basement game.

It sounded like Papa was running around upstairs, banging stuff around. CLOMP! CLOMP! CLOMP! He curled up in the pile of blankets and covered his head. He didn't want Papa. He wanted Nanny Judy.

Papa had spent all day taking pictures of him. At first, the basement game was fun because Papa had so many different make-believe areas set up for him to pretend. A hospital, a Western town, a circus. Make-believe was fun.

It was fun until the silly redheaded girl's parents from next door visited them. Then everything got all crazy.

At first, Sammy thought Papa was very angry about the neighbors' visit. But then he let him eat the plate of cookies. But only after he'd promised to take a vitamin. Yucky! It wasn't like the vitamins Nanny Judy gave him. It was big and felt like sand on his tongue when he bit into it. And it tasted funny. And Papa got excited. He said it was almost time to celebrate the bestest Christmas night ever.

Papa told Sammy that they had some work to do first. CLICK! CLICK! That Sammy had to play real hard while Papa took pictures. CLICK! CLICK! CLICK! Because he was making a special Christmas calendar for Nanny Judy and his parents. CLICK! And that it was a secret. CLICK! CLICK!

He thought Santa and his wife brought cookies about a cartoon ago, maybe two. But he wasn't sure because he fell asleep. That's how Nanny Judy taught him how to tell time. In cartoons. So he'd understand what it meant if they were going somewhere in an hour. Or two cartoons from now. It helped him understand how long he had to wait.

So they'd been playing the basement game together for hours all day, only now—the past one or two cartoons—it was different. Since the redheaded girl's parents came to visit, everything was fast, rushed. CLICK! CLICK! They'd run out of time to get the calendar done before his mom came to pick him up. CLICK!

His favorite play area was the Western town, equipped with a big, stuffed horse, a saddle for him to ride, and lots of cowboy hats, boots, and guns to shoot. The wall looked just like where a cowboy would live, all dusty with lots of old buildings, some cowboys, and ladies in fancy dresses walking on the wooden sidewalks with horses on a dirt street. Even though this was his favorite make-believe area, Sammy wished he had friends to play with in the Western town. Without a friend, he couldn't play Cowboys and Indians. Even without a friend, Sammy enjoyed pretending to be the sheriff, wearing the chaps, boots, cowboy hat, and silver badge and throwing the teddy-bear bad guys in prison.

Papa's cameras whirred, clicked, and flashed. He told Papa he was tired of playing, but Papa insisted he keep playing. And then when Papa told him they only had an hour left to play the basement game, Sammy was sad. He liked playing the basement game. Except for having no friends to play with. And except for Papa's rules about costumes and clothes.

Papa was a meanie about rules. Especially his rule that Sammy take off all his costumes before switching play areas. Everything. Papa told him this was part of the fun and that he would enjoy the game more if he followed the rules. So, he took off his clothes. He learned not to argue. If he did, Papa would spank his bare bottom, which stung. Sammy had never been spanked before. Until he went outside at lunchtime when he wasn't supposed to. It hurt. Sammy knew he would have more fun playing the game if he could keep his clothes on. And after he ate the cookies, Papa was in a big hurry and said to forget about the clothes altogether now that they were out of time. Sammy didn't argue. He didn't want to be spanked again.

Sammy was cold in the basement. But each time he shivered, Papa would turn on more spotlights. Eventually it would heat up. Sammy decided to make the best of his last hour here, even if he was tired of playing make-believe.

When he got hungry earlier, Papa told him to play in the make-believe area that looked like a kitchen. He even brought Sammy real food to eat and cold milk to drink, placing it on the table just like the waiters do where Nanny Judy took him for spaghetti.

One time, Sammy cried to get more cookies. Papa didn't get angry. Instead, he became all happy and silly. Papa told him that his crying was perfect for his pictures and—CLICK! CLICK!—his camera lit up the dark basement and hurt Sammy's eyes. Eventually, Sammy was so tired, he curled up on a sheepskin carpet and fell asleep to the sound of clicking, imagining the flashes to be fireworks. He dreamed of playing in the grass with Nanny Judy, having a picnic on the blanket, and waiting for the sky to get dark and the fireworks to pop in the sky.

And here he was.

Shivering in the dark. Awakened by the CLOMP! CLOMP! of Papa's big feet running around upstairs. There were no spotlights to warm his body. Sammy stood, trembling, and looked for his clothes. He groped in the shadows of the play areas, walls, toys, and props. He tried not to cry. Tried not to be scared. Tried to be a big boy. He tried not to scream in pain when he stepped on something scattered on the floor or when he stubbed his bare toes. He found the pile of play clothes at the bottom of the basement stairs. Slipping into his comfortable, warm sweatshirt and pants, Sammy took the stairs to the warmth above, knowing he might get spanked again. But he was so cold. With each step, Sammy could feel the funny taste of the thick air growing heavier. He wanted a breath of fresh air.

The kitchen, all funny orange and green, was filled with shadows. It was still nighttime, he could tell. He wondered if Papa went to bed, was already sleeping. Or if he was still locked up in the tiny room in the basement, the one Papa called his dark room. He wondered if he could just step outside for a second to catch a breath of clean air. Or open the window above the sink. Just for a second. Maybe Papa would never know. Papa didn't let him open the windows. Or step outside. Ever. At any time. And he didn't want to get spanked again.

Climbing up on the kitchen counter and kneeling at the small window near the sink, Sammy stared at the mountains in the distance, wanting to breathe the air and to play out in the cold snow.

"Sammy," Papa greeted him cheerfully.

Startled by his voice, Sammy slid off the counter into the sink. Papa laughed and lifted him from the sink, setting him gently on the floor. "Careful, boy. You almost slipped down the drain."

Sammy didn't smile. He had grown scared of Papa. He didn't like Papa. He didn't like to be spanked. He missed Nanny Judy. Papa's face was spongy like an old washcloth. "I'm hungry. Can I have dinner, Papa?"

Sammy watched as the man bent toward him. He could see the wet, sticky stuff that was always on his white skin. It was gross. Nanny Judy would have told him he needs a bath. When Papa opened his heavy lips to answer, Sammy could smell that funny smell from the basement. It stunk.

"You didn't like your special cookies?"

"I loved them. But my tummy is all twisty."

Papa laughed but he didn't think it fit his mood. He was all twitchy and sweaty like he was when the redheaded girl's parents came by with the cookies. He looked like the cartoon cat after sticking its claw in the electric socket poking around for the mouse. BZZ! BZZ!

"You worked hard today, boy. You can have anything you want for dinner. In celebration of our success. What would you like to eat?"

"McDonald's," Sammy said.

They were nose to nose. Papa's hands were on the kitchen counter touching Sammy's thighs with his thumbs. Sammy didn't like it. He thought Papa was going to yell at him again. Papa moved away. Sammy took a deep breath. Papa laughed. It was a weird laugh. Papa was fat. And ugly. Sammy could see up Papa's hairy nose and in his mouth that was filled with silver things in his yellow teeth.

Sammy wasn't so hungry anymore.

"How about if I make you a Christmas meal. You can take it with you in the car."

"Where are we going?"

"It's Christmas night. We're going to a manger, just like where Jesus was born. Nanny Judy is going to pick you up there. If you're really good. And really quiet. Can you do that?"

Sammy nodded.

"I'll make you a peanut butter sandwich. Like a picnic. Two if you'd like. That's even better than McDonald's. But you deserve it since we finished. You worked hard, Sammy."

Sammy didn't know why Papa kept saying this. He asked, "Finished with what?"

"With our project," Papa answered honestly. "Like I told you after the neighbors' visit, I'm working on a special calendar to give to your parents for Christmas. For Nanny Judy, too."

"That's good," Sammy said, his stomach rumbling. "Can I have chips and cookies, too? For later after my stomach stops wiggling and gurgling?"

Papa nodded. "You can. But we have to hurry now."

Papa leaned against the kitchen table, which squeaked on the wooden floor because he was so fat. He crossed his arms over his chest. The way Papa was staring at him, Sammy got a chill. He wasn't comfortable with some of the things Papa had asked him to do today and last night. He kept telling himself it was just that Papa had a different way of living.

That's what his mother said about all the strange and different people he met at his house in California. She had told him that he shouldn't feel uncomfortable just because someone was a little different from him. He had remembered her words when Uncle Aldo treated him bad. He had remembered her words when Papa brought him here yesterday. But Sammy didn't feel good about some of the things Papa had asked him to do while playing games.

Secretly, Sammy was glad it was over.

He didn't want to have his picture taken. His mom did. But maybe Papa was confused. Sammy wanted to play outside with his friends and go to school. He wanted to ride his bike and play ball. He wanted to play in the ocean again and on the playground in the park. He missed all of those things. Most of all, he missed Nanny Judy. He wanted to see her again. He needed her. Sammy would even play outside with the little redheaded girl from next door for a few hours, if Papa would let him.

While Papa made sandwiches, Sammy watched out the picture window in the living room and silently counted the infrequent cars that drove by on the quiet street beyond the lit sidewalk. He wanted to run away from this house. Real bad. He wasn't sure why. Papa had treated him okay. He had a nice quiet room, plenty to eat, and lots of toys. He just couldn't get rid of the feeling that Nanny Judy wouldn't like this. STRANGER DANGER! STRANGER DANGER! Maybe he should have said something when Santa Claus stopped by. Who knew Santa lived next door to Papa, had a redheaded child, a skinny Mrs. Claus, and a kid who didn't talk? He couldn't wait to tell Nanny Judy.

He looked out the window toward the house next door. Where that kid lives. The kid who didn't talk. Sammy wondered if he should at least try to sneak out of the house. Run over to Santa's house. But he was afraid the little redheaded girl wouldn't help him. She said she didn't want to be his friend and he remembered how she had stuck out her tongue at him when he was outside earlier. He sighed. It wouldn't do him any good to run away from here if all he had was help from the little redheaded girl next door.

"Sammy, our picnic is ready."

Sammy heard Papa whistling happily as he put the dishes in the sink, stuffed sandwiches in baggies and pulled chips out of the pantry.

"And cookies?"

Papa eyed him. "The cookies the neighbor brought over today are all gone. But I have some in a box."

Sammy watched as Papa stuffed all the food into a brown paper bag.

"Lots of napkins, too?" Sammy asked, seeing Papa stuff a fistful of napkins in the bag. "Where's Jesus's ranger?"

"Manger. Small building for shelter," Papa laughed. "It's in the mountains. What do you think about that?"

"It's snowing."

"Sure," Papa answered with his mouth full of something he'd eaten from the refrigerator. Nanny Judy wouldn't like Papa. "It's fun. Haven't you ever gone in the mountains when it snows?"

"Nanny Judy doesn't like the snow. We don't even go outside."

Papa frowned at him. "Well, that's no fun. Let's get going. I'll have everything packed in no time. You go upstairs and put everything of yours in the backpack. It's under your bed. Everything. Anything you've worn since you've been here and everything you own. Your toothbrush, hair brush, the works. Understand?"

"You . . . you don't mean all the toys, do you?"

As he shoved another handful of what looked like meat in his mouth, Papa answered, "Leave the toys. Just take everything else."

Papa was growing annoyed again. Sammy decided to obey and quit asking questions.

Sammy packed everything he could think of in the backpack. Just like Papa asked. He added a few more things, just like Nanny Judy had taught him. He stuffed a bottle of water in the backpack along with a handful of granola bars he'd snuck from the cupboard while Papa was downstairs, and the half-eaten bag of M&M's from yesterday at the airport, the first day he'd ever met Papa, just in case he needed more snacks for later.

Still shivering from his nap in the basement, Sammy slipped on a second layer of clothing, then a third since they were going up in the mountains to a manger, before grabbing his coat, several hats, and plenty of mittens and stuffed them deep into his backpack. He did not want to get cold waiting in a manger in the snowy mountains for Nanny Judy. Sliding the straps of the backpack over his shoulders and hoisting the weight onto his small back, Sammy walked over to his window and stood on his tiptoes to see into the window of the house next door. He looked for the quiet boy, who laid on the floor by the window.

Sammy felt a little better, peaceful and happy, when he saw the kid straining to lift his weight onto his skinny arms, stretching his head to the sky to see outside. Sammy knew the quiet kid liked the outdoors almost as much as he did. He suspected the kid had about as much difficulty convincing his mom and dad to let him play outside as he had with Papa. Every time Sammy saw the kid lying at his window, he would wave to the kid, but the kid never waved back. This made Sammy sad because he really liked the kid.

For some reason, tonight more than any other time since yesterday, Sammy needed to see the quiet kid's dimpled smile.

Sammy's heart sank like a stone when all he could see was the empty bedroom window.

"Sammy!"

Sammy trembled. His tummy kept flipping and flopping. Maybe it was the plateful of cookies from earlier. Or the vitamin. He lowered his eyes, looked back out at the neighbor's window, and waved.

Sammy whispered sadly, "Bye, kid."

When he heard the loud footsteps of Papa coming up the stairs, Sammy called, "Coming, Papa."

CHAPTER 50

JACK FINISHED HIS NOTES and set his pad of paper aside. "We time-stamped all of it and narrowed down the tapes. We zoomed in on both the perp's face and the time sequence of his movement with the child."

"Did you find him?" Streeter asked.

Jack Linwood pointed to the time in the bottom right corner of the screen. "We think so. The time shows it to be almost twenty minutes after the Williams boy was last seen, fifteen minutes after the video taken at the exit I showed you earlier."

"The one where he was disguised to look like a girl," Chief Gates said.

Jack nodded, but I could tell the subject matter—a child abducted—was difficult for him. I suspected no one else in the office knew about him losing a six-year-old son. I sensed that Jack told me that in confidence. And with his attempts to keep his privacy, I had interpreted that as some kind of dark secret he wanted kept between him and me. There was so much I didn't know about him, really. I didn't even know his real name was John until I saw it on the list of passengers coming from Kansas City yesterday.

"We found correlating video at the toll exit. Long story short, the child is not seen in the video, but we retrieved a partial license number on the guy's car."

"A partial?" Streeter asked.

"The numbers on the plate were obscured. Frozen mud, if I had to guess," Jack said.

"Do we have the list of sex offenders yet?" Streeter asked.

Jack nodded and handed several sheets to Streeter. "From the DPD Sex Offender Registration Unit."

"Unit? There's an entire department assigned to these assholes?" I asked, hoping no one noticed my swearing and reminding myself that I must start following my New Year's resolution now that I was an FBI agent. "How many of them are there?"

"Hundreds," Streeter said, flipping through the list.

"Thousands," Jack corrected. "In the Greater Denver area."

I shuddered. "I'm not in South Dakota anymore."

"Sorry to tell you this, Dorothy, but you probably have the same problem up north, just in lower numbers." Jack held my gaze. I knew I could believe it. He probably made it his personal mission to know these things, given his background.

"Where do we begin?" I asked.

"Gates's people narrowed the list to offenses involving children, and we've been working with their unit to look at the offenders and the ages of children, just in case."

I shuddered again. I realized little Max was in grave danger. This guy in the dark coat on the airport video had no intention of returning the boy any time soon. Or ever.

Jack explained the series of color video clips from the toll area in, starting from the abductor's arrival to DIA, his dark coat draped over the front seat and what appeared to be the strap of a small backpack looped over the back. He was not wearing sunglasses. His hair was jet black. Like shoe polish. Jack explained the time lapses between segments. "It appears this guy was impersonating a janitor, loitering around the airport for hours. We have him changing clothes. He goes into the bathroom and comes out with a dowager's hump. Broom in hand."

Jack flipped over to the grayscale videos from inside the airport and showed us the clipped series with time stamps. The man wearing coveralls with a blue airport vest had a stocking cap pulled low on his head, earphones, and thick-rimmed glasses with what looked like sports tape on the nosepiece. His facial features were all but obscured, and if they hadn't been tracking the video of the man going in and coming out, we'd never have known it was the same man.

"The backpack? Under his coveralls?" Streeter asked, pointing at the man's humped back.

I thought about the backpack I'd found in the woods yesterday morning, which seemed like decades ago, and wondered if that child met the same fate as little Max. My gut twisted.

"That's my guess. You nailed it in the initial video, Streeter. Maybe he was lonely on Christmas Day. Maybe he was waiting for someone. Although we don't have direct proof, it appears from the direction he leaves the cameras' view that he heads directly to the airport's food court area, near the Buckhorn, where he apparently spent most of his time."

Streeter added skeptically, "My guess is he was looking for an opportunity to snatch a kid or had been paid to snatch the Williams kid, but my money's on the former, not the latter. He was just waiting around until a child wandered across his path unescorted. The fact that he had the hidden backpack with a girl's coat and hat in it will be evidence that this crime was premeditated."

Jack agreed. "It appears so. Watch."

As the time drew closer to little Max's disappearance, the man swept up spilt popcorn between the food court and the restrooms in the main concourse. After a forty-five minute lapse, just ten minutes before the Williams boy's disappearance, the janitor pushed a broom near Buckhorn Bar and Grill where little Max was last seen.

"Wearing what we believe are green coveralls, an airport employee blue vest, no overcoat, and a big hunchback," Jack explained. "From the DIA diagrams that Liv provided, this guy probably hovered under the overhang near the Buckhorn for forty-five minutes as he scoped the concourse for prey." Jack's voice cracked. "Probably used candy to entice the kid to come to him initially, just as Liv suggested. We're speculating since this guy avoided the cameras and obscured his facial features with the phony glasses, but we assume he spots the Williams kid and bolts to take advantage of the opportunity. Hard to watch."

The man reappeared on the exit camera wearing the dark coat, no longer carrying any backpack or bag, but holding the hand of a small child that was dressed in a pink coat and hat.

"We got him," Streeter growled, his eyes fixed on the screen.

Tony whistled and repeated, "We got him."

"How many names do we have so far on the narrowed list of violent sex offenders?" Streeter asked.

"Well, by process of elimination—those we could account for, such as those who are incarcerated—we're down to this." He handed Streeter the sheets. I peeked over his shoulder. Thirty-six names. None I recognized. A lot of people to follow up on.

"Any that fit the description we have on this guy so far?" Streeter asked.

Gates nodded. "Six of them. I have surveillance people in the field as we speak waiting to pull them in, if you'd like."

Streeter studied the list the chief handed him. So did I.

"Watch these clips," Linwood said as the images flashed quickly on the screen. He pointed at the image of the cars departing DIA. One image was of a lone man in a two-tone brown station wagon. "The time lapse would be about right for this guy leaving the parking ramps. I can't really tell, but doesn't that look like him? No dark coat, but aren't those the same coveralls he was wearing when he entered DIA? The sunglasses? The greasy-looking hair?"

"That's him," Streeter said confidently.

"Any sign of little Max?" I asked, nausea roiling.

"No."

Streeter answered, "He's probably got him hiding on the floor in the backseat, covered by a blanket or something."

"That's what we figured," Linwood said.

Streeter asked, "Jack, what does the profile from BSU look like?"

Jack shuffled quickly through his stack of papers and computer print-outs. "If I had to guess, this guy is probably an introverted preferential child molester, rather than a seduction or sadistic type, although I haven't ruled out the sadistic type altogether."

Jack was amazing. And smart. I asked, "What is the introverted type?"

Streeter said, "It means our guy is a dirty old man, the type of guy who gets off on targeting strangers and very young children. He's the flasher we find at playgrounds and school yards."

"That's sick," I said, grimacing in disgust.

Jack added, "Introverted preferential child molesters tend to range in age from sixteen to eighty, are typically male, engage in minimal conversation with their victims, prefer hanging around places children frequent like playgrounds as Streeter suggested, and target total strangers, particularly the very young. Although introverted types often engage in passive sexual encounters with their victims, such as exposing themselves, they can become more aggressive, which is why I said I haven't completely ruled out that this guy may indeed be more of the sadistic type."

Streeter said, "The good thing for us is that if this man is an introverted preferential child molester, that means he will likely have left a trail. It's so hard to prove child molestation cases, but with repetitious behavior patterns, it makes it a hell of a lot easier."

"Precisely," Jack agreed. "He has taken a big risk to acquire his victim at DIA. He might move unexpectedly after this. He's probably never been married, lives alone, lived with his parents most of his life, has a nearly nonexistent social life, never dates, has no relationships with his peers, and has an obsession with young children, treating them almost as if they were his possessions. If I had to guess, it's highly likely he was sexually abused as a child and has already molested several, maybe dozens of young kids already. Most likely we will never know how many children this guy has molested because he's probably a master at manipulating young children to get what he wants from them, and seduces them with attention and gifts to assure their silence."

I added, "These perverted ass . . . asinine people have a sixth sense for sniffing out the vulnerable," I added, noticing Jack's and Streeter's stares. I ignored them. "It's almost like a predator's instinctual ability to single out the weakest of the prey before pouncing."

Holding up the reports Jack had handed him, Streeter added, "These people can single out the one child in a crowd who comes from a broken home or who has been molested before."

Jack turned back to the video and the grainy image of the creep in the overcoat. "This guy reminds me of a vulture who circles his prey from miles above. He targeted little Max once he sensed the young boy was suffering from parental neglect."

"Oh my gosh, Streeter! You were right all along. Your instinct. This isn't a kidnapping for money. Never was," I said.

"And my instinct tells me we won't find anything with these six violent sex offenders, but Gates, tell your surveillance teams to get going and move in on them," Streeter said. "This is no time for my instincts to be wrong. In the meantime, let's focus on the nonviolent list of sexual predators involving children. Lengthy, but I bet our guy is on this list."

Gates hurried to the other side of the room, cell phone in hand, and started barking orders. Streeter set the short list aside and studied the long list of offenders. Names. Addresses.

At the thought of poor little Max's fate, my voice squeaked, "This creep has no intention of returning little Max." I felt the color drain from my face as quickly as I spoke the words.

As if on cue, Tony's cell phone rang at the exact time my cell phone rang.

I answered and Frances's voice said, "Liv, I need help."

"Not now, Frances. I'm in the middle of something."

"It's Noah. He thinks he talked with the missing boy." Her words were choppy, troubled. Serious. She hadn't called me Boots, which alarmed me.

"Sis?" My eyes flew up to meet Jack's, then Streeter's, both men studying me carefully.

To remain focused, I lowered my eyes to the long list in Streeter's hand. An address popped out at me, one in nearby Wheat Ridge, Colorado, on the street where my sister lived.

Gates ended his call first. I could hear him tell Streeter and Jack, "Sorry for the interruption, but a man called who thinks there's something suspicious with a little girl who's visiting at his neighbor's house, and he wants to meet with me."

Jack said, "Are you going?"

He shook his head. "I'll let my chief deputy handle it until we're done with our raid on the short-list suspects. Experience tells me that when something like the Maximillian Bennett Williams III abduction floods the networks and media outlets during the holidays, we'll get plenty of people whose imaginations have run away from them."

Everything came flooding toward me at once. I could hear the men talking while I was trying to decipher my sister's story about Noah crying, having a seizure, banging his knuckles on the glass, banging his head on the window, the five-finger message of "girl," and the laugh. Something about Dad polishing his shoes. And the address on Streeter's list. Something gnawed at me. As Frances ended her call with me abruptly, my sense was that my sister was hysterical and was headed to the Denver Police Department to make a report, to meet Gabriel. I stood for a moment staring at the phone in my hands, then at the list in Streeter's.

"Wait!" I said, stuffing my cell phone in my pocket. Tony was leaving, and I had only half heard what was happening. I asked him, "What was his name?"

"Who?" Tony asked, stopping just short of the door.

"The guy who called you."

"Hogarty. Why?"

"Gabriel Hogarty's my brother-in-law." The men swung their gazes toward me. I pointed at the name on the long list of suspects in Streeter's hand. "2291 Hedge Road in Wheat Ridge. Jason Horace Fletcher. That's my sister's neighbor. Noah says he talked to the girl with black hair. But he thinks she's really a boy. He heard her laugh and thinks it's not a girl at all but little Max in disguise."

"Who's Noah?" Chief Gates asked.

"A very brave, very smart little boy, and my nephew."

CHAPTER 51

Noah

MOM HUNG UP THE phone with Auntie Liv and ruffled my short brown hair. I arched my back and tried to stretch my bent arm toward her, succeeding with one quick, spastic movement long after she had walked away.

I talked to my mom as she hurried through the house grabbing last-minute items and turning off lights. A string of vowels was all I could manage, but my thoughts were clear. I wanted to tell her to calm down and to hurry up at the same time. She was doing the hurrying just fine, but I didn't sense her calm. She was mumbling as she moved about.

Normally, I preferred being with my mom over anyone else because she listened to me as if my moans and gurgles were more than that, as if they were words in conversation, even if it was all just in my imagination. I loved being alone with her. Not that I didn't love being with the rest of my family. I did. It was just that my mom was always so calm, open, and attentive when we were alone. Nothing distracted or troubled her. She was usually totally relaxed. She was the most beautiful when she was relaxed.

This was a side of her I don't think I'd ever seen before. Totally not relaxed. Not calm. She was frazzled. She'd already put two sweaters and a coat on me and seemed to have forgotten she'd done it. Scatterbrained. I'm glad she'd managed to call Auntie Liv because it seemed to have calmed her enough to think. At least a little bit.

My mom leaned against the kitchen counter and combed her long hair with her splayed fingers, holding her palm against her forehead. She was stressed and deep in thought. The top three buttons of her denim work shirt were unbuttoned, revealing the white cotton T-shirt underneath. Her faded blue jeans hung loosely on her thin frame and had the initial frays of a hole above her right knee. She wore oversized white cotton socks on her feet. Her fair skin had a glow, not like the one after her early morning workout, but instead due to the tension of worrying about the child next door. Although she normally wore mascara, today was a holiday and she hadn't planned to go anywhere, so she'd skipped it. Her clear blue eyes, normally so pure and kind, looked wild. Even still, she was a striking beauty, just like my dad says.

But stress didn't look as good on her, if you ask me. She looked more like a caged animal. And it was kind of scaring me.

The nine o'clock news program was blaring from the living room and the anchorwoman recounted the top news of the day, which of course was about the missing boy from yesterday. The news reporter was saying " . . . and closer to home, the top news story in national news is the disturbing story about the disappearance of Maximillian Bennett Williams III from the Denver International Airport yesterday." Images of the boy and the airport flashed on the screen as the woman summarized the story of the boy's mysterious disappearance.

Mom grabbed the handles of my wheelchair and pushed me toward the door that led to the garage. I heard her go back to the counter and grab her car keys and then go into the living room.

" . . . unconfirmed reports that it might be a kidnapping. No news so far on the boy. It has been more than twenty-four hours since his disappearance and all of America is hoping and praying for his safe return . . ."

"Noah, I am so proud of you for sticking with it."

Great, but Mom, we've got to move, I demanded in my head.

"I didn't understand what you were trying to tell me. Now I understand. You were trying to tell me that Sammy was the missing boy from the television, weren't you?"

I smiled tenuously at my mom, my eyes darting upward. *Move fast, Mom.*

"Well, I'm proud of you, Noah." Her voice was shaky. "Now, let's get that boy some help."

Finally!

I felt my mom unbuckle my harness and slip a coat over my arms—again—and a cap on my head. She tucked a thick blanket around me and strapped me back into my harness, scooping my blue chair from the wheelchair frame and carrying me into the garage.

I heard the little blond boy on the television run back and forth from the camera to the slide, wave and greet his parents, giggling throughout the clip. I heard the giggle. It was a very distinct giggle. Contagious. Happy.

"Oh my God," my mom choked. "It really is the same child."

Yes, Mom, I said, flashing her a sad smile.

While she strapped me into the backseat, Mom explained, "We're going straight to the Denver Police Department, Noah, to tell them all about this. That the girl, Sammy, is really Maximillian Bennett Williams III. I told Auntie Liv on the phone and she said she'd look into it right away. Dad's meeting us down there. They'll want our statement. They'll want to talk with you."

I moaned, offering a smile.

She closed my door and ran around to the driver's side and slid in behind the wheel. I saw the garage door open as she started the car, easing us out of the garage into the dark night.

"Oh, darn it. I forgot the bath. The water's running."

My mom opened her door, dashed back inside the house through the garage, leaving me in the purring minivan in the driveway.

Then I heard it.

The garage door creaked open next door and a car pulled out. I heard the car stop in the driveway and the garage door close. As the car idled, I heard screaming from inside the car. It was Sammy. Little Max. I was sure of that. Mr. Fletcher was taking him somewhere.

I started to yell for my mom but all I managed to do was push my stocking cap over my eyes again. I felt tears welling in my eyes and my throat go raw from my screams. I couldn't help it. I was scared. For Sammy. For myself.

The next thing I heard chilled me to my bones.

A car door opened.

Boots crunched through snow coming closer.

I quit my attempts at yelling and held my breath to stop the tears so I could hear what was happening outside the minivan. A rush of cold air blasted my face.

Someone had opened my car door.

Clammy, unfamiliar hands were unbuckling my seat and pulling me into the cold air.

And it wasn't my mom.

CHAPTER 52

IT WAS TIME.

He hated to do it, but it was time to say good-bye. It was not his fault. It was that nosey neighbor lady and her husband. They had seen Sammy earlier today playing outside and then came over with the cookies to check on Sammy.

But her eyes had betrayed her.

And then she made a mistake, a big mistake. She ran off and left her son alone in the car. And the broken boy had seen everything. He would have ignored the entire mess, but the boy's eyes made him nervous. Actually, this kid's haunting gray eyes totally freaked him out. It was his mother's ghost, he was sure. She had come back to haunt him, to judge him, after seven relatively peaceful years, through the broken boy.

The lady next door was the reason his time with Sammy had been shorter than he'd planned. He wanted more.

So much more.

She would lose her boy just like he had to lose his. He didn't want to draw more attention to himself and was already terrified of getting caught. The smart thing would be to ignore the boy, pretend he didn't exist. But then when he came back home, the broken boy would still be next door, judging him with those eyes.

He tried to decide what was best.

Surely the kid wouldn't be missed. He was broken. His parents had the redheaded girl. They would forget about the broken boy in time. Besides, this kid was possessed. By his dead mother. They shared the same murky gray eyes.

And without Sammy, there was no proof that he had done anything wrong.

But he would be thankful for the time he'd had with Sammy.

Sammy was special.

A gift.

He was different from the others.

Sammy was the son he'd never had. The son he wished he could have been for his own parents. Innocent and good. Compliant and carefree. Maybe if he'd been more like Sammy when he was a kid, his parents would have treated him more kindly. Maybe. If only he'd been obedient. Like Sammy.

Obedient to the end.

The screams of his parents still ricocheted in the corners of his mind.

The sound would quiet, eventually.

It always did.

CHAPTER 53

I DON'T KNOW HOW long I was with Frances and Gabriel, but it seemed like an eternity. My sister was a mess and I wasn't much better. Noah was their world and my earth angel. My mind could not wrap itself around the idea that his fate was in the hands of a monster like Fletcher.

As the story unfolded, we all realized Noah had figured it out. He'd known all along. I should have listened more closely to Frances earlier today, asked more questions. She was thinking the same thing. Blaming herself.

I had to make this right.

Elizabeth and Michael were upstairs with Emma in her room. Gabriel had called them right away. We might have needed Emma's help, but she certainly didn't need to be a part of all the drama that was going on down here. She didn't need to know that her big brother, Noah, was missing.

Frances grabbed my hand right before I left the house and had me say a prayer together with Gabriel. She prayed for little Max. She prayed for Noah's safe return. She prayed that while Noah was gone he wouldn't have a seizure or need his medication. She prayed for me, thanked God for having me here with her on the case to find Noah.

I felt totally helpless and inadequate.

Frances was another one of my earth angels. But even God couldn't keep me from getting booted off this case. I was too personally involved. Way too personally involved. And despite all my sister's prayers, there was no way her dream that I help would come true.

I had to face the music and let Streeter do what he needed to do.

As I approached the car parked in front of Fletcher's house, I wiped my puffy eyes and took a deep breath. Streeter was standing by Agent Steve Knapp, who was sitting quietly behind the wheel of the Bureau car with his window rolled down.

I heard Streeter ask, "Any word from Mills?"

Knapp shook his massive head. "Nope. He's around the corner watching for Fletcher."

They saw me. Their expressions changed. I hadn't seen either one look like this before. I must have looked frightful.

Streeter wrapped his arm around my shoulder. "You shouldn't be out here."

"I have to be out here."

I thought he would send me back inside, reminding me this case had just become a conflict of interest for me. I didn't think I could take it if he pulled me off the case. We looked at each other for a long moment. His blue eyes with a soft greenish tint to them were filled with understanding, not judgment or pity.

"We're going inside," Streeter said to Knapp.

Somehow, I knew Streeter would understood what I felt, what I was going through in a situation this personal. And he knew I had to follow this through to the end. He knew I needed him to bend the rules for me.

"Do you really think he'll come back?"

"Eventually. He doesn't know we're onto him about little Max. He'll come back and have some alibi for his whereabouts tonight that explains why he had nothing to do with Noah's disappearance. Remember what Jack described? He's bold, above the law. He thinks we're too stupid to figure this out."

"I hope you're right. It's been two hours since Noah was taken. And no one has seen Fletcher's car. It's too late, isn't it?"

Streeter wrapped his arms around me. I couldn't handle this. Noah was everything to me. I couldn't imagine a worse pain, even if he wasn't my own flesh and blood. And I understood why Jack refused to be here, wanted to stay with Chief Gates in case they found Fletcher. He couldn't bear to see the pain in my sister's eyes, in Gabriel's face, or in mine.

"Don't think that way, Liv," Streeter was saying, holding me in his arms, the horrors of the world falling away under his protection. "He'll be back. In the meantime, Tony has every officer in the city out looking for his car."

To Agent Knapp, Streeter said, "Park across the street at that house. Give us a heads-up if you spot Fletcher's car. Don't let him get away if he spots you or Mills. Hopefully he won't even notice you two and he'll drive right into the garage where we'll be waiting for him."

Knapp grinned and nodded once as he rolled up the window. It was nearly 10:30 and the temperature was dropping rapidly.

Streeter released me and hitched his thumb toward the house, saying, "Ready to see what Fletcher is all about?"

"Not really," I answered honestly. I would never be comfortable going into that monster's den. Worse, he was a monster who had my defenseless nephew at his mercy. I sighed, "But thanks for letting me stay on the case. Let's go."

Phil Kelleher had already picked the locks on the front door and was waiting for Streeter's instructions.

"Careful, now. If he thought we were on to him, the house could be booby-trapped," Streeter said.

Guns drawn, we entered through the front door.

My first impression was of the overwhelmingly stuffy and pungent odor that hung in the air. It was sweet and acrid at the same time. I was not at all familiar with this odor but thought for some reason I should be.

"What the hell is that smell?"

"You don't want to know," Streeter answered, searching the living room, moving quickly through the kitchen and every room on the main floor.

"Smells like a cross between Vaseline and body odor," I answered, wrinkling my nose in disgust.

"Close."

I got it. It was the smell of body odor, Vaseline, and semen. I thought I was going to lose it. If I did, surely Streeter would send me back to my sister's house to wait this out. I took a deep breath and moved forward. I had to focus on little Max and the monster, work the case, and pretend Noah wasn't involved.

"And bleach. Do you all smell bleach?" I asked, worried that we might be too late.

Streeter cut a look in my direction as he moved to the base of the stairs, shaking his head to indicate the main floor was unoccupied, clear. A faint, reassuring curl to his lip appeared. He understood that I was working hard to be an agent, not an aunt.

The house was decorated in burnt oranges and avocado greens, not a contemporary décor, but outdated and tired. The furniture was used and abused, chairs stained, table warped, and sofa damaged and sagging.

We walked up the stairs and into the two small bedrooms and bath, careful not to touch a thing since nothing had been dusted for prints yet or scanned for fluids. The first bedroom on the right was definitely Jason Fletcher's. It had a double bed, bedding bunched in a pile, and a single dresser with a thirteen-inch TV on top, with a hanger sticking out the top wadded with aluminum foil. No cable. The walls were blank except for a crucifix and a picture of a man and woman, presumably Fletcher's parents. They looked like middle-class Americans, white-bread, God-fearing folks. The closet door was open and the clothes were askew. It looked like a bachelor's bedroom.

The bathroom was at the top of the stairs and was quite unremarkable—tub and shower, commode and sink. The wallpaper was white with gold and orange butterflies, yellowing with age and peeling away at the seams.

The second bedroom was small: another double bed and a small lamp beside the bed. The closet and drawers were closed, and everything was neat and tidy, except for some toys scattered on the floor. My gut wrenched for poor little Max. I looked out the window and saw Noah's room across the short stretch of lawns, which were separated by a wooden-slat fence between the houses.

"Little Max stayed in this room," I said. "Noah must have seen the boy yesterday. That's what he was probably trying to tell Emma and my sister."

And I noticed he'd made his bed, tried to clean up his room before he left, the covers rumpled as if a child had made it, not an adult.

I said, "He's not planning on bringing little Max back, is he?"

Streeter and Phil exchanged a look.

My heart sank. I swallowed hard so I wouldn't cry. Work, damn it! My eyes flew to the window, imagining a deep breath of fresh air.

I pointed out the window to the second floor of the house next door, my sister's house. "Gabriel installed that picture window so Noah could lie on the floor and see the outdoors. He loves the outdoors," I said with a tremble in my voice.

Streeter stepped beside me. "He probably did see little Max. And probably saw Jason Fletcher, too. Maybe Fletcher thought he saw too much, thought removing him as a witness might be worth the risk of a second abduction."

"Noah knew all along. He was trying to tell us."

"But Fletcher wouldn't know he couldn't talk, would he?"

"Not according to Frances. The neighbor knew nothing about them. I don't even think he knew Noah had cerebral palsy."

"Come on," Streeter said and led me down the stairs.

The upstairs and main floor cleared, we descended the stairs. Halfway down, we both froze midstride. The basement was dark. Kelleher found a switch, illuminating a horrifying room.

"Oh my God," I gasped, and saw my every nightmare come to life.

CHAPTER 54

THE BASEMENT WAS ONE big room filled with different sets and backdrops, such as a hospital room, a school room, a Western village, a farm. Props and costumes were everywhere, organized in piles and hanging from dozens of coat racks.

"Sometimes I wonder if there is a God on days like this. When I get a glimpse inside the hell of people like Fletcher," Streeter said coolly. He began his descent down the stairs.

"What the hell is this place? Is this what I think it is?" I asked.

"Yes," Streeter answered simply.

"Twisted," I said. Jason Fletcher was the devil himself.

"You wouldn't believe the crap we found in this dump," Special Agent Kelleher said into his radio. He waved the riding crop and handcuffs above his head.

I added, "This place gives me the willies. How much longer do we have to stay down here?"

"Depends," Streeter said. "What have you found so far?"

"What do you want? This place is crawling in filth," Kelleher said. "Do you see all these sets? There are boxes and boxes of props and costumes—policemen, firemen, cowboys, superheroes, animals—you name it, he's got it. It's a regular dress rehearsal for a Village People's costume party. The costumes are of all sizes and shapes, most of them folded and boxed. The ones that were crumpled in the corner were for a child."

"Little Max's size?" Streeter asked.

Kelleher nodded.

"Bag it and tag it."

"And there's a darkroom over there." I pointed to the room behind us.

"We'll need the photographers in here, the crime scene techs to comb this place. Thoroughly. This isn't Fletcher's first time." Streeter was getting pissed, I could tell. His gravelly voice usually sounded like he had gargled with barbed wire, but at the moment, it was eerily low and controlled.

My unspoken thoughts were dark. I had a feeling that we were too late. A knot formed in my stomach and a lump rose in my throat. At least Noah hadn't been exposed to this.

"You okay?" Streeter whispered.

I nodded too emphatically, hoping to shake out all the images. I had to find Noah. I had to help little Max. My mind raced. "Where did he take them? And why would he grab a helpless boy with severe cerebral palsy from the car? Why? What is he up to? The heartless bastard."

Streeter held me again. "Why don't you go see how your sister's doing?"

"Just tell me why."

"Because he thought Noah saw something, knew something, was a witness to something."

I appreciated Streeter's honesty. Although I already knew the answer and the implication that Noah was in as much danger as little Max, I had to hear it spoken. I needed to hear it so I could move on and be an effective investigator.

Impossible.

"The smell is even worse down here."

He nodded. As he started to make his way through the backdrops, the toe of Streeter's boot caught on a leather strap and he lost his balance, falling to the floor onto one knee.

Kelleher called out to him, "You okay, Streeter?"

Streeter pulled on the leather strap that had entangled his boot and pulled up a cat-of-nine-tails. He answered gingerly, "No, I'm not okay. I've fallen in a sewer and I'm in up to my chin."

Just as he pushed himself up from the floor, Streeter hesitated. I saw him fishing around for something under the circus props. He reached beneath the edge of the canvas and pulled out a small dirty sock. We stared at his find in disbelief as Streeter held it by a fraction of the fabric, pinched delicately between the thumb and forefinger of his right hand.

As he rose to his feet, Streeter said, "Appears Fletcher missed something."

The child's sock was soiled at the bottom. Kelleher bagged and tagged the sock as evidence. We searched the area for its mate without any luck.

Streeter's cell phone startled us.

"Streeter, this is Tony."

"What's up?"

Streeter put Tony on speaker so Phil and I could hear.

"The Idaho Springs Sheriff's Department just called. An off-duty deputy sheriff spotted Fletcher's two-tone station wagon driving the back roads in an isolated camping area fifteen miles north of the Winter Park ski resort. He said that he had not been aware of the APB on Fletcher at the time, but recognized the partial plate number and description of the vehicle when he returned from his cross-country ski outing. The only reason he remembered Fletcher's wagon was because he had only seen cars around that day camp area in the summer months. The deputy sheriff thought it was odd that a vehicle was driving around in such an isolated area this time of year."

My heart raced.

"Thank God for small favors," Streeter answered, and gave me the "okay" sign.

"We sent a car up to check it out and they said Fletcher's wagon is no longer out there," Gates said. "I assume he's headed back home, Streeter. Are your guys still at his house?"

Please don't let it be too late, I prayed.

"You're talking to one of them," Streeter replied.

"Don't do something foolish, Streeter," Gates demanded. "Aren't you getting close to retirement, bud?"

"Aren't you?"

"Careful now," Gates answered.

"Tony, see what you can do about rounding up volunteers to comb the campground area right away. If Fletcher comes back alone, we need to know exactly where he's been. Have whoever is first on the scene diagram the prints in the snow."

I shivered at an unwelcome image. I couldn't handle seeing Noah in the snow. Or little Max. The thought, the smells, it was all too much. I had to get a grip. I felt the room close in on me and I sat down hard on a pile of props.

Kelleher and Streeter were staring at me. My vision was starting to come back. I took a deep breath, wiped my face, and pulled myself up from the floor.

Streeter didn't bother to cover the phone when he said, "You're as white as a ghost."

Gates said, "What?"

"Nothing. Liv just blacked out for a second. I'll explain later."

Gates added, "Let's just hope it doesn't start snowing again. If we're lucky, we can just follow his tracks in the snow."

"Good thought, friend. I'll round up a few of our agents and send them your way. Liv has Beulah next door and we can be up in less than an hour, depending on what happens with Fletcher. You are headed that way, aren't you?"

"Definitely," Gates answered. "I'll take responsibility for the search until you get there."

"Thanks," Streeter responded. "But Tony, it may be awhile if we get our hands on Fletcher. Leave some instructions for us on how to get to the campground site at the Idaho Springs office."

"No problem," Gates said. "Call me as soon as you can, if you get Fletcher."

"You got it. And call me if you see any sign of either boy." Streeter hung up and slid the phone back in his pocket just as his radio sounded.

It was Agent Kyle Mills.

"I've got a line on Fletcher. He's heading east on Chaparral."

There was a short pause.

Streeter shouted, "Get into position."

CHAPTER 55

AS THE THREE OF us ran up the stairs, Mills's voice said, "He did not see me. He's headed your way, Knapp."

Streeter keyed his radio, "Mills, were the kids with him?"

"Didn't see them."

Streeter let out a long breath.

I offered hopefully, "They might be lying down. Sleeping or resting."

"Stand ready inside this door with Kelleher. Turn off your radios once you hear the garage door open, got it?" Streeter stepped into the dark garage by himself.

Steve Knapp's voice sounded over the radio. "Got him. He's heading this way. I'm across the street in the neighbor's driveway."

"Once the garage door goes down, you two get your cars into position quickly," Streeter commanded.

"Got it."

"Yes, sir."

I saw the headlights of Fletcher's station wagon sweep across the darkened living room and heard the automatic garage door opening. As I heard his vehicle enter, I noticed the light growing from beneath the crack of the door to the garage.

"For God's sake, people, hold your fire if you can. We still don't know where the kids are. Radios off."

We switched our radios off as ordered so that Fletcher would not hear any static. We were all armed, weapons drawn.

I heard the garage door lowering just as Fletcher turned off the engine of his car. The light seeping through the crack disappeared as his headlights dimmed. The bulb in the automatic garage door must be out, I thought, which would make it even harder for the agents in the garage to see what Fletcher was up to. From my squatting position inside the house at the door to the garage, I could hear the pinging noise of the overheated engine in the deafening silence. I heard nothing. Fletcher hadn't opened the door. He must have been sitting behind the wheel of his car in the garage. For some reason, he was not getting out.

My heart and mind raced. I wanted to open the door and shoot the bastard. Make him pay. I wondered if Fletcher sensed our presence, noticed something out of place. I worried about Streeter alone in the garage with Fletcher. I suspected Fletcher was about to make a run for freedom and prayed that Knapp and Mills were slowly and quietly getting into position to block his exit from the garage.

I resisted the urge to rush through the door and shoot Fletcher in the gut. Just when I thought I'd waited an eternity, I heard the driver's door open and saw a faint light, which I imagined was the dome light flicking on in the otherwise pitch-black garage, giving Streeter a clear look into the car. I heard Fletcher clear his nose to gather the excess saliva and then heard him spit on the floor.

I grimaced. Disgusting bastard. Why not just shoot him now and rid the world of the cockroach?

Fletcher slammed the door of his station wagon and walked slowly around the vehicle to the kitchen door. The rubber soles of his wet snow boots squeaked on the concrete with every heavy step. I strained to hear noises from the car—stirring, yawning, or any sound that might be coming from an awakening boy or my scared nephew. I heard nothing beyond the labored breathing and squeaky steps of Jason Fletcher. When the footsteps were only a few feet from where Phil and I crouched near the door, the bright lights of the fluorescent bulbs in the garage hummed to life, light seeping through the wide crack into the dark space where we were waiting. Fletcher breathed heavily as he worked his key in the door and twisted the cold knob in his pudgy hand.

As he opened the door, Phil and I leveled our guns at his face and Streeter sprang from his hiding place in the garage. Our shouts of "Freeze!" rang out in chorus. Streeter had a gun to the back of Fletcher's head. Fletcher's pudgy, pocked cheeks oozed with perspiration.

I moved a step closer, pressing the barrel of my gun against his cheek. "Where's Noah?" I didn't recognize the sound of my own voice.

Something like recognition touched Fletcher's eyes. "The broken boy?"

"Broken?" I cried.

"Is that his name? Noah? Forty days and nights of rain. Perfect." His giggle was nauseating.

"What did you do to him?" I cocked my gun and slowly squeezed the trigger.

CHAPTER 56

STREETER GRABBED MY WRIST in one hand and gently eased my arm down to my side, my gun pointing at the concrete. "Not like this, Liv. We need to find the boys first."

My arms started trembling uncontrollably. Kelleher took my gun and Streeter slapped handcuffs around Fletcher's chubby wrists. Streeter hit the garage button, signaling Agent Gregory to join us.

Streeter reached around and held me steady, still pointing his gun at Fletcher. Once cuffed, Agent Gregory flicked the lights on and off in succession three times to signal Knapp and Mills that we had Fletcher in custody.

Within minutes, after a complete search of the vehicle, all of us agents and Fletcher were standing in his kitchen awaiting answers. There was no sign of the boys, but we had recovered a laptop and a locked, hardcover suitcase from the back of the station wagon under the seat. Streeter frisked Fletcher a second time and found the key. Piles of DVDs and thumb drives filled the case. Without even seeing any of the photos or videos, we had no trouble imagining what the content would be.

Streeter told Fletcher he was under arrest for the kidnapping of Maximillian Bennett Williams III and Noah Hogarty, for illegal possession and trafficking of child pornography, and for violating various probationary conditions from prior arrests. Streeter Mirandized him and stared into his lifeless eyes before saying, "You're in deep, Fletcher. We found it all."

Fletcher was staring back at Streeter, but did not appear to be looking at him. It was as if he was looking straight through him to something in the distance. The clammy-skinned, pocked-faced photographer did not seem the least bit fazed by his impending incarceration.

Streeter continued, "Everything, except Maximillian Bennett Williams III and Noah Hogarty. Where are they?"

Fletcher's face changed. It was like he snapped out of a trance he'd been in. "Noah?"

Streeter looked at me, but I was as confused as he was by the man's question. Kelleher shrugged his shoulders. Agent Gregory stared, adjusting his grip on the gun pointed at Fletcher.

"Noah. No, not Noah . . . more like Joseph," Fletcher said, pleased with whatever sick thought he was having. He started to giggle. "Only he'll never be king, no colorful coat as a final reward. No, not Noah."

"Crazy bastard!" I yelled as I lunged at him and punched him in his fat gut as hard as I could. Couldn't help myself. He went down. I felt Gregory pull me off him.

Streeter helped Fletcher to his feet and ignored my outburst. "Look, Fletcher. You're in enough trouble as it is. You don't want murder charges added on top of everything else or you'll be looking at your own execution by lethal injection. That's what happens in this state to pedophiles who kill their victims."

Fletcher's smile reminded me of a twitchy slug on a platter. Worse, he began to giggle again. Like a child. His breath smelt as acrid and disturbingly foul as the stuffy house when we had first arrived. As bad as the basement.

Streeter said in disgust, "Put him in the car."

Agent Knapp and Gregory escorted Fletcher to the caged backseat of a squad car parked next to their Bureau-issued Crown Victoria.

As Agent Gregory was about to close the door, I heard the slug call my name, after picking it up from the agents who had coaxed me out of killing Fletcher with my bare hands. I walked over to the open door, looming above him as he slouched against the vinyl seats.

He licked his lips. "I'll be thinking about you tonight. What you must have looked like when you were Noah's age. Nine? Ten years old?"

I kicked the car door shut in his face and mumbled, "Freak."

Streeter grabbed my arm, pulling me away from the car.

To Knapp and Gregory, Streeter barked, "Tell the officer to get him out of here." To Mills and Kelleher, Streeter ordered, "Bring the crime tech team in. Kelleher, you're point man. Focus on the spare bedroom with the toys upstairs. The boy must have stayed in that room. Dust it for prints. Tear the station wagon apart, too. The boys' prints will be there. Make sure everything is by the book on this one, because we're going to need it. Finish the bag and tag, box everything up and take it back to headquarters. I don't care how long it takes. Once you finish up, check in with me at the office because I may need you to help with the search. Looks like we're in for a very long night."

Streeter's cell phone let out a piercing shrill. He checked the number and said, "It's Linwood."

"While you talk to Jack, I need to tell Frances and Gabriel what's happening. I'll be right back."

I didn't know the woman with my sister. She was a psychologist, recommended by Tony, who specialized in dealing with victims and the bereaved. My sister was a mess, but I didn't have time to deal with that at the moment. I told her what had happened and that we had Fletcher, but that I needed to go find Noah. I collected Beulah and her gear and threw everything in the back of my SUV. As I was walking toward Fletcher's house, Chief Gates was pulling in, his sweeping headlights striking something shiny in Fletcher's driveway that caught my eye. As the chief stepped out of his car, I pulled off my gloves and reached down, plucking it from the snow. Brushing off the ice, I realized what I was holding was the football pin I'd given Noah.

"Wait!" I shouted and the rest of the agents who were gathering up equipment froze like statues. "This pin. It's Noah's. Queue it up. Queue it up!"

They were all staring at me, dumbfounded.

Streeter walked toward me. "Liv?"

"It's an audio recorder. With memory. I gave it to him. He left it for me."

The men gawked.

In a hushed tone, Gates said, "Liv, it probably just got knocked off in the struggle when Fletcher grabbed Noah from the car."

I knew they didn't believe me. I knew they thought I was crazy to think a child with severe cerebral palsy had the ability to stay cool and capture audio of a crime in progress. But I knew Noah. He did. He would. He made sure he left that pin for me to find.

"Queue. It. Up," I demanded, ignoring Gates.

Streeter nodded at Jon, who fired up his laptop and removed the memory from the pin, plugging it into the port. There were muffled noises, lots of muffled noise. The agents slowly disappeared from Fletcher's kitchen to go back to work, retrieving evidence.

"He has trouble controlling his movements. It's on and off. He probably rolled over on the activation button a few times. Fast-forward, Jon, use the graphs to show voices."

Streeter's expression was one of pity. But I knew Noah. Jon did as I instructed, reluctantly. About twenty minutes into the recording the graph jumped and the screeching of fast-forwarded voices sounded from his speakers like chipmunks.

"There!" I shouted. "Listen."

Little Max's laugh rang out, everyone recognizing it from the press releases. More agents and officers gathered in the cold on Fletcher's front lawn.

"It's him," Streeter said, his voice soft, his eyes wide. He gave a nod to Gates.

The laughter was replaced by Fletcher's voice, scolding the boy for disobeying and warning him that if this kid—meaning Noah—had been more than a vegetable, little Max would be in trouble. The conversation ended before Noah's wailing began. Jon was about to turn the recording off.

"No! Fast-forward. There might be more," I insisted.

He did and the bars of the graph jumped again with a short conversation near the end of the memory. Jon Tuygen queued up the last conversation from the beginning.

"There you are," Fletcher's voice sounded. Noah whimpered. I bit my lip so as not to cry. The heavy breathing of Fletcher repulsed me. Noah's weight proved too much for the pig. "Your fault, really, broken boy. Sammy was all mine until you interfered. He won't stop crying. Says he wants you to go with him. So you will." Giggling from fat Fletcher like we had heard a few minutes ago. More rustling, more of Fletcher's panting. "See how much help you are to Sammy in the woods tonight. You'll probably end up like the others. Besides, I know it's you, mother. Hiding inside this broken boy. Judging me. Know how I can tell? Your eyes. They gave you away." The panting noises were of Fletcher carrying Noah and a thumping noise soft against metal, probably Noah's blue Styrofoam chair being pushed against the car. "But I'll be rid of you soon. Forever. I doubt you'll be as lucky as Clint was." Then a door opened, and Fletcher said, "Here you go, Sammy."

Little Max's voice sounded like a siren, the wailing, as he cried, "Oh, Papa! Thank you! Thank God you're here, kid!"

There was the sound of fumbling, scratching, and rustling before silence and the recording ended.

"Clint! Did he say Clint?" I wondered if it could possibly be the same Clint that Noah and I had been talking about, the owner of the lost camo backpack.

Chief Gates said, "Probably in reference to the boy who was abducted last year after school just after the Thanksgiving break. He was found near Idaho Springs in the woods naked, but otherwise safe. We never did learn what happened to him. He's still in counseling from the trauma and almost froze to death."

The GPS location that Michael took from the encounter with the mountain lion was where I'd found the backpack.

"Tony, tell me." I was nearly frantic. I could feel my muscles trembling. I gripped his forearms in my hands, knowing I was gripping him too tightly, and held his gaze. "Was Clint a fifth grader? Last year, maybe? At Pennington Elementary School?"

"How do you know about Clint?" Gates asked.

"I know where Fletcher took Noah!"

CHAPTER 57

Noah

I DON'T UNDERSTAND WHAT'S wrong with little Max. It's like he's been kicked in the head or something. He keeps whimpering but falling asleep, dozing off, and then wakes up screaming. He's scared to death and so am I. I wonder if fear does that, if it makes you sleepy.

I don't know what more I can do.

I'm starting to get really, really scared myself.

I've stayed brave as long as I could. It's cold. And dark. And the smell is horrible! Worse than anything I've ever smelled before. Worse than any mess I ever made in my utility britches. I can hardly stand it.

And something keeps moving in the dark. I can hear scratching or nibbling or squeaking noises. I thought I could stay brave. I thought I could handle all this spy stuff. But I don't think I want to be a spy at all. Not anymore. This is too scary. And I'm just a boy. Like little Max. I can't help him. I've done everything I can.

After Mr. Creepy left us here, little Max seemed so happy that "Papa," my neighbor, was gone, he actually talked and talked and talked. He told me all about his mom and his dad and his nanny and his friends and playing in the park and on the slide. It made everything seem so much less scary and cold to me when he was telling me all those stories.

When I wouldn't answer his questions, he started calling me "broken baby" and talked to me like an adult would to an infant. He layered me in all sorts of clothes from his backpack, huddled close to me to stay warm. He even tried to feed me a peanut butter sandwich, until I started choking, which made him cry. Made me cry, too. Eating is difficult for me even when someone like my mom or dad feeds me. I can hardly swallow and choke often. And peanut butter sticks in my throat. But how could this poor kid know that? He's just a baby. Through his sobs, little Max said he didn't know what to do, which is how I felt, and his crying made me cry. And my wailing moans scared him even more.

I feel so helpless.

Thankfully, I managed to settle down. So he settled down. But then he got really cold, said he was feeling sleepy again, like he did after Papa gave him that big old vitamin. I don't know much about vitamins, but I'd never heard of them making kids sleepy before. I wondered what it was that Mr. Creepy made him eat. Little Max kept coming in and out of sleep, occasionally saying he felt drowsy-wowsey-woo-woo, which made me laugh. Then he'd giggle. And he'd fall asleep again. At least he fell asleep happy. But he's been asleep a long, long time now and I can't hear him breathing anymore.

And he hasn't moved.

I tried to scoot my chair toward him, to nudge him, but the pain in my leg made me start crying again, and things skittered away from me in the dark. I felt something on top of the blankets, heard nibbling noises. I think they might be rats. But what if they're mountain lions? Or bears? And they've come to eat us alive?

I hope little Max sleeps through all this. Because it's so scary I can hear my heart pounding in my chest.

What if something terrible has happened to him? Like maybe he's frozen stiff. Or a bear has already eaten half of the boy, leaving the other half leaning up against me.

I'm so scared. I hate the dark. I wish I had Auntie Liv's luminescent flashlight she gave me last Christmas. The one that got taken away from me because Mr. Creepy complained. I hate that man. I know I'm not sup-posed to hate anybody, but God, hear me now. I hate him. You can take his soul anytime and hurl it into hell.

I started crying again.

I don't want to be here anymore. I don't want all this responsibility. I want to go home.

To make things worse, I can feel the giant's finger thrumming the inside of my ribs again. It's already too dark here. Too cold. I'm alone. A seizure may scare little Max to death. And with no family here, no one who will know what to do, I might not fight off God taking my soul this time.

This time, I was just too weak to fight back.

CHAPTER 58

I HAD CONVINCED STREETER to ride with me, since Beulah's kennel was in the back of my vehicle and Streeter had asked me to bring her, just in case we'd need her in the woods. I had tossed him the keys, thinking he'd drive while I sulked.

When Streeter climbed into the passenger seat at my sister's house, asking me to drive, he surprised me. "Forget about him. He's messing with you. It happens to a lot of people. Not just you. Now focus and drive."

I slipped another oversized FBI-issued sweatshirt over the rag wool sweater before getting into the car and reached into the backseat for my coat, which I draped across my lap. The layers were to help me stave off the chill that Fletcher had imprinted as he tried to violate me with his eyes, taunting me with what he'd done to my poor nephew. And on top of all that, he had said he'd be thinking about me tonight—what I must have been like when I was Noah's age—whatever that meant. I have not a clue what he was talking about, but there was no mistaking the wolfish look in his evil eyes.

The layers were not enough to ward off the chill. Never enough. I pulled my hands far inside my sleeves to cover any exposed skin.

I was glad Streeter made me drive, forced me to focus. I can count on

Streeter never to baby me; he treats me like an equal. His special way of being both compassionate yet holding me accountable empowers me.

With the steady beat of wiper blades sweeping away the large flakes that continued to fall on the windshield, I worried about the weather's effect on the search that was just getting underway. I assumed that Tony Gates and his officers had already mapped the tire tracks and the foot-prints, if any, before they were completely covered by this steady snow. I hoped that by the time we arrived, the search teams would have already found the boys. Alive.

Quantico training had warned me to prepare for less.

Letting out a sigh, I focused on more practical matters. If the snow had been falling in the mountains all along, which was likely, the search would not be quick. I hoped that everyone had brought several layers of warm clothes and plenty to eat and drink. I suspected this search would last well into the night and for the entire next day. If I were honest with myself, I would admit that the search would probably last for several days. I looked in the rearview mirror, straining to see Beulah in her kennel in the backseat.

I admit I had convinced Streeter to ride with me for selfish reasons. I didn't want to be alone. And I felt safe around him. I couldn't call on Jack, since he was working downtown at the Bureau and was told to meet the other officers who took Fletcher to the holding cell for interrogation. Plus, I knew Streeter hadn't had a nap going on two long days. So I was glad he'd asked me to drive. He could take a catnap on the way up to the campground. I'd stolen a nap earlier that day after my search of the airport parking lot and now it was his turn.

He had fallen asleep almost immediately. I was enjoying watching him sleep, his face serene and chiseled. Awake, every taut muscle of Streeter's face was lined with the maps of his history; his slightest movements were more expressive than in any other man I'd known.

We were almost there when his phone rang.

Streeter's head snapped up and I could see him trying to work through the confusion that fogged his sleep-deprived brain.

"Your phone. We're almost there."

His fished for his cell in his pocket and answered, "Yes."

"This is Blake Riley with security."

I could already hear the voice on the phone in the stillness of the nighttime drive, but Streeter hit the speakerphone button anyway.

"Got some bad news for you," the voice said. "Or maybe it's good news."

"What is it?" Streeter asked with a groan, as his fingers brushed through his short, white hair.

"Fletcher hanged himself sometime in the last half hour," Riley said with little emotion.

"He what? How did it happen?"

I could see that Streeter was wide-awake with that news.

"You're not going to believe this. He had a rope, tied it to the top row of bars in his window."

"A rope? Where the hell did he get a rope?"

"Well, not a rope, really. More like thick twine or something, but strong enough to hold. We don't know where he got it or how. We've seen sheets ripped before, but he didn't even have any bedding yet. This guy wasn't on suicide watch according to the chart. Should he have been?"

Irritated, Streeter answered, "Well, obviously he should have been, Riley. The man committed suicide. But if you were asking if there was a mistake made on his chart, the answer is no. We had no idea that Fletcher was suicidal when we brought him in earlier. Was he frisked?"

"Yep. But no one found the twine." Riley continued past Streeter's long pause. "I don't think there were any mistakes made in security. Not that you guys make mistakes or anything. You know what I mean," Riley fumbled with his words. "We did follow procedure. I mean, we did take away his belt when we locked him up. He deserved to die, the nut job."

Annoyed, Streeter asked, "Why would you say that? No one deserves to die."

"It was the way he did it. He jacked himself off before or during the hanging. Who does that shit?" Riley asked. "Nut jobs. He had his khaki pants around his ankles, his boxers around his shins, and his pecker sticking out for the whole world to see. There was a puddle of semen beneath him and a goofy grimace plastered on his dead face. His eyes were still open and everything. Looks like he died a happy man."

"Could he have hanged himself accidentally? Was it autoerotic asphyxia or something?"

"You mean that oxygen deprivation thing that some weirdos get off on? Maybe," Riley considered.

Streeter closed his eyes and asked, "You haven't touched anything, have you?"

"Not no, but hell no."

"Are you sure it's been within a half hour?"

"Yeah. Within thirty-five minutes, for sure. That guy from Control Ops, the bigwig who escorted Fletcher to his cell about an hour ago, stayed with him about twenty minutes longer than the rest of us. Was the last one to see him alive, as far as we know."

My stomach flipped.

"Control Ops. Jack Linwood?" Streeter asked.

"Yeah, that's the guy."

"What was he doing down there?"

"Beats me," Riley answered. "Oh, yeah. Sorry. Didn't mean that as a joke or anything."

"Get the techs in there, then cut him down and clean him up. And send the report directly to me. No one else," Streeter said before ending the call. Streeter mumbled, "What is going on? First the nanny loses it, then Fletcher. What a mess."

Worried, I said, "Fletcher was alive after Linwood left. He would have told us, right?"

Streeter said nothing.

I remembered the last thing Jack whispered to me was that I shouldn't worry a thing about Fletcher. And now Fletcher was dead. No worries.

I wondered.

I also remembered the last thing Fletcher had said to me as he sat handcuffed in the backseat, in the driveway next to my sister's house. "I'll be thinking of you tonight."

Had he intended to commit suicide? It made sense why he had become so peaceful, placid, calm as we put him in the squad car. I wouldn't lie to myself. I was glad Fletcher was dead. Spared us all a trial. Spared me from ever having to look at him again.

"No matter how loathsome, he shouldn't have been allowed to commit suicide. That was too easy. And where did he get the twine?" Streeter asked.

I didn't answer, knowing it was a rhetorical question.

After a long moment, Streeter said, "It doesn't mean anything."

I did not take my eyes away from the Rocky Mountains that loomed around us. My voice was strong, but cold. "Yes, it does. He told me that he would be thinking of me tonight. He would be imagining what I was like when I was Noah's age."

Streeter had started to protest and I knew he thought better of it. His initial reaction was to protect me and I appreciated that. But in the end, he knew this was my battle to fight. And I appreciated that even more. I wasn't going to let scum like Fletcher win. Streeter knew that.

"He knew I'd find out. He wanted to get into my mind and then into my nightmares. Seep under my skin like a fungus."

"He's a sick bastard."

"Was a sick bastard. And it does mean something." Streeter put one hand on my elbow. I neither resisted nor responded to his touch. Instead, I continued to stare out into the distance. I'd been through worse than Fletcher.

After several moments, I turned to face Streeter. With defiance, I said, "I won't let him. I won't. He can't win."

The silence that followed my statement was as loud as a crash of cymbals.

Eventually, as we wound along the mountain road, I vowed, "Instead, I am going to go out there tonight and hope for a miracle. We'll find little Max and Noah and give them the proper homecoming they deserve. Fletcher can't keep me down."

My lips tightened with resolve and indignation.

In his deep, gravelly voice Streeter said, "Guys like him never win. People like you and little Max are too strong for creeps like him. And Noah's the hero in all this. He kicked Fletcher's sorry ass. So let's focus on finding him."

He was right.

CHAPTER 59

EVEN THOUGH IT LOOKED different at night than it had yesterday morning when I was up there working with Beulah to find my brother-in-law Michael, I knew we had found the right campground area. I would have known we were in the right place even before I saw the faint indents in the snow from a single set of tire tracks going off the road into it. Fletcher had been here. I could feel it. He had dumped the kids an hour ago, maybe two, before heading back home where we were waiting for him. I just knew it, even though in my headlights I could see the tire tracks had long since been covered by the falling snow.

Gates and Streeter directed the search party to park their cars along the unimproved gravel road that led to the area, instructing them to line up single file. Michael's GPS coordinates would lead me to where I'd found the camo backpack, several yards up into the woods to the north. My brother-in-law had decided he would stay at Frances's house, helping her and Gabriel manage their grief and allowing Elizabeth to spread the news to our large family about what had happened. I was grateful Michael still had the coordinates in his GPS from yesterday morning when we'd been out tracking.

The faint stars shining through the sparse clouds lighted the dark night. Large snowflakes slowly descended. It was a peaceful evening—the type of evening that reminded me of home in the Black Hills as a child with my brothers and sisters, sitting on the front porch with our nine sets of tiny fingers wrapped around our individual cups of hot chocolate.

Streeter leaned forward, studying the landscape that shone in our headlights. I looked back over my shoulder at the line of cars and the dozens of search and rescuers pouring from them, donning layers. I could hear the humming of my engine and the beat of my windshield wipers as I studied the landscape, grateful that Michael hadn't deleted the coordinates from his GPS where I found Clint's backpack. Chief Gates had set up in the right place.

Within seconds the thrum of a light generator plant sounded and a shower of light spilled across the snow, the campground lit up like a miniature baseball field. Everyone hung back awaiting Streeter's next order, most huddling around Gates's cluster of official vehicles just behind us.

"There's Tony," Streeter said, looking in the rearview mirror. I turned back and saw Tony's handsome black face as he leaned up against a midnight blue pickup with his arms folded across his wide chest. He appeared annoyed. Not just a bit. A lot.

Streeter mumbled, "I wonder what he's miffed about."

Streeter jumped out of my SUV into the below-freezing temperature and greeted Chief Tony. I made sure Beulah was okay, put on my coat, and followed him.

"Fletcher wasn't any help," Tony said to Streeter. No hello, no how ya doing. Straight to the point. "Your team just told me he committed suicide."

They both cut their eyes my way. To see how I'd take the news.

"How many do we have for the search?" I asked, ignoring the rising dread I felt.

"We've got twenty-eight guys out here, including the three of us," Gates continued. "I lost a guy. His wife went into labor."

"Twenty-eight is good," Streeter said.

"It's snowing," Gates said sullenly.

"Let's go look," Streeter said, and the three of us started off toward the campground parking area alone as everyone watched.

The trees near the road had preserved the tire tracks, but the farther we walked into the campground, the more the fresh snow had been free to cover the tracks.

"Not good," Gates said.

By the time we made it to the large clearing, the snow fell in blankets, and the tracks of Fletcher's vehicle had been completely erased. There were no tire tracks, no footprints, and too many humps and lumps in the snow that could be rocks, logs, or bodies.

"Shit," I said. But deep down I knew Fletcher had been here. Sensed it. Likely comfortable with his chosen dump site, even if Clint had survived.

Streeter said, "Here's the plan. Gates, get everyone to fan out and check this area first. Lock arms and uncover every inch of snow in swaths to make sure nothing's been buried."

The "nothing" meant my nephew and little Max. The thought made me sick.

"Snow is a concern. For all of us. Because if we don't get moving, it won't just be Fletcher's tire tracks that are covered." His eyes flicked toward me. "It will cover up any fresh footprints, too. Let's move."

I knew he meant the boys' bodies, not just their footprints. Noah could not walk. And little Max had no hope of carrying him. Noah was slowly being covered in snow as we spoke. And he would freeze to death if we didn't get moving. Our only hope was to find little Max's tiny footprints, hoping he'd taken off to find help for Noah.

Within seconds, Gates had a search party gathered and walking in step along the opening that was the campground, kicking at mounds of snow and shoveling off layers from the picnic tables, outhouse, benches, and stumps that surrounded the area.

Stunned at the sight of it all, my mind still reeling from the thought that Noah might be out here in this frigid cold, I melted into Streeter, who held me upright. Within minutes, Gates had converted one of the picnic tables into a makeshift command center. A light plant—powered by a noisy generator nearby—was relocated closer to illuminate the entire area.

Gates swept his arm across the table, brushing all the freshly fallen snow from the surface. Laying the map on the clean table, he showed us the nearby terrain using the topography lines.

"This is where we are. On our initial search, we send out three teams to the north, where Liv found Clint's backpack yesterday." Gates turned and pointed over to the hilltop. "It's the most difficult terrain, but that's where we'll start. I'm assuming the child would have run from Fletcher, who headed out to the road in the opposite direction."

The searchers kicked at and quickly stamped down the fluff of freshly fallen snow.

"I think the opposite side of the road to the campground area, to the south, might prove more lucrative for our search, because it's the easiest terrain and has fewer trees. Assuming Fletcher led them in a direction. He wasn't in the best shape, so he'd take the easier route. We'll search that on our second sweep."

"How long will the teams be out?" Streeter shouted over the generator.

"Once they finish up here, I'm sending the teams out and telling them to turn back in an hour and a half."

"No tracks, no footprints," Streeter said.

Gates shook his head. "And it's still snowing."

"Not good," I said.

The falling snowflakes were small and fast. That meant it was going to snow for a long time. Tolie Sharpfish, a Lakota Sioux, taught me that when I was a little girl. Flakes large and slow, the snowfall wouldn't last long. Flakes small and fast, prepare to get buried.

"On the second sweep, they should be able to complete their search of the area south of the road. After that, we can send them out on sweeps to the east, and then west."

For the first time, Gates noticed me staring at him. I had been admiring Gates's focused determination. He reminded me of my little brother, Jens. Tall, smart, determined, soft on the inside, steel on the outside. Knapp and Gregory, who had followed Streeter and me from Wheat Ridge and who had parked their car down the road, emerged from the dark shadows beyond the light plant and walked over to the picnic table.

After shouted introductions—the generators too loud to hear much else—Streeter suggested to Gates, "Liv brought Beulah. Want her to try the north before everyone starts tromping out the scent? If there is one?"

"It's your crime scene."

I hoped Beulah and I didn't blow this.

"Besides," Streeter added, "We have a half hour or so before the search team finishes their campground area sweep, wouldn't you guess?"

We all watched as the searchers tromped through the snow, brushing off even the smallest of mounds and buried objects.

"Can she do that? In the dark?" Tony hesitated and studied my face. Looking up at his face, I smiled back at him and nodded respectfully. He frowned. "You best get started. I don't want you out there on your own."

"We'll get started right now," Streeter agreed. "Keep the rest of the searchers in the lot or out on the road so she can get a clear trail determined. Agreed?"

"Agreed," Gates said reluctantly.

Preparing for the search, I grabbed bolt cutters, a shovel, and a crowbar.

"What are you doing, Liv?"

"Nothing's getting in Beulah's way. Or mine. Come hell or high water, I'm finding Noah."

CHAPTER 60

"READY?" I ASKED.

Streeter nodded. Gates gave us a wave and leaned against my SUV with Knapp and Gregory at either side of him. Streeter called to him, "Keep the search teams in the campground or on the road, okay?"

Gates waved his hand in agreement.

"Stay right behind me the whole time, okay?" I said to Streeter, who nodded in response. "Oh no, Streeter."

"What?"

"I gave Jack little Max's beret. I don't have a target scent for Beulah."

"I kept the sock I found at Fletcher's house. Will that help?" Streeter searched his coat pocket and pulled out the plastic bag.

"Let's hope it's little Max's and not some other kid's," I said. I extracted the sock and knelt beside Beulah. I held it away from the dog's nose and commanded, "Beulah, find."

Beulah trotted around the packed snow of the parking lot and circled a small area several times. The lead was loose between the dog and me. I looked back at Gates. Gates nodded his encouragement.

Over the sound of the generators, I yelled to Streeter, "It's definitely little Max's sock."

I could see the word form on his lips, "What?"

"His sock. This is most definitely little Max's sock," I shouted.

I jerked my head in Beulah's direction to explain. Beulah had lowered her nose for an instant, and then she lifted it up in the air and was circling a small area repeatedly. She started pulling on the lead straight into the campground area.

Over the rumble of the generator, I shouted the command as support, "Find!"

The lead went taut. Beulah strained against the harness to follow the scent. I stepped through the deep snow as quickly as I could with my snowshoes. Beulah only went a few hundred yards, directly to the out-house, and bayed excitedly. Her front legs were stiff and the hair on the scruff of her neck was standing on end.

Streeter looked at me. I gave him a beats-me look. "She only does that when she's found the target."

Streeter asked, "Let me look inside."

"Go ahead," I said, as I shortened the lead and knelt beside Beulah, encouraging her with long strokes and kind words.

Streeter slowly pushed the door of the outhouse open. His headlamp swept across the inside of the outhouse. He looked behind the door and peered cautiously down the black hole and up at the ceiling beams. He came out of the outhouse and shrugged his shoulders.

I suggested, "Look around."

Streeter circled the outhouse twice. With his headlamp sweeping across the dark woods, he knocked the snow off each mound he encountered with his boot, only to find mostly rocks and a few pieces of wood. He climbed on top of the outhouse to look on the flat roof and found nothing.

When he returned to where I knelt, he asked, "Now what?"

"Well, it could mean little Max stopped to use the outhouse and then went right back to the car," I explained. "But normally, Beulah would have backtracked on the same course, following from the oldest to the newest scent. And she wouldn't bay like she did. She only does that when she finds the actual person. I've seen her do it several times before. I'll restart Beulah. There may be several different trails. Or maybe the snow is bothering her."

Or maybe it's the mountain lion incident on Christmas Eve. Although she did fine in the airport and with the garbage in the parking lot, Beulah's confidence in the woods might be shaky.

We walked back to the parking lot with Beulah, where we were met with rumbles of chatter coming from Knapp and Gregory. I couldn't hear them over the generator, but I could tell they were concerned about Beulah. Rumor at the field office of her downhill slide as the best search-and-rescue dog in the country started circulating the second I'd set foot in the office three weeks ago as a new agent and assigned handler for Beulah. My self-confidence waned. Ignoring them, I knelt in the middle of the parking lot beside Beulah again and scratched behind her long, droopy ears.

"Good girl, Beulah," I encouraged her. "You're a good dog. Now, let's try again."

I extracted the sock from the plastic bag in my pocket and held it several inches from Beulah's nose. I ordered, "Beulah, find."

The dog immediately trotted through the parking lot to the same area as she had before and circled the exact spot where she had paused only minutes earlier. She lowered her nose again and sniffed deeply.

Again, I commanded, "Find."

Beulah took the direct route to the outhouse again, stopping short of the closed door and baying wildly.

I frowned and ordered, "Beulah, find."

The dog would not budge.

Streeter was watching along with everyone else. I gave him a shrug and he just shook his head.

"This is so odd, Streeter. I'm not sure what to make of it," I said.

Streeter replied, "Well, there is no way he's here, unless you see a mound that I've missed."

"I sure don't."

After three more identical attempts, Chief Gates shouted to us, "The search teams are ready to head out, guys."

Streeter nodded and waved. Turning back to me, he said, "What's next? Your call."

I shook my head. "I don't know. I've never seen it quite like this. The way Beulah is reacting I would swear she's found her target. She only bays like that when she finds what she's looking for. Other than the mountain lion incident on Christmas Eve."

"A mountain lion?" Gates asked, unfolding his arms.

"But that was because the mountain lion was between me and her," I corrected.

Streeter asked, "What mountain lion?"

"Long story. But maybe that's what has her spooked out here. That or the dark. I've never taken her on a night search. And she hasn't been back in the woods since the mountain lion incident."

Streeter said, "The scratches and sore ribs? A mountain lion, right?"

"A close call, let's just put it that way," I said. "I would swear little Max was in or around the outhouse." I couldn't even think about Noah. I had to stay focused on little Max. For my own sanity.

"But he's not," Streeter said.

"I know. The only thing I can figure is that Fletcher let little Max out to go to the bathroom, then took him by car to some other spot. But then she would have backtracked. I would bet money that these guys won't find anything out in the wooded area. If Max was out there, Beulah would have picked up the scent of a different trail on one of those attempts and followed it." I was convinced. I knew Beulah and she wasn't a quitter.

Streeter warned, "The search teams will be starting any minute. Want to go with them?"

"I'll kennel Beulah. I have a battery-heated blanket I'll throw over the kennel to keep her warm and I'll join you on the search."

Gates said, "Maybe it's the noise from the generator."

I kicked some snow with the toe of my boot. "Maybe I'll try again after the search."

Streeter called out to the teams, "Remember. Based on the time of Fletcher's departure from home and subsequent return, taking into consideration the driving time, and taking into account that he wasn't in the best physical shape, Fletcher could not have wandered very far from the parking lot. He did not have snowshoes, only snow boots. And he had a five-year-old boy in tow and would be carrying the other boy strapped in a bright blue Styrofoam car seat. Turn back in an hour and a half for the first sweep, and we'll meet back here in three hours. Go slowly and be thorough."

The teams took off in their respective directions, with Gates assigned to direct one, me the other, and Streeter the last. The searchers of each team linked arms to form a human chain and slowly kicked away the soft snow beneath our feet, looking beneath every tree, bush, and crevice we encountered. The chaotic sweep of headlamps was as mesmerizing as a well-orchestrated laser show. The mountainous, wooded terrain offered peculiar challenges to all the team members as we fanned our way through the woods.

Every time I kicked a clump of snow, I was praying I'd find nothing beneath.

CHAPTER 61

A CHILL GRIPPED ME.

Maybe it was the drop of melting snow that landed on the back of my neck. Maybe it was thoughts of little Max and Noah braving the elements all night. Cold. Alone. Scared.

I told Steve Knapp to take charge of my line, broke from the search party, and told him I had to stay back. I was thankful for the bright moonlight in the clear Colorado sky that would soon surrender to dawn. It was five o'clock. I noticed that our extensive search had eroded the hard snow in the campground, but revealed nothing but frozen earth beneath. The stubborn foliage and sparse rocks poking through the surface somehow gave me hope.

I lumbered back through the snow. Alone. Nearing the parking lot, the curving line of cars shimmered in the rays of the waning moonlight, like an eel. The imagery tugged somewhere dark in the recesses of my mind. Shallow waters. A fish or eel. Just below the surface. In the mountains where it shouldn't be. Water everywhere. Forty days and forty nights. Lots of rain. Just like in the Bible. Noah. Where he shouldn't be.

I pulled Beulah from her cage again. I slipped on her harness and attached the lead. I was going to try this one more time. Only this time,

I was going to search for Noah, not little Max. I don't know why I didn't think to try this before. I fished in the backseat for one of Noah's stocking caps he'd left in my car this week. I knelt down beside Beulah, took a deep breath, and held out the stocking cap.

"Find, Beulah. Find!"

The persistent bloodhound circled the parking lot, hesitating at a spot about three feet from where she had in her search for little Max. I realized Noah had been in the backseat. That made sense. Fletcher would have put little Max beside him in the front and Noah in the rear to make a quick getaway. Beulah pulled me to the exact location as before, directly in front of the outhouse. Again. Not far behind the bloodhound, I stood rubbing my forehead. The hell of it was that all I could think about was Fletcher's comments about forty days and forty nights and lots of rain. Crazy how the mind works. The all-nighters were beginning to take a toll.

"Stubborn," Streeter grumbled as he walked across the trodden snow toward me.

I hadn't heard him at first because the generators were so loud. The crunching of the hard-packed snow beneath his feet as he approached ripped me back to the previous night. Fletcher's wet boots across the concrete floor in the dark garage. Why hadn't I shot the son of a bitch when I'd had the chance? Made him die the slow, painful death he had deserved. My mind slid to the image of Fletcher dangling from his makeshift noose, his stained pants and underwear bunched around his ankles. The fury of my lost opportunity in that garage fueled my body despite my exhaustion.

"She's not stubborn. She found her target. I just don't understand what she's telling me."

"I wasn't talking about the dog. I meant you." He smiled.

"I knew you'd come back," I said, staring at the outhouse as if it were a giant wooden tarot card.

"I told you to forget about this."

I brushed a loose strand of my hair from my face. "I'm sorry about breaking ranks. But I just couldn't let this damn thing go."

"That's when mistakes are made. People can die from mistakes."

"It won't happen again."

And that's all it took. He was back to helping me again.

"What's your gut telling you?" he asked.

"Beulah's not the rusty one. I am," I answered.

"And?"

"Look at her."

Beulah stood directly in front of the outhouse door, howling.

Streeter folded his arms as he watched the persistent hound.

"This time I used Noah's cap, not little Max's sock. Beulah tracked Noah to the exact same spot. Again."

"Maybe it means something totally different."

"Like?" I grabbed Beulah by her harness, crouched beside her, and rewarded my hound with strokes across her red coat. Her howling stopped and her tail thumped against the frozen ground.

"Well, we've looked all around this outhouse several times, right?"

I nodded again.

"And there are no boys."

I shrugged.

He persisted. "Fletcher couldn't have buried the boys' bodies because the ground is frozen. What if Fletcher left the boys right here and someone else picked them up? Would Beulah still return to this spot?"

I shook my head, rubbing my chin. "She would track the scent to the car or snowmobile or whatever picked them up. There were no tracks, except in the parking lot. If they went back that way, so would Beulah. She'd follow right up to where the boys got into the car or whatever. That would be a more recent scent."

"In the parking lot?"

I nodded.

"But it had snowed. Maybe the snow covered the tracks."

"True."

"Sorry, Liv, but I have to ask. What if Fletcher killed them right here, then carried them off somewhere. Would the scent stop when they died?"

I shook my head.

"If a wild animal got them, say a mountain lion or a coyote dragged them from this spot sometime before we got here? Is that possible?"

I shook my head again. "If a wild animal dragged them off somewhere, Beulah would have followed the boys' scent."

"Dead or alive?"

"Dead or alive."

"Even if it was a mountain lion, considering her scary experience on Christmas? If she was spooked by the cat?"

"I think so."

"And the scent of a mountain lion or some animal doesn't overpower the boys' scent?"

"Maybe if the animal ate them whole. Right here on the spot." I turned my head and made my last meal public. It was all too much. I wiped my mouth and said, "Sorry."

Streeter patted me on the back. "We would have seen some signs. Carnage of some sort. Blood. A shoe. Something." Streeter paced the trodden snow.

I told Streeter the whole story about the mountain lion, how Michael and I had been out on a training exercise. I didn't leave anything out. I explained that Beulah didn't act upset or even seem to know what danger she or I was in.

"Liv, you could have been killed."

"Yeah, I know."

"That's why you've been walking so gingerly, protecting your ribs?"

"I bruised them, I think."

We sat on the log in the center of the campground and said nothing. I adjusted the lens of my mind's eye several different directions until I could focus my thoughts. The string of cars looked like an eel. Fletcher's words about Noah being more like Joseph, only not a king, no colorful coat. Bible references. Beulah fixed on the outhouse. Something kept eluding me.

"If the boys are dead, Fletcher probably didn't kill them. He caused their deaths, but didn't actually do it," Streeter thought aloud.

"But the bleach at his house?"

Streeter shook his head. "I don't think so. He was too much of a coward to kill them. And too cowardly to let them live."

"Didn't think about it that way, but you're right," I said. "After all, Clint lived."

"Fletcher was so much of a coward that when he was caught, he killed himself to avoid any suffering. Any embarrassment or pain he may have had to endure during the trial or in prison," Streeter continued. "So if he was too yellow to kill the boys and was scared to death of little Max telling someone who he was, he would have left them for dead. Out here in the woods. In the middle of winter."

"How could he be sure the boys would never be found, like Clint? Or that little Max wouldn't walk out of here alive? Would he tie them up?"

"Maybe. Restrain them or incapacitate them somehow," Streeter suggested. "Little Max knew too much. He was with Fletcher too long. He wasn't sure what Noah knew. He snatched him from the car, probably because he saw your sister pull out of the garage and go back into the house. Who knows?"

"Do you think Fletcher worried about someone seeing him out here?"

"I doubt it. From what he said on that audio your nephew took, it sounded to me like Fletcher was crazy. Claiming his mother was trapped inside your nephew. I don't think he was all there."

"Noah's eyes are gray. One is quite cloudy. Blind. It kind of freaks people out."

"Maybe his mom had gray eyes. Or was blind. But I don't think Fletcher worried about anyone seeing him up here. And if he did, he may have figured he couldn't risk having someone stumble across the boys. After all, he thought this was a remote location, isolated, a summer destination. He never imagined seeing another car. And who knows what he might do if he did?"

"He may have decided to abort his plans and get rid of the boys somewhere else. A different location," I guessed.

"No," Streeter said with confidence. "We timed his trip. Remember? He wouldn't have had time, based on your sister's estimate of when Fletcher took Noah."

"He must have panicked."

"And was desperate," Streeter added.

"Desperate enough to overcome his cowardice? To kill the boys?"

"Maybe."

I couldn't stomach the thought. Beulah whined. I stood and tugged on her lead. "Come on, Beulah. Let's get you back in the car." Beulah resisted, planting her paws firmly in front of the outhouse. She looked at me with sad, droopy eyes as I insisted, "Beulah, come. What's the matter with you?"

When I leaned against the lead, Beulah bolted for the outhouse. The lead slid through my hands, the nylon burning against my scabbed palm. "Beulah!"

She ignored me, scratching at the door until it opened enough for her to squeeze through. Streeter scrambled to his feet and ran after me toward the outhouse. When we arrived, Beulah was howling, standing with her front paws straddling the seat.

Streeter and I crowded into the outhouse with Beulah. Our eyes met and our mouths fell open with recognition.

"He panicked," I repeated.

"He needed to find a place for little Max and Noah where no one would ever find them and where they could never get out."

"In the shit hole."

"Alive," Streeter said.

"Not Noah, but Joseph. He'll never be a king, never have a colorful coat," I recalled. "Straight from the Bible."

"What?"

"Joseph's brothers," I explained. "They were jealous and threw him down a hole to die."

CHAPTER 62

DURING THE NIGHT, WE had looked down that hole many times and seen nothing. We still couldn't see any sign of the boys down there, even with our headlamps shining all the way to the bottom, which had to mean they were alive after they were dropped down the hole. *If* they were dropped down the hole.

"Little Max would have scrambled to the edge to stay dry and get out of the shit. Who wouldn't?" I speculated, pulling Beulah off the seat. "He must have helped Noah."

Streeter peered down the hole. He shouted, "Max! Max, can you hear me?" There was no answer. "The bad man's gone. Papa's gone! We're here to help, Max! Noah?"

Stillness settled in the expected stench below.

Streeter ushered me out and closed the door. He must have seen the expression on my face of the dread I had been feeling. He added quietly, "No. Don't think that. Come on. Help me."

He rammed his shoulder into the side of the dilapidated shack, hell-bent on tipping it over as if it were a gravestone pinning the boys' fate. I ran beside him on his second charge. Rage coursed through my veins. The worn, gray wood groaned in protest. We charged again and again until we both doubled over to catch our breath. My ribs ached and my lungs burned. I was having trouble catching my breath.

"Fletcher probably figured no one would ever find the boys until they froze to death," I panted.

"No one would ever find the bodies. Or notice the smell of decay. It's a perfect hiding spot."

Beulah sidled up to me and licked my face. "Good girl. Come on. Kennel."

Streeter caught his breath. "Do you have a rope? Blankets, too. Bring anything you think might help."

I streaked toward the car, slipping on the packed snow and landing hard on my left arm. Wincing from the pain in my ribs and my arm, I pushed myself to my feet.

"You okay?"

"Fine," I lied. I gave him a pathetic little wave and bolted for the car.

Beulah barked at the commotion, sensing our mounting excitement. I kenneled her, tossed her a handful of snacks, and rummaged through the car, grabbing several blankets, including the electric blanket that had draped Beulah's kennel.

I carried everything Streeter had asked for in my right arm, except for the blankets, which were draped over the left. I was hurt, but I wasn't about to say anything now. We had more important things to do and he needed my help. He had his head stuck down the hole, his shoulders preventing him from going any further.

"No rope," I said. "Will this work?"

Streeter nodded his approval at Beulah's harness and the twenty-foot lead that I held up.

"It'll have to do."

Streeter flung open the outhouse door and wrapped the dog's lead around his chest, throwing the other end over a support beam. He had eased the two latches off their hooks and threw the entire hinged bench back like a lid to a treasure chest. He took a step up to straddle the box.

I hoped that Fletcher had dropped Noah still strapped to the spongy, blue chair. The chair would at least cushion his fall. And it would have easily fit in the opening if Fletcher lifted the bench as Streeter just had.

I hoped he hadn't taken Noah out of his cushion chair and dumped him down the hole with nothing. He really would be broken.

Streeter answered my unspoken thoughts, "If they're down there, it could mean they're sleeping."

"Or unconscious," I braved.

I watched as he started to step in and lower himself.

"Streeter, wait!"

He hesitated.

"Let me go. If you go down there and find them, I don't know if I can pull them up with one arm." His puzzled expression made me explain. I removed the blanket draped over my arm and showed him my limp arm. "I think I messed something up. When I slipped just now and fell on my arm."

He pulled himself back up and untied the harness from his chest. "This isn't long enough for me to leverage them up from the bottom."

Standing nose to nose with one another in the cramped space of the outhouse, I said, "My turn."

There was really no other answer. He knew it. But he tried anyway. "We'll wait until the other guys get back and we'll send one of the guys down there."

My desperate words were choked, "If they're down there, we can't wait. The other guys won't be coming back for at least another hour and a half, maybe two hours."

He had no argument.

"But I can hold on to the rope with one hand while you lower me down the hole." I added in a whisper, "If little Max and Noah are down there, we've waited long enough. Come on. I need your help."

I straddled the open bench seat wearing my thick winter coat, Streeter's rag wool sweater, Phil's too-tight charcoal gray suit pants, and my snow boots. I pulled on my insulated work gloves and wrapped Beulah's lead around my chest. I looked down at Streeter and offered him a tentative smile.

"Ready?" I said and stepped in.

Streeter gripped the rope. I groaned as the lead tightened around my chest and my ribs were compressed as he lowered me down into the outhouse pit.

I called up to Streeter, "I'm down far enough. Stop for a minute and let me look around."

I felt Streeter hold tight to the lead. I pulled the rag wool sweater over my nose and mouth.

When I turned my head to sweep the headlamp's beam across the dugout walls and floor, all I could see was the heap below. The foul odor crowded my senses. My beam swept across the bottom of the outhouse pit and along the walls, searching for any sign of the boys.

Dear God, let Noah be here. Alive.

I thought I saw something on the bottom and slowly swept my beam back and forth. It settled on a drag mark through the slimy, semifrozen piles of excrement. The mark was about a foot wide and flat. I followed the drag mark beneath me over toward one corner.

I gasped.

Little Max had dragged Noah's chair to the side.

"They're here! Ease me down. Quick," I called up to Streeter.

I could feel Streeter fumble with the lead and begin easing me down the hole. I saw a lump of different colors in one corner of the dugout structure and a patch of shiny bright blue.

Noah's chair!

CHAPTER 63

"**THEY'RE HUDDLED IN THE** corner. I think. All I see are colors. Mostly pink. It looks like a pink hat or something." I swallowed hard and told him the truth, "And they're not moving."

Down to the last two feet of the twenty-foot lead, I reached bottom. Streeter called down, "How far to Max and Noah?"

"About six feet or so. Maybe more." I loosened the lead and tied it around my good wrist. I trained my eyes at the pile of many colors so the beam would stay steady and thought of the Biblical story of Joseph. Wearing his coat of many colors, he had been tossed into a pit by cowards. Selfish cowards. I trudged through the thick muck that was stiff with cold, like oatmeal left in the refrigerator too long.

I felt the lead tug my arm.

Streeter called, "Don't let go of the lead. I'm hanging on. Just to be on the safe side. See if you can reach them. Without slipping."

Too late.

My feet slid out from under me and I wrenched my arm again. I groaned and righted myself, trying not to let my boots get sucked right off my feet with every other step. Where the excrement wasn't frozen slick as snot, it was thick like foul quicksand.

How in the hell did little Max pull Noah through this?

As I narrowed the gap, I held my breath. Not because of the stench. Anxiety constricted my lungs and I felt an overwhelming desire to hear every sound in the dark hole. I wanted to hear sounds of life, but all I could hear was the thick sloshing of my boots. My headlamp bounced with every step, my head jerking. The lead grew taut just as I reached the mound of colors. I was literally at the end of my rope. I untied the lead from my wrist and baby-stepped my way toward the corner.

A screeching rat scampered across the pile of colors.

And the colors moved!

"I hate rats. Don't you?"

Streeter called down, "Did you untie the—"

"My name is Liv."

Streeter would figure it out. I wasn't talking to him. I was talking to little Max, or to Noah, whoever it was that was moving under the layers. And I didn't want to scare him by hollering back up at Streeter. He was scared enough.

"You boys shouldn't have to stay down here with these rats. Max? Let's get out of here. Together. Would you like that?"

I heard a small sound from one of the boys.

I tossed back layers of colors, clothing that little Max must have stuffed in his backpack and piled on top of himself and Noah to stay warm. They had huddled together beneath the mound. Noah wasn't moving. I tried not to look at him, because I knew I'd start crying. And little Max was barely moving, blue. Scared. And right now he needed me to be strong. So I was. I swallowed hard. One at a time, I told myself. One at a time.

"Okay then, little bud. Let's get out of this yucky place . . . Max? Can you hear me? Wrap your arms and legs around me. Can you do that honey?" I coaxed him in a soothing voice. "Max?"

Max wasn't answering me. He had slipped away. Don't let it be too late, I prayed.

"Liv?" Streeter called down.

I didn't answer him.

"How about I just scoop you up and carry you? Would you like that? I'll hold on to you. I'll come back for Noah. I'm Noah's aunt."

"Broken baby? His name is Noah?" His words were nothing more than a harsh whisper in my ear as I bent to lift him. He stared at Noah, who was listless, but breathing.

I nodded. I was conflicted. I wanted to scoop Noah up first and come back for little Max. Get my nephew help immediately. But after my quick and initial assessment of both boys, little Max appeared in worse shape, dehydration and hypothermia causing some delirium. His skin was much bluer than Noah's and I knew I had to get little Max out first.

"You call Noah broken baby?" I asked him, hearing Noah groan a dull laugh, which made me realize my choice was wise. Max didn't answer. I was starting to panic as little Max was starting to fade. "Thanks for keeping Noah warm last night, Max. And for pulling him over here with you. Noah, sweetheart. I'll be right back."

I yelped with pain as I scooped little Max into my arms, feeling something pop in my forearm. It wasn't a natural sort of pop. Max didn't make a sound, his head lolling against my shoulder. "Look at that, Max. The rats are scattering," I said, trudging my way back to the center of the pit. "Can you wrap your arms around my neck, Max?" No answer. "Max?"

I reached for the lead and tugged. Streeter pulled all the slack out of the lead as I neared the center. He stared down the hole, pulling the lead taut.

"That's my friend, Streeter, up there," I said. "He's going to get us out of here."

Cradled in my arms, looking more like a filth-encrusted runt pig than Maximillian Bennett Williams III, the boy stared up at Streeter.

"Not Papa?" he asked, listless, but alive.

Streeter smiled at the boy, offering him a little wave. But I could see all the pain Streeter felt for the boy in his wide blue eyes.

"Not Papa. I promise. He's gone. You have been so brave and strong. I'm so proud of you. Your mom and dad will be proud of you, too," I said.

Max lifted his heavy eyelids. A hint of a smile played around his lips.

"But I need you to be brave and strong for a little bit longer, okay?" I pointed up the hole at Streeter and said, "See that man up there, Max? He's my friend. And he's your friend, too. He's going to lift you out of this hole and wrap you up in a warm blanket. Would you like that?"

The little boy's eyes widened with fright. He hung limp in my arms.

I added, "I need you to be brave for me while he pulls you up. You'll need to hold on tight."

For the first time, the child moved. His filthy pink sleeve slid around my neck.

"Not to me. To the rope," I explained.

Max's grip on my neck tightened.

I shushed him. "It's okay. I promise. I'm going to have my friend pull you out first. Then I'll come up and hold you some more. Okay?"

That didn't quiet his fear.

"Besides, I need to get your friend Noah. And we don't want to stay down with these stinking rats anymore, do we?"

Max's little arm eased from around my neck. I kissed his soiled cheek.

I looked up at Streeter. He pointed at the lead, made a motion of winding it around little Max, and shook his head. I nodded. Winding the lead around Max's chest in his weakened condition may cause further damage. I looked back into Max's exhausted eyes.

"A blanket? Your coat?" Streeter said.

I answered, "That might work. I can wrap him up like a cocoon."

"How about this?" he said, holding up Beulah's harness.

"Perfect. Toss it down."

He did, careful not to let it fall too far from me.

I caught it and slipped the harness over little Max's chest, pulling his hands from my neck, threading each of his arms into the shoulder loops. I latched the lead to the harness and gave the thumbs-up sign to Streeter. He pulled the boy upward, slowly. The boy's head lolled to one side, which concerned me. Max stiffened and squinted in the bright light that Streeter shone down the hole. A good sign. The boy had some reflexes.

Once Streeter had him, he quickly stripped the boy and wrapped him in blankets, setting him on the floor beside the bench. Streeter dropped the lead and harness down the hole and motioned for me to get going. I trudged back through the heap to Noah.

"Noah?" Startled by his ashen appearance, I felt for a pulse. "Noah, it's me, Auntie Liv."

He had a pulse, but it was so weak I wondered if it was my heartbeat pounding through my fingertips. I pried open his eyes, moving my head so the light flashed across his face. His pupils responded. He was there. Buried deep, but there.

Noah's skin was a pale gray, his face sagging and sallow, and his lips had that haunting bluish tint. He had a dirty pink sweater draped across his legs and a small coat spread across his chest. Little Max had layered everything he could over Noah to keep him warm, including a pink stocking cap pulled over his head. He was still strapped in his chair, wrapped in a blanket, with his snow pants and coat, just as Frances had described putting on him late last night when they were headed to the police station, before he'd been taken from the backseat of her minivan.

Fletcher had dropped Noah down the hole, chair and all.

"Are you okay, bud?"

No smile. No response.

I knew he wasn't going to make it if I didn't hurry. I prayed both boys would live, that we'd found them in time.

"You're my hero," I said, swallowing the tears that were welling inside me and I kissed his forehead.

I scooped his chair into my arms, feeling the sharp pain in my left arm, the ache in my ribs, as I did. I wanted to scream from the pain. But I didn't want to scare Noah. If my arm wasn't broken before, it was certainly broken now. I wondered if any of Noah's delicate little bones had been broken in the fall, if his spine had buckled, if he'd had any seizures. And if so, how many. How bad was the damage? How much could this kid take?

I hooked Beulah's harness around my nephew's chair and watched as Streeter pulled him up through the hole.

When he made it to the top, I saw Noah lean over in his chair, his forehead wrinkling as he looked for me down the hole. Even clinging to life, he was more worried about me than himself.

And I cried.

CHAPTER 64

Noah

SHE DID IT!

Auntie Liv found me and saved little Max. I was hoping she'd find my football pin and figure out that creepy Mr. Fletcher had little Max the whole time, but for the life of me, I don't know how she figured out where he took us.

I knew Mr. Creepy drove us a long time, went way up in the mountains and out in the woods, a really long drive from our house, somewhere where his tires crunched in heavy snow, on back roads that weren't paved, because I could hear the gravel under his tires. But the Rocky Mountains are a big place and if I was really truthful about it, I didn't have a clue how Auntie Liv would figure out where he took us. And I was scared. Really scared. The pain in my broken leg made me feel angry and alive but mostly I was trying to hold on to my "mad" so little Max's whimpering and shivering wouldn't get me down. I knew if I cried, if I started worrying too much, I'd cause myself to have a seizure. And that would have really scared little Max. I was trying to stay brave because he needed me. By the time I did have my seizure, little Max had already passed out. Or at least that's what they told me.

And Auntie Liv found us. Found me. But I was just coming out of my seizure and it was all a blur.

Now that we've had time to talk, Auntie Liv said this is where she found the kid's backpack. Said the kid was an older boy that Mr. Fletcher had kidnapped a couple of years ago. When she told me his name, I remembered him. He was the "Boy Who Had Disappeared."

I'd heard about Clint at school. He was a legend. The kids all said he disappeared because he always stuffed his food in his milk carton at lunch and threw it in the garbage so the lunch monitors couldn't make him eat all his food. They'd warned him many times to eat everything on his plate. But he didn't. And after three warnings, the boy simply disappeared. POOF! Someone started a rumor that he got lost in the woods and was eaten by a bear. We all thought the lunch room was haunted, that Clint's ghost wandered from table to table, stole our butter pats, took cookies, or made our goulash taste yucky.

None of that was true. Auntie Liv told me Mr. Fletcher had kidnapped Clint and left him out in the woods, near the hole where he had dropped me and little Max. But Clint eventually made it out of the mountains to a house. His parents sent him to school at a different place the next year and no one ever told us. So I wonder who's stealing my cookies at school? Well, it's not the "Boy Who Disappeared," that's for sure. 'Cause Auntie Liv promised me Clint didn't die, so he can't be haunting the lunch room.

The doctor is just about done wrapping up my leg with the wet plaster. He told my mom and dad that I'll have to wear this cast for several weeks. I think it's so cool! It's blue, like my school's colors, and it matches the frame of my wheelchair. Everyone here at the hospital is so nice. I'm glad the doctor's keeping me overnight for observation. He said they want to make sure I didn't hit my head, receive a concussion, or suffer any trauma from hypothermia, whatever that means.

Okay by me, as long as they don't have to poke and prod and keep me up all night like they usually do when I have to stay here. And as long as they don't feed me goulash. The food here is actually good, but I'm full. Emma brought me a Dairy Queen Butterfinger Blizzard—my favorite—which Mom fed me while we were waiting for x-rays so the doctor could set my leg. Now that the doctor is finishing up, I'm excited about going back to my room because I told Emma to let Mom and Dad know I wanted some time alone to talk with Auntie Liv. If she ever gets here and has her arm x-rayed. She said she's busy wrapping up some loose ends on the case and will be here pronto to stay the night with me in my room, so my mom and dad can go home and get a good night's sleep.

I can't wait!

I have so many questions about what happened out there, and she promised to tell me the whole story, leaving out no detail. That's what I was hoping because how am I ever going to get better as a spy if she keeps things from me? Yeah, I know I said I didn't want to be a spy anymore. But I do. I just have to grow up a little bit so I'm not so scared.

Special Agent Pierce called me a hero and told me how proud he was of me. Denver Police Chief Gates gave me a special police officer's badge and told me to apply for work when I got old enough. But I think I was most excited about Special Agent Linwood. Auntie Liv calls him Jack. He took me aside and told me how brave I was, how lucky little Max was that I was there to care for him, to protect him like I did. He didn't talk to me like the others did. He treated me like a fellow spy. When he talked about how lucky little Max was to have me and said not all kids are that lucky, I think I saw a tear come to his eye, but I'm not so sure. I don't think FBI agents cry. Spies sure don't. Besides, I was so excited because Agent Linwood gave me his FBI cap, snugged the strap and put it on my head, as the ambulance was taking me off to the hospital. I think he knows kids. Knows I'm not invisible. He's a lot like Auntie Liv. Has the gift.

I like Agent Linwood. And I think Auntie Liv does, too.

Anyway, although all the rescuers and emergency people have been so nice to me, I'm glad to have some time alone with the doctor. It sure seems like a lifetime ago when my rainy day began and turned to sleet once Mr. Fletcher dropped me and little Max down that hole. I was glad I broke little Max's fall and even more glad that he broke my leg. It will be a great story at school. Most of all, the single ray of sunshine in my rainiest day ever was when I heard my name called in the slimy pit of that frozen outhouse.

By my Auntie Liv.

CHAPTER 65

THE GENTLE PURR OF Noah's soft snoring was the best Christmas music I'd ever heard in my life. And seeing him warm and snug, tucked in the hospital bed beside mine—both of us relatively unscathed from the horror that was creepy man Fletcher—was the best gift I had ever received. His tiny little cast from his knee to his toes was covered in signatures from well wishers, whereas my cast from my elbow to fingertips was unmarked as yet.

My sisters and brothers-in-law had just left; Frances was happy that I was planning to stay with Noah overnight, even though my injuries didn't warrant the attention. She would get a good night's sleep for once, not worried about the care Noah deserved. And she would be well rested to prepare a second Christmas Eve dinner so that we could all gather around the table together tomorrow night. Mom and Dad were on their way, driving to see for themselves that little Noah was well, and that I was, too.

I hadn't heard Jack come into the room, let alone step up to the bed where I was sitting, watching Noah sleep across from me. Jack's kiss startled me. Without a word, he sat beside me, his arm around my waist. I was grateful that Frances had brought me a fresh set of clothes and that the hospital let me take a shower in the employee changing room. Otherwise, I would still be wearing the clothes I'd borrowed from Phil that were soiled from the outhouse and too formfitting for my taste. I smelled antiseptic, sterilized, but at least I didn't smell as bad as I had before I changed. Jack didn't seem to mind one bit.

"How are you?" he whispered.

I nodded, smiled, and glanced over at Noah who was fast asleep, wearing the FBI cap Jack had given him. "Great, now. You made his day."

"He made mine."

A long silence passed between us as we sat watching Noah sleep.

"Do you want to talk about it? Your son?"

"Someday," he said, sighing and kissing me on the cheek. "For now, I hope it's enough that you know how much I love you."

Stunned by his heartfelt admission, I turned to him to reply. But he had already moved off. I turned just in time to see him step away, put his finger against his lips to hush me, and offer a wave good-bye. I closed my gaping mouth, wondering what I would have said if he had stayed, realizing a good night's sleep might clear my swimming head.

I don't know how long I sat there, letting the words "I love you" hang in the air, but I was pulled from my wistful reverie by an energetic voice.

"Noah!"

With my back to the door, I heard little Max call before I saw him run toward the hospital bed, his dad following into the room. Noah's eyes fluttered open and a smile instantly appeared on his face. Little Max jumped against the bedside, latched onto the metal bed railings, and climbed over the bars as if Noah's bed was a playground jungle gym, cuddling up beside Noah before Max or I could stop him. Noah's laugh erupted, causing little Max to do the same, contagion in the room.

"You were so brave," I said to little Max. "I'm proud of you."

"Noah's the brave one. You should have seen how brave he was with Papa cursing and yelling and slamming his fist against the steering wheel on the drive to the woods. Noah just laughed. Which made me laugh. Which just made Papa even madder."

Max cleared his throat. "He's not your Papa."

"I know, Daddy. You are. It's just a name. We were just pretending until you came to pick me up."

Max smiled and touched his son's cheek. For the first time, I could see what Ida had seen in Max. He wasn't such an asshole after all. Little Max started to tell Noah stories, everything that had been happening since they left the outhouse. I noticed that little Max was sporting the same color wristband as Noah, a hospital band.

"Hey, Noah," little Max said. "Sorry I called you 'broken baby.' I just didn't understand why you weren't talking to me. Your aunt explained. She says you talk in smiles. Do you?"

Noah's smile was wide. Little Max started giggling and chattering, telling stories and asking Noah questions.

I mouthed, "Is he okay?"

Max stepped nearer and I rose from my bed, stepping closer to him so we could talk without the boys hearing us.

"He'll be fine. It appears Fletcher didn't molest him, which is a miracle. Based on those horrid photos they found, we all would have thought—"

I shook my head. "Me too, but apparently the boy who got away and lived to tell about it said that Fletcher never did anything sexual to him, either. Just took nude photos of him, slept with him in the same bed on occasion, but never violated him in any way. At least physically."

"Fletcher's lucky he committed suicide, Liv, because seriously," Max said giving me a grave look, "I don't know what I would have done to him after seeing those photos of little Max. You guys did a brilliant job."

"Thank you, but don't thank me. Noah did all the heavy lifting. If he hadn't told us about little Max, if he hadn't figured it out and left that audio recording on his pin, I don't know if we would have ever figured out what had happened. We would have been too late."

Max chuckled.

"What?"

"Liv, Noah can't even talk."

"Oh really?"

Max glanced at Noah, who was intent on listening to little Max and laughing when the boy laughed. "He's just going with the flow."

I sighed. "Max, sometimes you can be so dense. He is smart and courageous and communicates all the time, just not like you and I communicate. It's kind of like you understanding Noah as much as you understand someone who speaks Spanish."

That made him laugh. "Oh, that's rich. You remember? It's my Achilles' heel."

"I remember what an asshole you were. And she wasn't speaking Spanish that day, you idiot. She was practicing her song. Ida's opera was Italian, for Pete's sake, and you were supposed to feel the story, not understand every word. Yet you thought she was speaking in code about you," I said. "Your Achilles' heel is paranoia. What an asshole."

"I'll take your word for it. And thank you for still being classic Liv. It's what I miss most about not having Ida in my life anymore. I need someone around me who's not dazzled by money. I need someone honest like you. That, and I miss your mom sharing her Tootsie Rolls with me."

"From her magic purse," I agreed. I drew in a deep breath. "How's Melissa?"

"She's . . . she's changed. So have I. She's breaking up with Aldo as we speak. She wants to give us another try."

"Well, good for you. Try not to be such an asshole this time. Melissa's a nice young lady and little Max deserves parents who don't fight."

"Of course he does," Max said, crossing his arms and rocking back on his heels. "I'm a new man. And thanks for pointing out my flaws so succinctly. You could try to do it a little less often." He looked over at me. "But your honesty was exactly why I insisted that you be on this case, Liv. I asked for a list of the agents at the Denver Bureau and when I saw your name on it, I knew you could do this, even if you were a first-office agent and just out of Quantico. You're a 'no bullshit zone' for sure, and if I've learned nothing else, I've learned that I need more people like you in my life."

"No bullshit? Well, then let me give you some advice. I do think you can learn to be less of an asshole. I do think Melissa cares about little Max, so you need to cut her some slack. And I do think you have a child who needs you both in his life now that Nanny Judy isn't in it," I said with a grin.

He laughed. Little Max turned to watch his dad and started giggling. "Daddy, I've never seen you laugh like that before."

"And it's about time you did, isn't it little Max?" I asked.

"Well, champ, we better get going. My jet is fueled up and waiting on us. Come on, little Max. Bye, Noah. And Liv, I'll make sure Chandler knows how well you did, slips you a bonus this holiday."

At first, I decided to ignore his comment, but then as he was leaving the room with little Max in tow, I said, "Max?"

He turned, a quizzical expression on his charming face.

"Do me one better. Instead of a bonus, would you mind cutting a donation to United Cerebral Palsy in Noah's name? Since he's the real hero in all this."

Max looked over at Noah's hospital bed and offered a crooked smile. Little Max pranced around his dad repeating, "Please, Daddy? Please?"

Noah lay still, listening to Max's answer.

"How does a half million sound, Noah?"

Noah squealed, his arms and legs pulling into his chest, he was so excited.

Max looked back at me. "Maybe you're right."

And then Max and little Max were gone.

Noah truly had done all the heavy lifting on this case, leading me to solve the abduction of Maximillian Bennett Williams III despite so many disbelievers. Without his help, without him figuring out who Clint was, without him triggering the spy pin and recording Fletcher's voice with little Max, with Fletcher kidnapping Noah, we would have never been able to find little Max and close the case, allowing us to bury Fletcher's evil deeds along with his carcass.

The coward.

Jack had called me earlier before stopping by and told me what had happened during Fletcher's interrogation, where he had owned up to nothing and resolutely professed he had killed no one. Jack believed him. He concluded Fletcher was too much of a coward and calculatedly discarded the boys in such a way that killing them was unnecessary, leaving them to fend for themselves in the wild like he had Clint. There were unsolved cases to recover some of those missing boys' bodies, if ever, but now that they had located Fletcher's favorite haunt, where I had found Clint's backpack and where Fletcher had left little Max and Noah to die, the team would have a place to start looking.

And Jack also told me about how Fletcher committed suicide in his cell, how Jack was the last person to see him alive, and how glad he was that the world was rid of his filth and evil.

I thought about how Jack had told me he loved me for the first time tonight. And how he hadn't given me time to tell him I loved him back. I wish I had. I think. But my head was still swimming in all the confusion and with the lack of sleep.

It had been a very long day. Now that Noah was back to sleep, I snuggled up beside him in bed, closed my eyes, and counted Noah's smiles as I began to doze. Noah's gentle purr beside me led my mind to the memories of hearing little Max and Noah laughing, until the joyful laughs became like the rumble of a lawn mower, and made me recall a laugh that made my insides warm and my spirits lift. It was Streeter's laugh. And I was jolted awake.

He was standing above the hospital bed and I thought he was a dream. "You're always there, aren't you?"

His grin was real. The five o'clock shadow was rough against my fingertips as I instinctively reached out to touch his face as I had done so many times since I'd first met him in Fort Collins this summer.

My eyes snapped open, realizing none of this was a dream and that Streeter Pierce was actually standing by Noah's bed. "Oh, sorry! I thought I was dreaming."

I slipped out of bed and rose to stand next to him, looking down at Noah.

Streeter's grin widened. "It's okay. Just wanted to see how you're doing."

"Great! Never better. The good news is my rib is *not* broken. Told you so." I drew in a breath and sat on the unoccupied bed, where he joined me. "The bad news is my arm *is*." I lifted the cast for him to see. "Want to be the first to sign it?"

"I see everyone's been lining up to sign Noah's cast. Sorry I missed the celebration. He deserved it. He's a hero. And so are you."

I lowered my eyes. "I'm no hero. And no one believes that Noah actually solved anything. They don't get it."

"Well, I do. And I talked to the mayor. They are dedicating this year's New Year's Eve parade in Noah's honor and want him to be the Grand Marshall. Think he'll be up for it?"

My smile was easy. "Of course. He's the strongest kid I know."

"Clever, how you figured out where to find the boys, Liv. We would have been too late, if it weren't for you connecting the dots to Clint from last year."

"I didn't. I swear. That was Noah. All I did was find Clint's backpack. Luck, really."

Streeter shook his head. "Not luck. Skill. And you'll both be joining the mayor on the lead car in the parade, my dear. So dress warmly."

He smiled and I sensed he was about to leave. But I didn't want him to. "Streeter?"

He arched his eyebrows and smiled.

"I don't know if I made the right decision," I said.

For a long moment, he simply stared at me. Then he scooted closer to me on the bed, put his arm over my shoulder. "About what?"

I looked over at Noah. I wanted to tell him about Jack. That he'd said he loved me and that I didn't know how to answer him. Instead, I said, "About the FBI. I have to admit, my mind wasn't on finding little Max at the end. It was on finding Noah. On family."

A tear slid down my cheek as I gazed over at Noah, asleep and at peace. I turned back to seek an answer from Streeter on my dilemma.

His crooked grin was reassuring somehow. He reached up with his thumb and wiped away the tear from my cheek. "That's normal."

He stood up and moved closer to Noah's bed, away from me.

"But what if I had made a mistake? This all came so fast, Quantico, my decision to leave the family business. You. Jack."

I saw his head droop. He remained silent for a long moment as I studied him. "It's not something you have to decide right now, Liv."

I wondered if he meant my decision about staying with the FBI or going back to my family's life of quarrying. Or if he understood that my confusion was much deeper.

Streeter reached in his jacket pocket, bent down to sign Noah's cast, and then turned to me. I would have sworn there was a tear welling in his eye. He leaned over to sign my cast and slipped out of the room without another word.

I noticed he had signed my cast upside down, so I could see it. But he hadn't signed his name after all. My eyes fixed on the single word he had scribbled indelibly on my cast.

"Always."

And I smiled.

ACKNOWLEDGMENTS

I AM HUMBLED BY the number of book clubs that volunteered to be "beta readers" for this book. Beta testing is a common term in business for benchmarking and measuring the volatility of something, and ever since I was introduced to book clubs across this country with *In the Belly of Jonah*, my first Liv Bergen story, and learned how honest and valid feedback from members of book clubs could be, I decided to choose a "beta reader" book club for each of my books before I sent the manuscript on to my publisher for editing. *Lot's Return to Sodom* was read by the Tough Ladies of Harding County, a combination of two book clubs from Camp Crook and Buffalo, South Dakota. *Widow's Might* was read by a book club I hijacked one night when the homeowner suggested I come to the front window and peer in on the group as they discussed *In the Belly of Jonah*. A huge thank you to sisters Ruthie Conway and Sara Gross for that fun experience and for volunteering as the beta readers for *Widow's Might*, which earned an ABA Indie NextPick.

The volunteers who read and made suggestions to improve *Noah's Rainy Day* were the wonderful Ladies of the Knight and the Rambling Mustangs book club in Chicago, Illinois. I thank them for their honesty and suggestions for improvement in fleshing out the story. A personal thank you to Denise Kreb, Jacqui Menich, Kim Cichon, Andrea Bonefas, Sandy Blethen, Christine Lussow, Terri Bauer, Patti Brock, and Julie Caporusso. They invested so much of their precious time to help me and I am so appreciative. Thank you, ladies!

Jeanne Thornton, bless you for coaching me through the edit process, and thanks to Elizabeth Chenette for her expert editing. Jenny Simonson, you provided the common thread throughout all my books, thank you!

And to Team Hoyt—Dick and Rick Hoyt—thank you for making me believe I could write this story and give a voice to the real heroes in this world: people like you, my nephew, and his parents. Warriors and angels.

READER'S GUIDE
DISCUSSION QUESTIONS

1. In a departure from Sandra Brannan's previous Liv Bergen novels, murder wasn't the central theme in *Noah's Rainy Day*. Did you find the change in story line and writing style refreshing or disappointing?

2. Liv Bergen is blessed with numerous siblings and a strong family. How effectively does the author use the character's family members to further the story in *Noah's Rainy Day*, using a newly showcased sibling, sister Frances, as the focus in this book?

3. The relationship between Liv Bergen and Streeter Pierce may be hindering Liv's desire to further her relationship with Jack Linwood. If you were Liv, whose bed would you jump into with both feet, eyes wide, and why?

4. The author raised several serious topics in *Noah's Rainy Day*. What are your experiences with the author's

perspective that people with challenges are often seen by society as "invisible" rather than having strong skill sets that may be unseen?

5. Brannan's FBI agents and DPD touched on the concept that child abductions can most often be linked to family members. The villain in *Noah's Rainy Day* was not typical. What do you think about publicly mapping where sexual predators live in certain communities versus the rights of convicted criminals to privacy?

6. If you had a child or family member with severe challenges and a high requirement for special needs, at what point would you consider institutionalizing your family member and what factors would you imagine most important in your decision?

7. The author found no way around introducing Noah's voice in the first person. Up until *Noah's Rainy Day*, Brannan had only allowed Liv Bergen the first-person perspective. Did you find the technique effective or off-putting?

8. The story of *Noah's Rainy Day* occurs over a two-day time frame and was less of a murder mystery than it was a cozier mystery with the thrill of a ticking clock: Will the good guys find the bad guys in time to save the boy? Did you like how the author changed her style?

9. Which of Sandra Brannan's books is your favorite?

> *In the Belly of Jonah* (2010)
>
> *Lot's Return to Sodom* (2011)
>
> *Widow's Might* (2012)
>
> *Noah's Rainy Day* (2013)